ADAM
AND
EVE
AND
PINOCCHIO

ADAM

A · N · D

EVE

A · N · D

PINOCCHIO

ON BEING AND BECOMING

— H · U · M · A · N —

WILLARD GAYLIN, M.D.

VIKING

VIKING

Published by the Penguin Group

Viking Penguin, a division of Penguin Books USA Inc.,

40 West 23rd Street, New York, New York 10010, U.S.A.

Penguin Books Ltd, 27 Wrights Lane, London W8 5TZ, England

Penguin Books Australia Ltd, Ringwood, Victoria, Australia

Penguin Books Canada Ltd, 2801 John Street, Markham, Ontario, Canada L3R 1B4

Penguin Books (N.Z.) Ltd, 182–190 Wairau Road, Auckland 10, New Zealand

Penguin Books Ltd, Registered Offices: Harmondsworth, Middlesex, England

First published in 1990 by Viking Penguin, a division of Penguin Books USA Inc.

1 3 5 7 9 10 8 6 4 2

LIBRARY OF CONGRESS CATALOGING IN PUBLICATION DATA

Gaylin, Willard.
Adam and Eve and Pinocchio : on being and becoming human / Willard Gaylin.
p. cm.
ISBN 0–670–82601–4
1. Man. I. Title.
BD450.G39 1990
128—dc20   89–40323

Printed in the United States of America
Set in Granjon
Designed by Fritz A. Metsch

Dedicated with delight, gratitude, and love to Sarah, Charlie, Laura, Emily, and David— who really are something special.

What is man, that thou art mindful of him? and the son to man, that thou visitest him?

For thou hast made him but little lower than the angels, and hast crowned him with glory and honour.

PSALM 8:4–5

ACKNOWLEDGMENTS

A TWENTY-YEAR INVOLVEMENT with my colleagues at The Hastings Center has influenced my thinking and attitudes beyond my recognition let alone acknowledgments. I am grateful to them all for the counsel and wisdom shared with me in what is the liveliest marketplace of ideas I have been privileged to attend. Special thanks for this project, however, must be extended to Janet Bower, Marna Howarth, and Bruce Jennings for their indispensable contributions.

My agents Owen Laster and Pam Bernstein and my editor Amanda Vaill are consummate professionals. One ought to feel blessed to have that. But they are more. They are advocates and friends.

Finally, at the core of this book, at the heart of my life is—as always—the supporting presence of my wife Betty.

CONTENTS

PROLOGUE

WHAT'S SO SPECIAL
ABOUT BEING HUMAN

~~~~~~~~~~~

WE DON'T MUCH LIKE OURSELVES these days. By "ourselves" I am not just referring to our individual selves measured by our personal feelings of self-worth and self-esteem—although, Lord knows, a truly self-confident creature is a rarity in our society—but our species and our nature. That special awe and reverence for humankind, for its power and potential, that sustained us for centuries seems now to be rapidly disintegrating.

The uniqueness of the human being has been under indirect attack for some time now from the implications of modern Darwinian biology. By establishing incremental linkages, a continuity, from the lower to the higher species, evolution has emphasized our similarity to lower creatures without explaining the enormous implications of those differences that do exist.

Currently we are witnessing from other sources an even more serious assault on the singular worth of the human animal. The ecological disasters and the threat of atomic annihilation have shaken our arrogant nineteenth-century confidence in human science and technology. We assumed that we had created the tools that would eventually eradicate misery and restore us to a new Garden of justice and tranquillity. Instead, we are hoist with our own petards.

We are a failure in our own eyes, and that is always a dangerous and unstable state, whether for the individual or the species. We are losing faith, not just in our institutions, but in ourselves. We view ourselves as the polluters of the environment; the brutalizers of animals; the warmakers; the potential destroyers of the planet.

Yet we continue to articulate our shibboleths about human dignity. "Respect for human dignity," "the right to dignity," "treatment with dignity," and even "death with dignity" are all catch phrases circulating in the current world of ideas, mindlessly repeated with no coherent sense of their specific meanings. Dignity has joined that group of concepts that, like difficult books with cachet, are paraded in public to establish one's allegiance to intellectual fashionability. They seem destined to be prominently displayed while remaining essentially unexamined and unexplored. No one has bothered to examine the use of "dignity" in these particular contexts to see whether this word still means what it had historically meant.

Traditionally the word "dignity" always alluded to an inherent nobility and worth that were ascribed to our species, *Homo sapiens, and to no other*. It referred to the specialness of humankind, which demanded separation, at least in moral terms, from all lower animals. Almost anything was justifiable when done to a lower animal if it was necessary for the survival of the human being.

The book of Genesis makes the quintessential case for human dignity. In the passages of this first book of the Bible, God does not equate the human being with other forms of life. We are not advised to live harmoniously with nematodes or viruses, or, for that matter, eagles and elephants. God commands that we subdue them. We are not directed to be one among creatures, but supreme among creatures: "And God created man in His own image, in the image of God created He him; male and female created He them. And God blessed them, and God said unto them: 'Be fruitful, and multiply, and replenish the earth, and subdue it; and have dominion over the fish of the sea, and over the fowl of the air, and over every living thing that creepeth upon the earth.' "[1]

The ancient Jews, unencumbered as they were by Hellenic concepts of hubris or Christian concepts of humility, saw human beings as supreme among God's creations. We were *not* the first among equals; we were awesome and wonderful. The unique worth of humankind was acknowledged both in our likeness to our Creator and in His injunctions to us.

The Greeks, despite their concern with hubris, also acknowledged, both implicitly and explicitly, the special worth of humanity. Sophocles wrote: "The world is full of wonderful things but none more so than man."[2] Antigone was prepared to die, not to save her brother's life, but to show respect for the being that once was, in the treatment of his dead body, the residue of his personhood. She asserted the profound claims of family and religious honor above the duty to the state—a duty not taken lightly in the Athens of Sophocles.

The human being, even in death, is different. The shell of the human being, the dead body, is still not a carcass and in almost all religions demands respect and ritual treatment. The everyday language of death affirms this fundamental distinction in its allusion to "the mortal remains."

This reverence for the human body had remained intact down through time and across almost all cultures. In the rough days of the early-American West, horse thieves were hanged, for the horse was crucial in that primitive hunting-and-farming society. Yet the same frontiersman would slaughter his devoted horse if necessary to feed his child. The horse itself might be loved, but there was no sentimentalizing its position in the real world of survival. It was an instrument to serve that survival. It was a means to a vital end, never an end in itself.

That same pioneer would not, however, butcher the body of one dead child even if it meant enhancing the survival of his others. When episodes of cannibalism occurred, such as the infamous incident at the Donner Pass—where pioneers trapped in the mountains in winter were reduced to eating the flesh of those who had died—they were almost universally perceived with revulsion and condemnation.

Since human life is so precious in the Western Judeo-Christian tradition, one would assume that to save human lives one ought to feel free to consume the remains of the dead. On a utilitarian calculus this might have some arguable merit. But human dignity transcends even life. The human being is of a different measure from all animal forms, in death as well as in life. The human being is an end in himself, never to be used as a means. The human being is "in the image of God."

The power of the imagery of Genesis sustained the concept of human dignity throughout the Middle Ages. Centuries after Genesis, Macrobius, an influential Latin writer and philosopher, still based his argument for human dignity on the premise that the human race was ennobled by its kinship with the Heavenly Mind, and that, of all creatures on earth, only a human shares the mind with heaven and the stars.

For the most part, human dignity was not to be redefined in nonreligious terms until relatively modern times, but the Reformation did produce one important and subtle change. The concept of dignity was gradually expanded to include not just the species as a whole but every single member of it. Axel Stern, among others, dated the rise of the individual to the Protestant Reformation, stating that, whereas the specialness of the human species versus that of other animals existed in antiquity, the dignity of personhood came to the fore only with the rise of mercantilism and capitalism. He saw this most manifest in the bypassing of the Church by the Protestant reformers, who insisted that each Christian had to face God directly.[3]

Ultimately Kant's writings were to produce the most profound changes in modern thinking about ourselves and our nature. His rationale for, and definition of, human worth were to become the supporting pillars on which much of modern moral philosophy would be built. Kant's position was very clear. The dignity or the worth of the human being as distinguished from all other animals was based not on our special reasoning powers, although he acknowledged we were quite different from even our closest animal relatives in this way, but on our freedom, our autonomy. "Man in the system of nature is a being of slight importance . . . but man regarded as a person—that is as the subject of morally practical reason is exalted above any price. . . . Autonomy then is the basis of [human] dignity."[4]

Following Kant, the literature of autonomy flourished and the concept of dignity declined. "Dignity" was to become an accepted term in modern writing without ever having been adequately analyzed, and it always implied the Kantian definition of autonomy. One supporting fact is that, in B. F. Skinner's *Beyond Freedom and Dignity*, the concept of dignity is never discussed. Even the word is not present. The book deals heavily with the nature of autonomy. When I asked him about this, Dr. Skinner responded that he presumed that our worth (our dignity) was vested in our assumption of autonomy.

Now that we are living in an era where science is the truest religion, and Darwin its reluctant prophet, the comfortable view of the animal kingdom is to visualize a continuum of creatures, all advancing in small increments up the hierarchical scale from the unicellular to the primate. In approaching the subject of human nature, we must dissociate ourselves from the accepted cultural wisdom of our day.

My central argument will be an attempt to demonstrate that this conceptualization is defensible only when considering the developmental line that stretches from the virus to the chimpanzee. But the order of change between the chimpanzee and the human being is of such a magnitude as to represent a break, a discontinuity, in this great chain of life. Mankind is that noble discontinuity. We are not the next step, or even a giant leap forward. We are a parallel and independent entity; a thing unto ourselves; in a class of our own; *sui generis*. This being so, the preservation of this species, our species, is vital not only to our selfish ends but also to the preservation of something extraordinary and unique in nature.

The illumination of our biological linkage to other, lower animals has been of extraordinary importance, the knowledge we have gained from comparative biology overwhelmingly valuable. No one now questions our animal heritage. No one can deny that we share whole biological systems with animals much lower and more distant from us than the higher primates. But what we have done with these various systems, and, beyond that, what nature has done with these systems, is profound and immeasurable. We are not dealing with more and better. We are different. The distance between man and ape is greater than the distance between ape and ameba.

We must come to understand how different we are from other animals, and how those differences will dictate different aspirations, different hopes, and different methods of survival.

The Old Testament prophets did not need to be reminded of our special role and our worth. The ancient Greeks and early-medieval philosophers understood the uniqueness of the human species. They would not have debated the fact of our being special, only the ways in which we are.

Modern biologists understand this, too, and stand in awe of our uniqueness. A major geneticist like Theodosius Dobzhansky pointed out that, in developing culture, humankind has outstripped nature and found the supragenetic. In all other animals, change can occur only through mutation. Mutation is generally destructive; the mutant will die. A positive mutation will rarely occur. And when it does, that change will be transmitted solely to the specific offspring—and only after hundreds of generations may it enter into the species at large.

Cultural changes, on the other hand, can be directly and universally transmitted to everyone in that culture. A change can occur within one lifetime rather than await the centuries that traditional evolution demands. Occurring so rapidly, the change will have a better chance of being established, for it is not subject to the unpredictable vicissitudes of time. The power and the peril are both magnified. Dobzhansky eloquently stated:

"By changing what he knows about the world man changes the world that he knows; and by changing the world in which he lives man changes himself. . . . Evolution need no longer be a destiny imposed from without; it may conceivably be controlled by man, in accordance with his wisdom and his values."[5]

We and the rest of the plant and animal kingdoms, for better or worse, live in a world that is at least in part of human design. We consciously, purposely, and often foolishly and shortsightedly change the actual world in which we and our fellow travelers on this planet must abide. But we also alter our environment in a second way. Our "world" is a product of our own perception; our imagination, feelings, sensitivity, knowledge, aspirations, self-deceptions, and hopes will create a "reality" that will command our lives beyond most strictures of actual events. How we interpret events and define happenings will be the primary influence on our behavior, our pleasures, our self-judgments, and our sense of purpose.

Animals live in a sensate world. We live in a world of our own imagination. What we choose to perceive may be radically different from that which is; what we choose to anticipate may be dictated by desire and denial rather than by rationality; but our perceptions dominate our existence.

And we are capable of changing ourselves as well as our world. We have always done this through culture and child-rearing, but now we can directly intervene in the genetic mechanisms of our children. No longer dependent on the crude "genetic engineering" of the past—prenatal diagnosis and selective abortion—we now have the capacity to remove, replace, or restore a missing gene. We exist in the awesome and frightening age of molecular biology and recombinant DNA. If culture is the "superorganic," the techniques of the molecular biologist, in their speediness and directness, represent the "superduperorganic." This technology can and will be used to reduce genetic faults and increase the opportunity for a normal, healthy child. It will also be used to effect changes whose merits are not so cut-and-dried, changes that will be seen as making a more nearly ideal or optimal child rather than simply a normal one: a child of a certain gender, size, superior intelligence, resistant to disease.

Eventually these ideals will become norms. Health care acquires a momentum of its own. We inevitably turn from the replacement of deficiencies to additions for enhancement and ennoblement. Cosmetic surgery and orthodontia are covered by our medical insurance. We are likely these days first to discover a treatment and then to invent the disease to go with it. Presbyopia would not have been a disease before the discovery of the lens; old people weren't expected to be still capable of fine work. The invention of psychotherapy presented the physician with a tool for dealing with unhappiness, which had not traditionally been viewed as a sickness. The modern psychiatrist spends little of his time dealing with conditions that were recognized as the domain of psychiatry in the nineteenth century. The feats of reproductive technology, from in-vitro fertilization to surrogate motherhood, boggle the mind. What may emerge next? The artificial placenta? At a time when the technology is moving so fast, when opportunities for change are so beguiling, we must carefully look to see what can be prudently changed and what might imperil our species and the world, whose fate now lies in our hands.

Even the most flexible of species, *Homo sapiens*, may be stretched to its snapping point. For this reason alone, the social scientists, psychologists, political scientists, and everyday persons on whom our future rests must learn what "we" are all about. This book represents one such attempt to examine ourselves.

We are in urgent need of reacquainting ourselves with our nature. Our self-respect as a species is alarmingly low. The late twentieth century has seen a confluence of events destined to diminish self-confidence and self-esteem. Along with the great wars, the Depression, the Holocaust, and the ecological disasters— enough to drive any introspective creature to self-doubts—have come a series of seemingly unrelated intellectual movements that have independently and unwittingly diminished our stature in our own eyes.

The "dignity of man" is attacked indirectly by those who, drawing from modern biology and using the principles of sociobiology, have consciously attempted to lessen the distinction between us and our fellow creatures. Anthropologists in particular—Lorenz, Tiger, Fox, Morris, and others—have tended to emphasize the hostile, aggressive, and territorial aspects of human nature while ignoring the caring and nurturing aspects. They have envisioned man at best as a naked ape, and at worst as a marauding beast.

Fortunately, some of our most literate, respected, and brilliant biologists, while marveling at, and honoring the lower animals, have had no doubts about the special quality of being human. Such great humanistic twentieth-century biologists as Dobzhansky, Tax, and Portmann have been elegant spokesmen within their disciplines for the special nature of human beings. They have not, however, gone beyond their disciplines to indicate the moral implications of our biological uniqueness.

The reputation of our species is also under attack, in a way that is half direct and half indirect, through what has come to be known as the animal-rights movement. The purpose of the people in this movement is not to diminish *Homo sapiens* but to protect the beast. They do so by elevating animals, often endowing them anthropomorphically with features the animals do not possess. Their purpose is noble—to protect helpless creatures from unnecessary suffering—but one untoward consequence of this decent enterprise is a reduction of the distance between the nature of people and that of animals. Animal rights advocates constantly emphasize the similarity between the human and the subhuman in a worthy attempt to mitigate our abuses of the subhuman. But in so doing they seriously undermine the special nature of being human.

Peter Singer, perhaps the most eloquent spokesman for animal rights, acknowledges a quantitative difference between the worth of lower animals and human beings. (Some of his colleagues do not.) He rejects, however, any suggestion that there is a qualitative difference, which would preclude *any* measurement of the worth of a human life against that of an animal life, seeing such a construction as immoral in itself. On the contrary, he insists, the failure to consider such a calculus constitutes a breach of ethics.

This leads him into the dangerous readiness to measure humans and animals on the same scale. Although he certainly would not equate the life of a rat with the life of a human being, he has inevitably been forced to take a position whereby thousands of rats would be judged more worthy of life than one child, since he is prepared to see differences only in degree.

I am not clear where on his social scale the cockroach would need to be in relation to the rat, so that we might extrapolate the number of cockroaches necessary to balance the life of a child.

I see a danger in the animal-rights movement that is more than theoretical. It is beginning to impinge on the lifesaving research necessary to solve such human miseries as AIDS, cancer, and degenerative diseases of the nervous system. I acknowledge my bias. In my world, trees may have standing but animals have no "rights." In the world of morality—as in the world of politics—the animate (and inanimate) exist—valued, considered, dealt with, or destroyed, all in the service of the purposes and interests of humankind.

This position has been attacked in the past as being unfairly anthropocentric. Anthropocentric it certainly is. But what else can a human being be? Beyond man are only the claims of nature or the hand of God. Though not a religious person myself, I have profound respect for religion, and I would point out to critics that the position I hold was most firmly established, not out of the anthropocentricism of science and psychology, but in the religious tradition of the Old Testament and as confirmed, in that same tradition, by such modern philosophers as Kant.

Kant was capable of a great tenderness toward animals, as Mary Midgeley observed in her excellent book *Beast and Man*, citing the following statement by Kant: "Liebnitz used a tiny worm for purposes of observation and then carefully replaced it with its leaf on the tree so that it should not come to harm through any act of his. He would have been sorry—a natural feeling for a humane man—to destroy such a creature for no reason."[6]

Yet the very same Kant, with the inherent self-confidence of his Lutheran morality, said: "The first time he [man] ever said to the sheep, 'Nature has given you the skin you wear for my use, not for yours' . . . he became aware of the way in which his nature privileged and raised him above all animals."[7]

I oppose the attribution of rights to animals not out of any religious conviction or invocation of divine authority, and not because I have no affection for animals, but because I fear animal-rights arguments diminish the special status of *Homo sapiens*. Respect for human beings requires that dignity be granted our species beyond any qualitative comparison with others. In insisting on that dignity, I do not shirk our responsibility toward other creatures.

A position of such privilege and power imposes a special moral obligation on our species. That is why only we human beings are capable of, willing to, and even obliged to agonize about other species.

It is directly within the purposes of humankind to treat animals with compassion, even empathy; to have reverence for those common qualities we share with the higher primates; and to be aware that, given the mutability of our nature, the way we honor and revere other creatures and other things will define the degree to which we have been true to our humanity. If human nature is so perverted as to be indifferent to suffering and blind to beauty, what is left is no longer "human" and therefore not worthy of its special role in the moral universe.

All animals are not created equal, however. Some animals have less value even than inanimate structures; some have negative value. I do not grieve for the destruction of *Treponema pallidum*, that beautiful and delicate spiral organism that is the cause of human syphilis. To destroy this entire species would be a blessing; whereas blowing up the Grand Tetons or willfully destroying Michelangelo's *David* would constitute a greater moral crime, these are inanimate "things."

Recently I was confronted with a difficult case of the ethical permissibility of using chimpanzee hearts in experimentation to facilitate human organ transplants. Chimpanzees have enormous charm, sensitivity, great intelligence, and a strong kinship to humanity. Should they be sacrificed for human ends? If so, what are the limits?

It seems to me that the implicit issue evolved into the following dilemmas. Assuming a promising and prudent research procedure, would you sacrifice a chimpanzee for a trivial human need? I suspect most of us would not. Would you sacrifice a chimpanzee for a child's life? I know most of us would. Would you sacrifice the entire species of chimpanzees for the entire species of *Homo sapiens*? I hope most of us would. Finally, the hard question: would you risk sacrificing the entire species of chimpanzees, a real and not just a theoretical possibility, to relieve the pain and suffering and premature death of many children? I emphatically would. Others would not. It is here that my bias for the specialness, for the extraordinary specialness, of the human being emerges.

Our current understanding of anthropology is replete with the suggestion of humanoid species—*higher* than the chimpanzee—that have become extinct for unknown reasons of climate or competition. Such is the moral indifference of nature. It is only with the introduction of human sensibility, human empathy, and human capacity for identification that we—alone among creatures—even consider the "rights" of other species.

The nobility of the human being is expressed in this readiness of some of our misguided members to sacrifice human children for the preservation of a kindred living creature. To these spokesmen the overvaluation of the human child is a form of "anthropocentrism" a prejudice like racism or sexism. I am pleased about the presence of such advocates—their unselfishness does honor to our species—even while I reject their sentimentalities. But with my coarser sensibilities, my willingness to sacrifice the chimpanzee, I am still within the limits of decency that define that glorious creature whom I defend, *Homo sapiens*.

To defend the principle that *Homo sapiens* is indeed special, one looks to antecedents in modern writings and finds surprisingly little. There is no major literature in philosophy and jurisprudence on the subject of human dignity, despite the increasing use of the term in legislation, litigation, and codes of ethics. We operate with an unexamined concept of human worth, where dignity has been subsumed under the banner of autonomy. To Kant, our worth lay exclusively with our autonomy. Such an equation creates multiple and serious problems.

First, modern psychiatry and psychology have begun to undermine and challenge our supposed autonomy. The concept of psychic determinism is not just an abstract philosophical construct. The assumptions of both dynamic psychology and behaviorism that present behavior is a captive to past experience, sociological as well as psychological, has cast grave doubt on the notion of human autonomy which supports the civil and criminal law. Beyond the insanity defense there now exists a panoply of mitigating conditions, from the serious to the ludicrous, to protect the offender from bearing the consequences of his actions. From poverty to excessive television watching, the arguments are marshaled to insist that we are all victims, if only of our own past. We are not responsible for what we do. Our mothers, or the absence of a mother, is. This concept of psychic determinism has profoundly diminished our sense of human responsibility and wreaked havoc with the law.

Second, with the exploding capabilities of the biological revolution, the old anxiety about tampering with Mother Nature has re-emerged with a vengeance. Since we are now capable of directly interceding in our genetic structure, a new *genetic* capability—instant, predictable, and specific—has been added to our already present capacity to modify our species *behaviorally*. A new imperative has been introduced to the old question of the nature of human nature.

Today, genetic engineering is in the forefront of our anxiety. In the 1960s, when we began to perceive the potential for influencing human nature through the use of drugs, electrodes, and direct surgical intervention in the brain, the suspicion and anxiety that this generated reached a point of hysteria. We are now less concerned about manipulating behavior than we are about the prospect of tampering with our genetic structure. These new capacities make it urgent that we understand the special and eccentric qualities that distinguish the human creature.

We have, of course, always been charged with designing ourselves and our descendants. One of the most singular of our characteristics is the incompleteness of the infant at birth. Environmental support is needed to allow normal development to continue, and its quality determines the nature of the emerging adult in many significant aspects.

This exaggerated state of prolonged early dependence, combined with our liberation from rigid instinctual patterning, mandates that we share in contributing to our own definition. "Tampering" is a misconception. We *must* mold the raw materials of the inchoate newborn into a pattern at least partly of our own design if we are to produce a mature adult human being. There are, however, limits. We must begin to define those limits, to stay within the borders of species survivability, and to ensure that what survives continues to be human.

Third, modern developments in medicine raise questions about individuals whose autonomy is limited, underdeveloped, or destroyed. These nonautonomous persons must continue to command a special respect. The infant and the child, the senile, the comatose, the retarded are still human beings and vested with the dignity of our species, even though they are not autonomous. The conflation of dignity and worth into autonomy threatens their position in the moral world and may compromise our treatment of them.

For all these reasons—distrust of the human stewardship over our environment, the attack on the concept of freedom arising from the social sciences, our increasing population of people whose autonomy is limited (facilitated by the newfound medical capacity to save life), our increasing technological powers—it has become crucial to explore and explicate those aspects of human nature, *beyond autonomy*, that dignify and elevate our species.

I have selected for examination eight special attributes, out of dozens, that define the unique and extraordinary species *Homo sapiens*. Even these, as will be seen, are often overlapping, interdependent, and suggestive of other qualities that might take precedence in the judgments of others. I will present an argument grounded in my knowledge of biology, psychology, and sociology. Seeking a means to structure this vast material, I chose two metaphors from literature: Adam and Eve, and *Pinocchio*.

The first three chapters of Genesis, dealing with the creation of human beings and their expulsion from the Garden of Eden, indicate that twenty-five hundred years ago all that was essential to human nature—all that was uniquely special about human beings biologically—was already apparent to the shrewd observer. The entire existential drama of modern life is played out in metaphysical terms in the myth of the Garden of Eden.

Pinocchio, while hardly a masterpiece, is an ideal legend to deal with the forces of development—to help draw the distinction between having human form and "being human." Pinocchio is nothing but potential, a block of wood that can speak. In order to become a "real boy" he must learn the dignity of work, responsibility toward others, and the capacity for love. In Pinocchio—written in the mid-nineteenth century for children—the author explores the nature of development by tracking the conversion of a talking block of wood into a real boy.

The form of my book explains the why of it. Under the heading of "Adam and Eve" will be discussed those attributes that are part of the inherent biology of the human being: human imagination; freedom and choice (or autonomy); the range of human feelings; the eccentric and romantic quality of human sexuality. In the Pinocchio section I will deal with the impact of development on our inherent potentials: the nature and significance of human dependency; the concept of human work; the capacity for morality and conscience; and, finally, the meaning of love. These define the process and the realization of becoming human.

Through the story of Pinocchio I will attempt to answer some of the questions of those who may with good reason take offense at my offering a vision of Homo sapiens as but little lower than the angels.

Is this glorious creature—in the image of God—the same person who rapes his five-year-old daughter, scalds his two-year-old infant, mugs the elderly to steal the meager contents of their purses, ignores the hunger and poverty of his neighbors while he attends to his hedonistic and narcissistic needs? How can we reconcile the potential human being as outlined in Genesis with the human being as we meet him on the mean streets of our mean cities?

This is the paradox of our plastic nature, of our need for becoming, beyond mere being. We are born incomplete, and, for good or bad, we share in our own design. God may have had it easier. Adam and Eve, after all, were created whole and adult. They would not have it so easy with their own children.

"I will greatly multiply thy pain and thy travail; in pain shalt thou bring forth children."[8] And God might have added: In sorrow thou shalt raise them.

This book discusses that which is special about being human. I approach the task as a psychologist and a biologist, not as a philosopher. I would like to draw a distinction between human nature and the nature of being human. An example might be the study of any species. If I were interested in earthworms and wished to describe to the uninitiated what the worm was—in order to understand why it behaves the way it does—I would not title the book *Annelid Nature*, yet I would be describing the nature of a worm. I approach the human being in the same way. I am not primarily concerned with the traditional "human-nature" discourse of philosophy, except where those wise theologians and philosophers were capable of intuiting what biology and psychology would "discover" centuries later. I draw on them to support my understanding of the special nature of being human.

Many of the most sophisticated and best-educated people seem to have little idea of the uniqueness of the human being in the animal kingdom. How can they understand our nature when they do not understand our workings? For example, ask any intelligent layman about the multiple function of that intriguing organ the liver and you are likely to get a blank stare. Most of them have no idea even of its size.

If one then extends the discussion beyond the purely physical (much of which we share with lower animals) into the complex areas of behavior, perception, and cognition that are uniquely human, the confusion is appalling. Many of us continue to think of the human being as something like a smart ape. No trajectory from the smartest ape can possibly prepare one for an Aristotle, a Newton, or a Jane Austen. If that seems self-evident, let me add the less obvious fact that no extension from the ape allows for the explanation of an ordinary Tom, Dick, or Mary.

By approaching the subject from a modern biological and psychological perspective, I hope that some increment of knowledge may be added to the understanding of human nature derived from philosophical speculation.

Let me admit to an underlying bias. With more than thirty years' experience of dealing professionally with human misery and

human contrariness, I still think of the human being with awe and
reverence. To some it may seem perverse to write an encomium
to human nature in such mean and ornery times. After the history
of the Holocaust, the famines in the sub-Sahara, the brutalities of
totalitarian regimes that continue to be the norm, the growing
narcissism and selfishness of the affluent democracies, the capacity
to destroy ourselves many times over with nuclear weaponry—
what is there about us left to love?

What is left to love is what there has always been—the magnificent *potential* of the human being to become something halfway
between animal and God.

At this juncture, where our technology seems to be expanding
our horizons for changing the nature of our species and the forms
of our lives, we must be unafraid of such changes and recognize
that our glory has always been not just in what we are, but in
what we can become.

ADAM

AND

EVE

———

ON

BEING

HUMAN

LIVING IN TWO WORLDS:

SYMBOL AND REALITY

~~~~~~~~~~~~~~~~~

"AND GOD SAID, Let us make man in our image, after our likeness."[1]

Many have no problem accepting a literal, albeit vague, image of God. Children generally will picture Him as a majestic, slimmer Santa Claus, with a flowing robe instead of a fur-trimmed suit. For many adults the anthropomorphic reproductions of Michelangelo's image of God, who brings life to Adam on the Sistine Chapel ceiling, is perfectly acceptable.

But what of the God who speaks to Adam; what of the God who reveals himself to Moses in the burning bush; what of the God who tests the faith of Job? To be created in the image of the Lord God, Jehovah, who dominates the Old Testament cannot possibly imply that our physiognomy, our limbs, and our loins are facsimiles of the Creator of the Universe.

For Christians, the problem of visualizing God was resolved with the coming of Christ. A human form and a human sensibility combined with divinity in the body of Christ made conceptualization easy. One could pray to Jesus—or Mary or Joseph, et al.—while staring at an image in stone or paint that was recognizable, that could be fused with memories of loving and protective figures in our life. Jesus and the saints are comforting intermediaries for those of Christian faith. The New Testament reversed the process of Genesis. Where the Torah saw man in God's image, Christianity gave a human form to God, creating a God in our image.

Jesus is an acceptable symbol for a vast population of the earth. Christian believers are not dismayed that in his physiognomy Jesus resembles the ignoble human self that needs food, defecates, sweats with the heat, is besmirched by the dirt of the land. This does not diminish the potential for godliness in him, or in all human beings. It is in his thoughts, his behavior, his ideals and vision expressed through his speech, that we see the reverse image of a God created in the form of man.

In this context it is worth examining the similarity between us and our closest relative. Allowing for the fact that the chimpanzee seems to share so many features with human beings, try to conceive what form of God could have served as an image of that charming creature. What Christ could we create for the chimpanzee swinging gracefully from the tree branch, picking the lice off his companions and doing *what?* What would be the idealized chimpanzee that would suggest immortality or godliness? What substance of thought, imagination, aspiration, will, sacrifice—what ideals exist in this creature that would permit the construction of a god in its image?

The authors of the Old Testament, battling against heathen representations of gods in the shape of animals or symbolic of the elements, were not about to accept *any* visual representation of Jehovah, the mighty, omniscient, single God whose very name was sanctified beyond representation. So holy was the name of God, so beyond ordinary identification, that it would never be written in the Hebrew liturgy, only suggested by code. Even *human* images would be banned from the synagogues of the Jews, for we are in His likeness. The ancient Jews created a God without form or representation; a God unseeable and unexplainable; a God of wisdom, justice, purpose, and mystery. To be in *that* image is extraordinary.

We are in His likeness, according to the scholars of the Old Testament, in our capacity for reason, choice, and morality; in our awareness of the cycle of life and death; and ultimately in our knowledge of, and capacity for, communicating with Him—in all those special functions that constitute the human mind or the human soul.

The specialness of the human being in God's purposes is manifest in Genesis through the language of our creation, so different from the chapters that describe the creations of the other living things: "And God said, Let the earth bring forth the living creature after its kind, cattle, and creeping thing, and beast of the earth after its kind."[2] God does not soil His hands with the creation of the animals. The lower creatures are born *of* the earth, not created by God *from* the earth.

In the very first telling of the creation of man, the opening words set a profound distinction in tone: "Let us make man . . ." The very language of the text establishes a special relationship between God and man. The animals are "brought forth," passively, it would seem, from the earth. God *makes* man. We are His creation by the explicitness of the term: "Let us make him . . ." And when that sentence is completed with those awesome words, "in our image, after our likeness," one knows a different order of intention is in operation.

From the beginning, the authors of Genesis rejected the idea of a continuum from beast to man. To them human beings are not "creatures of the earth," but something special. What they are is fashioned with knowledge, with wisdom. They alone can recognize—or find the need to create—a divine presence or a divine order. It is the human being that thinks in terms of meanings, futures, fates, not merely survival.

There is a touching playfulness in the relationship between the God of Genesis and His human creations. One sees a God who is not sure Himself about the creature He has made. But is this not the essential nature of that creature? God has made Adam and Eve unpredictable. Even He could not anticipate their behavior. They were autonomous creatures, something that will be discussed in detail in the next chapter.

God creates the animals for the amusement, for the companionship, and ultimately for all the purposes of human endeavor. "And the Lord God said, 'It is not good that the man should be alone; I will make him a help meet for him.' And out of the ground the Lord God formed every beast of the field, and every fowl of the air."[3] The central role of Adam among the living things is clearly established. Animals are his to use. The way he uses them will of course indicate his nobility or the erosion of his dignity, and the way he treats them will always be important in defining the kind of person he is. But they are there for his purposes.

God did not understand all of the specifics of Adam's nature or needs; the gift of the animals did not lessen Adam's sense of isolation and loneliness. "But for Adam there was not found an help meet [fitting] for him." What Adam needed was love and companionship with other creatures of his own kind; there was no true companionship with other animals. So God "made he a woman, and brought her unto the man." God created Eve.[4]

Who were these innocents, these perfect beings, all promise and no problems? They were not yet the exemplars of modern man and woman. Adam and Eve were incomplete until they had tasted of the Tree of Knowledge, at which moment the moral human being would be fully created. In the first two chapters of Genesis they are innocent, still only partly formed. They exist like children, waiting to be completed by life experiences in which they would be active participants. But the raw materials were all there. Adam and Eve before the Fall contained all the elements essential to making our species an entity beyond what would be conceivable in a mere extrapolation from all the animal life that existed before. They represent the child who will be father to the man. They are reminders of what we were meant to be and what we can aspire to become. They are the Jewish alternatives to a Christ. They are the godlike in us—they contain all the elements of our perfectibility. In the case of Adam and Eve, as distinguished from Jesus, they represent what we once were rather than what we are capable of becoming. The opening chapters of Genesis are a way of describing the anomaly that although we may resemble the animals we are not one of them. In the midst of evidence of our inhumanity, Adam and Eve remind us of what we were and what we can be. They remind us that we *are* in God's image.

Central to any definition of a human being as distinct from all other animals is that we think differently from all other animals. It is not just that we think "better"—that is, that we are smarter than lower animals, which of course we are—but we think differently. We think about different things and we think in different ways. The nature of human cognition is in such opposition to the way other animals think that perhaps we ought not even be talking about the "thoughts" of these lower animals.

All definitions are arbitrary when speaking of the functions of the human mind, in part because the components of conceptual thought are interdependent and overlapping. It is difficult to define intelligence, imagination, perception, anticipation, reasoning, problem-solving, analysis, calculation, dreaming, projection, conception, questioning, doubting, symbolization, and language without recognizing that each term may be simply a synonym for another, or that each one somehow uses the others, and may depend on that capacity for its expression and realization.

The capacity to symbolize allows us to see the essential similarities among seemingly unlike things: to relate the ant to the elephant in the community of animals; to relate oxygen and iron in a periodic table of elements. It also allows us to visualize in abstraction the concrete representation of the thing itself. This aspect of symbolization is observed in the most sparkling example—human language.

Language, and how we use it, reveals some of the most extraordinary aspects of the human being. Language lends form to the substance of our mind, and out of that substance we create worlds for ourselves beyond the world into which our species was born. With language we define the nature and the boundaries of our world; we can exchange "information" with our fellow human creatures, who share our time and space, and through written language to the generations that will follow us.

Cicero based his concept of the uniqueness of the human being on language, or "eloquence." In his metaphor of evolution, history began when "Men wandered at large in the fields like animals and lived on wild fare." During this season in man's history, he was guided by brute strength and unreasoning passion. "At this juncture a man, a great and wise one . . . introduced them to every useful and honourable occupation." They resisted the burdens of the honorable life until "through reason and eloquence" they were "transformed from wild savages into a kind and gentle folk."[5]

Rousseau, too, saw language as the vehicle that separated primitive man, who was little more than a beast, from the human creature who was to emerge. For Rousseau, language was the central coordinating attribute of the human mind, on which all the other human attributes of culture—science, the arts, history, and even identity—would be based.[6]

These days it is fashionable to observe in animals as different as dolphins and robins, chimpanzees and dogs something that is called "language," but while the debate continues it is becoming increasingly apparent that only human beings have true language—the capacity to communicate abstract thoughts and ideas.

All sorts of animals communicate with one another: insects, fish, birds, herding animals, and primates. But do they converse with one another? Noam Chomsky has pointed out that every animal communication system that is known consists of a very fixed and limited number of responses which are essentially signals directly related to specific behavior. Human language is not "characteristically informative," to use Chomsky's term. We can, perverse and wily creatures that we are, speak to intentionally *misinform*. In addition, our speech may be totally unrelated to anticipated actions or real events.[7] In other words, there are human but no animal storytellers in either sense of that phrase, neither entertainers nor liars.

True speech is not merely the utterance of sounds to communicate emotions or needs to your fellows. Obviously any dog lover knows when his dog is hungry, wishes to play or go out. But the dog does not make it explicit by his utterances, although the owner may know through his intelligence and experience what Spot would like to do, what particular games he would prefer to play, or where he wishes to go and for what purpose.

It is not chance that examples of animal speech are uniformly drawn from domesticated or research animals. Animals who "speak" inevitably speak to human beings. Beyond the rudiments of survival—the signaling of the approach of a predator, the call to food or water—of what use is the nature of true speech in even the relatively advanced chimpanzee world? Much of this could be equally well performed through pheromones, the secretion of coded scents that are responded to by the olfactory senses rather than the auditory. In fundamental life-supporting activities, such as warning of the approach of a predator or announcing sexual receptivity, chemical communication or a specific cry would have a distinct advantage over speech. It is immediate and unambiguous.

True speech is a form of symbolic abstraction and therefore interpretable in multiple and idiosyncratic ways by different human beings, from separate cultures and with a variety of personal development. It requires cognition and analysis: "What does he mean by that? What is she trying to tell me?" True speech is bound to other unique attributes of human thinking: imagination, foresight, symbol formation, consciousness of time, space, purpose, and destiny.

It is true that with diligence and labor we can teach the higher primates to tell us what they wish to eat, whether they wish to play, why they wish to go out. It has even been stated that they communicate such messages to one another, although what response they would get from another ape is questionable.

"Speaking" animals are reminiscent of those old circus acts in which trained dogs were dressed up as bride and groom and minister and a mock marriage ceremony was performed. They marched down an aisle bedecked with flowers; they knelt on cue; they looked like the real thing. Animal speech is akin to canine nuptials: all form and no substance. As the philosopher Jonathon Bennett wistfully said, as though talking of some dreadful dinner companions, "They never say anything complicated, and their range of themes is small."[8] They will never say anything that bears repeating.

Some early researchers assumed that human speech had evolved as an elaboration of the guttural noises of certain animals; the grunting, gesturing, introjectional, projectional sounds gradually became modified into words. This theory, first and probably best expounded by Democratus in classic times, had an appealing quality

that captivated the imagination of generations to follow. It is not
readily accepted these days. Modern understanding of comparative
anatomy confounds it. We can identify the shrieks of pain and the
purrs of pleasure in our pets as well as in some of the animals of
the wild. Over hundreds of thousands of generations, these utterances have never developed, and in all likelihood will never develop, into anything like true speech. The brain configurations of
lower animals are so different from the human being's it is inconceivable that they could support true language.

In considering the way human speech develops through childhood, E. O. Wilson concludes that the human mind is innately
structured so as to string words together in certain arrangements
and not others. This "permits a far more rapid acquisition of
language than would be possible by simple learning. It is demon-
strable by mathematical simulation alone that not enough time
exists during childhood to learn English sentences by rote."[9]

Many of the pioneers in animal communication have now come
to recognize that what they have accomplished with animals is a
form of sophisticated conditioning or learning, not the initiation
of a latent trait for language. Herbert Terrace, a pioneering researcher in this field, finally concluded after many years of study
that primates were not capable of true speech, agreeing with Chomsky that human language appears to be a unique phenomenon,
without significant analogue in the animal world.[10] What we have
most likely done in our attempts to teach language to higher primates is dissimilar only in form and complexity to what the average
dog owner does in domesticating his pet. The evidence of this
procedure's artificiality lies in the fact that these animals always
seem to have more to say to us than to each other.

The unique gift of speech is an important theme from the
beginning of the Old Testament. The power of the name and
the capacity *to name* is a mystical and oft-repeated ceremony in
the Bible. Naming will be used to mark a new identification, a
transformation, a rebirth of a spiritual form. It is always a symbolic
and profound action. God will use the process of naming to indicate
a mission and a blessing. When God chooses Abraham to serve

His purposes and to sustain His laws, the covenant is symbolized by a change of name.

"Neither shall thy name any more be called Abram, but thy name shall be Abraham; for the father of a multitude of nations have I made thee. . . . And I will establish my covenant between me and thee and thy seed after thee throughout their generations for an everlasting covenant. . . ."[11]

When God rewards Sarah for her love and fidelity by blessing her with fertility at the age of ninety, her name is changed from Sarai to Sarah, so that "she shall be a mother of nations; kings of people shall be of her."[12]

And after Jacob struggled with the messenger of the Lord, he extracts a blessing from the angel. The blessing is expressed in the change of his name:

"Thy name shall be called no more Jacob, but Israel; for thou hast striven with God and with men, and hast prevailed."[13] Jacob, who stole his brother's birthright, who achieved his position by stealth and deceit, is implicitly forgiven. His devotion is rewarded. Jacob the supplanter becomes Israel the prince of God. God Himself will later directly confirm this change of name as a further reaffirmation of the potential for redemption through service and behavior that is so central to the philosophical values inherent in Genesis.[14]

God shares with Adam the profound privilege of defining through names. Adam exercises his authority over the animals by using that precious gift. It is for him to decide what they shall be called, and in that process how they shall be considered. In giving name to them he is defining a species: God "brought them unto the man to see what he would call them; and whatsoever the man would call every living creature, that was to be the name thereof."[15] By granting Adam the power to name the animals, God is clearly announcing that they are Adam's creatures. They have no separate entity in the scheme of His design. They will not be concerned with His divine justice nor in the carrying of His name or word.

I use language as an introductory example to elucidate the special quality of the human mind that also includes the related capacities of abstraction, symbolism, and human imagination. I use naming specifically because it is the first example of the power of the symbolic world offered in Genesis, and also because the power of "the name" is often underestimated.

To name something is to identify it. To identify something is to endow it with certain traits rather than others. In the symbolic world in which we live, definitions become realities. We will starve in the presence of abundant protein in the form of human cadavers, because in our tradition the human body will never be defined as food. The debate over whether the fetus or even the eight-celled zygote is a "person" is testament to the continuing power of the name. We label something "good" or "evil"; we identify someone as friend or foe; we treat some seemingly trivial but symbolic piece of behavior as essential to our honor—and we may offer our lives to uphold these distinctions.

To call a human being a higher primate, or even the highest primate, is to place him in a context of values associated with animals. To say he is in God's image is to set different values on his treatment and his behavior. In the beginning is *always* the word.

According to the values of Genesis, the capacity for language was a fundamental attribute of human nature even before the exercise of free will. Spiritual man is conceived and made possible through our ability to speak with God. This powerful asset allows us to make and keep covenants. Language supports a world of ideals that transcends the "real" world of survival.

We live in at least two worlds. We are blessed and cursed with an awareness that transcends the sensate. We can escape from the strictures of self and survival. Beyond the world of appetite and satiation, fear and rage, life and death is a world of hope and imagination, of ideals and purpose. Those of us who have passed beyond the state of struggle against starvation, beyond levels of brute survival, will spend our days in this world of our perceptions. Our awareness of God may be a legitimate recognition of that which truly is or merely a product of our imagination. In either case, it is a stunning example of our potential and need to understand the meanings of life, rather than just to accept and experience

the conditions of life. "Man is of God," declared Rabbi Akiba:
"And what is far more, he *knows* he is of God."

Ovid, in examining the uniqueness of man, also emphasized our
questing mind, while commenting on another unique aspect of
Homo sapiens, our upright posture: "And, though all other animals
are prone, and fix their gaze upon the earth, He gave man an
uplifted face and bade him stand erect and turn his eyes to
heaven."[16]

Animal activities that seem imaginative, brilliant, or intelligent
are none of these. The organized behavior of insects is fixed by
instinct, not by choice, and the stupid mechanical quality of such
behavior can be revealed by its lethal persistence even when environmental conditions have changed, making the formerly life-
supportive behavior deadly. The insect, whose behavior seems so
efficient, so rational, so purposeful, cannot make a minor change
to accommodate to a life-threatening change in the environment.

Even the "tool-making" monkey, prying the termites out of the
rotting log with his bent stick, attests to the difference between
humankind and the animals. The monkey's tool is discovered, not
created, nor will it ever be improved upon. A million generations
of monkeys will never create an iron probe. And, like the com-
munications of all animals, the tool is survival-oriented. How does
this activity relate—in any significant way—to the creation of the
telescope? What bizarre "animal" expends the energy for such an
abstract and nonutilitarian purpose as examining the stars? Perhaps
the investigation of the heavens was, indeed, originally utilitarian—
driven by our need to understand the nature of God. Then the
question may be restated: what bizarre "animal" has the need or
the capacity to discover theology and cosmology?

The building of the pyramids is in its complex way a metaphor
for all that is singular in the activities of the human species. It is
a testament to religious conviction, vanity, cruelty, wastefulness,
esthetics, imagination, and technology. In all of these aspects, it is
characteristically and purely a product of the human imagination.

"Imagination" may be the best general term to capture this
quality of the human mind. "Intelligence" seems too mechanistic

and exclusive, being defined as the capacity to acquire and apply knowledge. "Imagination" embraces and describes a richer range of mental activity: the capacity for learning and analytic reasoning; the capacity for creative reasoning; creativity itself—science, technology, the arts; the ability to build cultures—to accumulate knowledge and transmit this knowledge from one generation to another; true language; abstraction; fantasy and long-range anticipation— the discovery of the future.

Our imagination creates two other, quite distinct worlds for us. First, through our application of knowledge, imagination transforms the actual world we occupy into a different world of our own design; second, our imagination will transcend reality and create a world of our own perceptions in which we will be forced to live.

The World of Our Own Creation

The lamprey occupies the same marine environment that it has for hundreds of thousands of years, constant, unchanged by any actions of the species. The Londoner lives in a world that could not be imagined by his antecedents of only a thousand years before.

These days the blessings of science and technology seem to be ungenerously dismissed as we live in the midst of its metaphoric and literal fallout. Inheriting the transformed world of our manufactured culture—our arts, science, technology—we forget that these are gifts to us from past generations, inheritance from our ancestors. We take for granted the progress of the past and focus on the problems. We must remind ourselves that, although the privileged few might have had a more elegant existence in some romanticized past, the average person lived a life of such misery as to be unimaginable and unsupportable to the sensibilities of the average citizen of our Western democracies. Absorbed with the anxieties of the technological world we occupy, we ignore the privileges.

Science itself seems to have conspired in contributing to our diminishing self-confidence and self-esteem. Astronomy exposes our relative unimportance in the broader scheme of things; we are an ephemeral speck occupying an infinitesimal moment in an insignificant space in an unmeasurable universe. The anthropological descendants of Darwin proclaim our kinship with the chimpanzee. Biology in its current molecular phase may, through careful analysis of our DNA, establish an essential relationship between us and the lowest form of animal. Modern physics and chemistry may even reduce the distinction between us and inanimate, inorganic things by defining at a molecular level our particular nature.

Yet science is the product of our rationality and our reach, and whereas the possibilities for our survival may be reduced by our increased knowledge and its applications, the uniqueness of our species is only enhanced by them. And the quality of our lives is better than that of people forced to suffer the pains and torments of prescientific existence.

The technology that supplies us with warmth in the most frigid winters and sustenance through extended droughts is a product of the human mind. It is another example of the basic capacity for abstraction and symbolization that allowed us to discover the *principle* of the wheel, more significant than inventing the thing itself. The ancient Mayans had discovered the wheel without discovering the underlying principle, without fully appreciating what they had created. Using wheels only in toys, the Mayans were forced to construct their magnificent cities without the advantage of carts or pulleys. Moreover, they built their temples under the limiting conditions imposed by their failure to recognize the power inherent in the arch.

By fathoming the true meaning of the wheel, we were free to arrive at an understanding of the pulley and to discover in the relationship of the wheel to the pulley—and the gear and the lever and the inclined plane—the abstract concept "machine." God had dictated that man should earn bread "In the sweat of thy face," but the knowledge that would mitigate the burden was also the gift of God. We invented machines that efficiently reduced the labor imposed upon us so that, in Western cultures at least, most of us need not sweat in the air-conditioned offices of our work-places. That we suffer in other ways, perhaps with greater agony, will be discussed more fully in the chapter on work.

Beyond the world of technology, esthetics is another specifically human contribution to the transformation of the world in which we live, a testament to the particularly human capacity for feeling, imagination, and symbol formation. Animals do beautiful things but not for the sake of beauty. They contribute to the existence and presence of esthetics in this world, but the esthetic sensibility is within our eye and the esthetic purpose is ours. The display of the feathers of male tropical birds is gorgeous, but its purpose is to attract a mating female not to create beauty. The display is a means, not an end, fundamentally related to the survival needs of the bird and its species. Such adornments and performances are thus fixed and determined by nature, not by the choice or mind of the birds.

Only *Homo sapiens* adds elements to existence independent of their utility. Sometimes for vain and foolish reasons. The purpose of the fig leaf was to cover the shame of human sexuality. And the garments of skins that God made for Adam and Eve were for protective covering in anticipation of the rough world—the thorns, the thistles—that awaited them outside Eden. The "esthetics" of clothing that has evolved is more likely to occupy modern man and woman than considerations of modesty or protection from the elements. Yves St. Laurent is a long way (whether up or down is a matter of taste) from fig leaves and bear skins. The immense amount of money spent on clothing—and cosmetics and jewelry—preponderantly serves other needs beyond the utilitarian. To use the words of fashion itself, these items are selected to make "a statement."

But all is not vanity. Certainly other aspects of esthetics—poetry, music, sculpture, architecture, painting, and dance—enrich our lives and serve to soften the harshness of survival by adding light and glory to the cold industrial landscape we have created. The joy in the arts, our creations, rivals the pleasure of nature, God's creation, in its capacity to nurture the souls of human beings. The world of esthetics may be the purest and most singular expression of the difference between us and the animals. No animal looks with wonder either at the beauties of nature or in appreciation at its own artistic products. The feeling of awe, with its commingling of wonderment and fear, is testament to our awareness of our own finitude and a tribute to the uniquely human awareness of a world beyond our own purposes and even perceptions.

Every specifically human attribute is rooted in a corresponding biological substratum. Similarly, every unique biological aspect of the human being will contribute to the forms of human institutions. Consider one seemingly irrelevant but peculiarly human attribute—the prolonged postreproductive life of our species.

The human animal spends a much larger percentage of life after its reproductive capacity than is imaginable in other species. There is a fertile period of some thirty years in the life of a woman, from fifteen to forty-five, but the life expectancy of a woman in our culture is now about eighty. In almost every other animal group, an animal dies off quickly after its reproductive age has ended. The postmature period for a woman is at least as large a percentage of her life span as the fertile period.

This extended postreproductive period, when added to the already long life span of *Homo sapiens*, longer than traditional in higher animals, allows for another attribute of the species. In human populations, two, three, and sometimes even four adult generations may coexist. This facilitated transmitting acquired knowledge across generations well before the discovery of writing. It would not be necessary for each new generation to rediscover the wheel.

This coexistence assures that a powerful Lamarckian mechanism—whereby acquired characteristics *can* be transmitted—will coexist along with the Mendelian mechanisms that support all animal genetics. We are capable of passing on acquired characteristics. We are not dependent on mutation to introduce change; we do not need to reinvent the pulley, nor do we need to have some specific pulley-inventing capacity fixed into our genetic nature.

Culture has become a more efficient and powerful genetic device.

As one great biologist, S. Tax, put it: "Culture is part of the biology of man . . . even though it is passed on socially and not through genes. It is a characteristic of our species, as characteristic as the long neck of the giraffe."[17] Through our culture, we inevitably alter the world we occupy, and also the world of our children's children, for better or for worse.

But I have said we alter the world in two distinct ways. First, as has just been described, we create the actual environment, the facts of our existence. Second, we occupy a world of perception that becomes for us more "real" than the actual world.

The World of Our Own Perception

The philosopher Ernst Cassirer, in his *Essay on Man*, saw the creation of a symbolic world as central to the distinction between human and animal perception of the worlds they inhabit: "In the human world we find a new characteristic which appears to be not only quantitatively enlarged; it has also undergone a qualitative change. Man has, as it were, discovered a new method of adapting himself to his environment. Between the receptor system and the effector system, which are to be found in all animal species, we find in man a third link which we may describe as the *symbolic system*. This new acquisition transforms the whole of human life. As compared with the other animals man lives not merely in a broader reality; he lives, so to speak, in a new *dimension* of reality."[18]

Cassirer then states that man no longer lives merely in a physical universe, he lives in a symbolic universe.

"Language, myth, art, and religion are parts of this universe. They are the varied threads which weave the symbolic net, the tangled web of human experience.

". . . No longer can man confront reality immediately; he cannot see it, as it were, face to face. . . . Instead of dealing with the things themselves man is in a sense constantly conversing with himself."[19]

Cassirer seems unaware that this idea of a perceptual world, more real than any actual experience, is the central thesis of Freudian psychology. Freud took the concept of subjective idealism that seemed so abstract and metaphysical in the writings of Bishop Berkeley and made of it the stuff of everyday reality. Berkeley held that there is no existence of matter independent of perception; only God makes possible the apparent existence of "real" things. Freud assumed the existence of a real world yet found it essentially irrelevant, since we do not engage or react to the actual event but only to our perceived construction of it. For most of us, the real battles of survival occur in our internal world. It is internal conflict that produces neurosis, and its resolution that brings peace of mind.

The Freudian view of human experience has become a central construct in our modern view of ourselves, the world we occupy, and the relationship between the two. It is a cliché of modern psychiatry that we live in a world of our own creation. Once we leave a life of struggle for the basic stuff of survival, we enter into the world of perception. Joy, despair, security, and terror will be fed by our view of who and what we are in relation to those around us. This is often in complete variance with measurable reality.

In our everyday activities, instead of responding to the actual events that compose our lives, we will impose a distortion from the past that will color or cloud what we choose to see. For example, our capacity for symbolic recall will allow that memory of a stern, unyielding, and unforgiving father to dominate and influence all relationships, even with the most loving, protective, and generous of authority figures. The past is both a distorting and a filtering lens through which the present will be visualized. We will selectively "forget" painful events, invent others, and distort what happens today to conform to our expectations as shaped by our past. Our self-image, which is a profound element in shaping our aspirations and behavior, is more closely related to what we *think* we are, what we *once* were, or what we were once considered to be than to what we may actually be. One of the most beautiful women I have known was convinced of her plainness because "everybody" knew her sister was the beauty in the family. A man who was a giant success, having not just succeeded but triumphed in multiple careers, was haunted by dreams of exposure. A "gifted child," he grew up "lazy and undisciplined," according to his adored father. Since things came easily, he had not worked hard as a child. He worked prodigiously hard as an adult. No matter, he carried around the internalized self-image of a lazy boy who had gotten away with it and who might imminently be exposed as the fraud he assumed himself to be.

Sigmund Freud's most profound contribution was not in the area of mental illness but in his illumination of normal human sensibilities. His examination of pathological states was most productive as a magnifying lens to reveal through their exaggerated extremes the mental functionings that underlie normal human behavior. In this spirit, I would like to offer a clinical example to illustrate how we live in a world of our own perceptions.

Like Freud, I have seen, in constantly repeated examples, the tragedy of patients who suffer the anticipation of events that will never arrive. Almost all psychic distress is the product of a distorted perception that transforms our present reality, undervalues our strengths, and anticipates a dreaded imagined doom that tragically may arrive—precisely and only because it is anticipated. When misery is proportional to actuality it is not defined as emotional illness. Psychologists and psychiatrists may help such patients through times of true privation and misery, but only in the fashion of a supportive friend, not as a professional.

The paranoid personality offers a dramatic example of the relationship of perception to reality. He lives in a world of hostile individuals by whom he is—I mean really is—always cheated. To begin with, he will always recognize those incidents in which he was short-changed in life in a way that most of us will not. Most of us are not that sensitive to exploitation. We will, blessedly, ignore or fail to see slights of little consequence. The paranoid will detect the least slight. He is a professional grievance-collector and, like the antique-collector who can spot the genuine article amid the collection of imitations, he will sense a trace element of scorn in a bedrock of admiration.

Second, whether or not he is demeaned or cheated, he will assume that he has been. The paranoid interprets each ambiguous, nonmeasurable, arbitrary action as a calculated decision against him. If he plans a picnic, he is sure that it will rain. If it does rain, he will egocentrically interpret the rain as being an action against him. Though statistics will ensure that he gets neither more nor fewer rainy holidays than the rest of us, in his reconstruction of the past he will perceive himself as having been singled out by bad luck and bad weather. In his view, he is always given the dirty end of the stick or the smaller piece of the pie. If this is his perception of the world he lives in, what difference does it make if it is "real"? It is his reality, and his suffering is real.

Finally, I would assume that usually he *is* given the smaller piece of the pie. The paranoid always assumes that the trusting person will be taken advantage of; therefore he dare not be trusting. In actuality, a trusting, naïve, generous individual is likely to bring out the best in most of us. We want to give, we want to share with that kind of person. And even if we do not respond with generosity, what about *his* reality? He will go through life convinced that people never take advantage of him, and ultimately that may be more important than what actually happens to him.

A sullen, paranoid, resentful individual—always assuming that he is not being well served, expecting that no one will treat him fairly—will tend to elicit the worst in those around him. He invites exploitation. We give him what he asks for.

The formulations of both Cassirer and Freud are rooted in the philosophical idealism, from Kant through Fichte and Schelling to Hegel, that dominated the German culture from which they both emerged. In the world of the idealists, all reality is the creation of the mind or spirit. Idealism was constantly being rediscovered in each new age. As Cassirer himself points out, it was Epictetus who had said: "What disturbs and alarms man are not the things, but his opinions and fancies about the things."

Our capacity for symbol formation permits us not only to learn from the past but to anticipate a future. We need not wait for the actual event. We exploit our experience, our knowledge, our acquired history. We can approach the symbols and extrapolate from them. We can see connections and even at times understand the nature of the connections. We can deal with future events as though they were at hand. This is part of the power of anticipation, or, to use the term of the French philosopher Rousseau, "foresight." Characteristically, Rousseau emphasizes the pessimistic rather than the creative aspects of this unparalleled gift. He identifies it as the source of much of our misery: "Foresight! Foresight, which takes us ceaselessly beyond ourselves and often places us where we shall never arrive. This is the true source of all our miseries."[20]

The most profound effect of anticipation on us lies in our awareness of the inevitability of the termination of our lives. Animals experience fear, but it is unlikely that any of them have a sense of the relationship that leads from pain to illness to mortality. Though they fear predators, they do not know, or cannot conceive, the ultimate pain involved in the human awareness that we will die—and, worse, that the world will go on without us.

The knowledge of death leads to elaborate methods to deny death. Ernest Becker, in his book *The Denial of Death*, beautifully describes the extraordinary price we pay to avoid facing our mortality.[21] The knowledge of death is seen by many psychologists as underlying almost all neurotic anxiety. Many of the terrors and irrational anxieties that plague our existence are simply displacements from the ultimate terror of our own inevitable end.

The institutions of religions have been explained by Freud, in particular, as an attempt to deal with our finitude and our vulnerability, and to make bearable sense of the idea that something so central, so pivotal to our own personal world—our very existence—can be but an ephemeral and passing phase. Such a narcissistic injury, such a blow to our own inflated self-worth, is simply intolerable. Freud postulates religion as an illusion that supports an existential world of vulnerability and anxiety, and reinforces the need to deny our mortality.[22]

The dynamics of *neurotic* life were used by Freud to adduce the principles of normal behavior from which it evolved. None of us lives in the actual world. We all create our own dramas. We are all the authors of our own existence. The symbolic world is the environment of the healthy as well as the ill. It is the adaptive value of our perceptions, not the fact of them, that distinguishes mental health from mental illness.

With the natural inclinations of the physician, I, too, have started my discussion of anticipation emphasizing the negative aspects of anxiety and survival before introducing the positive and life-enriching aspect of anticipation. Anticipation is a source of immense joy. The anticipation of a desired event—a child's Christmas, a romantic liaison, an honor or a promotion, a vacation—may support us with pleasure that transcends the actual event. First, it is often extended over a longer period of time. Second, the real event may prove less delightful than the fantasied one. Third, the event may never come to pass, but the anticipation will nonetheless have produced a delight on its own.

There are three aspects of travel that most of us enjoy: (1) the preparation, planning, and anticipation; (2) the actual events of the trip; and (3) the nostalgia and reminiscence. We love reading about a strange country, poring over maps, relishing the expectation of surprise and delight. Then the gratification of a trip is always compounded by the reminiscences. In nostalgia, the "disaster" that was—a flat tire, a missed ferry, a wrong turn, a sleepless night— is converted into a shared source of humor and delight. The trip itself is often another matter: the chaos of an international airport; the charming little town that has become commercialized and overrun by monstrous tour buses; the hotel that does not have the reservation and indeed never heard of you and denies that such a person as you even exists. For me, there is no question that the anticipation is the most pleasurable, the nostalgia is the second, and the actual event of the trip is the least pleasurable. I have often thought what a wonderful convenience it would be if I could find some mechanism that would allow me to have the first and third and eliminate the trip altogether.

Beyond the enhancement of pleasure, anticipation supports our very survival. It allows for strengths and stabilities beyond the mere fragility of human cartilage, sinew, and bone. We need not resort to evasive action to protect ourselves from a danger anticipated in the near or distant future. We are not limited to the options of reacting to what we know is coming. We can prevent its coming. We are to a remarkable degree determinants of our future, not merely passive subjects or victims of it. We can anticipate dangers before our senses can possibly monitor them. We know the normal predicted rainfalls, for instance. When the reservoir levels are dangerously low, we can restrict consumption to essential needs, thereby protecting ourselves from a potential disaster. By predicting the future, we can make contingency plans. Anticipation leads us to build homes, store fuel, domesticate animals, ration supplies, build walls and fortresses, discover armaments—and, finally, build atomic weapons, which make the destruction of the entire species yet another dread to add to the loss of our own selves, to our recognition of our own mortality.

Some animals seem to anticipate. They hoard, put food away, hibernate through the winter. Yet this is not anticipation but a fixed mechanical action genetically built in. It bears no relation in form or in purpose to the mental functioning of anticipation. The building of burrow after burrow after burrow by the groundhog, spaces beyond his possible use, may give him sensate pleasure, but not in anticipation of their function. This need to burrow is built into his biological pleasure mechanism and his instinctual drives as a protective device in times of danger. He can no more decide not to do it than he can decide to do it. Animals do not make decisions about survival-enhancing mechanisms. Nature would not put the species so at peril. Only *Homo sapiens* can risk their own destruction. But only human beings will be capable of adapting to natural disaster.

Domesticated animals in particular seem to practice what is labeled "anticipation." Yet, if a jumper who has had trouble with a particular fence shies when approaching that jump again, this is nothing more than a conditioned response. In form it is related to the salivation of Pavlov's dog on hearing the bell, not to the concept of an old-age pension or fire insurance. The distinction between the animal and the human consists in part in the complexity of human anticipation, of course, but that is not the fundamental difference. The so-called anticipation of the animals is always related to a previous experience; it is behavioral learning. Only the human being can imagine both a past he never knew and a future he can barely imagine. All of this is independent of experience but intricately linked to human culture, intelligence, and imagination.

Imagination and anticipation are guidelines useful only to an animal who is free to shape his own future. They are not by accident the exclusive and treasured possession of the human being, the only creature blessed and cursed with freedom and choice.

Rousseau recognized the power of imagination as a motivating force that drives and directs human behavior: "It is imagination which extends for us the measure of the possible, whether for good or bad and which consequently excites and nourishes desires by hope of satisfying them."[23] Imagination brought us out of the caves and into the universe. Imagination drove us to build cities and rockets to the moon. Imagination is the force behind culture and creativity. It drives us from the world of everyday experience to seek the world of the possible in a future that exists only in human imagination. To the animal, the present is a clone of the past, and the future does not exist. The future is the discovery of the human being.

Of course, the future we imagine may be *only* of our imagination; it may never come to exist. We may be preparing for something that will never come, or, worse, we may be facilitating that which we dread. This is the risk we run, the inevitable cost of vision. But vision will as often save us. Besides, we do not live to survive, we survive in order to live. Beyond physical survival is the stuff that dreams are made of. Anticipation is a golden thread woven into the tapestry of human existence. Fantasy can sustain us through times of boredom or pain, soften the harsh present with the expectation of a better future, lend mystery and romance to the humdrum and banal.

Kant, in struggling to define the special quality of human thinking, drew the illuminating distinction between knowledge of the "real" and knowledge of the possible.[24] This awareness of the possible, that which might become, is an acknowledgment of the power inherent in human imagination when yoked to human plasticity.

This grants us the power to design the multiple worlds we occupy.

We feed our souls on the products of our imagination and perception. They are at the root of the most treasured of human capacities, hope. Hope will support us against the ravages of disappointment and depression. It will allow us to endure and, beyond that, to aspire. When God banishes Adam and Eve from the Garden, a miraculous transformation occurs. Adam looks into the terrifying abyss of the future and discovers hope.

"Dust thou art, and unto dust shalt thou return" is the awful pronouncement of God. Adam's response is immediate, incredible, and glorious. He turns to the woman who has participated in his defiance of God, who will share his journey into the unknown, and triumphantly proclaims their future: "And the man called his wife's name Eve; because she was the mother of all living."[25]

With the power of the name, Adam transforms their banishment into triumph. From the ashes of despair, hope emerges. The end will become the beginning. The future is announced. And Eve will become the mother of humankind.

FREEDOM AND CHOICE

~~~~~~~~~~~

RATIONALITY AND REASON ARE ATTRIBUTES without sense or purpose if not accompanied by autonomy. To understand what the banished Adam and Eve meant to the author of Genesis, we must know something about the inhabitants of the Garden before the Fall— although, admittedly, that pure and perfect pair are difficult people to comprehend.

All of our proudest achievements could have conceivably existed within the Garden. We were already endowed with intelligence, rationality, and imagination—the ingredients necessary to create an intellectual, technological, and esthetic life. But it is difficult to imagine an esthetics free of doubt, pain, and uncertainty. It is difficult to conceptualize any aspect of human activity without conflict or shame, without grief or frustration; with choice but without the exercise of that choice. The innocent human pair, Adam and Eve before the Fall, are not identifiable with the kind of human beings we are likely to encounter in our everyday life. To those of us who occupy this world of vice and virtue compromised, they remain as enigmatic and elusive as the spirit and form of angels.

As Adam and Eve were the creations of God, we are the creatures of Adam and Eve. The human being we know today was born at the moment when Adam and Eve audaciously and willfully ate of the forbidden fruit of the Tree of Knowledge. In their defiance our ultimate identity was shaped. Genesis describes the biological singularity of our species, the double birth of *Homo sapiens*. We are shaped by God in our potential and reshaped by human choice—nature and nurture; genetic endowment and the forces of environment. This primal pair, in selecting knowledge over safety, chose the risks of autonomy over the security and restrictions of dependency. By so doing they also assumed responsibility for their own completion. They became parents to themselves. Each human being is constructed in such a way that as an infant it will be born incomplete, awaiting the impact of the parent-controlled environment to determine whether it will develop into a fully mature human being or something less.

Thinking people, scientific people, creative, relating, and loving people could all have existed before the Fall. The moral human being certainly, but also the complex psychological human being that occupies this latter half of the twentieth century is the progeny of parents transformed by autonomy exercised against authority.

"And the eyes of them both were opened, and they knew they were naked; and they sewed fig leaves together, and made themselves girdles. And they heard the voice of the Lord God walking in the garden . . . and the man and his wife hid themselves from the presence of the Lord God. . . . And the Lord God called unto the man, and said unto him, 'Where art thou? And he said, 'I heard Thy voice in the garden, and I was afraid, because I was naked; and I hid myself.' And He said, 'Who told thee that thou wast naked? Hast thou eaten of the tree, whereof I commanded thee that thou shouldest not eat? And the man said, 'The woman whom Thou gavest to be with me, she gave me of the tree, and I did eat.' And the Lord God said unto the woman, 'What is this thou hast done?' And the woman said, 'The serpent beguiled me, and I did eat.' "[1]

Now, here is a couple with whom we can identify. We know these inquiring, defiant, ambitious, inquisitive—and ultimately confused—people, the mother and father of us all. Ashamed, frightened, guilty, expecting punishment they know they deserve; whining, blaming each other—she did it, he did it, they did it, it wasn't I. In all of this we recognize the child that we once were and the child that remains within us always. It is not difficult to read the story of Adam and Eve as the story of development from the innocence of childhood to the guilt of adulthood—from dependency to responsibility. That may be one intended message of a complex tale that can exist on multiple levels. At any level, the text is a story of the birth of morality.

There cannot be a moral creature without autonomy, and choice. A freedom that is designed always to choose good is no freedom at all. Out of the act of defiance and the failure of the test, shame, guilt, and fear will emerge. These emotions constitute the stuff of which conscience will later be built. But why the test?

Biblical scholars see this challenge to will as establishing, beyond the moral self, still another facet of human beings, the spiritual self. "Man's most sacred privilege is freedom of will, the ability to obey or to disobey his Maker." This sharp limitation of self-gratification, this "dietary law" was to test the use people would make of freedom; and it thus begins the moral discipline of humankind. Unlike the beast, man has also a spiritual life which, under the relationships established in Genesis, demands the subordination of human desires to the law of God. "The will of God revealed in His Law is the one eternal and unfailing guide as to what constitutes good and evil—and not man's instincts, or even his Reason."[2]

Freedom of will has meaning only within the broader structure of the kind of thinking that is exclusively the function of the human brain, different in kind, not just in quantitative capacity, from that of all other animals. The kind of choice that is available to lesser animals is trivial and insignificant. Only human beings are capable of making important decisions. The survival of the human species will inevitably depend on them. The choices of lesser animals (Shall I eat the banana or the mango first?) can have only accidental significance for their survival and none for their species.

Other animal species are destroyed by chance, by a catastrophe of nature, or often by the simple alteration of their environment, but never by elective behavior. No animal will refuse food when it is plentiful and choose hunger for some long-range purpose. Overgrazing during a period of prolonged drought may destroy a species of cattle, but they are driven by hunger to graze. There is no cattle Joseph to interpret the dreams of a cattle pharaoh. There will be no rationing, no storage, no enduring of hunger in the presence of plenty, and therefore no eventual lifesaving allocation in a period of want.

There is nothing in lower animals equivalent to the freedom of will of the human being. There is nothing that can mitigate the command of instinct. "Instinct," Kant has said, is "that voice of God that is obeyed by all animals."[3] By Kant's definition, the human being is not an animal, for we are constantly disobeying. This is explicated with authority and elegance in Genesis. A generous Creator offered Adam the world, literally, with but one condition: "Of every tree of the garden thou mayest freely eat; but of the Tree of the Knowledge of good and evil, thou shalt not eat of it."[4]

We disobeyed, and we were created anew in that disobedience. We continue to defy the call of instinct, often to our peril, but also to our ennoblement. Perhaps the concept is not defiance but being true to our nature. In *Homo sapiens*, while crucial survival needs are supported by basic drives—thirst, hunger, sexual drive—which are genetically coded into the species, the power of our will is such that we can sacrifice or corrupt even these, for purposes both noble and venal. With animals, things that are necessary for survival are immutable.

Genesis clearly makes the case for the autonomous and therefore responsible (accountable) human being. For fifteen hundred years or more, this vision was to remain dominant and surprisingly unchanged in the world of ideas that constituted Western civilization. And it was always supported at its base by the lessons of Genesis.

With Descartes, a modern philosophy was born freed from the constraints of theology and scholasticism. Doubt, speculation, and intellectual analysis were to replace revealed truth. The ambiguities of human nature would be re-examined, and the autonomous nature of the human being would come into question. The battle of free will would be eloquently argued, to no firm conclusion. Locke would defend it against the reasoned assaults of Hobbes and Spinoza. In the following generation, Hume would attack the notion and be answered with equal intellectual vigor by Rousseau and Kant. These were heady days for philosophy.

Eventually the philosophical battles would become secondary and academic. The battle would be won on another playing field altogether. The emerging economic and political demands of the Industrial Revolution would give birth to Western democracy as we know it today. The arguments of the philosophers became incidental to the necessary assumptions of such new philosophies as mercantilism, consumerism, individualism, free enterprise, participatory democracy, and the imperatives of rule by law. For us to exist in such a world, autonomy and accountability were essential assumptions. In the real world, human autonomy was assumed, independent of the vicissitudes and fashion of philosophy.

By the end of the nineteenth century, a scientific vision of human destiny was poised, ready to replace both the philosophical and the theological image of human existence. Scientific optimism was at its peak. Granted that the technological age was still more promise than reality, the future was in sight, and the future was in our own hands.

The scientist was the new Prometheus. There was no problem that technology would not eventually be able to solve. We were too arrogant to recognize even arrogance. We did not have to fear God; we had replaced him. The whole of history seemed to be contrived to serve the purposes and glorify the name of *Homo sapiens*. The new philosophers that would rule this world would emerge from science, economics, engineering, and the social sciences. The human being would be re-created, not in the image of God—or, for that matter, Kant—but in the images of Darwin, Freud, Marx, and Einstein.

But while we were building this brave new world of the twentieth century, technologically far beyond our most extravagant expectations, the tools of our own destruction were being fashioned. Our self-confidence would be eroded by this joyless and cold technical world. We would be diminished in the distorted mirrors of our own creation.

In recent times, the most concerted challenge to the concept of freedom or autonomy has emerged from the field of psychology. In the psychology market, freedom has few buyers. The two major influences here, behaviorism and psychoanalysis, may be antagonistic in every other way, but they have traditionally joined in blissfully embracing determinism.

Both see behavior as a complex end-point, a mathematical result of a number of forces and counterforces, or experiences and conditioning, accumulated over the years and patterning the individual in such a way as to produce one logical and inevitable result.

Before psychoanalysis, psychiatry was a descriptive science without a psychology—without any explanation of mental mechanisms in health or disease. Modern psychiatry now uses general psychological principles borrowed from psychoanalysis. Although many psychiatrists reject psychoanalysis as a treatment technique and dismiss some of its developmental concepts, two axioms of psychoanalytic theory are so widely accepted that they are now represented in almost every psychiatric frame of reference. The first: Every individual act of behavior is the result of a multitude of emotional forces and counterforces; this is the "psychodynamic" principle. The second: These forces and counterforces are shaped by past experience; this is the principle of psychic causality.

Taken together, these two principles dictate a way of viewing any act of behavior. Suppose three men are threatened by a man with a gun. One flees; one stands paralyzed with fear; one attacks. The stimulus for all three is the same. But the stimulus is only one factor in determining the resultant behavior. Acting on the complex machinery of the human being, the stimulus triggers associations, perceptions, and response patterns already "programmed in" by previous experience. This view of behavior rejects the possibility of an isolated and voluntary action and, whether we like it or not, places psychiatry in the camp of determinism. The way one behaves when confronted by a crisis will be determined by the multiple influences of one's background. We will "explain" Mary's courage—or Jack's cowardice—by the fact that Mary's mother did such-and-such, or Jack's father did so-and-so. In psychoanalytic theory, all acts—healthy, sick, or not-sure-which—share one property: *they are predetermined.* Many psychiatrists in fact do not like it, and are personally unhappy with determinism; they "believe in" free will. But professionally they have not been able to incorporate "chance" as a relevant phenomenon into the theory of psychiatry.

Behaviorists do not believe in an unconscious. They eschew the "nonscientific" assumptions of dynamic psychiatry. They see behavior, not perception or ideation or emotion, as all. They envision complex behavior as the sum total of individual pieces of conditioned responses, behaviors built into the organism over the years of development. They see perceptions as a product of behavior, whereas Freudians see behavior as a product of perceptions. Both, however, see present behavior as being determined by past events acting on the individual. In both of these areas, the cause-and-effect model of physics has been applied to human behavior. Never mind that the analysts and behavioral psychologists see one another as putting the cart before the horse. It really matters very little. They are both concerned with the same cart and the same horse, and neither has any doubt that the problem is a cart-horse one or a horse-cart one, depending on the orientation.

Ironically, though rejecting free will in theory, in practice a psychoanalyst demands it. This somewhat illogical dualism has been the only way the analyst could function as both a theorist and a therapist. The compromise that was reached—and I do not offer it as an elegant one—is that freedom of behavior does not actually exist, but that the illusion of freedom is essential to effect change. This is why a psychiatrist may insist that his patients can give up their addiction to food, drugs, or cigarettes. The assumption, coming from a figure vested with power and authority, becomes one more stimulus that will determine the inevitable, now desired, response.

Psychic determinism may richly enhance our understanding of individual development but it is a mischievous concept in a society that aspires to justice. One need only consider the relationship of psychoanalysis and law to see the sterility of this construction. With

the decline in the power of the religious vision and our abandonment of religious values, we began to approach questions of right
and wrong sociologically and psychologically. Rules of conduct
became fudged by consideration of the events that led up to the
conduct: the state of mind of the individual, his perceptions of
right or wrong. Our relativism began to erode previously held sets
of absolute principles. We began to individualize our concepts of
justice, and in so doing we inevitably made them more subjective
and relative.

Modern psychology contributed to a more compassionate and
sophisticated understanding of transgression and to a more refined
sense of justice. But the extension of sociological and psychological
exculpations would eventually prove self-defeating by becoming
all-inclusive. Psychoanalytic theory ultimately became a useless tool
in the system of justice, because it could not differentiate between
grotesquely different qualities of behavior.

When a judge in a court of law is forced to distinguish between
a free act and a compelled act, he is not helped by being told by
either a psychoanalyst or a behaviorist that *all* acts are compelled.
Civilized society requires that there be a distinction between a
coerced and a voluntary action. In other words, autonomy is a
necessary postulate to the assumption of individual responsibility.
A free society cannot function without the assumption that for the
most part we are responsible for our own actions.

Dynamic psychiatry may have been the leading agent in the
assault on autonomy in the law, but behaviorism was the dominant
force in the field of education. Behaviorism, given its pseudo-
scientific involvement with measurement and the methods of conventional science, had held a particular appeal for educators and
social scientists who aspired to scientific respectability. In this age
of the computer and computer graphics, anything that could be
represented in charts and tables, any data that could be quantified
would carry the illusion of objective truth. The quantifications of
the behaviorists proved comforting to those who were offended by
the irrational and complex world of the Freudian unconscious.

But human behavior is not and never will be analyzable into all of its components and cannot be usefully considered to operate on the model of causality supplied by physical scientists. Most human actions, particularly in areas of volition and cognition, will involve so many variables as to make predictability almost impossible.

Let me offer an example. A man is five pounds overweight and has decided to diet. One unconditional and inviolate principle is that there will be no snacking. It is the first night of this resolve. He is seated at a dinner meeting. He has been ultra-careful during the meal and, as his diet dictates, he has finished still feeling somewhat hungry. The waiter places in front of him a bowl of petits fours and miniature chocolates. Within ten seconds the subject has an impulse to take a chocolate. The problem is to predict whether he would take the chocolate or not at the time of the first impulse.

Obviously no one of scientific mind would accept this test case and make a prediction. There are too many unknown variables for us to determine this particular piece of behavior. It is no different from being given a complex problem in physics with incomplete data. We could not know.

Now let us examine the next step. You are given the crucial information that he does not follow his impulse. He does not take the chocolate. Without analyzing the variables, you know that an entire lifetime of complex inputs toward taking the candy have been placed on one side of the scale, and an entire lifetime of training and conditioning to resist it on the other side. We are asked to believe that, given this particular individual, this particular lifetime, and these particular conditions at this particular moment of time, the refusal of the candy was predetermined in precisely the same way as if balancing weights were added to one side or the other. I doubt it.

To complicate the matter further, you are then told that three seconds later he has a second impulse. You now have the enormous advantage of knowing the first decision to resist the impulse. Are you prepared to predict the response to the second impulse? You are not. Even though you now start by knowing the result of the immense number of factors before the first decision, and all you have to balance against that are three insignificant seconds of time.

If you were presented with the pattern of fifty impulses, leading both to the acceptance and the rejection of the chocolates, you would be no better at predicting the fifty-first. Even if the interval were reduced to one-tenth of a second. The number of variables that could be introduced in that fraction of time are as incalculable as those in the mass of time preceding the first decision.

The same is not true of weights and measures. That is what makes prediction of human behavior different from prediction of the behavior of inanimate things or of simple animal forms. Whether this is truly a "free" choice or not, it is an incalculable one, and as such can pass for freedom.

We all know we can condition a man to reject chocolates. My example has nothing to do with simple conditioning. It has to do with the predictability or inevitability of behavior. It might even be argued that, given an ape with a bowl of peanuts, a bunch of bananas, some lettuce, and a variety of other comestibles, we could not predict the ape's action in the sequence and choice of eating. But, given a hungry ape, we know that he would eat. If a starving or hungry ape refuses food, we assume some gross abnormalities. Every single ape will eat when hungry.

The man's decision with the chocolates has nothing to do with hunger. It has to do with a concept called "dieting," a concept totally inconceivable to any animal except the human being. His behavior is the product of his characterological capacities for impulse and impulse control, his specific passion for the object involved, the relationship of passion to reason, of appetite to knowledge, his attitudes about pleasure and safety and how they are balanced, his capacity for rationalization and how it intrudes on his capacity for rationality.

No ape understands health, longevity, or life expectancy, or is vain about his thirty-one-inch waist. There are practically no conditions involving human volition that can be titrated and measured regardless of how simple they might seem. Impulse and resistance, instinct and learning, motives and countermotives, thought and action are all aspects of the complexity of the human mind that deny predictability and make programming, at least at an adult level, extremely difficult.

The concept of psychic determinism, whether derived from behaviorism or psychoanalysis, simply will not hold water. Even if there is nothing called true autonomy, there has to be something recognized as freedom from the specific instinctual restraints that bind all subhuman animal behavior.

Having made a case for autonomy, one must acknowledge the data that drive psychologists into the arms of determinism. Much of adult behavior is automatic, patterned, and tenaciously resistant to change, mechanically operating, independent of rationality and choice.

Traditionally, geneticists use two technical terms to differentiate the interplay of nature and nurture: "genotype" and "phenotype." "Genotype" refers to the genetic constitution of an organism, the genes you inherit that determine whether you will have blue or brown eyes, will be right- or left-handed, and, beyond that, whether you may have special musical, artistic, or athletic skills. In the latter areas, all one inherits is the potential. Whether such potential is fulfilled will be determined by the environmental forces brought into play during the crucial years of development and afterward. "Phenotype" refers to what the organism becomes, the product of the environment's playing on the genetic capacity so as to encourage the expression of one set of characteristics as opposed to another.

In all animals except the human being, the genotype is almost fully expressed in the phenotype and therefore is predictable under standard conditions. And standard conditions are predictable, since in the natural environment of the zebra there are minimal variations in the patterns of behavior of the parents. The adult animal is true to his genetic design. Only in the human being is this not true. This is perhaps most eloquently expressed by Rousseau in his discussion of the perfectibility of man.[5]

Rousseau saw in every animal "only an ingenious machine to which nature has given senses in order to revitalize itself and guarantee itself, to a certain point, from all that tends to destroy or upset it." He asserted that the same exists in the "human machine," with one essential difference. With the beast, nature alone does *everything*. With man, he himself, by being a free agent, cooperates with nature. The beast "chooses or rejects by instinct" and man "by an act of freedom." "A beast cannot deviate from the rule that is prescribed to it even when it would be advantageous for it to do so, and a man deviates from it often to his detriment. . . . Nature commands every animal and the creature obeys. Man feels the same impetus, but he realizes that he is free to acquiesce or resist."[6]

Rousseau asserts that man is born essentially empty and must fill himself, and construct his own motivations from very rudimentary beginnings. At first he will do this willy-nilly and inadvertently, without design and perhaps without knowledge. Later, with his awareness of what is happening, he can rationally shape ideals and values and design institutions that serve those ideals and values. These institutions will then alter the very course of his own development and "fill in" what nature has left blank. Rousseau then goes on to demonstrate how this quite remarkable difference will be further magnified by the special consciousness of the human being. This awareness that he is free introduces a spirituality into his soul. It is this that Rousseau calls the perfectibility of man. In one precise statement, he sums up the immense difference between beast and human that is predicated on human autonomy and self-perception.

"An animal is at the end of a few weeks what it will be all of its life; and its species is at the end of a thousand years what it was the first year of that thousand." The exclusively human faculty of self-perfection will over the centuries bring to flower man's "enlightenment and his errors, his vices and his virtues," and in the long run makes the human being "tyrant of himself and of nature."[7]

No new knowledge emerging from the complex vision of modern scientific biology contradicts this brilliantly reasoned insight of two hundred years ago. Autonomy is complex, genetically determined, and multiply defined. It refers not just to the freedom inherent in the species, but to the freedom of each individual to behave in certain ways that are unpredictable and idiosyncratic. A species that can shape itself also has the potential to shape itself into relatively fixed and rigid patterns.

The human child is subject to an extraordinarily prolonged period of dependency. This serendipitously allows the parents sufficient time to mold the raw materials of the child into their models of a proper adult. Even here the unpredictability of these efforts is only too apparent to anyone who has raised a child. Still, our children are our products, for good or bad, and we shape them to our conscious or unconscious designs. These designs will be profoundly influenced by the standards of our culture and the selective values within the subculture of the particular family, further modified and reinforced by our behavior and attitudes as parents, and, of course, limited by the genetic nature of the child. By the time the average child reaches adulthood, he will carry within him certain values and sensibilities that will force much of his behavior into automatic patterns. He will, in other words, have been so indoctrinated that there will be a set of limitations on his freedom of action, imposed by his inbuilt set of values and propriety, his conscience and his self-image.

This early modeling has its most noticeable effect in two areas that seem at opposite ends of a spectrum: the first, manners and mien; the second, character and values. Manners and mien are expressed in apparently unimportant behavioral differences—forms of dress, social conduct, the "superficial" behaviors that distinguish one country or one time from another. Character and values will control the most profound aspects of our behavior. They will determine whether and under what circumstances we will sacrifice self-interest, or even self, in behalf of others or in the service of ideals that transcend survival.

René Dubos expressed his awareness of this early conditioning on himself: "From the beginning, I have felt completely at ease wherever I have worked in the United States. I doubt that I could have been as healthy, successful, and happy anywhere else in the world. Yet, after more than forty years of continued residence . . . I still have some mental reservations when I say that I am an

American. This is not for lack of allegiance to my adoptive country, or regret at having become an American citizen . . . but because I have not outgrown and do not want to discard the attitudes that I acquired in the small French villages where I spent my formative years and in Paris during my student days. The subtle quality of the skies, woods, and fields of the Ile de France country, and the intellectual discipline of French culture, have left an indelible stamp on my biological and mental being."[8]

We constantly modify behavior during the "formative" years, and thereby restrict autonomy. Those modifications set early in life will seem to have the fixity of instinct. Toilet attitudes and concepts of modesty are only two examples of behavior that are formulated early and dreadfully difficult to change, but there are many other fixed patterns of behavior. Those of us who have been taught to brush our teeth every morning and every night experience discomfort if we cannot do so. If evidence were forthcoming that fluorides made brushing completely unnecessary, many would find rationalizations to continue the practice because of a sense of irrational unease accompanying the abandonment of the habituated behavior.

"Manners" was the word that had traditionally been used to describe "the socially correct way of acting; polite bearing or behavior; etiquette."[9] The term now has a quaint and old-fashioned ring to it, which is a significant statement about the changing relationship between the individual and the community.

Manners instilled in young children made for automatic behavior, often inexplicable to them. At one time children "instinctively" rose when an adult entered the room. They may have had no idea what purpose was served by this behavior, but would rise in the same way that a yo-yo would rise when tugged. With maturation, many would recognize the reasoning behind the behavior: the sign of courtesy or attention; an act of respect; an acknowledgment of the status of the other person; perhaps an offer of services, such as making a seat available.

Although there were rational reasons for this convention, in other cases the reasons may have disappeared, the acts being merely a preservation of form over substance. Men were instructed from childhood to walk on the outside of the pavement when accompanying a woman, long past the time of mud roads and rambunctious horses. It has become a mechanical and meaningless behavior. One of the advantages of manners is that, being addressed to unimportant and trivial standards of social behavior, they freed us from having to analyze each and every situation and allowed us to concentrate on decision-making where it was important.

Manners became the substitute for instincts or instinctive behavior. That they were mostly concerned with specific trivial aspects of life did not mean they did not add a kind of elegance to life in general. Many acts of manners were designed to express courtesy and respect. There was a more civilized, somewhat more gracious quality in those days—before the dictum "Every man for himself"—when an adolescent boy would automatically rise to offer a seat in a train or trolley to an older woman, or, for that matter, to an older man.

These manners contributed to civility by defining, logically or not, a public behavior to which we all were expected to conform. In that sense, they were far from trivial. Manners paid homage to the public space, and acknowledged a limiting force on self-indulgence and impulse.

Clearly, the routine and mechanical behavior of manners is related to an esthetic of "civilization." Manners carried within them a set of values and expressed a concern for decorum and decency. Manners were an attempt to maintain a distinction between the behavior of human beings and animals. British movies depicting the upper classes of the 1930s inevitably contained the scene of a couple dining alone at opposite ends of one of those baronial tables that seemed to stretch into infinity. Of course they were in "dinner dress." To a middle-class American fifty years later, with a different concept of civilized behavior, this scene seemed "funny" and was reminiscent of all the safari jokes involving the stereotypic Englishman dressed for dinner alone under his tent in the jungle, with the buzzing mosquitoes and the sounds of the night creatures in the background. The peculiarities of others are always more apparent than our own.

Although the automatic nature of social behavior does limit autonomy, it is still not the fixity of the social behavior of insects. Changing conditions can lead to the rapid reversal of such behaviors. We saw it in every so-called social revolution, whether the sexual revolution of the sixties or the biological revolution now still in progress. The poor ant is stuck with his social behavior even under conditions that guarantee his destruction if he does not change.

In human beings, however, the profound fixity of behavior related to values and conscience transcends that of social mien, for it often reinforces a biological and genetic directive. The almost reflex readiness of most parents to risk their own survival recklessly and willfully to save the life of their dependent child is but one extreme example. For most of us, such behaviors are automatic, so dovetailed into our intuitive responses that they seem immutable. We assume that it is the genetic nature of the beast to behave in this "normal" way, and we are shocked and bewildered when we discover those among our kind who violate such patterns with unnatural acts.

The power of early conditioning to facilitate the development or the dissipation of our human potential is incalculable. It is demonstrated in the existence of the distorted few who abuse their children. They violate the biological directive on which the future of our species is built, the compassionate concern for the dependent child.

The battering parent is but an extreme example. What of the adolescent who can calmly hit a fellow human being over the head with a lead pipe to gain the contents of a purse or for no reason at all? The absence of any constraining guilt or shame in his behavior implies a defective conscience mechanism which is unlikely to be reparable. When a conscience-free individual emerges because of an inadequate or corrupting early environment, no amount of good will, understanding, compassion, or for that matter psychotherapy is likely to rectify the problem. Self-control in these individuals will reside in fear of retribution, not in remorse.

In matters of conscience and values, early conditioning, enforced through the emotions of fear, guilt, and shame, is a powerful influence in determining automatically the most profound aspects of human life. This being so, why not press for social engineering to ensure the development of human beings who will contribute and conform to the kind of civilization we respect? Why leave the phenotype to chance; why not preselect the kind of creature we would like to represent our species, and make sure to maintain a climate that will encourage the evolution of such a paradigm? Why not design our descendants? Since the human being is a construction of nature and development—a collaboration by two authors— why not, as one of the authors, predetermine the product? That was precisely the position taken by one of the most distinguished social scientists of our time, B. F. Skinner.

The most powerful assault on the principle of autonomy derived from behavioristic psychology occurred with the publication of Skinner's book *Beyond Freedom and Dignity*.[10] Skinner had the courage to take what was implicit in behavioral psychology and make it explicit. He extrapolated the inevitable political and sociological consequences of the psychological assumptions of behaviorism. Coming from the most respected student of behaviorism in our time, these ideas demanded serious attention. They remain the definitive statement of behaviorist philosophy.

In *Beyond Freedom and Dignity*, Skinner went further than an exposition of the implicit philosophy of behaviorism. He offered a political agenda based on the assumptions of that philosophy. The swap that he asked us to make was freedom for security. Professor Skinner attempted to ease the pain by reflecting that this exchange was not only necessary but a free lunch: we gain a great deal and we give up nothing. Freedom, he asserted, is only an illusion that we maintain to protect our vanities. We pretend that we differ from the lower animals, building our special worth on an erroneous assumption of autonomy, propagandized by prescientific philosophers and theologians.

By the time we have reached adult life, Skinner said, we are no freer than the jackal. But we have been conditioned with no specific program and therefore no rational purpose. This chaotic state has led us to the brink of the abyss. Give up the illusion of freedom while there is still time to save ourselves and begin the process of self-design with at least the same intelligence and planning that we would use to build a machine or train a dog. He offers a political agenda based on this set of assumptions.

This is not the theory of an academic philosopher speaking to his own esoteric audience of fellow academicians. Educational institutions are designed under Skinnerian principles these days, and suggestions for child-rearing continue to use behavioral theories. Why not extend these theories into the public-school systems and into the homes? Why not ensure preferred behavior and proper values by early conditioning?

Unrestricted personal liberty has rarely been offered as an ideal for social living by any intelligent thinker. From the dialogues of Plato to the last decisions of the Supreme Court, one can see debates that will pit the autonomous rights of the individual against the public interest.

Freedom and control are not a moral polarity in which one represents good and the other bad. The entire social structure is built on the right and need of society to control—indeed, coerce—certain behavior. Organized religion, organized morality, codified ethics, style and fashion, public education, civil law, constitutional law, criminal procedures all operate within a whole range of explicit and implicit control mechanisms.

What, then, is wrong with Skinner's agenda? On at least three grounds, I believe it is counterproductive.

First, human autonomy is not a myth. But the assumption that it is can lead to a diminution of both our personal autonomy and the freedom granted us by society. Dr. Skinner has said: "No theory changes what it is a theory about; man remains what he has always been." This is an incredible view from a psychologist. The assertion it denies has been described as one of the crucial distinctions between psychological and physical definitions. It is true that if we define a solid as a gas it nonetheless retains its solidity. The atomic weight of an element is what it is despite our ignorant assumptions. But the human being is a product of the environment—which is something I thought the behaviorists believed—and therefore becomes what the environment makes him. Our view of ourselves will create a person consonant with that perception even if it is false. Although culture is man's product, it is also his producer.

Second, the behaviorist model inevitably leads to massive manipulation of the environment (it has been most effective in controlled institutions for the mentally retarded) and is extremely susceptible to political exploitation. Think of the massive use of the big lie and the techniques of behavioral brainwashing employed by tyrannies of the right and left, the most recent examples being the "re-education camps" of the Chinese Communists.

Third, although it is possible to modify environment so as to encourage certain traits and discourage others, it is impossible to guarantee any given results in precisely those more complex areas that are essential to survival, such as imagination and flexibility. What it is possible to control may not warrant the excessive price that might have to be paid to do so.

The desire to view human freedom of will as a myth is as much a product of anxiety as of scientific understanding. The appeal of Skinner's argument is not that we are entitled to condition man since he is not really free at any rate, but that we must condition man because he *is* free and such freedom includes the freedom to be aggressive, immoral, and destructive. I suppose that, if we came to the conclusion that the very survival of our species demanded we abandon our concepts of freedom or, indeed, freedom itself, behavioral conditioning to that end would be justifiable. The question is, are we at that point?

The fear of autonomy-gone-bonkers is understandable in this age when macho superpatriots like Oliver North and his nameless liege lords—who command the use of atomic weapons and other kinds of force— place themselves above the law and beyond accountability; when the lawless and perverse destroy our public spaces, converting the parks of our inner cities into no-man's-lands where even the police are reluctant to enter; when a self-indulgent middle class is destroying our forests and countryside with acid rain to satisfy their irresponsible desire for ever bigger automobile behemoths; when industrial leaders, by selfishly focusing narrowly on "the bottom line," contaminate our rivers and streams and beyond that the very oceans that for centuries have been seen as the incorruptible purifier of all things. Maybe we could have prevented many of these creatures by universal conditioning. But we have at this point many cultural and political maneuvers available that are less risky than an abandonment of autonomy. We could ruthlessly punish such offenders. We could hold them culpable under an enhanced vision of autonomy that placed the public good at the center, rather than the periphery, of our moral concerns.

Skinnerian conditioning could in itself be more destructive than the risks of freedom. The dangers of conditioning may not be so apparent at first consideration. When behaviorists say that behavior is "determined," they do not use this word in the sense of "influenced by," but in a fixed and absolute mathematical sense. Beyond this, when they refer to "environmental circumstances," they are talking about something quite different from the generalized environmental influences that psychoanalysts are concerned with, such as parental attitudes and cultural models. Behaviorists think in terms of smaller units of behavior. They see all complex behavior as being multiples of tiny aggregates, conditioned responses. To achieve their purposes would require rigid controls and detailed prescriptive maneuvers of a sort that would dwarf the Leviathan state of Hobbes.

We may inevitably be moving to a more homogeneous and predictable behavior, independent of the psychologists, driven by the social and economic realities of our time. Conditioning in early life undeniably modifies future behavior. Inescapably, it will be used even more in this era when we are heading toward the collective education of the child. Skinner may yet triumph.

The liberation of women from the kitchens and laundry rooms of life was traditionally accomplished not by enlisting the cooperation of men, but by exploiting other women. We are running out of everything these days, including exploitable women. The only solution is a less labor-intensive system. We are discovering collective caretaking. With the advent of the single-parent household (often a euphemism for the nonparent household) and the financial need for two working parents in those families that are still intact, there is pressure for earlier and earlier child-care programs. Children a year of age or younger are kept collectively under the tutelage of professional help for as long as eight hours a day. In a family setting, where the ratio of caretaker to child is small, the power of identification and personality development through role modeling is enormous. The average child will pick up his character traits wholesale through emulation. He is more likely to become the parent, rather than what the parent instructs him to become. Heterogeneity, that bête noire of the engineers, will be encouraged. In institutions, things are different; conditioning is more cost-efficient.

A crucial fact to keep in mind when considering early "education" is the plasticity that exists in early life. In changing behavior, age is a lever that becomes progressively shorter. At birth, the inchoate child is all potential, awaiting and demanding modeling into behavior patterns; the arm of the lever is extraordinarily long. With a proper fulcrum and the proper position, Archimedes said he could move the world. The parent has that fulcrum and that position, particularly in the first few years of life.

Parents know that by the fifth year of a child's life the essential personality and character traits are so firmly fixed that, short of heroic or professional efforts, they can barely be modified. My concern about social engineering does not mean that I do not subscribe to the right and, even more, the obligation to modify behavior through proper training. Such training has generally been vested in the family that controlled the infant and shaped his values during the intense crucible of learning that is the first five years.

Obviously most of us are not planning to turn over our newborn children to be shaped in the character models of others. But day care, like television, will be one more reduction in the heterogeneity, already limited, that the family introduced into character and personality. Homogeneity offers less opportunities for survival than heterogeneity. More may survive the predictable, but there will be none left to survive the unpredictable.

One other obstacle that seems insurmountable when contemplating either an engineered individual or an engineered society is the nature of the design. In order to proceed to build a person, one must first construct a model, a pattern of correctness or normality. The attempt to define normality has been one of the conspicuous failures in psychiatry. The nature of virtue has not even been considered. What characteristics shall we include in our design, and who shall be the people to decide?

This was a primary concern of Dr. Skinner in *Beyond Freedom and Dignity*. He always operated from a humanistic and democratic sensibility, despite the abuse and accusations of totalitarian attitudes that were heaped on him by his later critics. He had explicitly said that the problem was to design a world that would be liked not by people as they now are, but by those who would live in it.

How in the world is that possible? How will he do that? How can anyone do that? We live in a technological age in which things move fast and generational life is shortened. The average college student often does not recognize a common identity with his own high-school-age sibling. Technology speeds up change to a frightening degree. We cannot condition, starting with the newborn, in order to guarantee the adult behavior in some unknown culture twenty to thirty years later—a culture that may not be inhabited by the designers and cannot be anticipated by them.

Of course everyone wants a good life, but thousands of years of philosophy have been testimony to the changing definitions of the nature of the good society. Nonetheless, most of us, excluding some extreme ideologues from left and right, could agree on an agenda, a set of basic principles, to define a just and decent society. We could also, I believe, come to consensus on the qualities of a good man and woman. What is not at all clear is that any technology for inculcating such attributes in the developing child is yet available as efficient as the traditional family.

The history of scientific and institutional approaches to controlling behavior offers little comfort about the future of such endeavors. In many ways, we have been better served by happenstance than by social design. One need only look at the state of some of our designed institutions today—our public-school systems, our prisons—to question the wisdom of social science and social engineering.

Besides, the most intimidating paradox remains. The attribute of human behavior that must be most scrupulously respected is the mutability of our nature, our freedom from instinctual fixation. Although we may modify certain behavior, we must not try to produce a human machine—machines rapidly become obsolete. Nor should we compensate for nature's gift of autonomy by imposing a developmentally induced predictability. We must not look with envy at the order and stability of the insects. We could not endure the life of the ant. Nineteen eighty-four has come and gone—many times. It has never produced a stable, let alone a happy, society.

There are other ways to compensate for the balance between individualism and social good. In a democracy such as ours, social controls are better left in political hands than psychological ones. There are areas of activity in which a blunt instrument is superior to a precise one; this is such an area.

In times of war, when we knew that the survival of the state was thought to be in jeopardy, we have suspended highly respected rights and privileges—the right to change jobs, to consume unlimited supplies of scarce foods, to use energy on "unessentials," to travel—without abandoning our belief in individual liberties. Political changes—provided they are within the boundaries of a democratic contract that respects human dignity and is seen as inviolable—are reversible and open to periodic review. They are *constraints*, not changes in the structure of the individual. These constraints limit what a person can do without suffering from punishment; they do not alter what the person would like to do, or is free to do. When the emergency is over and the prohibitions are removed, the individual goes forward with his freedoms restored. The same is not true for changes that are products of early conditioning.

We dare not shackle the autonomous capacity of the human being to shape his future behavior. Our freedom, our variability, our malleability—these are our ultimate safeguards. They will allow us a chance to survive even in the dangerous and fragile future that we may now be generating through that autonomy. If there is to be a greenhouse effect that will melt the polar caps, we will have been fools to allow it to develop. But we are the kind of fools who can recognize the concept of a greenhouse effect and would most likely invent a means of surviving it. The cost might be a regression to a culture that resembles the stone age, but, given the flexibility of the human species with its capacity to retain knowledge from the past, we could reinvent the twentieth century.

I recognize that we may go further than that. An atomic holocaust could conceivably destroy the entire species. It was this above all that frightened and motivated the humanistic Skinner. I assume there are ecological disasters even beyond my present anticipation that might prove irreversible. Yet I think the risk of either is less than the risk of an immutable human nature within a rigid, paternalistic state. We have yet to see what a heightened awareness of and commitment to community and environment can do. We can be proper Aristotelians and recognize our indebtedness to the community without denying our autonomy or abandoning essential freedoms. We can change our philosophies and our political convictions through education and, where education fails, through fear of immediate and certain punishment. We can acknowledge that individualism and freedom may have been overvalued in our society to the neglect of community, without going to the opposite extreme exemplified by the fascist and communist Leviathans with which we have coexisted.

We in the Western world *are* suffering from the ill effects of a rampant individualism. We *must* rediscover the community. This can be done, however, within the respected confines of a concept of autonomy. All power has the potential for corruption. We have in the past used some of our powers unwisely and unwell. The capacity to do evil is a risk of freedom, but it is also a component of a definition of the good. If we sacrifice that freedom, that special capacity to look to the stars, we may cease to be a species worth saving.

In attempting to improve the human condition, we must not destroy that which is uniquely human. Our primary strength is not, as some have suggested, our science and technology. They are only our products. The badger in *The Once and Future King* expressed the uniqueness of the human condition best when he had the Creator say: "You, Man, you will be a naked tool all our life though a user of tools. We will look like an embryo until they bury you but all the others will be embryos before your might. Eternally undeveloped, you will always remain potential in Our Image, able to see some of Our sorrows and to feel some of Our joys."[11]

Human autonomy is dangerous stuff, but it is the very stuff of humanhood. The abandonment of security for freedom was the choice and the heritage of Adam and Eve.

FEELINGS[1]

~~~~~~~~~~~~~~~~~

AWE, WONDER, DELIGHT, AND HOPE, grief, anguish, and despair all are part of an extended repertoire of feelings that embellish the lives of human beings, and only human beings. This range has no counterpart in any other animal.

Considering the central importance of feelings in our everyday lives, the amount of confusion that still exists about them is surprising. Our feelings determine the quality, value, and ultimately the judgment we make of our existence. If we feel a preponderance of happiness, joy, and pride, the sum of our material advantages becomes irrelevant. If we are dominated by fear, guilt, shame, humiliation, frustration, rage, and depression, no truly pleasurable retreat is purchasable with the goods of "success."

I will be using the term "feelings" rather than "emotions" because "emotion" as traditionally used in psychology is a complex amalgam. Beyond the subjective experience, the feelings, emotions also consist of physiological responses which, while important, are not central to a discussion of human nature.

First, despite what some self-styled experts may say, there are no "bad" feelings. There are obviously painful feelings as well as pleasurable ones; different feelings serve different purposes; but they are all designed as aids and signals for survival. The painful ones are aversive stimuli, serving either the adaptation of the individual or the survival of our species. Anxiety about heights, for example, is almost universally present in childhood and may

be seen in its progenitor, the clutching reflex of the newborn
infant.

The range of human feelings is a product of our autonomy, and
the consequent need to make important decisions. Feelings guide
us in those functions. For this reason, some feelings are uniquely
human, shared by no other animals. Some animal forms have no
feelings all. Distance yourself from your own experience for a
moment and try to visualize what life must be like for the simplest
creature on earth, the ameba. This one-celled animal has a survival
mechanism—as simple as it is—that puts to shame many of its
more complicated relatives. The ameba, it is fair to assume, is free
of emotions. It survives by a simple trial-and-error mechanism of
ingesting everything around it in a haphazard fashion, less dis-
criminating than even the most indiscriminate adolescent. If what
the ameba takes in is a nutrient, it is broken down and absorbed.
If what is taken in is poisonous, it is repelled or rejected.

As one moves up the scale of animals, one sees an increasingly
complicated regulating mechanism, usually built on pain and pleasure, that helps to ensure survival of the organism. In order to
distinguish between pain and pleasure, a more elaborate nervous
system is required that must have receptors to mediate these sensations. Pain is a sensation, not a feeling, as I am using the term.
There is an inevitable confusion between sensation and feeling.
We use the same words for both. We will ask, "Do you feel any
pain?" Or, conversely, we will say, "I felt such a sense of shame."
All perceptions are mediated physically and biochemically—what
else is there? but sensations, while subject to some psychic
elaborations, are primarily simple and direct physical responses—
touch, smell, vibration, et al.—whereas feelings are the sensory
and perceptual consequences of our thinking and perceiving
selves.

The pain-pleasure apparatus enhances survival by serving as an
indicator of proper adaptive behavior. It "tells" the creature what
is safe and what is harmful. That which is painful in the broadest
sense of the word is survival-endangering, and we tend to avoid
it. That which is pleasurable is survival-enhancing, and we seek

it out. An animal *could* have developed through mutation in which destructive impulses were enjoyable, and nourishing and sustaining ones were disgusting, but it would not have survived long. That is the nature of change through mutation.

Pain and pleasure, then, are the common mediators of survival in the lower forms of animals. To speak of pain and pleasure in some of the lowest species is to indulge in an anthropomorphic projection of our own feelings. That an animal will avoid a noxious stimulus does not necessarily imply any perception of what we would call pain. It is unlikely, for example, that the oyster we swallow live is distressed even as it is being digested. It does not have a nervous system that would support such a sensation. The response of avoidance may be reflexive. We human beings contain the residual capacities for such responses. Think of the immediate response to touching a hot stove. In a simple situation like that, the response is simultaneous with the sensation of pain, or may even precede it. When a trauma is sufficient, there is often a surprising respite for a few seconds before one is flooded with the painful experience, while the conditioned reflex, a primitive mechanism, short-circuits the brain. For simple defensive actions, perception, judgment, and volition are not required; immediacy of action is preferable to contemplative analysis.

The existence of a brain, particularly an advanced brain like the human being's, allows discernment to a point that may overrule the mechanical conditioning response. The brain, with its multiple functions of examining, evaluating, and controlling behavior, can allow us to steel ourselves to the prick of the physician's needle without withdrawing our arm. This is an example where rationality overcomes reflexive and emotional response. It is not, however, the inevitable consequence of the interplay between feeling and cognition.

Feeling is too often represented as the opposite of rationality: you either behave emotionally or you behave reasonably. Within the complex structure of human behavior, exactly the opposite is more often true. It is the presence of rationality that requires the development of the finely tuned feelings of the human being. Because we are intelligent creatures, we are freed from instinctive and patterned behavior to an unparalleled degree and must make difficult choices.

In fact, in the complex world of the human being, we often will endure pain for a higher rational purpose. We will endure present pain for later good, or we will pursue an unselfish action that brings pride or joy. Through our perceptual capacity to weave a past and future together into a blueprint for the present, we know that some pain is worth enduring for higher values, future pleasure, or pride of service.

Imagine an alligator, so dependent on its jaws and its teeth, voluntarily enduring the pain of root-canal work. Aside from the fact that the animal would by genetic design be incapable of conceiving or executing such an action or understanding the nature of dental caries, it simply would not have the capacity to endure the pain for the sake of some future which is not conceivable in the animal mind. It is because alternative futures are recognizable to us that we human beings plan for a future even while knowing that it is never really absolutely predictable. We take out life insurance, hoping that we are wasting our money and will not die prematurely. All other animals must operate under the often false assumption of a predictable future, and any unpredictability may mean the end of their species.

Pain and pleasure are common regulators that serve survival in many forms of animals. It is reasonable to assume that pain occurs somewhat lower in the animal line than does pleasure. Pain, however, is still not fear. A sensory perception, not an emotion, it can be mediated through a much more primitive nervous system. It is considerably less effective as a survival mechanism.

Pain requires intimate physical contact. As such, while it can help one avoid ingesting the wrong things, it does not help much in avoiding one's being ingested. Pain has a limited escape value. By the time the jaws of the tiger are at your throat and you feel the pain, the perception does you little good. What will be necessary to enhance survival is a way to anticipate the tiger's arrival. This occurs with the emergence of modalities that are known as "distance receptors"—as distinguished from touch and pain, which require actual contact.

The distance receptors are the organs of smelling, hearing, and seeing and in some animals the sense of vibration. These distance receptors give all animals an edge in the battle for survival. They allow them to locate—before physical contact—that which is about to destroy them or to be destroyed by them. They enlarge the environment; they expand awareness and improve the animal's control over an increasingly large world. Distance receptors make possible physical anticipation, if not ideological anticipation, and even this limited anticipation is a remarkable increment in the struggle for survival. Anticipation buys time. What we do with the time, flee or attack, will be determined by the mix and quality of feelings that are generated by the awareness of the specific impending threat.

Many animals feel some emotions, and reviewing the emotions we have in common with lower animals will further dramatize the differences that occur with the emergence of emotions that are specifically human.

Fear and rage are the most common emotions of animals. They usually emerge together, as part of a continuum. The fear-rage response—including its feelings and physiological reactions—is the basic mechanism that prepares an animal for fight and flight. These emotions trigger large, programmed, involuntary responses, such as the redistribution of blood supply (a face livid with rage), the sweating of one's palms, or the dilation and constrictions of the pupils. Observe a cat threatened by a dog and you witness the fight-and-flight mechanisms in the arching of the back, the alert and focused position, and other external changes indicating that the cat is crouched and ready for action. What you do not see are the complicated and extensive internal reactions, the autonomic and involuntary responses that are preparing the innards of the body for that fight or flight.

We, too, have an emergency system built on fear and rage that is a basic part of our physiology. The pioneering work of the great American physiologist Walter B. Cannon[2] showed the extent to

which many human ills were related to these primitive and automatic emergency responses and their conflict with more specific
and contradictory signals of civilized life. Human beings, with our
capacity for learning and for symbol formation, go beyond the call
of our distance receptors. First of all, we do have a whole range
of conflicting emotions, like shame and pride, which conflicts with
desire to run from danger. We might not run, even though our
bodies were straining to do so, if it would make us seem cowardly.

Even if we had only the emotions of fear and rage, we would
still behave differently from most other animals because of our
extraordinary powers of imagination, and also because of our potential for implementing our survival needs by using other talents.
We need not wait to see the predator charging down on us. We
need not even wait to see it on the horizon. We can respond to
symbols, signs, or antecedents of the event as though they were
the actual occurrences. We can understand the life patterns of our
natural antagonists and educate ourselves and others about the
nature of danger. We can avoid the jungles where the powerful
predator lives, or enter his territory armed. Our unparalleled ability
to anticipate allows for strength and stability beyond those afforded
by our sheer weight, size, and normal power. The advantages of
anticipation and prediction in matters of survival are obvious. Aside
from preparing ourselves for the assault or running from it, we
can at times modify the situation so there is no assault at all: we
can build fences and fortifications and institute all sorts of other
preventive measures— quench the fire, dam the stream, support
the collapsing tree, mollify the antagonist, ingratiate the boss, lie,
cajole, seduce, and so on.

So, unlike most animals, who use their limited anticipation only
to enhance their capacity for flight or fight—that is, to escape or
conquer a fixed reality—we can change the reality itself. This is
but another affirmation of the fact that we are coauthors (with
nature and chance) of our future, not merely passive subjects of it.
Our intelligence is a super distance-receptor. Our imagination and
synthetic reasoning permit us to anticipate threats even during
periods of maximum security and comforts: to prepare in the best

of times for the worst; to recognize that there are seasons, that the balm and plenty of summer will inevitably give way to the cold spareness of winter. And because of our intelligence and imagination, we need not see the first frost before we store the harvest.

We do not endure pain simply to enhance our survival. We do not live only to secure our lives and to perpetuate our species. We lead a life of perception and imagination, and that life involves values and ideals that will even transcend the urgent claims of survival. For these purposes we require a broader range of emotions; we need guidance to help us in a decision-making existence that complicates questions of safety versus danger with questions of good versus evil. We will endure pain for pride, for pleasure, for vanity, for service, for altruism.

Most of us in the middle-class culture of the Western world devote more energy and activity to matters of quality and meaning of life than we do to the acts of survival. A significant part of our symbolic world is supported by our activities in behalf of others. This sense of the human being as an altruistic, giving, and caring creature has been lost and forgotten in the hedonistic and narcissistic philosophy of recent years. Lost, too, is the complex sense of the nature of human pleasure.

Pop psychologists insist on defining pleasure in the most simplistic terms, such as freedom from worry, or achieving sensual gratification. They play on the confusions of the average person and exploit them with a continuing flow of "how-to" books that guide the perplexed and despairing to inner peace by conflicting and contradictory pathways. All seem designed to liberate people from the "useless" emotions of shame and guilt. But shame and guilt are the noblest emotions, those that specifically define the human being, and are essential in the maintenance of civilized society. These feelings most profoundly shape our personhood and are most central to being human. They are vital for the development of the most refined and elegant qualities of human potential—generosity, service, self-sacrifice, unselfishness, love, and duty. They support our abilities to feel remorse. They are the building blocks of conscience, the core of the moral animal. It is for this reason that I will focus on those few emotions—shame and guilt and their opposite, pride.

The emergence of shame is the dramatic climax of the human story in Genesis. It can be argued, however, that emotions do exist before the Fall. God expresses delight when He has created the world, the beasts of the earth, the cattle and their kind, and "saw that it was good." He expresses greater delight when He considers the balance of the world with man and woman at its center; when He has seen "everything he had made" and found that "it was very good." Is there not a feeling implied when God made grow from the ground "every tree that is pleasant to the sight"? It may even be seen in God's touching statement: "It is not good that the man should be alone; I will make a help meet for him." And surely there is the suggestion of disappointment and loneliness in Adam's response to the creation and the community of animals: "But for Adam there was not found a help meet for him."[3]

Loneliness, or a sense of isolation from one's own kind, may truly be the first human emotion dealt with in the Bible. It is consistent with the significance of community in the Old Testament. And the first explicit mention of emotion is shame. "And they were both naked, the man and his wife, and were not ashamed."[4] Shame is an emotion that is at the very foundation of communal living.

The individuals who existed before the eating of the fruit of the tree of knowledge felt no shame. They may be our kin, but they are not our kith. They do not share our inner life and therefore occupy a different world from ours. The psychological human being as well as the moral life begins with wrongdoing, the knowledge of having done wrong, and the feelings of fear, guilt, and shame that accrue from that awareness.

The emotion of shame is essentially and exclusively human and communal. It is not devoted to personal pleasure. It is primarily concerned with the survival of the group and the values of the group in opposition to the selfish interests of the individual. The precedence of shame over guilt is consistent with the difference in emphasis between the Old and the New Testaments. Here, so early in the old Bible, we see the Jewish commitment to community. The individual must serve his community. It is the people who are pre-eminent, for they have been chosen to receive and preserve God's Law. Justice and community hold central sway here, as love and individual salvation will dominate the New Testament.

It has been commented on that the ultimate irony of the story of Genesis is that eating of the tree of knowledge, instead of bringing wisdom, only brought shame. The first response to their transgression, even before fear, is shame:

"And the eyes of them both were opened, and they knew that they were naked; and they sewed fig leaves together, and made themselves aprons." Shame is quickly followed by fear: "And he said, I heard thy voice in the garden, and I was afraid, because I was naked; and I hid myself."[5] That shame and fear are linked in all of us is but another indication of the extraordinary insight of the framers of the Bible.

It is safe to assume that everyone reading this book has felt fear. I cannot assume that you have all felt shame or guilt; some people have never experienced these feelings. They are not, however, the lucky ones, and we are unlucky in having them in our midst. The failure to feel guilt is a basic character flaw. It is the hallmark of the psychopath or antisocial person, who is quite capable of committing the vilest crimes without feeling any emotion of guilt.

What, then, is the feeling of guilt? What will distinguish it from related feelings? If you were to ask a group of people to define a situation in which they recently felt guilty, it is likely that at least half would describe something else—guilty fear. The qualities that characterize guilty fear fall into the caught-in-the-act, or about-to-be-caught, category.

We all know that panicky feeling when we are in the process of an immoral, illegal, or disapproved action and we feel the hot breath of authority down our neck. That rush of sickening feeling that we are to be apprehended imminently and punished is not guilt but guilty fear. The primary emotion is fear. It is *guilty* fear, because it is fear that is clearly related to some wrongdoing that we acknowledge. If you are casually driving at sixty-five miles per hour (when you know that fifty-five is the legal limit) and suddenly hear the unmistakable sound of a police siren as you catch a glimpse of the highway-patrol car in your rearview mirror, that fluttery feeling through your chest is guilty fear.

Here guilt is only the modifier, "guilty" the adjective to describe the kind of fear you have. The emotion is not the product of having been bad but of having been caught at being bad. Suppose now, to return to the scene at the highway, that, as you apprehensively watch the approaching police car, you find that he passes you by to flag down a car that whizzed past you only moments before. What do you feel? If it is relief, the emotion experienced with the first sound of the siren was guilty fear. If there are a few strange ones among you who are disappointed, then I grant that you felt true guilt.

The distinguishing test between the two is in the relationship to exposure and apprehension. When guilty fear alone is present, getting away with it brings immediate relief and delight. Guilt, however, wants exposure. It needs exposure, because it needs expiation and forgiveness. Maxine Hong Kingston, in her memoir *The Woman Warrior*,[6] describes guilt as an unbearably constricted feeling in her throat. I myself always experienced guilt as a nauseating feeling somewhere between the upper chest (reserved for fear) and the abdomen. The most profound and immediate relief for this feeling is to confront the individual who is both responsible for the feeling and capable of relieving it.

Guilty fear, then, is relieved when the threat of punishment disappears. True guilt often seeks and embraces punishment. The purging power of the confessional, so clearly recognized by the Roman Catholic Church, acknowledges the central role of guilt, both in Christian theology and in everyday life.

Guilt represents the noblest and most painful of struggles. It is between us and ourselves. It is alleviated or mitigated by acts of expiation. Guilt is also exclusively a human emotion. Guilty fear is obviously not. It is most evident in household pets. I have had a running intellectual battle with colleagues and close relations on this subject. Pet lovers consistently humanize their devoted companions, and they pamper them. Since dogs in particular are no-torious transgressors of decorum and public decency, a loving caretaker will be eager to find signs of contrition. These are difficult to come by. A dog may be trained to bring you the daily paper, but he is unlikely to see this as an act of devotion or service, and not likely, therefore, to offer it as a gift of repentance.

Dog owners in particular are offended by my assertion that animals never feel guilty, and inevitably offer as proof the "guilty" behavior of whatever disreputable dog they happen to own. As a lifelong dog owner and lover, I know whereof they speak. One particularly rambunctious terrier would always follow up his typical outrage with slinky, slippery, slithering, ingratiating tail-between-the-legs, whimpering, and altogether disgusting behaviors, which to my wife and children were the ultimate expression of guilt and inevitably reduced them to a state of forgiveness—and amnesia. Gone was the outrage. Out came the sympathy. Since his miserable behavior was interpreted as guilt and therefore implied contrition, it demanded forgiveness. I, on the other hand, remained unconvinced. I never remember this dog approaching me, confessing his transgression, and "asking" to be punished. If anything, quite the contrary. I knew immediately when he had violated the code of canine conduct. He was nowhere to be found, hiding under or in or behind some barricade. And I never found that this presumed guilty feeling and behavior were diminished by punishment. My family remains unconvinced to this day.

On my side, however, I have Martin Buber. In his discussion of guilt he states that guilt and conscience are evidences of a specifically human nature and a capacity to distinguish not only current but past and future actions and decide which of those should be approved and which disapproved. He makes the interesting point that human beings can punish themselves for acts of omission as well as for deeds of commission. Failures to measure up, even wishes, can cause a feeling of guilt. For most of us, these dominate our guilty feelings. The failure to visit a sick friend, the neglect of an ailing parent, the call not made, the flowers not sent, the note unwritten, the work pushed to the back of the desk—

these are the products of everyday guilt for those of us who lead a generally quiet and moral existence.

Buber sees in this tendency to feel guilty even about omitted acts our capacity to set at a distance—beyond things in our environment—our very selves. This capacity to distance oneself from oneself is specifically human. Having become a detached object about which he can reflect, "he can from time to time confirm as well as condemn."[7]

Buber upbraids Freud for not having developed a full-blown theory of guilt and its role in human behavior. In this he is correct. Freud's first mention of the counterforces that keep us from being purely selfish were brief and unanalyzed discussions of shame, disgust, revulsion, loathing that emerge from the unconscious. Freud focused his clinical attention on the drives rather than the counterforces. He labeled his central thesis a "theory of instincts." The counterforces drifted in a limbo of neglect and casual acknowledgment.

Only when Freud began to analyze culture did he start the process of building a theory of the conscience mechanisms. His pioneering work in this area was *Totem and Taboo*,[8] where he begins the analysis of inborn fear and guilty fear. He shrewdly and intuitively assumed that there was a genetic imperative inherent in the structure of the human being for unselfishness, for good. Certain taboos were not taught but inbuilt, and human beings violated these only at their peril.

Conscience was regulated by fear. We acted as though a punitive parent were inside us, watching carefully all of our wrongdoing. Like the view of God held by some children, we view the parent as an omniscient Peeping Tom who, in seeing all, is prepared to expose all and punish the same. Fear of retribution and retaliation is the dominant force for social order described by Freud in *Totem and Taboo*.

It is obvious, then, that guilt is a different order of emotion from fear. Fear and rage are emotions oriented to the survival of the organism. They served as the primary protective devices for the individual in the days before law and civilization. In the primitive society there were predator and prey. In that struggle for survival the emotions fear and rage signaled whether it was appropriate to flee or fight, and the proper and timely behavior elicited in response to those emotions would enhance survival.

Guilt, on the other hand, is an un-self-serving and peculiar emotion. It is a social emotion. What survival purposes are served by feelings like guilt, love, or caring? Would we not survive more adequately if unencumbered by such sentiments—if we greedily fought for each scrap of food even to the point of personal gluttony in the presence of the starvation of our weaker neighbor?

The presence and power of these social emotions are testament to the fact that, for the human being, community, the presence of others, is not some ideal, some entertainment, but a biological necessity. There is no such thing as individual survival. The human being is *human* because of the nurture of other human beings and will not survive without them. Or, if love and caring are supplied only minimally, he may survive biologically but without the qualities of humanity that elevate him above the common animal host.

If at any point an individual is withdrawn from contact with his kind, he will attempt to re-create social relationships in his imagination that will sustain him for a time, but if there is sufficient deprivation, he survives at the risk of being reduced to an animal state indistinguishable from lower forms. There are touching moments in *Robinson Crusoe, The Count of Monte Cristo*, and William Golding's *Pincher Martin*, as well as in such true stories of isolation as the personal accounts of Jacobo Timmerman[9] and Nadezhda Mandelstam,[10] which speak to the depravity and deterioration that ensue when memory ceases to counter the despair of the isolated self.

We are so constructed that we must serve the social good on which we are dependent for our own survival, and if we do not we will suffer the pangs of guilt. In that sense, guilt and its imperatives can be seen as paralleling, in a reverse direction, the sexual drive. The intense personal pleasure of sex—as distinguished from the pain of guilt—drives us to perform the function that alone (at least until the recent perfection of in-vitro fertilization) ensured the survival of the species. In a similar way, guilt and its fellow emotion, shame, bind us to those who are needed for our own survival. Our seemingly unselfish acts serve the self in a way that is not always apparent in the everyday individual battle for survival.

Beyond and above serving survival, guilt is a guardian of our goodness. It is an internal judgment that forces us to endure pain to do good. "Guilt becomes a way of putting oneself before a sort of invisible tribunal which measures the offense, pronounces the condemnation and inflicts the punishment."[11] We have judged ourselves and have been found wanting.

Guilt is the pain of self-disappointment. It is a sense of anguish that we did not achieve our standards of what we ought to be. We have somehow or other betrayed some internal potential self. Guilt is a more internalized and personal emotion than shame. You-against-you allows no buffer and no villain except yourself.

Shame is a sister emotion to guilt. They both serve the same purposes, facilitating the socially acceptable behavior required for group living. Both deal with transgressions against codes of conduct and are supporting pillars of the social structure. But whereas guilt is a more inner-directed emotion, shame incorporates the community, the group, the other directly into the feelings. This is why Aristotle, in defining shame, focuses on it as a pain in regard to "bad things [often translated "misdeeds"] . . . which seem likely to involve us in discredit [often "dishonor"]."[12] He goes on to describe shame as the feeling that involves things that are disgraceful to ourselves or to those we care for. "Bad things," "misdeeds," "discredit," "dishonor," "disgrace" all reflect the elements that define shame, and all entail both a misdeed and its exposure.

Shame requires an audience—if not realistically, than symbolically. Shame is fear of a public exhibition of wrongdoing, of being exposed in front of the group. Guilt often drives us to seek exposure, but shame begs for privacy. Again, Aristotle recognized this when he said: "Shame is a mental picture of disgrace in which we shrink from the disgrace itself and *not* [my emphasis] from its consequences."[13]

In the most direct way, shame serves the purpose of preserving the community. It supports the enforcement of community standards and community judgment as determinants on our behavior. As such, it requires for its effectiveness a respect for the community. Shame also tends to encourage behavior that binds the comfort and good of the individual to the community's survival. Shame allows the community to join in the enforcement of moral behavior, rather than leaving this up to individual responsibility and internalized models. The shame and disgrace of imprisonment, a form of punishment seen as most humane by our society, is important in controlling the parts of the population that are capable of feeling shame. White-collar and middle-class people should go to jail even when it serves no rehabilitative purpose. It is an announcement of a violation of community standards, and the shame is part of the punishment.

Now that I have attempted to tease out the distinctions between guilty fear, guilt, and shame, let me introduce another related and intertwined emotion, the definition of which confounds us by including the word "shame." This finally brings us directly to the literal usage and meaning of the expression "they were both naked . . . and were not ashamed."

Here I draw a distinction between "feeling ashamed" and a "sense of being ashamed." The two are obviously related, but it is worth examining their differences. One of my first personal memories of the use of shame involved the jingle "Shame, shame, everybody knows your name." I have no idea what this means or why it was so upsetting, particularly when accompanied by that gesture: pointing the index finger of the left hand at me while stroking the index finger of the right hand across the surface of the extended finger of the left.

What can it mean? Of course everybody that I was playing with knew my name. Perhaps it is a corruption, and my recall is incorrect, and the actual expression was "Shame, shame, everybody knows your game." This would have made sense, meaning perhaps, Everybody knows what you are up to. But the memory is so distinct, and I have found friends who recall it precisely the same way. I suspect now that it does have a legitimate meaning and it may speak to an essential distinction between the private and the public sphere that brings us back once again to Genesis.

There *are* cultures where the knowledge of one's name is kept secret. With certain Chinese groups and some Indian tribes, there is magic assigned to one's name that must be protected. Even here the name suggests a metaphoric relationship to an inner self which is never truly revealed. For someone to know your name is to know who you are at the most basic level; to expose your name is to expose that core of yourself for which you have no public responsibility and which need not be popularly shared.

This private self may set the limits for the sense of shame. It may represent the most personal area of our unconscious and our fantasy life, for which we owe no public accountability and need no public apology. This sense of a private self introduced a different sense of shame, which may be what Adam and Eve felt, or whose absence was commented on earlier in Genesis. It may represent the innocence of the early Adam and Eve, who on examination begin to seem progressively more like children. Children are indeed unashamed of their nakedness and at certain ages enjoy exhibiting themselves, taking obvious pleasure in the public display of their private parts. Freud saw this exhibitionist tendency as an essential step in the development of the libido. It was a "component instinct." By adulthood, these components are expected to be submerged into more mature sexual activities. When adults are exhibitionists, we tend to see them as aberrant.

It is hard to talk about this sense of shame in our current environment, in which everything is open to the public. Everything now seems suitable for group discussion, and in matters of behavior "anything goes." But there were earlier times in which a sharp distinction between the behavior permitted in the public and the private spheres was mandated.

One example of shame that is often mentioned by classicists is the story of Gyges. Herodotus tells the story of a king of Sardis who was so in love with his wife and so proud of her beauty that he insisted that his favorite lieutenant, Gyges, view her naked. Gyges is no fool. Recognizing the inherent danger in such action, he resists. Only after intense pressure is exerted by the king is Gyges forced into secretly entering the bedchamber in which the royal couple sleep. The queen comes in and undresses, and Gyges looks at her. In passing, however, she sees him: "And instantly divining what had happened she never screams as her shame impelled her." She suppresses her shame and sets about her vengeance. It is made clear that in this culture of the Lydians it is reckoned a deep disgrace even for a man to be seen naked. The queen extracts her revenge by having Gyges kill her husband on the spot where her nakedness was exposed.[14]

When I first read this account, it did not strike me as an example of shame at all but, rather, of its close relative humiliation. Shame, by my definition, is the sense of exposure *before* someone. Humiliation is the sense of exposure *by* someone. Shame always carries with it a small kernel of guilt; it is the public exposure of some failing, implying an inadequacy or a responsibility. On the other hand, humiliation is more often fused with anger, for the exposure has been done *to* us. If there is no implication of either wrongdoing or humiliation, we are dealing with an entirely different emotion—embarrassment.

What this, then, exposes is the distinction between a feeling of shame and a feeling of being put to shame, a "sense of shame." The sense of shame contains within it a specific emotional feeling, but it is strongly related to the feeling of being ashamed. Arising out of our conviction that things *are* and *ought* be private, a sense of shame not only guards our private area from public examination, but also protects the public space from contamination by private matters. It is normally we ourselves who are the primary guardians of our private selves. What then is the connection between these two distinct feelings that share a common name?

A sense of shame is related to the feeling of shame in that both feelings are dominated by a concept of exposure of that which ought not be exposed. We feel ashamed when it is our misdeed or deficiency that is exposed. With the sense of shame, it is some part of ourselves, usually our bodies—often sexual aspects but not necessarily so—that has been compromised by public view; it is the exposure itself that is seen as morally wrong, not necessarily what is exposed. Still, we are apt to feel some culpability, in that each individual is seen as the keeper of his own privacy.

A sense of shame is therefore bound closely to the now old-fashioned concept of modesty. It encompasses a multitude of feelings: guilt, even if it is unwarranted; humiliation when we are exposed by others against our will or without our permission; embarrassment when chance is the only culprit. The unzipped fly, which many adolescent boys and some postadolescent men have experienced in public places, produces something closer to a sense of embarrassment than the more profound feeling of shame.

I recall one poignant example that illuminates the interrelationship between feeling ashamed and the sense of shame. During the Vietnam War, I was visiting a group of young conscientious objectors who had chosen prison over service in the war. Among the many hardships of prison life for these young men was the deprivation of sexual outlet. This was a young group, at their prime sexually and still young enough so that their sexual identity and confidence had not yet been firmly established. Since they had no opportunity for sexual intercourse and they eschewed the homosexuality rampant in most prisons, the only obvious sexual release was masturbation. These men discussed their masturbation with me, and their masturbatory fantasies; almost to a man, they bemoaned the lack of privacy, which made masturbation so difficult.

Unlike the terrifying image most people have of prison, with single locked cells, in modern prisons few prisoners are locked in individual cells. This is particularly true in federal prisons and minimum-security facilities. More often than not, the problem is precisely the opposite of isolation. There is no place to retreat— no sense of privacy, no escape. Barracks are the traditional prison abode. Men in this environment, though knowing and even discussing among themselves their need to masturbate, would lie awake at night, each waiting for the others to fall asleep so he could masturbate in private. To a man, they expressed their feeling that they were not guilty about the masturbation; they talked about it freely; but they were ashamed to do it in public.

Certain things are reserved for our private sphere of activities. How much the sense of shame is an inbuilt mechanism and how much is culturally determined and taught to the child has always been open to question. In either case, the sense of shame is generally very closely tied to sexuality. In Genesis at least, the argument is made that this sense of shame, particularly over body parts and a sexual act, is part of our genetic makeup.

In almost all cultures, sexuality is a private affair. To enforce this privacy and protect the public sphere, the sense of shame is extended beyond the act of sexuality to the organs of sexuality, and beyond that, a form of shame by association, to the entire pudendal (from the Latin *pudendus*, meaning "ashamed") area. This sense of shame as applied to the exposure of the genitals has traditionally been viewed as a controlling mechanism in tribal society necessitated by the nature of human sexuality, which is liberated from estrus and season. The persistence of sexual potential throughout the day and the season could be disruptive to social and family life. Further, shame could be seen as reinforcing the almost universal taboos against incest. Freud saw incest taboos as part of the genetic endowment of the human being, and he viewed the desire to reinforce these taboos as the driving force in much of primitive culture and religion.

A debate has raged between anthropology and psychoanalysis about whether cultures exist in which no sexual guilt occurs. Abram Kardiner, in attempting to counter the idea of genetic roots and instinctual behavior, pointed out that in some cultures, like that of the Trobriand Islanders, genital exposure and nakedness were common but eating was a private practice that had to be done back to back.[15] Despite such exceptions, what is impressive is the similarity of attitudes about sex and the interdiction of incest across diverse cultural barriers.

Whether there is an inbuilt mechanism or not, it is clear that the two kinds of shame have a relationship. They both protect the public space from contamination and help the individual distinguish what should be public or private. One classic case of an attempt to violate that distinction is in pornography. Central to the concept of pornography is an *intention* to shock with its insistence on blurring the boundaries between private and public. Those who defend unlimited free expression often neglect the importance of the equally respected right to be left alone.

George Steiner worded this beautifully when he said: "Sexual relations are or should be one of the citadels of privacy. . . . The new pornographers subvert this last privacy. They do our imagining for us. They take away the words that were of the night and shout them over the rooftops, making them hollow. The image of our love-making, the stammering we resort to in intimacy come pre-packaged."[16]

For many of us, the viewing of sexuality in pornography, if too explicit, becomes antierotic. There is something ludicrous, undignified, and embarrassing about the random feet, legs, arms, exaggerated motions, and grunting noises that becomes only too apparent when viewed by a distant observer. All of this supports eroticism in the actual acts of sexual intimacy, where one is into it rather than outside of it. Philip Roth was aware of this when he described in *Portnoy's Complaint* an orgy that he had devoutly desired in fantasy but that turned out in reality to be something like a traffic jam.[17]

The feeling of shame and the sense of shame share the common bond of something being exposed that ought not be, and the feeling that the exposure somehow or other reflects badly on us. When we feel ashamed, it is because of our own wrongdoing. When we have the sense of being shamed, it may be that we have violated the boundary between private and public through our own lack of vigilance. Even when the violation is by assault we may feel ashamed because somehow what has been done to us, still exposes *us*. In many ways this explains the tragic sense of guilt and shame women often feel when they have been raped.

Human social behavior, however, is driven not only by the aversive force of painful emotions. There is a positive reinforcement that encourages us to sacrifice our selfish needs for a common culture- or species-survival service. Life, for the human being, is more than the avoidance of danger. We are reward seekers. And, unlike the lesser creatures, the beasts of the field, we seek rewards that are not just the nutrients supporting our own individual biological survival. We are created as aspirers. We crave achievement, mastery, and purpose, because they are the stuff that extends the meaning of human survival beyond the mere perpetuation of the biological shell. There is a unique experience of pleasure in performance, and pleasure in doing good, that is in its way the ultimate driving force for noble behavior. That is the experience of pride.

To a psychoanalyst, pride in self is the ultimate goal of all therapy. Erosion of self-confidence and self-esteem humiliates and distorts the life of the mentally ill. To restore self-pride is a noble purpose. Given this therapeutic orientation, I have always been shocked to find pride not just listed among the seven deadly sins but heading the list.

Why in the world isn't it one of the cardinal virtues? Self-respect, self-esteem, self-confidence, all ingredients of pride, are essential elements to human flourishing. They serve our capacity to perform in life and the pleasure we receive from that performance. Part of the contradiction is that pride, like shame, has two distinct meanings. Unlike those of shame, pride's meanings are not related but almost oppositional.

There has been a dramatic difference over the years in our attitudes about pride. To the Greeks, a special form of pride called "hubris" was the cardinal affront to the gods. It might be close to our use of "arrogance" or "haughtiness." The great Greek tragedians are all joined in their central concern with human hubris. Greek tragedies were written for the privileged and powerful citizens of Athens in the fifth and fourth centuries before Christ. Those who have power must always be cautioned against the misuse of that power by those who are the spokesmen for morality. This is what the Greek playwrights were doing: warning against the arrogant use of power by the powerful. They were cautioning the indulged citizens served by serfs and slaves that a just ruler must identify with the ruled, must recognize that the distance between the mightiest and the merest is as nothing when compared with the distance that separates the most powerful of mortals from the gods.

The playwrights of classical Greece were moral preachers. Their message was a constant reminder that the great threat to those in power was the sin of pride. Unforgivable in the eyes of the gods, hubris would bring destruction and humiliation to them and their families. It was the emotions of the powerful that interested the politically oriented Greeks, because their mood established life in the state.

The Christians, however, directed their message not to the powerful leaders but to the abused masses of the postclassical period. Whereas the Greeks had only four primary sins, Christianity added three more for good measure. Even here pride led all the rest. Obviously the message of pride must somehow have been transformed. Christian leaders were speaking to an oppressed minority in a desperate age where no hope flourished, for whom the afterlife became the only source of solace. It must have been a comforting reflection that humility and poverty were not only your lot but a ticket to the beyond. Since we are told that "It is easier for a camel to go through the eye of a needle than for a rich man to enter into the kingdom of God," there was a value in poverty. But, whether intended or not, the preaching of pride as a sin and humility as a virtue led to acceptance and passivity and served to protect a social order of inequity.

With the powerful, I suppose, humility is still a requisite virtue. But times have changed. The number of the securely powerful are few indeed. Anxiety has become the great democratizer. Of course there are still strutting creatures, puffed up with self-satisfaction, but the few arrogant power brokers who still survive are not generally our heroes. Tragically, most of us see ourselves as among the unpowerful, the alienated, or at least the anxious.

With this majority it is humility that ought to be a sin, for it leads to despair and encourages a tolerance of injustice. We no longer fear that our overweening pride will offend the gods. For one thing, we have handled that by diminishing the role of God; for another, the world, which is now viewed as our own creation, is in such a mess of uncertainty as to discourage any excess of self-confidence.

The alteration in the meaning of the word "pride" can be seen in the attitudes toward the feeling by seminal thinkers over time. In the seventeenth century, Spinoza attributed pride to "man's thinking too highly of himself." In the nineteenth century, Schopenhauer saw pride as "an established conviction of own's own paramount worth." And finally, to *The American Heritage Dictionary*, in the twentieth century, pride is "A sense of one's own proper dignity or value." We have moved our definition of pride from "too high" a sense of worth to a "paramount" to a "proper" one.

There is yet another set of complications in considering the nature of pride, even more closely parallel to the discussion on shame. As with shame, there is both a "sense of pride" and a "feeling of pride." The sense of pride is a general awareness of one's own worth, of being decent and proper. It can thus be synonymous with self-respect, for it defines our proper sense of self and worth.

This pride of self-acceptance is usually not a conscious matter. We wear it with our clothes, in public, although we are likely to wear it without thinking about it. Nonetheless it sticks out all over us, and with its absence we advertise our self-contempt. A sense of pride is important—it affects our bearing, our manner, our aspirations, the way we face defeat, and the way we accept victory. It will also determine how we are treated by others. The self-respect or contempt with which we endow ourselves is like a sign hung around our necks, demanding appropriate treatment, and usually getting it, from those we meet.

The conscious *feeling* of pride, on the other hand, is most often experienced in terms of specific activities. We feel proud when we become aware of having done well. That second feeling is defined by *The American Heritage Dictionary* as "Pleasure or satisfaction taken in one's work, achievements, or possessions."

God said: "Let there be light: and there was light. And God saw the light, that it was good."[18]

"And God called the dry land Earth; and the gathering together of the waters called he Seas; and God saw that it was good."[19]

"And God made two great lights; the greater light to rule the day, and the lesser light to rule the night; he made the stars also . . . and God saw that it was good."[20]

And after the creation of the living creatures, the whales, the cattle, and the creeping things, "God saw that it was good." And finally, "God saw every thing that he had made, and, behold, it was very good."[21]

This is pride or satisfaction taken in one's work. Granted that it is God's work, but we are in God's image and we, too, can have that enlarging sensation. This marvelous feeling of pride is not reserved for the creation of the earth or the conquest of nations or the grand talents of the select and artistic few. It can occur for all of us, and does, with each sense of mastery and achievement. We see it in the face of a child when he has completed a task for the first time, even if the task is dropping a clothespin into a bottle.

Normal feelings of pride are generally quiet, although warming, experiences. They are experienced in the minor measures of our value, in our small daily victories. Often we are not even aware of the emotion. We simply feel "good" or "gratified." Pride can be augmented by public acknowledgment, but it is the nature of the activity itself that brings the pride. Thus it combines the mechanisms of both guilt and shame. It is driven by public and private endorsement.

But it is not really the antithesis of guilt and shame. Guilt and shame are exclusively moral judgments. They are the emotional signals that we have not done good. Pride tends to be more involved with doing well than with doing good. It is true that there can be pride in moral achievements, but this tends to diminish the moral character of the act. To do good ought to be part of the fabric of one's being. One should feel pain in the deviation from the good and simply feel normal in the performance of the good. To do good for external approval is goody-good.

Since pride is involved with achievement and mastery, the whole area of doing and creating, it is generally a sign not that we are good but that we are competent. More: it is the esteem in a self that we can depend on. While pride is evident early in childhood, it must be nurtured into proper channels. The development of innate tendencies will be either encouraged or discouraged, depending on the responses they elicit from parents. A child's actions will be influenced by parental attitudes so subtle, so artfully and unconsciously signaled and received, as to create the impression that they were "innate" and not taught.

This interplay between child and parent is a potent factor in the way a child learns to distinguish between the good and the bad of his early random behavior. When he does something, he will almost invariably look to his mother for approval or disapproval. That *looking to the mother* is surely an organic part of the adaptive process. Even if the appeal for approval is answered only with a smile or a perfunctory "I'm looking" or "That's lovely," a response is required. Externally reinforced pride will eventually become internalized in those who are offered the proper cues. We will continue throughout life to feel pride in terms of the good things we produce and the good things we do—in our productions and in our performance.

Internal pride is an essential ingredient of maturation. It is our incentive and at the same time our reward for abandoning the pleasures of dependency. The advantages of being an adored and protected child may be too seductive, and the alternative of self-reliance may seem too dry. Pride is the pleasure of achievement that supports independence. It is an added incentive to abandon the ways and the pleasures of childhood for the more elusive gratifications of maturity. Pride, then, like guilt and shame, is one of our vital signs. An emotion basic to the survival apparatus of the thinking and social animal that is the human being.

These emotions of guilty fear, guilt, shame, being ashamed, and pride, linked and admittedly difficult to differentiate, guide us to our better selves and ensure our safety by supporting the group upon which we all ultimately depend for our survival. In the possession of these emotions, we leave the general animal host and enter an emotional domain that is exclusively human. These emotions will become the ingredients of conscience.

Although these inbuilt potentials for social feelings all support the development of conscience, they do not guarantee it. They are necessary but not sufficient conditions.

We are not born with a conscience, only with the raw materials with which to build a conscience. It remains for our development to nurture and to exploit those ingredients to a point where we can become civilized, human, and mature beings.

SEX

~~~~~~~~~~~~~~~~~~

"And God blessed them, and God said unto them, Be fruitful, and multiply, and replenish the earth. . . ."[1]

To be fruitful and multiply, an organism does not have to use sexual reproduction, let alone copulation. Sexual reproduction is only one, and perhaps not the most efficient, form of multiplying. The self-sufficiency of the unicellular animals who multiply by simply dividing themselves in half is a formidable asset in the reproduction of their own kind. What can be the possible advantages of sexual reproduction?

The extraordinary advantage of all sexual reproduction is that, unlike reproduction by division or fragmentation of the self, or subdivisions of the self, whereby particles can grow into whole animals, each creature that is the product of sexual reproduction will combine the features of both "parents," thus creating multiple and variable individuals all differing genetically from one another. The advantage is comparable in every way to the advantage (and certain disadvantages) of free will over fixed instinct. Certitude is abandoned for variability.

With cell division, a "perfect" organism can be perfectly reproduced in exact mimeograph; it can clone itself. This allows for constancy but not for the inconstancy of nature. The species improves through mutation and "survival of the fittest." A superior mutant will emerge and through competition with a variety of similar species will dominate its environment. That species will have been "designed" by chance to master survival in its milieu.

98

The most successful mutations will survive, *given the conditions at the time of the mutation*. Dramatic or even slight variations of conditions—temperature, winds, rainfall—may destroy the fixed conditions of the inflexible and nonadaptive organism. The only hope for survival is through the process of mutation. Since most mutation is of a destructive and maladaptive nature, this is an iffy mechanism. The success of unicellular organisms is explained by their tendency to inhabit relatively uncomplicated and fixed environments, and their ability to run through thousands of generations in a relatively short period of time.

Sexual reproduction is in the service of variation. Diversity will produce a wide range of creatures, differing in their capacities to cope with differing conditions. Some will be more poorly equipped for survival under standard conditions, but the variability is likely to ensure that *some* creatures will survive to renew the species in case the environment is significantly altered.

Our diversity will permit us to be the widest-ranging of all species. Our species occupies an extraordinarily distant and varied landscape, larger by far than that of any other animal. This contributes to our also being the most variable of creatures. Highly pigmented dark skin was a protection against the blazing sun of the equator, but the black African is sister under the skin to the blond Aryan. This extreme variability in sizes, shapes, and colors—allowing for adjustment to different climates and nutrients while still remaining one species— is exclusively a human capacity. Domestic animals may have an extended variability, but less than it seems, and only through human guidance.

No other creature has managed to develop on its own the variability present among human beings without splitting into related but different species. What defines a species is the capacity to reproduce its own kind. The seven-foot Watusi can mate with the four-foot Pygmy were they so inclined and produce a child with intermediate or mixed characteristics, but still a human child.

Sexual reproduction, with all of its advantages, is independent of any need for copulation. In the technical sense, sexual reproduction requires only a species that is divided into male and female members, each of which contributes half of the characteristics of the new offspring. In many marine animals, the male and female have no physical access to each other except in their mutual presence at the breeding site. The eggs are laid; the female departs; the male appears and sprays the sperm over the eggs. Not romantic, but nonetheless efficient.

In plants, even this minimal cooperation is not necessary. The pollination is often dependent on the elements, or unwitting third-party participants like bees, who, while they are pursuing their own independent designs for living, will willy-nilly and unwittingly be satisfying the trees' or plants' need for pollination. The bees, in seeking nectar, hopping from one flower to another, will be the unknowing but essential intermediary in the reproductive needs of the male and female plant.

This admittedly simplified introduction to sexual reproduction is intended to dispel an anthropocentric view that "sex is sex," and that what we do is not essentially different from what lower forms of life do. Sexual reproduction is defined by the necessary union of male and female gametes, not the union of male and females, to produce offspring. Nonetheless, most of us are unprepared to see the apple tree as a participant in any sexual activity. What the dog does in the street, however, seems sufficiently similar to what we are likely to do in the privacy of our homes that we are prepared to equate these two activities. Again, as in other more complicated activities, looks are deceiving; there is a world of difference between these two forms of copulation.

God's injunction to be fruitful and multiply, stated before the Fall, indicates that sexual intercourse, at least for the authors of Genesis, was considered an innate endowment of the human being, to be judged good, certainly within the relationship of a loving couple, as represented by Adam and Eve in the Garden. Yet even in Genesis human sexuality is not the "natural" or ordinary function that it is in animals, or that it has been represented to be by modern liberationists. It does not emerge, like equivalent biological drives for food and water, unencumbered by psychological ambivalences. And although all human activity is filtered and altered through imagination, sex seems particularly vulnerable to distortion through symbolic elaboration.

The special nature of human sexuality among the drives is explicitly acknowledged in Genesis by the dramatic transformation that occurs in Adam and Eve after acquiring knowledge of good and evil. Before knowledge, "they were both naked, the man and his wife, and were not ashamed." Indeed, the subsequent text reveals that they did not know they were naked. The concept of nakedness did not exist for them any more than it does for a buffalo or a baboon. After they ate of the Tree of Knowledge, "the eyes of them both were opened, and they knew that they were naked."[2]

At this juncture, then, there was an attempt by the authors of Genesis to explain this peculiar paradox, the existence of a basic mechanism essential to the survival of *Homo sapiens*—the sexual drive, which seemed to carry a natural shame attached to it, or imposed on it by the members of this species, as though it were illicit, unnatural, or ignoble.

Expressions of the holy naturalness of sexual passion are present throughout the Old Testament. Puritan Christians have always had difficulty with this and have attempted to desexualize the Bible by use of revisionist metaphors. It is generally a losing battle. Interpreting the lush sensuality of the Song of Songs as symbolic of the human adoration of Christ is perhaps the most extreme example. Solomon says:

Thou hast ravished my heart, my sister, my bride;
Thou hast ravished my heart with one of thine eyes,
With one bead of thy necklace.
How fair is thy love, my sister, my bride!
How much better is thy love than wine!
And the smell of thine ointments than all manner of spices!
Thy lips, O my bride, drop honey
And the smell of thy garments is like the smell of Lebanon.[3]

In these statements, as in those that precede and those that follow, most of us will resonate to Solomon's sensuality and see in their

inclusion in the Bible a sense of the honor for romantic love held
by the ancient Jew. But even Jewish scholars have attempted to
deny the explicit sexuality everywhere present in the Torah. Rashi
interpreted the "nakedness" of Adam and Eve as symbolically
expressing their absence of gratitude to God for all that He had
bestowed upon them, by defying Him in His one stricture. Although the purposes of the writers of Genesis may have encompassed broader meanings, the explicit sexual nature of their actions
and their shame is paramount. After all, Adam and Eve covered
their loins, not their faces, in shame.

The unique role of privacy in human sexuality is part of the
biology of human sexuality. It is but one aspect distinguishing the
sexual behavior of human beings from their closest primate relatives. There have been numerous attempts to understand and reconcile the contradictions inherent in the peculiar facts of human
sexuality. Here is an animal as dependent on copulation for its
survival as the pigeon or the rat, who nonetheless approaches sexuality with modesty, shame, a need for privacy, and often guilt
and trepidation. There seems an essential contradiction, if not a
downright maladaptive quality to this peculiar mix. Why should
sex not be as unencumbered by these psychological trappings as it
seems to be in most other animals? For that matter, why should
sex be so different from the other drives that sustain life, thirst
and hunger?

The most comprehensive attempt to examine human sexuality
from both a biological and a psychological framework occurs in
the writings of Sigmund Freud. When Freud developed his ideas
about sexuality, he was fully aware that human sexuality differed
significantly from animal sexuality. He was particularly interested
in the appearance of sexual guilt and shame. He developed two
separate theories of its origin, one drawn from his inquiries into
human developmental, and the other from an anthropological and
sociological point of view.

In what has come to be known as the libido theory, Freud
postulated a genetically fixed, biologically driven theory of normal
human development in which the primary energy, the force that

drives all human activity, is the sexual instinct.[4] According to this theory, the human child is a hedonic animal driven by his pleasure needs, and these are always specifically and uniformly sexual. At first his sexual interests are centered on his own body parts, and if left to his own devices he will enjoy masturbation, exhibitionism, voyeurism, and the like without shame or guilt. By age four or five, the child integrates his sexual drive and begins to seek an object other than himself. It is at this point that he attaches his sexual interests to the parent of the opposite sex. The attraction of the little boy to his mother and the little girl to her father is understood by Freud to be instinctually determined. This sexual interest initiates an incest dread, which Freud also assumes to be both universal and biological.

The incest dread produces guilt, shame, and fear of retaliation from the parent of the same sex. To avoid this perilous condition, the child suppresses all sexual desire and enters into a latency period, where sex is permissible only when sublimated into seemingly nonsexual activities. Sex remains hidden in the unconscious until the power of puberty drives it back into consciousness and, with luck, toward a nonincestuous object. The incest dread will always dictate a precarious balance in sex between desire and shame, which will then require that sex be secretive and private, as distinguished from such other survival-serving drives as hunger and thirst. The privacy that shapes the sexual behavior of the parents will reciprocally protect the child from his compelling incestuous appetites.

Freud covered the same territory of sexual guilt and shame from what would now be labeled a "sociobiological" point of view in his book *Totem and Taboo*. Freud postulated that, in its primitive beginnings, the human social structure resembled that of the hordes of primates. A dominant male copulated with a female group, which consisted of his "wives" and his daughters. Male offspring were banned from the primal horde on reaching puberty, to keep them away from the father's sexual consorts. Eventually the banned brothers joined together, forming a secondary group. With aging, this group became powerful enough to raid the primary horde, kill (and eat) the father, and appropriate the mating females. In time, Freud stated, these memories (through mechanisms now discredited by modern biology) became imprinted on the unconscious of the new horde leaders, resulting in religious taboos. These taboos forbade eating certain foods associated with tribal totems, forbade the killing of the father or leader, and protected against incest by regulating marriage within the various totemic units. This is a brutal oversimplification of a fascinating speculative work.

Freud's conclusions in this book remain identical to those expressed in the libido theory. Incest dread and incest taboos are universal parts of the human conscience, as compensation for genetically determined incestuous appetites. Shame, guilt, privacy, and the other rituals of human sexuality are part of an apparatus essential for the survival of a species with contradictory demands. Sexual drive is as essential for species survival in the human being as it is in lower animals. But *individual* survival demands suppression and repression of sexuality, given the eccentric factors of human birth and development: the continual sexual drive; the prolonged dependency period—demanding a tight-knit family and a great potential for individual diversity. These distinguishing traits demand the special environment of privacy and the shame that inevitably characterizes exposure of our sexuality. We pay a price for our sensibilities. Our sexuality is less fixed and more fragile than that of the lower animals.

Before considering the profound vulnerability of our sexual behavior to sociological and psychological influences (this vulnerability being one of the more extraordinary of the distinguishing features), we must look at the biological characteristics of human sexuality.

It is strange that sexuality is so often seen as a quality of human beings at their most "bestial." The assumption is that in our sexuality we come closest to our animal forebears. Is it not instinctually determined? Is it not the same rutting, obsessively driven, genetically derived, somewhat ludicrous procedure that we recognize in

other primates and such lower animals as horses, dogs, and sheep?
Again, it is not.

It is true that many lower forms of animals engage in sexual
reproduction and copulation, but even here the difference is more
intriguing than the similarity. The most dramatic difference is that
the human being is the only continually—although not, thank
goodness, continuously—sexed animal. We have no mating season
and no distinct estrus.

Most animals, male and female, live out their existence with
isolated and single moments reserved for their reproductive functions. Certainly this is the model that prevails in the insect community. As we climb the ladder of complexity in animals, we find
that many *male* animals, particularly among mammals, are also
liberated from a periodic and isolated time of sexual arousal. But
since it still takes two to copulate as well as to tango, the mating
season could be established simply by controlling one-half of the
copulating pair. This is effectively accomplished in many animals
by having a restricted, isolated, and relatively brief period of receptivity on the part of the female.

In the female animal, sexual desire and sexual receptivity are
always linked to the potential for reproduction. As a result, a mating
season is defined according to the occurrence of ovulation and a
fertile period in the female. In some but not all animals, female
estrus will also influence and control the sexual appetites of the
male, who will require the pheromones, the specific sexual olfactory
stimulants secreted by the females only during estrus, to trigger
the brain centers initiating his sexual appetite.

Estrus, then, establishes two conditions central to animal sexuality. First, sex, though it may be pleasurable, never serves pleasure
alone but is closely linked to reproduction. Second, all sexual activity is limited to a severely restricted period of time, a mating
season. The differences between human beings and animals in even
this shared "instinct" is now becoming only too apparent.

Of course, the primary function of sexuality built into the human
being is also to ensure the survival of the species. The intense
pleasure of the sexual experience for the individual is the driving

force that will guarantee the performance of this species-serving function. But the activity of human sexuality is now so divorced from its reproductive function that, for most people at most times, the reproductive aspect is an annoying and limiting imposition on the now transcendent pleasure purposes of sexual intercourse.

The advantages of estrus are obvious. During the period of mating, but more particularly during the period of tending the young, the animals are at risk from predators. The young nursing animals are particularly vulnerable, but the species depends on their survival. There is a distinct advantage to having all of the young born at the same time, when the herd is together and the males present for maximum protection; and there is a further advantage to having this time limited to a relatively short period of the year. If the herd can be kept together during these limited, specific periods, not incidentally during times where food is abundant and extensive grazing is not required, the length and extent of vulnerability is narrowed.

It is not difficult for most of us to imagine the pleasure advantage of a sexual function that can operate twenty-four hours a day, seven days a week, all year long, but what adaptive end could this characteristic of human sexuality have served? And what does it say about the human condition?

E. O. Wilson has seen this continuing capacity for sexual activity as assuring the bonding that was the predecessor of marriage, as does the elaboration of sexual activity and the forms of sexual pleasure. The everyday and heightened hunger for sex links the mating couple in desire through the years:

"Human beings are unique among the primates with their intensity and variety of their sexual activity. Among other higher animals they are exceeded in sexual athleticism only by lions. The external genitalia of both men and women are exceptionally large and advertised by tufts of pubic hair. The breasts of women are enlarged beyond the size required to house the mammary glands, while the nipples are erotically sensitive and encircled by conspicuously colored areolas. In both sexes the ear lobes are fleshy and sensitive to touch."[5]

Wilson tends to see sexual love and the satisfactions of family life—like almost everything else—as based on "enabling mechanisms" fixed genetically into programmed behavior in the physiology of the human brain, but he almost reluctantly introduces the concept of human imagination as an influence on the sexual drive.

"Human beings are connoisseurs of sexual pleasure. They indulge themselves by casual inspection of potential partners, by fantasy, poetry and song and in every delightful nuance of flirtation leading to foreplay and coition. This has little or nothing to do with reproduction. It has everything to do with bonding. If insemination were the sole biological function of sex, it could be achieved far more economically in a few seconds of mounting and insertion. Indeed, the least social of mammals mate with scarcely more ceremony. . . . It is consistent with this trend that most of the pleasures of human sex constitute primary reinforcers to facilitate bonding. Love and sex do indeed go together."[6]

Wilson assumes the importance of human bonding, without explaining why it is so essential to our species. It is the extraordinary nature of human infancy that demands the full occupation and cooperation of at least two adults— or did so, at least, in the hundreds of thousands of years that antedated the development of a culture that could provide child-care services. The human child is born so utterly helpless, and remains thus for such a ridiculously long time, that a full-time caretaker is required. The infant would encumber the wide-ranging hunting activities necessary to feed and support the incipient family unless an arrangement were made for a division of labor, with part of the family structure dedicated to the care and feeding of the child while another representative seeks the wherewithal of survival. In the early history of our species, when we were essentially a hunting-and-gathering society, a dedicated pair, at least, were required to support the needs of the helpless creature. The role of human dependency in shaping our natures, our psychology, and our institutions is so central that it commands a chapter of its own.

Male animals in most primate groups have no special interest in their own progeny, if, indeed, they even recognize or acknowledge them as such. The protective devotion to the specific child is the purview of the female. The male is responsible for the collective safety of the horde. In nonherding animals such as the tiger, the mother must defend her young against male tigers—including the father—who represent one of the major threats to the offspring. This is not so in *Homo sapiens*. The overvaluation of one's child is gender-neutral. It may be argued that, given the traditional patterns of caretaking, it assumes a greater intensity in the mother, but the human father knows and zealously guards the interests of his own.

The bonding of the male to the female assures that he will support her needs above those of the general host. Beyond bonding, desire and love will drive him to return to the waiting mother and child. The bonding of the female supports her fidelity to the male during his absences. Unlike other monogamous creatures, who cling together only during the mating period, humans have a mating period that is forever and continuous, even surviving long absences, since food gathering demands a wide-ranging male. The female of this species experiences sexual appetite whether or not she is ovulating, and whether or not her mate is physically present. It is the emotional elaborations of sexuality that bind the couple together in commitment and love.

This need for a family setting, combined with the continual nature of sexual appetite, may help to explain further the paradox presented earlier: why so essential an activity as sex should require privacy and be endowed with a mantle of shame. One hypothesis is that the covering of the genitals so common across cultures is an attempt to inhibit or constrict sexual arousal in order to facilitate such other essential activities of life as building shelter, getting food, and rearing children. Modesty is also a public statement about the nonpublic aspects of the genitalia and their sexual activities. For human beings, sexuality is never a casual public affair.

The dramatic conditions distinguishing human sexuality from animal sexuality are rooted in the biological liberation of women from the limiting conditions of an estrus. This separation of fecundity and appetite resulted in the emergence of a continual sexual appetite, around the calendar and around the clock. This alone was quite capable of transforming human sexuality into something entirely different from the models of other animals. But, as in all things human, the essential biology is but the raw material that will be shaped and transmuted by the psychological and sociological forces forming our perceptions and behaviors.

Human beings will always defy laboratory analysis. Laboratory analysis is a legitimate and helpful means of viewing human behavior; it is not necessarily a truer vision than a poetic, philosophical, or dynamic psychological vision. The view our culture has of our "proper" functioning will determine not just the way we judge our behavior, but the nature of the behavior itself. We all aspire to normality and respectability. The cultural attitudes about sex become as critical as the biological facts in determining sexual mores. Speculative thinkers in various cultures across time have struggled in the same way that the authors of Genesis did with some of the seeming contradictions inherent in human sexuality. In the *Symposium*, Plato describes Socrates and his friends discussing various aspects of love. At a banquet, Pausanias distinguishes two contrasting aspects of love that he defines as the earthly and the heavenly Aphrodite. The earthly Aphrodite is what we might now call animal instinct or pure lust, and the heavenly Aphrodite the bonding aspect of love. These two contradictory images had occupied the poets and philosophers of Greece well before the time of Plato.

On the one hand, love was seen as a passion that was in opposition to, and that threatened, order and rationality. It was therefore a destructive force driving human beings beyond reason, the residual animal aspect of our nature, striving for gratification and requiring constraint, not far from the uninhibited libido that Freud was later to describe. This earthly aspect of Aphrodite was expressed beautifully by the chorus in Antigone:

"Love, unconquered in the fight, Love, who makest havoc of wealth, who keepest thy vigil on the soft cheek of a maiden . . . ; no immortal can escape thee, nor any among men whose life is for a day; and he to whom thou has come is mad.

"The just themselves have their minds warped by thee to wrong, for their ruin: tis thou that has stirred up this present strife of kinsmen."[7]

The concept of a disruptive Eros was not idiosyncratic to the Greeks. Throughout ancient mythology, the symbol of a disuniting, malicious, and maddening Eros is a constant presence (often visualized as a blind Cupid, an impish and mischievous boy) and would only be replaced with the conversion of the Roman Empire to Christianity. Virgil, in his *Aeneid*, describes the awesome destructive power of the unfortunate Dido's passion: "Unlucky Dido, burning, in her madness roamed through all the city, like a doe hit by an arrow. . . ."[8]

From the classical period forward, the history of ideas and attitudes about sex derive primarily from theological studies presenting us with a morass of contradictions. The confusion about the proper role of sex in human relationships was to be drastically muddled by later religious interpretations, particularly from Christian sects that were to discover a virtue in celibacy. Despite God's injunction to be fruitful and multiply, as revealed in Genesis 2, and despite the Roman Catholic Church's reverence for the Old Testament, Catholicism compounded the problem and confused all of us by elevating celibacy to the highest standard of human behavior.

Elaine Pagels admirably traced the confusing process that initiated a model of celibacy to the forefront of virtue in Christian theology. For my purposes, the most interesting aspect of her book, *Adam, Eve, and the Serpent*, is her focus on the extended debate between Augustine and Julian.[9]

Augustine is the champion of celibacy, elevating it to a virtue beyond even marital sex. His disgust with sex of any sort, even within the confines of marriage, is explicit and has left its mark in modern Christian thought through that peculiar concept inherent in modern Catholic teaching that sex must be exclusively and specifically tied to childbearing and the desire for procreation.

Julian, in his gentle rejection of Augustine's arguments, points out that desire was natural from the beginning, inherent in our very design. "God made bodies, distinguished the sexes, made genitalia, he bestowed affection through which bodies would be joined, gave power to the semen, and operates in a secret nature of the semen—and God made nothing evil."[10]

Fortunately, I do not have to enter the convoluted Byzantine labyrinth of Christian theology. I am not interested here in the philosophical or theological nature of human behavior, but in the biological and psychological roots. I am interested in how we are created: what is given to us by our genes and how we modify it through our culture and development.

To a biologist, Augustine seems perversely in opposition to the precise element that distinguishes human sexuality from animal— its liberation from the procreative function. To a psychoanalyst, his position is contrary to a lifetime of experience in dealing with human beings, where the evidence is overwhelming that the true power and nature of human sex is in its role as a component of a romantic life that facilitates the binding together of couples. Procreation is for all practical purposes both statistically and theoretically a minor agent in the drama of everyday sexuality.

The personal history and development of these two antagonists, Augustine and Julian, may offer some help in discovering possible explanations for their violently antithetical attitudes toward sex. Augustine, in his confessions, reveals himself as a man obsessed with sexuality—a man of enormous passion who wrestled, one suspects, with his own version of the Angel of Death until his own death. Augustine loathed this "diabolical excitement of the genitals."[11] "Behold the vital fire which does not obey the soul's decision but for the most part rises up against the soul's desire in disorder and ugly movement."[12] No such passionate indictments could exist except in a sexually driven and sexually dominated human being.

By contrast, Julian sounds middle-aged. He had, after all, had his fling with marriage. He had enjoyed his sexual life, one presumes, within the institution of marriage, and therefore within the permissible limits of the Church.

It is not just the thought and conclusions of Julian and Augustine that are different; it is the intensity and the passion of the arguments. Ironically, Julian defends sexual desire with a pedantic and passionless tone. Augustine attacks it with a maniacal and desperate passion.

It was Augustine who was to leave the more profound mark on the modern Roman Catholic Church, but not without its costs. The insistence that sexual appetite is sinful if separated from pro-creation, even when it is related to love and marriage, has continued to plague the relationship between the Church hierarchy and its constituency. Nowhere in Church teaching is there so flagrant and willful a disregard of authority and dogma as in issues surrounding birth control. The Church fathers may speak with the imprimatur of the powerful, but they are impotent when what they preach seems discordant with popular wisdom.

Despite the orthodoxies of many religious groups beyond the Roman Catholic Church (Puritanism is after all the pinched and peculiar offspring of Protestantism), sex has prevailed—and with a vengeance. The twentieth-century orthodoxy about sex rests not on the teachings of the Church, but on the "verities" and dogmas of modern psychology.

Modern behavioral scientists are, whether they acknowledge it or not, the latter-day disciples of Thomas Hobbes. Alan Ryan, in his study of human nature, saw this clearly. Hobbes was, in his attitudes toward human nature, the antithesis of the writers of Genesis. He saw human actions as determined and predictable, denying the existence of free will. As an inevitable corollary, he saw all human behavior as selfish, dismissing even the possibility of any altruistic capacities in the human being. Hobbes's insistence on purely mechanical explanations for all human action is mirrored in such diverse modern-day determinists as Sigmund Freud, B. F. Skinner, and Edmund O. Wilson. As Ryan said: "During this century, the goal of toughminded scientists has been to reduce the psychological vocabulary of desire, purpose, intention, to something akin to the austere vocabulary of mechanics."[13]

In the beginning as in the end of modern sensibility, there is Freud. The sexual revolution was, if not initiated by his theories, certainly justified and rationalized by his imaginative and brilliant observations and constructions. Freud was the twentieth-century apostle of the new sex. The re-evaluation of all values that occurred in the new climate of ideas following World War I and World War II, and the technological advances of the twentieth century, ushered in the biological revolution, demanding a new vision of purpose and destiny. No one contributed more to that vision than Sigmund Freud.

Freud not only resurrected sex from the hypocrisies of Victorian Puritanism; he elevated sexuality to a transcendent position as the universal life force. In Freud's view, the human being is driven by a motivating force that is for the most part instinctually fixed and determined. Originally this was conceived of as a dual force, consisting of two instincts—one serving survival, and the other serving pleasure. Eventually Freud fused the two into the concept of the libido, a sexual force that managed through its reproductive end to serve group survival and through orgastic pleasure to serve individual motivation. The sexual drive, the libido, dominated and controlled all human action and all human behavior, all human performance and all human pleasure. As sexual energy, the libido was the only fuel that drove the human machine, and its discharge, in one form or another, produced the pleasure that underlay *all* pleasurable experiences. The vicissitudes of the libido, its permutations and transformations, supplied the energy that drove art, science, intellectuality, friendship, religion, and love. For good and ill, modern attitudes about human sexuality were recast in the crucible of a Freudian dynamic.

The libido theory views all behaviors as products of the driving force of the sexual instinct and of the counterforces that kept it in check. The environment and the events of the child's experience had meaning only as they were internalized, and as they could influence the genetically patterned libido. The intrapersonal life of the individual was to become the exclusive focus of the psychoanalysts. Conflict became the central thesis, and intrapsychic conflict at that. It was a world of psychodynamics, forces and counterforces and the emotions were incidental fallout, ultimately uninteresting scientifically. Attachments were neglected as psychoanalysts busily charted the topology and the structure of our struggles with our only important adversaries—ourselves.

Modern psychoanalysis had, without his eloquence, anticipated Pogo and discovered the enemy in ourselves. All attention was directed to internal conflict: desire versus fear; impulse countered by conscience; id against superego. These were the areas of interest to the psychoanalyst. He was, in a sense, observing a flower through a microscope, and although he learned a great deal about the structure of the self, the inner world, he tended to ignore the environment in which the isolated self would be nurtured or deprived. Interpersonal relationships were only reluctantly and recently elevated to serious consideration by Freudians.

In a world in which relationships are secondary phenomena and all emotions are derivative, love will never be discovered, and sex will be everything. All attention was placed on the instinctual drive and the counterforces that contained it. Pleasure was defined strictly in terms of sexual release, pain in terms of sexual frustration. This was a model built on a hydraulic principle more suitable for explaining the mechanisms of urination and bladder function than the complex subject of human pleasure and human motivation.

The drive for instinctual (sexual) gratification, labeled the "pleasure principle," was for a preponderant time in psychoanalytic theory the sole motivating force by which all human behavior was presumed to be driven. It was a hedonic view of life, regarding the human being as driven by an urgent need for sexual gratification that was constrained only by the institutions of society, civilization, and certain ill-defined counterforces within human nature.

But what of the counterforces that created the dynamic tension out of which neuroses were born? Well, they were confusing, and never adequately analyzed by Freud. And that is too bad, for it is in the counterforces that we find the binding elements of the social being: the conscience mechanisms, unselfishness, the emotions, and, finally, love.

The definition of pleasure in this pleasure principle was simplistic and peculiarly negativistic. It may be perfectly suitable to define pleasure purely in terms of the relief of tension when we are speaking of animals hedonically regulated at a mechanical, subcortical level. Of course people experience pleasure in the satiation of hunger, and of course there is pleasure in orgastic release but the human cortex informs and modifies all activities that involve conceptualization. The concepts of pride, esthetics, sensibility, and fantasy—to name but a few that Freud was both cognizant of and interested in—will never be explicable in a vocabulary and framework so limited and mechanistic as the libido theory.

Since the feeling of love is, in my mind, the highest form of human pleasure (albeit more than that), in order to understand the nature of love and its influence on sex from a psychoanalytic point of view it is necessary to re-evaluate and expand the concept of pleasure. The traditional psychoanalyst attempted to confine us to a loveless theoretical world. Sex was everything. Friendship, creativity, work, and beauty were simply sublimations, reaction formations, derivatives, and disguised forms of our instinctually driven animal sexuality. But the modern psychoanalyst has suffered the misfortune of surviving the victory of his philosophy and must now suffer the humiliation of living in this unlovely world that is in great part of his own creation. Though the final score is not yet in, the results of the sexual revolution so far are less than reassuring. The liberation of the sexual drive from the repressive forces of a puritanical environment has brought no surcease from neurotic anxiety and despair. The loveless world of casual sexuality is surely not the healthy environment to which we aspired.

Freud, of all people, understood the role of human imagination in shaping human experience. He was a product and a part of the broad tradition of German idealism, which held that the world as it actually existed was less important in the psychic affairs of the human being than the world perceived. Surely even human appetites are influenced by the human imagination. Sex cannot be the automatic and animalistic mechanism described in the libido theory; pleasure cannot simply be the physiological product of released sexual tension. Sex must be placed somewhere, somehow, into its proper position within a broader, more sophisticated concept of "attachments" and—yes—love.

What Freud saw was there. He was an extraordinary observer. He recognized that many of our activities carried a hidden sexual charge. Unfortunately, from these specific and brilliant observations he persisted in constructing a universal, generalizing theory about all human behavior. Such pursuit of universal truth inevitably brings down even genius. Freud made the generalization that all behavior, beyond having the capacity to contain covert sexual aspects, was in essence pure sex. That was an error.

There are other powers as urgent as the sexual that drive our behavior. There are, for example, those emotions that serve our survival. Freud was inspired in recognizing that a woman dreaming of a gun might well be dreaming of a phallus. He should have been equally aware that a woman dreaming of a phallus might really be thinking of a gun. The great insight of Freud was his recognition that all things are not what they seem to us to be, not that all things are sexual; his awareness that we are driven by unconscious irrational motives as well as and perhaps more than our conscious rationalizations. But not all unconscious motivation is sexual. Power, vanity, fear, rage, and other forces drive our behavior beyond our knowledge.

That which joins Augustine and Freud was much greater than that which separated them. What an odd alliance was formed! Both Freud and Saint Augustine saw an unbridled sexuality as threatening human tranquillity and therefore demanding cultural control or modification; both felt that social order rested on the civilizing of the sexual instinct. The crucial difference lay in the cure. Augustine demanded celibacy and constraint; Freud invented the concept of sublimation and reaction formation, whereby the power of the libido could be released through its transformations into disguised forms of sexuality. According to Freud, play, creativity, work, all expenditures of energy were driven by the sexual instinct and resulted in the release of sexual tension through its various permutations.

Both equated human sexuality with the instinctual drive of the beasts. Augustine saw this as diminishing our dignity unless restricted to the essential biological purpose of survival—procreation—whereas Freud saw the release of sexual tension as the driving force of life, the fuel that fed all of humanity's ends, higher and lower. Indeed, "higher" and "lower" became terms that had no significance. Since underneath all activity, whether prayer or profligacy, lay the hidden libido, no moral distinctions could be made. "Healthy" as opposed to "neurotic" displaced such old-fashioned terms as "good" and "evil" and became the foundations of the new twentieth-century morality. "Sickness" replaced the principle of sinfulness. This is precisely what Philip Rieff described as the "Triumph of the Therapeutic."[14]

The one most essential difference between Freud and Augustine resided in the fact that Freud, by enlarging the functions of sex, by making sex the only fuel available to drive all the machinery of human action, would end up visualizing the binding forces of sex as at least as crucial as its procreative ends.

What of the essential assumption that joined the two men, the belief that human beings are instinctually driven by a powerful sexual force that must be controlled by civilization? Wrapped into the rituals and romance of human love, is there not something operating in *Homo sapiens* that is equivalent to the pure sexual instinct that drives the lower animals? If there is, the term "lust" is likely to be used these days to describe the aspect of human nature that we share with the animals—an automatic sexual drive uninformed by human imagination or sensibilities.

C. S. Lewis explained it perfectly when he said of lust: "Sexual desire without Eros [love] wants *it* the *thing in itself*, whereas love wants the lover. . . . We use the most unfortunate idiom when we say of a lustful man prowling the streets that he 'wants a woman'. Strictly speaking, a woman is just what he does not want. He wants a pleasure for which a woman happens to be the necessary piece of apparatus."[15]

Lust is the desire for a casual and anonymous sexual feeling—the erection that occurs without intention of necessary pursuit or even valuation of the object. Certainly both men and women have experienced a surge of sexual excitement on seeing an attractive member of the opposite sex. Roberto Unger defined lust as "Sexual attraction untransformed by love or generally uninspired by the imagination."[16]

Such is "love" among the animals. An observation of animals "making love" is often a disquieting experience. Although the courtship and competition may be elaborate and intriguing, the copulation seems stereotyped and passionless. Considering the exhausting and often dangerous maneuvers to gain permission to mate, the action doesn't seem all that much fun. Further, it is amazing that the same stereotyped behavior exists all the way up the line from simple to complicated animals: copulation remains the same dull (to the observer, at least) and predictable entity whether one is watching guppies or our "cousins" the chimpanzees.

With the sexual liberation of the past two decades, we have seen an attempt to detach sex from love and commitment. The emptiness and unfulfilled nature of such sex is only now beginning to be appreciated by large parts of the population. These days it is easier for many young people to go to bed with one another than to form trusting or intimate relationships. It is easier for them to expose their genitals to a stranger than to expose their feelings. Such exposure has become less frightening now that we socially condone it. The resulting confusion is beginning to be sorted out in psychoanalysts' offices around the country.

But it would be a mistake to think that by detaching sex from commitment and attachment we have liberated it either from all of its symbolic meanings or from all of its emotional charges. It is always metaphoric, always more than just instinct, always accompanied by past memories and future expectations, always compounded by desires, fears, aspirations, self-deceits, and vanities.

It was the conceit of psychoanalysts in earlier times to assume that freeing sexual conduct from the artificial strictures of the puritanical society of the late nineteenth century would make sexuality an easier and simpler event. Conventional psychoanalysis assumed that one could reduce the amount of emotional agony and neurosis that were presumed to be the product of the complicated struggle of the inhibited individual with his sexual desires. Well, one need only look around at friends and colleagues to recognize that despite our sexual "liberation" human misery has not diminished, neurosis is still all-pervasive, and, though the forms of anxiety related to sex may have changed, the amount probably has not.

It is true that the sexual revolution has liberated women to a point where they no longer bear an extra burden of pain and humiliation for their sexual appetites. It has made sexual appetite in women respectable, and that is no mean achievement. But the complexities of human behavior mandate that such disparate drives as power, security, love, the need for love, and sexuality must be joined to give some meaning to the life we are leading and the world we are occupying. Most of us need to weave the threads of our life together so that we can integrate our various selves into a life of whole cloth, a life of value, a life that stands for "something." We are frightened that "Getting and spending, we [may] lay waste our powers," fading from existence without a trace of memory, reputation, or influence on the lives of others. Sex becomes an integrating force that unites us to others in pursuit of shared joys and honorable activities.

Given the importance of relationship and the power of the sexual experience, it is rare to find human beings in whom sex is pure, unadulterated instinct. The most passionate lovers might like to think so, but they do not behave like rutting bears or bitches in heat. All human sexuality, like all human behavior, is shaped by emotion and imagination, by fantasy as well as reality. Only in animals and in the animalistic behavior of such aberrant people as rapists does one see pure sexual drive unadulterated by other sensibilities. With the rapist, sex may be totally separated from affection or knowledge of the other person. But even here one may be surprised. Careful study of rapists shows that sex is frequently a secondary factor in the attack. Rage and fear of women may motivate the rapist more than lust.

Some subcultures in our society have attempted to separate sexuality from the sexual partner completely. This isolated and sad sexuality exists, among other places, with male homosexuals who are attracted to the anonymous sex of public toilets and public

baths. These men have an obsessively driven need for a sexual—
or, more exactly, a phallic—experience stripped of all human association. The pseudonymous William Aaron describes his experiences in this world. The desire for anonymous sex leads to activity
whereby one may be anally penetrated repetitively or perform
fellatio on twenty to fifty "partners" a night.[17]

In this kind of sexuality, the anonymity does not make for
freedom from fantasy but is an essential ingredient of it, a major
part of the excitement. Another human presence intrudes on the
fantasy—it is the isolated phallus that has meaning, that is desired.
Sexual pleasure is totally incidental to some secret scenario of power
and humiliation, dominance and submission, anxiety and reassurance. The driven behavior is only barely sexual. That the sexual
act is not gratifying is evidenced by its insatiability and the need
to repeat it constantly. Sexuality, divorced not just from affection
but from human contact (the heterosexual equivalent of this has
been described by Erica Jong as "the zipless fuck"), turns out to
be sexual in form only. Such aberrations are also distinctly human,
though not characteristic of human sexuality. For animals, sex is
sex, not a symbolic substitute for anything else. Of course, power
struggles occur in the competition for a mate, but procreation is
the ultimate goal. Power and dominance are in the service of sex,
never the other way round.

With human beings, while sex may be detached from love,
romance, or even another human being, it is never separated from
human imagination. The indiscriminate sexual behavior previously
described is rarely sexual. It usually represents a compulsive use
of sex to fulfill other, quite different, unconscious needs. The real
motive force behind these activities is part of the complex domain
of male competition, dominance, submission, and dependency crav-
ings in our culture.

To repeat, then, the only time human sexuality is expressed as
pure appetite—independent of the nature of the partner—is in
certain pathological and perverse states. Most of us perceive such
sexuality as being beyond human norms.

Pure lust, or pure sexuality, operating as a release of tension in the same way that urination releases the tension of the distended bladder, is a rare phenomenon. Even at its most distorted and perverse, perhaps still more so in such cases, sexual appetite and behavior are laden with obligations to the past and hopes for the future. Sex is a symbolic and metaphoric act never completely separable from needs for security, approval, self-esteem, safety, pride, etc. Sex is rarely expressed or enjoyed independent of other emotional relationships with the sexual partner. We will not generally have sex with people who repel us.

Some among us, despite the evidence of their own experiences, assume that for others some pure sexual appetite—something akin to hunger for food—does exist. But most of us in this privileged Western world, in the bourgeois society of the writers and readers of books, have already separated the experience of eating from anything remotely resembling the behavior of a hungry animal. It is for this reason we use the word "dining" rather than "eating." Anyone who has attended one of the three-star restaurants of France or one of its many counterparts in America knows what a strange ritual "dining out" is and how little it has to do with the satisfaction of hunger. I ask you to remember the last time you went out to dine. What was involved? What were you seeking? Release from boredom, the pleasures of taste, being seen in the right place, a prelude to a hoped-for sexual seduction, an excuse for the leisure of conversation, an esthetic experience? Whatever it may have been, it had nothing to do with the experience of the lion tearing at the throat of an antelope or the chimpanzee eating a banana.

If eating has been so elaborately transformed by human imagination in modern culture, then what can we say of sexuality, which is infinitely more complex and metaphoric? It no longer bears any relationship to the exercise of the automatic animal instinct.

The rat, seeing and smelling a receptive female in its lurching movements, is not concerned with the esthetics, personality factors, or status of the particular female rat available. A male dog is attracted to a bitch in heat because of an olfactory stimulus, a pheromone, that operates like a chemical switch, turning on a mechanism so impelling that the male animal is driven toward the consummation of the sexual act often at the risk of its own life. A dog will get into fights with dogs twice his size and more powerful and terrible than he is when under the automatic spell of the sexual instinct. He is not thinking; he is drawn as though attached by a wire on a pulley. He does not care whether the female dog is well formed, misshapen, well bred, or mongrel, black or white, one-tenth his size or five times as large, old or young, his daughter, his sister, his mother, or simply the dog next door.

None of this is conceivable as a model for human lust, let alone love. It does matter to us whether the object of our desire is our mother or the girl next door. The sexual act, even when it is not a part of romantic love, is always modified by the imaginative aspects of the human psyche. The sexual object must be perceived as "attractive." She must be of a certain age, style, manner, or personality to elicit desire.

And what of the consummation of the act, once the contact between animals is made? It certainly doesn't seem to be much fun! Perhaps we misjudge the subjective experience of the animals. The male animal must derive intense gratification of some sort with ejaculation. Otherwise why risk life and limb for the privilege? But the female animal is not thought by most ethologists to achieve anything approaching the orgasm of women. To the casual observer, the mating of animals seems humdrum and tedious compared with the experience—or expectations—of human intercourse. The female usually seems fixed and staring. No moans of delight, no shivers of ecstasy. The male rhythmically pumps away until the charge wears down like the actions of a cheap wind-up toy. Sex among animals, whatever it is, seems genetically wired. Forget about romance; where is the passion? Only in the chase, not in the consummation.

Human sexual excitement, in contrast, is always an amalgam of endocrine and imagination. The response is more religious than reflexive. It always has and always will have an unanalyzable and mystical aspect. It is part of the union of man and woman.

When Adam and Eve defied God and ate of the forbidden fruit, they did it together. They shared the defiance. They would share the punishment. But they would also share a common future. And they would share it in hope. After God pronounced His punishments, warning man and woman of the bitter life they would henceforth lead, they left together, in love and in hope. Adam renames his wife Eve—in Hebrew, Havvah, "Life"—because she would be the "the mother of all living." He pronounces the future, and the future will be a race of free and aspiring creatures bound by few rigid and automatic drives. By gaining knowledge and freedom from instinctual tyranny, Adam and Eve created a new creature slightly lower than the angels. We are the children of that glorious, willful, curious, and questing couple. We share their passion and their curiosity. We suffer their shame and guilt. We will never again be innocent; nothing will be immune to our imagination and perception. Nothing, not even the drive on which the survival of the species is dependent, will ever be simple and automatic. All pleasure will be intermingled with pain and doubt. Sex will always be vulnerable, but precious. It will be bound, in romance, to commitment and expectations.

PINOCCHIO

—

ON

BECOMING

HUMAN

DEPENDENCY

~~~~~~~~~~

In 1881, Ferdinande Martini, a young Roman editor, had the inspired idea of creating a magazine devoted to the entertainment of children. Martini's *Giornale por i bambini* was evidently an instant success. Searching about for new contributors to a field that was itself a new one, he approached a journalist from Florence, Carlo Lorenzini, who, writing under the pseudonym C. Collodi, had already achieved a certain success in writing for children. In July 1881, the first story of what would become the adventures of Pinocchio was published under the title "La Storia di un burattine," "The Story of a Puppet." Collodi was to continue to publish these episodes for two years, concluding with their collection into book form in 1883.[1] Since then, the story has been translated into eighty-seven languages, according to some authorities, and as many as 162, according to the more expansive Italian publishers. There have been four hundred television versions, hundreds of doctoral dissertations, and even a papal letter.[2]

With *Pinocchio* we are dealing with a very different literary form from that of Genesis 1–3. A simple story written for children, it is the work of a single author rather than a group or succession of them—and that author, Carlo Lorenzini, was the product of a very specific culture, whose values are manifest throughout.

Pinocchio is not dissimilar in form to children's stories today. It is somewhat longer, more preachy and moralistic, and less sophisticated than most of today's literature for children. Nonetheless, the truth and genius in *Pinocchio* have allowed it to persist and

flourish for over a hundred years. The impact of *Pinocchio* undoubtedly surpassed the most grandiose of expectations of either
author or publisher.

Here, as with Genesis, it is not the literary work as such that
interests me. I am neither concerned with doing an exegesis of the
Pinocchio story nor involved in some "psychohistory" attempting
to reduce Pinocchio to the personality or neurosis of his author. I
approach *Pinocchio* as a parable, a framework on which to construct
the other half of the extraordinary story of *Homo sapiens*. Where
Genesis clarifies our natural endowment, *Pinocchio* explores how
development influences the expression of those potentials.

I presume that a rough knowledge of the Pinocchio story exists
for most readers. To allow for the fact that some readers may not
recall the story, let me briefly summarize. It starts with the discovery by a lonely carpenter of a talking piece of wood, a piece of
wood that laughed and cried like a child.

On rereading the first page of the first chapter of *Pinocchio*, I
became aware of how memory plays tricks. I had not remembered
the story as beginning this way but, rather, as being the story of
how a lonely carpenter, who desperately wanted a child, created
a puppet child for himself. What I was recalling was the Disney
version of *Pinocchio*, which does start this way, and in so doing
converts *Pinocchio* into something more like the Pygmalion myth
or the Frankenstein story. But the author of the book intuitively
starts in a simpler—and ultimately more sophisticated—way. It is
not a fantasy of the human creation of life, but of the everyday
miracle that is represented by human development. The parent—
in this case, atypically, a father—is given the crude form of humankind that is the newborn baby, with all its potential within it
but still hidden. He then carves and shapes it, guiding, setting
standards and examples that will inevitably determine whether and
to what degree that potential will be realized and expressed—
whether that talking piece of wood will become converted into a
"real boy."

In the course of this transformation, Pinocchio will learn many
lessons. He learns of his own helplessness when he falls asleep at

a fire and his feet are burned off. He learns about unselfishness
from Geppetto. He learns about the value of work and the agonies
of labor when he is converted into a donkey and must labor like
an animal. He learns of duplicity and exploitation from two con
artists, the Fox and the Cat. Pinocchio learns about the power of
lying, and its ultimate consequences and pain. He learns of the
multiple forms of love. He is made to understand grief through
the loss of that love.

Pinocchio ultimately is a parable of the processes by which a
caring and loving human being is created out of the narcissistic
self of the infant. It is not necessary that Pinocchio become obedient,
pure, or perfect. He wishes, after all, only to be human and only
a child. But he must learn to be a human child. He must appreciate
the specific qualities of identification, imagination, and empathy,
which are at the roots of human love. To become truly human,
he must first learn to hear the voice of conscience; to identify with
those who are hungry, poor, and in misery; to appreciate the
profound joy of giving that transcends the ephemeral pleasure of
receiving. Or, in the words of his guardian angel, the Blue Fairy,
to possess all that she subsumes under the heading "a good heart."

Margaret Blount, an authority on children's literature, sum-
marizes the story and its meaning brilliantly in her book *Animal
Land*:

"Pinocchio falls from grace with the monotonous regularity of
most humans, doll though he is. Again and again he is put on the
right road, again and again he behaves foolishly, tells lies to save
himself, resents advice, dashes here and there in pursuit of pleasure,
steals, is taken in by the simplest ruses, is filled with remorse and
repentance, and immediately goes wrong again—one wonders why
the Blue Fairy and Cricket don't give up. The moral message is
quite clear—one may sin many times and still be forgiven—but
the implicit allegory is that it takes a long time to grow up."[3]

It does take a human being an extraordinary length of time to
grow up. Created for greatness, we are nonetheless thrust into the
world impotent and unformed. The pitiful, helpless blob that is
the newborn infant is as nothing compared with other newborn

mammals. The extreme dependency of the newborn baby and the length of time he will remain helpless are unparalleled in the animal world. The infant is not even the talking block of wood that was to become Pinocchio. In *Pinocchio* we see the conversion of a talking block of wood into a real boy, and through his experiences we can appreciate why, independent of our inborn potentials, some of us will never realize our humanity, but will remain blockheads or worse all of our lives. In the process of becoming human, Pinocchio is exposed to the most inhumane treatment, both from other human beings and from animals. *Pinocchio* is an ideal parable to illuminate the process of "becoming" as distinguished from "being" human.

So much for the block of wood. Now let us turn to that helpless, wriggling mass of tissue and tantrum, the newborn infant. Comparative biologists like Adolph Portmann have expressed incredulity at "the peculiarity of our early development." What in the world, Portmann wonders, are we doing out of the womb so early? Considering our superior brain development, we are all born premature. He contrasts us with our fellow mammals who seem to be born with well-developed limbs and are able to move almost immediately after birth—young deer, calves, foals, elephants, giraffes, whales, dolphins, seals.

The human infant seems to defy the general order of things. Usually, uncomplicated and undifferentiated animals have a short gestation period. Within moments of birth, the young fish is faced with the threat of its first predator—its own mother! Even the fish is one notch above the sea urchin, who must be prepared for a hostile environment only hours after the egg has been fertilized. Nature handles more complicated animals by increasing the amount of time they stay in the uterus to allow for the completion of the minimum protective mechanisms, such as the capacity to run with the herd.

But as Portmann pointed out, it is "a peculiarity of man that despite his higher level of differentiation he has to meet his environment far earlier than the elephant does."[4]

How is it, then, that the human baby is born in such a helpless state with practically no instinctual capacities for survival or self-preservation? The answer lies in the organ in which resides so much of our potential humanness—the brain.

The giant size of the human brain in relationship to its body, and the extreme narrowness of the human pelvis (accentuated by the upright posture, which facilitates our technological advances), demand birth at nine months of gestation. Otherwise the rapid growth of the brain would make it impossible for the baby to pass through the birth canal.

The human brain weighs roughly 350 grams at birth. If birth were delayed until the human infant were capable of walking, as is the case with almost every other land mammal—that is, until the end of the first year of life—the brain would grow to 825 grams. By two years, when the toddler is secure in his movements, the brain weighs a thousand grams. This, mind you, out of a total adult brain measurement of fourteen hundred grams! It is the potential wisdom, the capacity for art and industry, the nature of human imagination, wrapped up in that giant human cortex, that makes birth difficult and mandatory at a precariously early stage of development. Genesis is not only metaphorically but literally accurate here: a difficult delivery *is*, after all, the price of knowledge.

I know that we analysts have been accused of overemphasizing the first year of life, and perhaps we have done so; but it was the genius of Freud to point out a developmental basis for the poet's understanding that "The child is father of the man." Freud was trained in biology. He was not a psychoanalyst—such a profession did not exist in nineteenth-century Vienna. He was a neurologist concerned with human behavior and the human nervous system. Of all the lessons he would bring forth, and after all the modifications he was to make in theory, he was steadfast in his assumption that the most crucial biological fact of life was "the long period during which the young in the human species is in a condition of helplessness and dependence."[5]

The period of dependency will also tell us a great deal about the nature of the normal human adult. Whereas a mother guppy is likely to view her newborn as an ideal postpartum meal, most human mothers are not prepared to view their infants thus. The newborn elicits an almost universal protective attitude in the typical parent, male or female. Even in that period of human history before there was an understanding of the relationship of copulation to parenthood, when biological paternity had not yet been discovered, the human infant was still safe from the marauding male. The hungry male, being physically stronger than the protective mother, could have seen the small objects as a sop to carnivorous appetites in periods of hunger. Yet cannibalism, particularly of the young, is almost unheard of in the human species. A protective attitude toward the helpless newborn is unquestionably part of the human genetic endowment.

The newborn human infant is totally incapable of survival and must be tended to constantly and completely. But he must be more than physically tended to. What happens in that first year will determine whether he grows into a person who loves and is lovable, who has emotions and relationships, who is capable of altruism and hope. And though all of these attributes are biologically rooted in our nature, they will fail to develop unless they are psychologically and sociologically encouraged in that early year of dependency and extended helplessness.

Realize, too, that it is not only the utter state of helplessness in which we are born that makes us unique in the animal kingdom, but also the extended time it takes us to mature into adults; the time between birth and self-sufficiency is by almost any standard extreme to a point of ludicrousness when considered vis-à-vis other species.

We can define self-sufficiency, or independence, in a number of different ways. If one arbitrarily uses sexual maturity as the index point, since this is the time at which we are capable of reproducing our own kind and ensuring survival of the species, the human being spends roughly 20 percent of his natural life reaching that particular position. The dog arrives there at around nine months out of a life expectancy of about fifteen years, or by the time he has lived out 5 percent of his life expectancy. The dog is much more characteristic of mammals than is the human being.

Our culture has not mitigated this one bit. If anything, it has compounded the problem, so that, whereas an individual may be biologically capable of reproducing his own kind at puberty, usually from thirteen to fifteen years of age, we know that boys and girls of this age are incapable of assuming either the social or the economic role of parents—or even of autonomous, self-supporting adult individuals—in our modern technological society. We have extended the period of childhood, and we define it at a still higher level than the already extended biological base.

What can possibly go on in the mind of the infant in the earliest days of his abject dependency? Alas, this will always be unknowable, although to the psychologist it remains one of the most intriguing questions—and one of the most frustrating ones. In order to make some sense of development, conjecture and speculation in this area are rampant. Numerous, presumably contradictory theories have been offered, but if one strips the technical language in which the ideas are wrapped from the message contained in the package, there is a remarkable similarity in most of the prevailing theories of developmental psychology, at least in those of the group of researchers who presume a consciousness and cognition.

The early stage is obviously dominated by sensation. The infant does respond to wetness, cold, hunger, pinpricks, loud noises, and the sensation of falling. But even here caution must be exercised in making assumptions. What is really meant when we say the child is "feeling hunger"? Certainly the concept of hunger cannot be known to the child in the first days. What he is probably aware of is a pain caused by gastrointestinal activity, the spasms of the stomach, a sense of distress. At that point he roots and sucks, expecting nourishment and the surcease from pain it provides. If the nipple is not immediately available, he will scream in discomfort, or perhaps even in anger. In time his scream will produce a warm suffusion of liquid into the gastrointestinal tract, magically relieving the distress.

The infant cannot possibly be aware of the complicated sequence of events that transpire between his screaming and the alleviation of his distress. He cannot possibly know that the cry had first to be heard by a sleeping parent, who then nudged the other sleeping parent, who then went through the detailed business of warming a bottle or preparing for nursing, muttering along the way. He cannot know the multiple scenarios of the night feeding. Only we parents know that. The cry of the hungry infant is not a primitive and arrogant means of ordering food. It is more likely a generalized expression of distress.

But what is the infant *thinking?* I allow that there may be no conceptualization, that the crying may be automatic. Very shortly the cry does become something like a call for attention, and parents, within weeks, will learn to distinguish the cry of pain from the call of a hungry child. But in these first days the baby knows no one but himself and must, if anything, feel himself in control of the satisfaction of his own needs.

If conceptualization by the child is possible at this time, it is most likely that the child—unaware of a world around him—assumes that his cry itself produces the satisfaction he desires. This stage has been called "primary narcissism" or the "stage of magical omnipotence."

Gradually, of course, the child will learn better—he is a consummate learner. Parents who are engrossed with their children can see changes from day to day. Weeks bring total transformations. The six-week-old is like a different animal from the newborn; the six-month-old is in a different world. As the child begins to differentiate himself from the environment, he must become aware that, whereas once he may have thought of himself as magically omnipotent, it was a woeful, dreadful distortion of reality. Not only is he not omnipotent; he is totally impotent, powerless, incapable of ensuring any of his creature comforts, let alone his basic needs for survival.

Nothing can be more dramatic than this fall. It rivals the Fall of the angels, and perhaps inspired that mythology. To be reduced from the highest of creatures to the lowest, and in so short a time, could be a devastating blow to all future pride and self-confidence if this awareness were not softened by the recognition that there are other figures in that environment who *are* strong and capable, who are all the things we thought we were and are not, and who are prepared to take care of us.

The infant will discover his mother. And though the child's sense of himself at that moment may be undermined, his sense of her full powers will be magnified. Here is truly the Garden of Eden, where the pomegranates will fall into our lap, where a benevolent God will support our needs without pain or even effort on our part, out of love and generosity.

What saves the child from dread and despair is the awareness of that first supporting network—mother, then perhaps father—who fortunately do have power over the environment, and fortunately use this power to serve the child's purposes.

The capabilities of the mother are more than adequate to satisfy totally all of the needs of the infant. Will there ever be another time in life when one individual can sense such complete trust, such total security, such complete and unearned devotion from another? It is unlikely. But that does not mean that many of us will not persist in the search.

This rapid early development will lead the neonate to the crucial inference that is the primary lesson of infancy: survival depends on the beneficence of some protective others, not yet identified as parents. Terror, therefore, is equated with abandonment, separation, or even simple isolation. Separation anxiety is the model on which all later insecurities will be elaborated.

Psychoanalysis in its earlier years had all but ignored the concept of separation anxiety, by focusing on an alternative source called "castration anxiety." What is meant by this term? Forget the particular phallic representation; it simply means a loss of power, a sense of impotence. It is the diminution of confidence in the self's ability to cope. It was called castration anxiety because power was equated with the sexual drive, specifically with the phallus. Remember, however, that there are no instruments of power for a child in the first year of life. He cannot suffer "castration" anxiety. He cannot fear that his power will be taken away from him. His source of power is in the other. If there is any early sense of power, it is experienced through the vicarious joy and capacity to endear or ingratiate the all-powerful mother, thereby ensuring her loving presence. The look of terror seen on the face of a two-year-old child momentarily separated from his mother in a crowd is testament that we see our security, our very survival, as vested in the figure of the parent.

Even with loving parents, a child will come to learn that those figures not only have the power to give pleasure, support needs, satisfy desires, but as a corollary have the power to withhold all of this. The child learns that this willingness to please him is somehow or other related to the parents' relationships with him and their feelings for him.

In a normal home, the early love and care are unconditional. The infant does little to earn our love. He defies scheduling and disturbs our sleep at night, and we do not punish him for it. He does not defecate or urinate in appropriate places, and though we may be chagrined, his behavior is seen as within the nature of an infant. The infant is afforded unconditional love—pure nutrient, if you will—to flourish in these vital early few months of its existence. Given the vulnerability of the human infant, we can assume that the protective environment is not left to chance. The response of the adult to the helplessness of the infant could not have been a culturally created institution. We could not have survived to a point of inventing culture unless this protective and nurturing response were genetically built into most of us.

Slowly and gradually, during the period of dependency, the child will begin to build perceptions that link dependency to love to survival. These linked associations will last an entire lifetime and will condition the way he behaves in adult relationships. To be helpless is not necessarily to be in danger; to be helpless and unloved is the matrix of disaster. The "power" of lovability will inevitably lead to such diverse concepts as the longing for popularity, the need for group approval, the dread of group rejection, the desire for fame, and the fear of humiliation.

As the child grows older, his discriminatory capacity, his ability to fine-tune his behavior to the parents' readiness to give or withhold love or approval, will become a model for shaping his behavior to them. This is the device that permits parents to construct a child that conforms to their definition of good behavior. But these childhood patterns, designed to please the parents, will become part of the character structure of the developing adult and will eventually shape all his social behavior. Parental attitudes toward the child will become the models that will shape the emerging adult's attitudes toward all authority figures, and will determine our characteristic behavior toward all significant others with whom we interrelate.

The child is not entirely helpless, nor a passive instrument of his environment. A child who is not granted direct access to power may use the manipulation of parental love to get what he wants: he can be cute, charming, ingratiating, or whatever works. Conflicting parental attitudes about the use of direct power and anger by their offspring will inevitably produce adults who conform their behavior to their parents' values and biases. Aggressive and combative parents can create children with similar attitudes, as can shy and retiring parents. Incidentally, this also becomes a means of differentiating behavior by gender. Although genetic differences between genders unquestionably exist (of course "different" need not imply "better" or "worse"), we can and do encourage gender stereotypes during this period of prolonged dependency that may not be rooted in biology. What the little boy does to gain approval may be different from what the little girl need do to gain approval from the same set of parents. To certain parents, what is "adorable" and "cute" in a daughter may seem "unmanly" and "offensive" in a son. He may be encouraged to use other sources of ingratiation—generally in the areas of performance and competition.

The child's sense of his own personal power, no less than his sense of the proper uses and expressions of power and assertion, will also be influenced by the responses of the parent to the child's early experiments in self-assertion, particularly when such independent moves are in defiance of parental injunctions and standards. A set of parents who are too indulgent will fail in shaping the moral character of the adult-to-be. An overly constrictive set of parents will encourage the development of an anxious and constricted adult.

Freud, in discussing how crucial the period of dependency is in forging human nature, stated: "The dangers of the outer world

have a greater importance for it [the infant], so that the value of
the object [the mother] which can alone protect it against them
and take the place of its former intra-uterine life is enormously
enhanced. This biological factor, then, establishes the earliest situation of danger and creates the need to be loved which will
accompany the child through the rest of its life."[6]

The dependency period imposed on the human child may have
been an "accident" resulting from our development of a cerebral
cortex, the necessary consequence of the immense size of the human
brain and the large head necessary to accommodate it. But this
prolonged period of helplessness is also admirably suited to facilitate
the maximum use of that brain capacity. Our dependency is therefore both an adaptation to the kind of creature we are, and a
potentiating factor in the kind of human being we are capable of
becoming.

We need that extraordinary period of dependency. While others,
perforce, are taking care of us, enabling our survival through their
labors, we are freed to devote ourselves to full-time learning. We
must learn so much because we are capable of learning and have
designed our lives with the assumption of knowledge, whether it
be specific data—reading, writing, and arithmetic—or general capacities for speech and reasoning. We must learn so much because
so little is built into us.

In this crucial first year or so of life, our self-image will be forged
and our capacities to relate to one another will be nurtured or
destroyed. Our self-confidence, out of which the very fabric of our
life will be spun, and our potentials for joy, pride, and creativity
will be either enlarged or diminished. The nature of our nurture
in the first years of life will determine all the specifics of our
behavior that are left genetically undefined.

The biologically uninitiated often assume that the newborn is a
miniature adult, at least on the physical level. But this is not the
case anatomically: the newborn is an *incomplete* adult. Those adorable little wrists that are so appealing to doting parents are not
wrists at all. They represent absences, for the wrist bones are not
present at birth. The complete pattern of eight wrist bones will

not be fully present until the child is close to five years of age.

Similarly, essential parts of the nervous system are not completed at birth. The child is incapable of performing certain activities, not because he has not learned them but because he does not have the equipment to do them. Beyond that, many of the undeveloped parts of the newborn will never develop unless they are stimulated to by the environment. In an inappropriate environment they will atrophy and be destroyed. This is also true of the less vulnerable infants of other species. If a newborn cat is deprived of visual stimulation in the first days of life, he will never develop the power of sight. The visual cortex of the brain fails to develop when deprived of visual stimuli; there is an actual organic failure.

It is not just physical development that can be damaged by early deprivation, but also social behavior, the capacity for thinking and learning, the development of a sexual life, the range of activity and playing, and the vitality and emotionalism of the creature. The human infant requires nurturing to survive, and beyond that it requires a whole host of cuddling, caressing, cooing, human contacts with caring adults Withhold heat, food, or oxygen, and it will die. Withhold other essential nutrients, and development will be distorted. A lack of vitamin D will cause rickets and lead to a hopelessly deformed adult. Factors necessary for the infant's emotional and psychological growth are particularly at risk because of the enormously rapid and intensely concentrated growth of the human brain in the first two years of life.

If enough of those affectionate human contacts are withheld, the child will grow to be a cripple at its core—not in its physical abilities but in its psychological nature. It may look like a human but will have a diminished capacity for true humanity, less potential for love, caring, consciousness, duty, responsibility, and moral judgment. Even Freud, who eventually was to decide that all of life was dominated by sexual experience and sexual instinct, placed oral gratification as the central experience of the infant's life. Granted, he made of it something subsidiary to sex; but Freud, shrewd clinician that he was, knew that the feeding situation dominated the perceptions and sensibilities of the newborn.

The feeding process is necessary for survival, yet it also has profound psychological and sociological meaning to the child. It is the most intimate relationship between him and the person who, he quickly will learn, supports his life style as well as his life: his mother. That confusion and fusion between oral needs and security lasts throughout our lifetime. It is at the foundation of such diverse human behaviors as nail biting, cigarette smoking, alcohol and drug addiction, obesity, anorexia, and many other phenomena. When the adult experiences anxiety, he is likely to turn to an oral defense.

Certainly every adult recognizes in himself some of this confusion. Imagine the best-stocked refrigerator of your most gluttonous friend. In that refrigerator there may be an example of almost every taste sensation imaginable. Roast beef, savory pickles, cheeses, jams, peanut butter, milk, champagne, beer, fruit, the works. A bored, tired, or anxious person may open that refrigerator with all of its bounty and find nothing appealing. What does that mean? It means that he misread his hunger for "something" as a hunger for food. What he really wanted was nourishment. Nourishment might also mean love, affection, companionship, entertainment, stimulation, or sex. Even the best-stocked refrigerator is ill equipped to supply these ingredients unless a person suffers from obesity, in which case he will see the ingestion of comestibles as symbols for all of the above.

There are special foods that hold a central position in the symbolic life of most of us. For many it is the sweet treat that seems a special indulgence—the forbidden fruit, or maybe just the reward for having been a good boy and eaten our veggies.

For those with eating disorders, each calorie of food consumed beyond experience of hunger is somehow a reassuring message of worthiness, lovability, strength, and ultimately survivability. Because the ingestion of food does more than satisfy hunger, however, orality involves more than the ingestion of food. The amount of human irrationality connected to sticking things in our mouth is appalling. A cure for cancer would increase the average life expectancy *less* than an alteration of our oral habits so that we ate less of the wrong things, or simply ate less. And there is no better example of the compulsive urge to stick something in our mouths to replicate early feeding than the smoking pattern that has dominated our culture until very recently.

The early-feeding situation is incorporated into the psyche of the human child because of the capacity for imaginative and symbolic thinking, reinforced by the extraordinary length of time in which he is dependent on others for his survival. Since the first link forged between mother and child is through feeding, food and oral gratification become equated with safety and survival. No other animal forges these symbolic linkages.

Before the 1950s, almost all developmental psychologists focused on orality in early infancy. But close examination of the feeding situation shows that what transpires between the feeder and the child is more than merely the transfer of nutrients from one vessel, the breast or bottle, into another receptacle, the infant's stomach. The feeding situation encompasses embrace, body pressures, contact, flesh-to-flesh engagement, fondling, cooing, tickling, talking, stroking, squeezing. It involves the transfer of body warmth, the pulsation of the mother's heart, the brushing of her lips, the smell of her secretions. All of this was early recognized by developmentalists, but until recently the tendency—and a logical one at that—was to think that these latter activities became pleasurable *because* of their association with feeding.

Over the past forty years, data have began to emerge from research in animal psychology suggesting that feeding is only one of many interactions between mother and child that are crucial to development and maturation. Animal psychologists had noted for a long time that the grooming contact between mother and offspring was not nearly as random as had formerly been thought. It was not simply a matter of nuzzling or licking indiscriminately, nor was it purely a matter of affection. The licking and nuzzling activities of the mother are often required to initiate activity of primary importance in the young. A bitch will lick the perineal areas of her newborn puppies to initiate the process of urination. Without that stimulation, urinary retention will occur and the puppy will die. A mare or a cow licks her newborn all over to stimulate circulation and maintain body temperature. All this suggests, then, that skin contact, touching, proprioception, nuzzling may be as significant a component of the nurturing transferred from the mother to the child as the food.

The vital link between human behavior and animal behavior was established by the pioneering work of Harry Harlow and his various collaborators on infant monkeys.[7] Harlow divided the function of mothering between two different surrogate "mothers." One "mother" supplied "nourishment" in the sense of food but was a cold, nontactile, wire-mesh machine. Present in the environment at the same time was a warm, soft, terry-cloth "mother" that supplied no food at all.

The studies demonstrated that the infant monkeys raised by these artificial surrogates inevitably preferred (loved?) the warm and soft cloth mothers even though they received no nourishment from them but got all of their life-sustaining food from the wire-mesh mother. It was with the terry-cloth mother that the infants chose to spend most of their time, clinging fiercely—possessive, jealous, desiring her presence. As startling as this, however, is that, when exposed to any threat or danger, the infant monkeys retreated to the terry-cloth mother for reassurance.

Building on this early, amazing discovery, Harlow extended the amount of deprivation by isolating newborn monkeys from any contact with adult monkeys, demonstrating the profound influence of tender and loving social contact in early life. These newborn monkeys were given all the necessary ingredients for physiological development: food, water, proper temperature, protection against disease, everything one might say a good institution would supply. All that was missing was contact with an adult figure of their own kind, a true parent or live parent surrogate.

What emerged out of these studies were strange creatures, almost unidentifiable in psychological and social terms to their fellow monkeys. Their social behavior had been destroyed. If they had been children, we would have said they had lost their "humanness."

Anyone, regardless of how unknowledgeable of the research,

could have walked through the laboratory and seen these strange creatures and recognized in them something terribly disturbed and distorted. They indulged in odd, isolated, bizarre, autistic behavior not unlike what one sees in neglected, backward patients in mental hospitals or in the most severely retarded. They do not seem quite alive.

These animals were raised with the better surrogate (the warm, cloth one); they were, in addition, supplied with the necessary physical climate and nutrition—everything, that is, except the companionship and caring of their own kind. The surrogate gave them some comfort, but what it gave them was insufficient to guarantee the development of a normal adult. Present were the necessary but not the sufficient conditions for the survival of the infant to adulthood; they produced an adult incapable of interrelating with its own kind that could not sexually reproduce.[8]

The studies showed, further, that the effect of isolation depended in great part on the time and duration of the deprivation. Up to three months of deprivation seemed to allow a certain reversibility in these animals, but animals isolated beyond this point, even for six months, were permanently damaged.

One would normally speculate that if the monkey is this vulnerable the human infant would be even more vulnerable; these monkeys were deficient in precisely the features that are most closely associated in the human being with his humanness: the capacity to enjoy the company of others, to relate socially and sexually, to become a member of a social unit, to have "feelings," to play and learn. We can only imagine what might happen to children exposed to this kind of treatment. Obviously we did not replicate the experiments with children. Developmental research on human beings must exploit chance sociological events. Two corroborative studies did just that and confirmed that similar damages occur in human infants when they are prematurely and severely deprived of human contact during their early years. René Spitz did his pioneering studies on children in institutions,[9] and John Bowlby did his extensive research on children who were separated from their parents early in life and evacuated to the country to protect them from the dangers of the Blitz in London during World War II.[10] Both sets of data, though quite different in the techniques of observation used, and in the accidental experiments that produced them, confirmed that nurturing for human beings demands contact, love, affection, not just food, water, air, and protection from danger.

These early researchers stressed the importance of the *quantity* rather than the *quality* of time the infant was in the company and care of adults. A careful analysis of the various forms of attention and contact offered children—holding, playing, talking, and so on—led most researchers to the conclusion that the kind of contact was less important than the amount. The mother did not need to play with her children; she needed merely to hand them the toys. It was her being there that was important.

This body of research profoundly influenced the attitudes of social scientists who were designing instruments for child care. Sparkling institutions no longer seemed more attractive than shabby foster homes. Attitudes about "proper and approved" adoptive parents began to be re-examined in light of the importance of human contact with the child during the prolonged period of his dependency. Simple intimacy was found to be an irreplaceable ingredient in child-rearing.

A further set of data related the affectionate physical presence of the mother to the fundamental conditions of survival. Neonatologists began to note that certain premature babies tended to survive better than others of the same birth weight. Dr. Marshall Klaus was instrumental in bringing many of these observations to the attention of the pediatric community.[11] It became apparent that more "attractive" babies, or even more rambunctious ones, seemed to have a higher survival rate in the premature nurseries. Klaus and others decided it might have been related to the amount of attention, fondling, and general handling they received. Arbitrary instructions were given to nurses to pick up babies periodically and hold them briefly; incredibly, mortality rates decreased.

The attachment of the child to its mother is not a parasitic one but rather a symbiotic one, in which giving and taking are indistinguishable and a joyous and nourishing fusion exists. As helpless as the newborn infant may seem, he is not at the mercy of a chance response. His very helplessness will stimulate certain stroking, caressing, and tender responses in the parent, which, reciprocally and wonderfully, are the necessities for his survival as a human being. It is necessary for the child to be loved in a specific, caring way if he is to develop into an adult who can give care and love to others.

I have said that the potential for loving and caring is genetically fixed in the human being. The teleological argument that supports this contention is that no species constructed with such a prolonged and totally helpless early phase of childhood would survive if the adult did not possess powerful and genetically determined inherent responses to the helpless child. This is supported by every opportunity for empirical corroboration. Geppetto, one feels, would forgive Pinocchio anything. In this sense, he is in the grand tradition of literary history. The prodigal son and the forgiving parent are dominant themes that thread their way universally through the literature and the mythology of diverse cultures and disparate times.

We see the evidence of the power of parental caring manifested elsewhere. In history and literature, the sacrifice of the child is often the highest price that can be asked of an individual, a request usually reserved for the Creator and generally occurring in a religious context. This sacrifice transcends the sacrifice of one's own life. The tenth and most dreadful plague visited by God on the House of Egypt was the death of the firstborn. And when God wished to test Abraham, it was the sacrifice of Isaac that He demanded. The horrible price that Artemis extracted from Agamemnon to ensure victory in the Trojan War was the death of his daughter Iphigenia. In Christian theology, the only suffering sufficient to demonstrate the extent of God's love of man was the sacrifice of His Son.

We are people vulnerable to the helpless and sick. We *are* caring people, even though it is fashionable now to deny it. I acknowledge we may be less so than we once were. We respond not only to the child but to the childlike. We respond to the helpless, whether animal or human. Particularly forms that have an infantile representation touch us. There are certain features that identify the infant—the head too large for the body, the softness and roundness of form, the large eyes. And, like certain primitive instinctual birds that respond to the yawning, open mouth of a fledgling bird (even when it is not their own but a usurper's giant infant), we respond instinctively to these features.

An example that I have occasionally used because it seems so obvious is the campaign to preserve the harp seal, which inevitably features pictures of the plump, sad-eyed, and cuddly creatures. Consider for a moment if this endangered species had the same name but a different form. Would the campaign have been as effective? Visualize, for example, a young harp seal, a thirty-pound animal, that looked like a giant cockroach. Would we have responded to the pathetic plight of this "baby" if he were depicted full-blown in *The New York Times* with his beady eyes, his hard shell, his antennae, and his overenlarged incisors? I doubt it. I am sure that the shrewd organization, desiring to protect the endangered species, would have found a different approach for their campaign.

We associate innocence and vulnerability with a certain visual image—a baby face—that must derive from biological derivatives. The handsome young choirboy type, soft-spoken and boyish-looking, elicits different expectations from the onlooker, even in a courtroom, than his homely, coarse-featured, and tough-looking equivalent. This esthetic bias can facilitate the Ted Bundys[12] of the world in committing their mass murders, because we are reluctant to suspect them. They look so sweet. Even when we begin to suspect them, there will be a powerful sympathy and compassion for this "innocent-looking" young man. After all the evidence had emerged that, never mind dozens, there may have been hundreds of women that he brutally killed, tortured, and raped, some young women (who you would have assumed would identify with the victims) burst into tears when the jury finally found him guilty of murder. The same phenomenon was a prominent feature in the trials of Robert Chambers and Richard Herrin.[13]

The biological evidence is now incontrovertible: human children, with their prolonged dependency period, require caring and an extended commitment of time and energy beyond parallel in the animal kingdom. The propensity for such caring is part of the genetic endowment of our species. There is no evidence that the care must be provided by a woman rather than a man, or that a biological parent is required to nourish children. But human children need caring, not just caretaking. Our survival depends on it—because of the extreme condition of helplessness at birth. Our happiness depends on it—because the lessons that we will learn in our dependency period will shape our self-esteem, our self-confidence, and our capacities for love, work, pleasure, and performance, which are contingent on a basic pride system. Finally, our ultimate fulfillment as a species depends on it—because our biological directive for attachment, identification, and love is a necessary condition for the survival of a species that is dependent on community to survive. To be fully human we must exist in relation to others.

The communal nature of *Homo sapiens* cannot be overestimated. In adulthood, all meaningful existence requires relationship and community. David Hume recognized this when he said:

"A perfect solitude is perhaps the greatest punishment we can suffer. Every pleasure languishes when enjoyed apart from company and every pain becomes more cruel and intolerable. . . . Let all the powers and elements of nature conspire to serve and obey one man: Let the sun rise and set at his command: The sea and rivers roll as he pleases, and the earth furnish spontaneously whatever may be useful or agreeable to him: He will still be miserable, till you give him some one person at least, with whom he may share his happiness, and whose esteem and friendship he may enjoy."[14]

Symbols of separation have traditionally been used in literature to represent the most dreaded state of human existence whether it be in the banishment from country or isolation from kind. Ulysses the wanderer or Leopold Bloom, "the only Jew in Ireland"; the Flying Dutchman or Ishmael—the lonely person separated from home, from his own kind, is inevitably a tragic figure.

In childhood, we see that such separation is envisioned as a fate comparable to death, because such separation would be death. The child cannot survive without caring adults. It may be that the principal way the human being is capable of visualizing death is through separation. Death is so terrible an absence that we tend to deny its existence. I believe we are incapable of conceiving our world without ourselves since we ourselves are the perceiving agent. Instead, I think we see death not as the absence of ourselves but as the absence of everything except us. This explains the horrifying dream of being buried alive. One knows that a child will be more threatened by the withdrawal of love than by a parent's foolish threat to kill him. "I'll kill you" becomes a figure of speech to a child, which he ignores. It is part of the culture of his parents' hyperbole. He doesn't believe it, in part because he cannot visualize death—at least not for himself. Death is something that happens to flowers, pets, and old people. The concept of death does not exist for the child. I am not sure that it does for the adult.

The lessons we learn in the dependency period are never forgotten. They are part of perceptual apparatus which will shape our view of reality. Every person reacts to the present as though it were an extension of the past. It is worth examining some pathological conditions here, since pathology is only an interesting deviation from normal behavior, not a new entity. Neuroses, because of their enlarged and exaggerated forms, were the clinical conditions that allowed Freud to draw his extraordinary and more prescient insights about normal human behavior. Let me give two clinical examples to illuminate the degree to which the lessons of dependency permeate our perception of the present and alter our behavior.

In obsessional neuroses, a patient will be driven to repeat a single piece of ritual behavior to a point where his life may be dominated and eventually destroyed by the neurotic symptom. An obsessive hand-washer may rationalize his behavior, at least at first, with assumptions about the need for hygiene in a germ-infested environment. But by the time the hand-washing is at a point that it must be repeated at three-to-five-minute intervals, all rationali-

zations are usually abandoned. The behavior may eventually lead
to the abrading away of entire fingers. Most obsessive symptoms
are not so severe, and most obsessive behavior is insufficient to be
labeled a symptom. The ultra-fastidious, the superorganized, and
the perfectionistic among us may be benefiting from these character
traits, as well as paying for them.

What is characteristic of obsessional behavior, whether it is at
the level of a symptom or simply a trait of personality—what is
so revealing about this behavior—is how inevitably it relates to
actions that were rewarded in childhood. The obsessive will focus
on habits of cleanliness, bowel training, straightening, tidying,
awakening, and bedtime. These are the activities that earned him
the reward of being called or seen as a good boy in early childhood.

Even the least compulsive of us tend to be most compulsive in
areas of behavior that dominated the first few years of life. We are
doing the things—or, more exactly, adult equivalents of the
things—that garnered rewards from our parents. We are being
good boys or girls, according to our adult interpretations of our
parents' directives during our childhood.

Phobias represent another clinical illustration of the symbolic
power that separation holds even in adult life, when the survival
needs of early dependency no longer have validity. In the early
days of psychoanalysis, we were much more fanciful: we tended
to see each symbol in dreams as always having a specific and
universal meaning. Similarly, phobias were inevitably related each
to its own special fantasy and dynamic. We are—at least most of
us—more sophisticated now and less grandiose. We do not know
why one person fears heights and another fears tunnels and a third
fears elevators and a fourth superhighways. But we do see a common thread that binds this diverse symptomatology into a pattern.
Almost all phobia-inducing situations suggest a sense of entrapment; they involve scenes and settings in which escape is difficult
or humiliating. The phobic patient cannot return in dignity to the
safety of home. He is caught in a "no-way-out" position, at least
as he perceives it.

The airplane, the subway, the tunnel touch a responding cord of anxiety in most of us. We tend to think the fear is of the real danger and the real nightmare of being trapped. But the same panic will arise in a phobic in as nonthreatening areas as barber shops and beauty parlors. It is not the fear of the razor or hair dryer. It is the ludicrous position of being half lathered or half shaved or wet-haired. In all of these situations, one senses there is "no way out" (we should say, more precisely, "no way home") without losing dignity or pride, without suffering shame or humiliation.

The phobic is distressingly similar to the two-year-old separated from his mother in a crowd. Safety for him is, if not his parents, at least the symbols of parental care represented by the concept of getting home. Thus neuroses, in their hyperbole, show us that there is no escape from our early period of helplessness. The past will always be an active force in the way we perceive the present and respond to what we think we are seeing. This should not be viewed as an exclusively negative or maladaptive dynamic merely because I have used two such examples to dramatize the influence. The psychological linkage between attachment and security also serves constructive ends: it reinforces the biological need for community so essential for human life.

Since at birth we are all unaware of environment, or at least incapable of differentiating ourselves from environment, we can safely assume that this first stage of self-involvement, labeled "primary narcissism," is a universal experience. Certainly the second, brief stage (if one wishes to honor it as a stage) the awareness of our own impotence, is also universal. But the third stage, the reassuring sense that all is well, that we need not worry about our survival because "someone" out there is caring for us, is not universal. Too many children are not being taken care of, have no one out there.

How can this be consonant with my insistence that there is a biological directive to respond emphatically and protectively to the helpless and the childlike? What are we to make of the abysmal conditions, beyond mere neglect, of children who are sexually abused and battered? Once again one must confront the contradictions and complexities of human nature by recalling that the human being is the least instinctually fixed animal on earth. We are vested with very few genetic imperatives, and we are likely to ignore the genetically encouraged directives. It is a testament to the human power and uniqueness that even God, or nature, only suggests our future course of action. We presume that God, in Genesis, would have preferred that Adam and Eve not eat of the Tree of Knowledge. Yet He gave them the option to eat of that tree. He gave them freedom. Nor did He curse or abandon them in their defiance. Human freedom was part of God's design, and, therefore, one presumes that the defiance that is freedom's corollary was within the range of His purposes.

We are free to change our nature, including the noble aspects of our nature. We are free to change our nature even when we are unwittingly eroding that which may be essential for species survival. This is precisely what we are doing when we deprive a significant number of children of proper care.

A central thesis of the chapter on imagination was that an individual lives in a world of his own perception. He never or rarely experiences the actual world, only the distortion enclosed by his own personal experience. It is our past experience that forges the lens through which we will be forced to observe the present. A guiding, loving, nurturing parental figure is not an inevitable part of every child's environment. Children who are sufficiently deprived of warmth and attention will obviously enter adult life with different expectations from the environment and a different image of their place in that environment. Our capacity as adults to trust, our ability to be caring to our own children or to others in general, our openness or lack thereof, our level of paranoia, our optimism or cynicism, our level of generosity, empathy, compassion, and understanding will all be shaped by those early lessons about the nature of the human contract learned when we ourselves were children.

When the deprivation of caring is severe enough, either the survival of the small human being will be imperiled or the nature of its "humanity" will be diminished. It is quite possible, therefore, that many of us will have had our response to helplessness destroyed or obliterated. We will become as desensitized to helplessness as we have to other areas of life. This is a matter of more than theoretical concern now that an increasing number of our children will inevitably be turned over to professional caretakers. Unless we are forewarned to attend to more than the quality of *physical* care, they may receive less and less direct nurturing in a *psychological* sense. We must remember that whatever increments of deprivation we visit on the next generation will be compounded by their inability to give to the succeeding generation, for which they are responsible.

What does this say about the current sociological conditions in which children are being brought into this world? We have said that the child is vulnerable and dependent and needs more than physical nurturing in the first days of life. It will be seen in the subsequent chapters that he needs a relationship over an extended period of his life. What will happen to future generations as a result of the sociological changes we are now enduring? Surely the illegitimacy rate in black urban populations, where 70 percent of black children are born illegitimate and over half of them are born to children (teenagers) represents a real danger. It is a yoke of bondage that will inevitably trap those children unless we attend to their needs, needs that, again, during the dependency years go well beyond food and shelter. These deprived children will become a burden to society and a hemorrhage on the vitality and liberation of the black community for generations to come.

Beyond the massive problem of illegitimacy, in this age of the dual working family, something beyond traditional institutional care must be available for the intact families where both parents are working. Whatever child-care programs will be instituted, they cannot be just minimal warehousing; they must allow for human models and protracted intimacy with those models. The situation here is of course less desperate than that of the child born with one adult parent or no adult parents, and it is more easily remedied. The children, after all, will be reunited with their parents in the evenings. Experience with other cultures—the kibbutzim in Israel are but one example[15]—has shown that, although this type of development unquestionably influences character traits, it does not necessarily diminish humanity.

The human being is not a hothouse flower that requires perfect conditions and a model set of parents to survive and grow up human. It is tough to be a parent, but we are allowed plenty of mistakes, and we all make them. The idiosyncrasies of the parents, the proportion of affection and approval to punishment and rejections, the conditions that elicit pleasure or anger—all will vary with the personalities and culturally induced values of the parents. Children treated differently will emerge as different adults. "Different" does not mean either "better" or "worse." Different is good, as long as it falls within the generously broad range that we define as "normal." Human variability is unparalleled in the animal kingdom, and human children will flourish in a diverse range of settings.

But there are limits. If we are to ensure a socialized and civil community, we must design social institutions that provide not just for the primary survival needs of the infant but for the emotional needs of the child in that profound, extravagantly prolonged dependency. Biology demands it. This period, which is unique to the human species, is essential to allow for the development of those special qualities that define humanhood.

All of us, like Pinocchio, must act selfishly to learn charity; lie to learn honor; betray and be betrayed to value trust and commitment; toil to respect work; sacrifice self to become capable of loving; love to enrich self. Well before the child can even conceptualize these virtues inherent in the concept of humanness, the conditions that allow their development will be set by the attention devoted to him when he is totally helpless and dependent.

Pinocchio had only one parent, but a parent so adoring and devoted, so self-sacrificing and forgiving that he set a model that permitted a talking block of wood to become not a perfect child but a normal child. The mischief-making puppet remained a mischief-making boy, but a boy nonetheless. As the Fairy who gave him life said: "Boys who minister tenderly to their parents and assist them in their misery and infirmities are deserving of great praise and affection even if they cannot be cited as examples of obedience and good behavior."[16]

The prolonged dependency period is both essential and felicitous. We have much to learn in order to exercise the freedom of choice that is ours alone. It is not just knowledge that we must acquire, but the special skills necessary for empathy, identification, conscience, love, and self-sacrifice. The intimate contact with our parents, forced on us by the prolonged and utter helplessness of our infancy and childhood, represents the ideal environment to nurture our biological potentialities for a caring nature. The evolution of that caring nature will then guide us to the protection of the succeeding generation of helpless infants, thus guaranteeing the survival of that most complicated and wondrous of creatures, the human being.

In summary, to be human is not necessarily to be always good. This was the lesson of the first humans. If anything, it was in their disobedience that Adam and Eve exercised that essential trait of humanness on which all virtue and morality rests—their freedom to make choices. To be human is ultimately to have "a good heart." To be human is to be able to take the nurturing that was given us in childhood and, with a peculiar kind of linear justice, reciprocate by giving selfless nurturing to our children and beyond that to all of the helpless, infantile, and dependent in our community.

WORK

~~~~~~~~~~~~~~~~~~~

PINOCCHIO, IN HIS FIRST ENCOUNTER WITH CONSCIENCE, in the form
of the Talking Cricket, is warned that he who does not learn to
appreciate the value of work will be forced to labor. The Cricket
says, "Woe to those boys who rebel against their parents, and run
away capriciously from home. They will never come to any good
in the world, and sooner or later they will repent bitterly."[1]

Pinocchio defiantly advises the Cricket to sing away as he pleases;
he, Pinocchio, will not listen. He is not going to accept the fate of
other boys and be forced to study and work. He smugly says: "I
tell you in confidence, I have no wish to learn; it is much more
amusing to run after butterflies, or to climb trees and to take the
young birds out of their nest." Whereupon the Cricket pathetically
forewarns him: "Poor little goose! Do you not know that in that
way you will grow up a perfect donkey and that everyone will
make game of you?"[2]

Poor Pinocchio—he will be forced to replicate the travail of
Adam and his banishment from the Garden in his search for a
humanity. He, too, will defiantly leave the protection of his father
in order to establish his identity as a person.

One feature that distinguishes the life of the adult from that of
the child is the central role of work. Adults work. We spend
massive amounts of time at our jobs. Yet our understanding of the
nature of work—beyond its necessity—is minimal and contradictory. How is one to explain the paradoxes and dilemmas that
surround work? Why is work conceived of as an alternative to

155

play? Why is work seen as both the burden and the privilege of our species? Why is work so joyless in our modern culture? Is work an essential part of the nature of the human being, or only an inevitable development of a technological and consumerist society? Does it have value beyond being a vehicle for purchasing the means of survival and pleasure? How is it that work, even the same work, can be viewed as either ennobling or demeaning?

Pope John Paul II, at least to this moment, may be viewed at his most elegant and compassionate in his encyclical on the nature of human work:

"Work is one of the characteristics that distinguish man from the rest of creatures, whose activities for sustaining their lives cannot be called work. Only man is capable of work, and only man works at the same time by work occupying his existence on earth. Thus work bears the particular mark of man and of humanity. The mark of a person operating within a community of persons. And this mark decides interior characteristics; in a sense it constitutes its very nature."[3]

Pope John Paul II, with this statement, joins a long list of scholars who have viewed work as a singularly human occupation. For the Pope, work is the activity that defines the human species. Although many scholars would not go quite so far, most would agree that it is one essential characteristic of human nature, a defining glory and a central source of human pride. Yet surely everyone recalls that work was the punishment of Adam, not his reward. For God said to Adam:

"Because thou has harkened unto the voice of thy wife and has eaten of the tree of which I commanded thee, saying: 'thou shall not eat of it,' cursed the ground for thy sake in toil shalt thou eat of it all the days of thy life . . .

"In the sweat of thy face shalt thou eat bread till thou return from the ground; for out of it was't thou taken; for dust thou art, and to dust shalt thou return."[4]

In a brief, terrifying statement, God reminds Adam of the truth of his existence. He may have tasted of the Tree of Knowledge, but he has not yet eaten of the tree of life. He is and will remain mortal. He will be banished from the Garden, where all things are beautiful and life is easy, and he will toil until the day he dies.

But this is not the first reference to work in Genesis. Twice before, in a much more benevolent tone, God refers to Adam's role as a worker. "No garden was yet in the earth and no herb had yet sprung up; for the Lord God had not caused it to rain upon the earth, and there was not a man to till the ground." Only after God creates man will He create his garden and: "The Lord God took the man and put him into the Garden of Eden to dress it and keep it."[5]

This Garden was to be a collaborative effort between God and Adam, as all of human life would be. God would supply the elements, and Adam would shape the final product—he would till the soil. Presumably he would do so with little pain or effort, for this was the Garden of Eden, in which fruits abounded. And God made the fruits of the earth for Adam's pleasures.

Before the Fall, while still in a state of innocence and perhaps perfection, Adam was a workingman. It was his nature to do work. And why should he not—was he not in God's image? God Himself worked hard. "And on the seventh day God ended his work which he had made; and he rested on the seventh day from all his work which he had made."[6]

Pope John Paul II sees work as power and creativity. He interprets the mandate of Genesis that Adam must "subdue the earth" as having broad significance. Here certain environmentalists would be appalled by the absolute rights granted to humankind by the Pope. John Paul invests the term "subduing the earth" with an immense range. "It means all the resources that the earth (and indirectly the visible world) contains" are there for man to use.[7] It is good for man to transform nature. It contributes to his humanity—according to the Pope—because through work man becomes "more of a human being."

John Paul acknowledges that, with all its glory, work also contributes the hardship of life. He then draws the classic distinction between toil (or labor) and work. To understand the contradictions of Genesis—and, for that matter, the contradictions of *Pinocchio*

—it is necessary to draw some distinctions between labor and work and, beyond that, to understand the linked relationships of pain or effort and pleasure or satisfaction.

At this point, I think it is important to expand and understand the distinction between work and toil (or labor). Hannah Arendt brilliantly analyzed the difference:

"Labor is the activity which corresponds to the biological process of the human body, whose spontaneous growth, metabolism, and eventual decay are bound to the vital necessities produced and fed into the life process by labor. The human condition of labor is life itself."

"Work is the activity which corresponds to the unnaturalness of human existence, which is not embedded in, and whose mortality is not compensated by, the species' ever-recurring life cycle. Work provides an 'artificial' world of things, distinctly different from all natural surroundings. Within its borders each individual life is housed while this world itself is meant to outlast and transcend them all. The human condition of work is worldliness."[8]

Arendt herself draws the parallelism and distinction between work and labor from Locke's *Second Treatise of Civil Government*, in which he refers to "The labor of our body and the work of our hands."

Those familiar with *Pinocchio* remember the poignancy with which Pinocchio's ultimate conversion to humanity pivots on his five-month residence in the land of Cocagne, where he "grows a beautiful pair of donkey's ears, and he becomes a little donkey— tail and all." He is treated like a beast. The agonies of animal labor force Pinocchio to recognize the dignity of human work. Human beings, of course, labor as they work, but they quickly learn ways to minimize the labor in their work; after all, they left the Garden with their imagination and knowledge intact.

In the traditional semantic distinction, "labor" produces no lasting product. Labor is the activity of survival, the energy spent gathering food and firewood, which are made to be used up. "Work" in the traditional definition produces a product, "the work," which is independent of its producer's literal survival and

may outlast him. In this distinction, the "worker bee" is a mis-
nomer. Similarly, as busy as the beaver may be, he does not par-
ticipate in work. Work, as it is generally understood, is independent
of the toils of survival.

Work is not necessary for man; it is the special privilege of the
human being. Work is an occupation, a form of creativity. Nowhere
in the Bible is there mention of work for other animals. They must
scrounge for food, flee from predators, adapt to the environment,
migrate, burrow, build nests, dam rivers, cut trees, but none of
this is "work." We cannot conceive of it as either "congenial work"
or, for that matter, as a punitive task imposed as punishment.
There is no meaning in this animal existence except in species
survival. As has been said, the chicken is simply a convenient
machine for creating an egg that is capable of producing a chicken.

In the Bible, only the human species is given an occupation; only
in the human species is indolence somehow or other not to be
tolerated. This was symbolically recognized by early scholars of
the Bible. The Haftorah quoted Rabbi Nathan as saying: "See what
a great thing is work. The first man was not to taste of anything
until he had done some work. Only after God told him to cultivate
and keep the garden, did he give him permission to eat of its
fruits."[9]

If work exalts and distinguishes humankind, what are we to
make of the harshness and pain of the toil that inevitably accompany most work? The pleasure exists not *despite* the agony but
because of it.

The pleasure of animals is never quite analogous to ours. Theirs
is generally the pleasure of satiation, and occasionally the pleasure
of play. It is difficult to define human pleasure, but in whatever
form it exists, it tends to enhance, expand, enlarge, and elevate our
sense of ourselves. Under this common definition, there are discrete
categories of pleasure that differ in their source and quality.

Simple sensory pleasure corresponds most accurately to the pleasures of an animal—the pleasures from eating, from orgastic release, or from being stroked. But the human being also experiences
pleasure from the secondary elaborations of even a simple sensory

input. The joy in observing nature—the power of the sea, the majesty of the mountain, the delicacy of a flower—is not in the actual seeing but in the conceptual additions that transform that sight into a perception—a symbol. No animal contemplates the sunset or the chasm of the Grand Canyon with awe. The things that "delight" an animal are probably limited to the sight of the prey, the smell of a mate in estrus, and possibly the parent's view of its cub. The human eye *perceives* as it sees. It integrates the simple sensation into an embroidery of past remembrances, future anticipations, related events, and symbolic meanings.

A secondary source of pleasure is play. I suspect this is something we share with lower animals. For them, play may serve the same function as it was originally intended to serve for human beings, an initiation into activities that are essential for life. It becomes a device for sharpening the tools of survival. We test aggression with our siblings. We learn the limits of tolerated behavior within a group, whether human or animal. A pat across the butt from the mother is not dissimilar in form to the lioness's cuff of the rambunctious cub.

Play continues into adult life. Here it will serve a further function. It is an alternative to, and a simulation of, competitive areas of life that may now be too distressing or dangerous. Like the knights of the medieval world, we can joust with blunt spears and still savor victory. We may have to nurse defeat, but never a life-threatening one. We can test the limits of our capacities, compare ourselves with our colleagues, even dare be dangerous, without running the risks that would occur in the "real" world.

A third category of pleasure is discovery. To really appreciate the joy in discovery, you have to observe a two-year-old's almost frantic delight in poking, pulling, hammering, emptying, examining, upturning, and climbing. This delight in new experience is an essential part of the human being. In the toddler, it can be seen in the imitative play that will eventually enhance performance skills necessary to adult life, and also in the imitative babble that precedes (and rehearses) true speech. Later one will see the same need for discovery and intellectual curiosity in the incessant "whys" of the three-to-five-year-old. Delight in discovery is what Dr. Johnson called "the hunger of imagination which preys incessantly upon life."[10] It reaches fruition in the great discoveries of adult life. The creation of science and technology has led us to wander the earth until we conquered it, and then to set out on our journeys into space. Closer to home, the pleasure of discovery seems to be an essential ingredient in the process that will lead a child away from the protection of the mother and into the larger world—a separation that leads to autonomy and maturity. Was it not the same curiosity and need for discovery that led Eve, the first explorer into the unknown, to the tasting of the fruit of the Tree of Knowledge? This intrepid action would lead to separation from her parent, but in that process it would lead to the birth of modern woman—and man.

Very closely related to discovery is a fourth category of pleasure, which now brings us closer to the essential nature of work. I call this "mastery." Human beings love progress. We take gratification in change and growth. The delight of observing our mind in successful operation is in every way equivalent to the joy we receive in sensing our working bodies in athletic activities. And with both these joys, the very nature of the satisfaction involves effort and pain, the feeling "I did it." There can be great enjoyment in viewing a master's work. I recall vividly the rush of pleasure I received on first viewing Botticelli's *Primavera*. How could this compare with the joy of having *painted* it?

Viewing a painting is still not the equivalent of tasting a fruit or smelling a flower. What we are seeing is a work of art, the product of a painter's sensibility and genius. Whether we are viewing a painting, listening to music, reading a poem, or watching a play, we are cooperating with the artist in a shared emotional experience and a shared pleasure—a pleasure based on the artist's mastery.

Still, the perfectionism, pain, agonies, time, and effort the composer or artist expended on a work of art expansively reinforce his sense of "I did it" beyond our pleasures as appreciator and respondent to his efforts. Inevitably, therefore, the pride and joy in his work must be more profound than our pride and pleasure in sharing it.

Most of us are not creative artists in our daily life, but we still have some fortunate ones among us who have the capacity to receive enjoyment from their daily work; they are progressively becoming a small minority. Those less fortunate will find means of getting gratification through hobbies or simply extracurricular involvements. I enjoy gardening—the original work of Adam. Not the planting of seeds and the gentle and patient satisfaction of nurturing them to bloom—no, I am in for grander stuff. I like building retaining walls, moving bushes, battling against unruly growth, chopping, sawing, pruning, heaving, and sweating, until nature and I, in antagonism and collaboration, have created something I consider beautiful. It is not *despite* my bruises, my sweat, my scratches, my aching back, that I enjoy the activity, but because of them. Having done this difficult thing, I have proved something about myself and my worth.

By making Adam earn his keep by "the sweat of his face," God gave him the potential for a cherished gift, a capacity for mastery that would eventually become a source of his pride and an essential prop to his self-esteem and self-confidence. This pleasure in mastery and work would become necessary to sustain Adam and Eve in the independent existence they would have to endure outside of the protective environment of the Garden of dependency.

One might speculate that paleolithic man was not distinguished from the animals; that he did no work for its own sake. It is conceivable that all of his time was occupied, as is that of certain animals, with securing the means of subsistence. Although we can never completely know the nature of the earliest history of human beings, every new increment of knowledge seems constantly to reinforce the belief that early humans managed to "find" work, or to manufacture occupations. The slim evidences of the paleolithic period reveal remarkably diverse examples of the need to accumulate things, not for their survival needs but for their imagery, their suggestion of status, power, or wealth, or simply for their esthetics. Only recently a further discovery was made that revealed that human beings twenty thousand years ago—ten thousand years before the human being had learned to cultivate the earth and domesticate the animals—were already stringing together beads of animal teeth and claws, manufacturing artifacts of adornment, accumulating symbols of wealth and power. And there is evidence from the paleolithic period that an early esthetic also existed. The European cave drawings are testimony not just to man's imagination, but to his need to create, to do things, to make things that involve what we may falsely conceive of as an esthetic or even spiritual life, but certainly bear no relationship to physiological survival. These early records of our artistic endeavor are testament to the strangeness of our species. Here was an animal who—beyond subsistence and survival (often to the detriment of these two)— was preoccupied with the *significance* of existence and the *meaning* of survival. Even if, in their earliest primitive existence in the caves of Africa, before tools and fire, before agriculture and manufacturing, *Homo sapiens* only had time and energy to labor for survival, they managed in an incredibly short time of discovery to develop technology. Through the development of this technology— through the use of their hands and their minds—they created an existence that spared their bodies. The human being became, as Benjamin Franklin called him, "the tool-making animal."

The human species quickly moved into a period where it could conceivably have supplanted all labor with work. Here the development was really remarkable. A clam shell might be the model for a sharpened stone and ultimately would lead to the forging of metal tools. What may have started out as the chance use of a sturdily bent branch of a tree to upturn roots and edible tubers would soon give way to much more sophisticated instruments. The piece of wood, so conveniently bent to provide a lever, would lead to the construction of the lever and then, with the grandest leap that truly defines our species, to the discovery of the *principle* of the lever. The lever is the simplest of "machines." A machine is a mechanism for taking a small force and allowing it to move a larger load. Try opening a lid with your hands, and then use an old-fashioned bottle opener to appreciate the enhancement of power.

The discovery of the principle of the lever would lead to the awareness of the pulley, the inclined plane, the screw, and the wheel and the axle. These five simple machines are all there are. The entire complicated machinery of modern life consists simply of variations and elaborations on these five themes.

Eventually human beings, through their keen, observing eyes, would also discover the relationship of the seed that falls to the plant that grows to the production of the grains, the seeds that nourish. They would discover agriculture. The piece of wood would then be converted into a primitive hoe, and the human being could evolve a culture where he need no more go in search of food, but could actually cultivate food himself, and in his own "backyard." That extraordinary mind was operating in exactly the same way as we do today as we penetrate the molecular nature of living things.

The horizons early man was probing in the discovery of agriculture and the domestication of animals were in no way less dramatic than our flights into space and our Venus probes. The domestication of animals required the same time and patience, the same imagination and intelligence, the same abilities to accumulate data, synthesize them, draw conclusions, and then test the conclusions to separate the false ones from the correct ones. It took thousands of years for human beings to discover the relationship between copulation and procreation, in themselves as well as in lower animals. There have been primitive tribes existing in the twentieth century who still did not acknowledge this relationship in either man or beast.

Perhaps the first animals to be domesticated were seen as a form of living tools, dogs to assist in the relentless pursuit of game. The dog could be regarded as an extension of the same intelligence that developed spears, javelins, bows and arrows. But sooner or later the human beings would realize that the exhausting activity of the hunt was itself no longer necessary. As one domesticated the dog to facilitate in the hunt for the food animal, one could also domesticate the food animal. Compared with domestication, hunting was unreliable and energy-inefficient. Sheep would be slaughtered, pigs roasted, and cows milked, all, again, at one's own convenience and out of one's own backyard.

There were still further ways in which man could extend his dominion over the beast and by so doing reduce his toil. In addition to eating them, he would exploit *them* to perform his labor. The bent twig which had become a tool for digging could then become a plow to be drawn by oxen, who were gelded specifically for such uses. All of this paved the way for a life that was conceivably free from toil and sweat. Yet it was not to be, and the "why not" becomes a critical question in illuminating the nature of the human being.

Suppose for a moment that, after all these discoveries, men and women had stayed in the cave, had not, so to speak, been upwardly mobile, but had maintained their early, primitive standards of living. Suppose all the conditions of existence had been the same: we stayed in the cave, did not build cities—or even huts—did not advance our culture, aspired to no more than did the lion or the ape, worked only for food, air, water, and protection from the elements. With our discovery of technology and agriculture, we human beings might well have existed—despite God's injunction—without pain or exertion. But that is not the history of the human species. The questing beast that is *Homo sapiens* insisted on upping the ante at each turn, as he persists in doing to this very day. The cave would give way to a thatched or mud hut, which in turn would give way to a primitive stone or wooden lean-to, which in turn would give way to the palace, which in turn was a direct antecedent to the cathedrals of Chartres and Mont-Saint-Michel.

The history of human culture seems to be a perverse one, the human being constantly expanding his definitions of what is "necessary" for life—life clearly being not survival but implicitly the good life—and in so doing fulfilling the prophecy that he must earn his bread by the sweat of his face. The young men and women graduating from Ivy League law schools who are seduced by a major Wall Street law firm's offer of $75,000 a year will earn their money. They will be sweated out with seventy to eighty weekly hours of work of extraordinary tedium, which will generate a despair so vast that the majority of them will quickly develop a loathing for their profession and a cynicism about the law. Only a small percentage will persist in the field with pleasure and gratification.

Hannah Arendt contemplated this intensive expansion of our "needs" and came to the conclusion that they were an integral part of a requisite—beyond desire—need for work. She had originally defined work as producing goods not essential for survival, goods that would indeed last beyond our survival. She traced the influence of consumerism on our work. There is, after all, a limitation on how much we can consume, but we *must* continue to consume things if we are to continue producing them, particularly when there is an inexhaustible labor force. How can we rev up consumption when we seem already to have an unlimited accumulation of wealth and goods? she asks. The solution "consists in treating all use objects as though they were consumer goods so that a chair or a table is now consumed as rapidly as a dress, and a dress used up almost as quickly as food. . . . The Industrial Revolution has replaced all workmanship with labor, and the result has been that the things of the modern world have become labor products whose natural fate is to be consumed, instead of work products which are there to be used."[11]

This quotation, perhaps more than anything else, explains literally as well as figuratively what we mean when we say that we now live in a consumer society. In the battle between what Arendt has labeled as *homo faber* (man the worker) and *animal laborans* (man as laborer), the laboring animal has won. We live in a throw-away world. Everything is to be consumed, nothing saved. But in the process of doing this, we have paid an enormous price. We have changed our normal work into labor. No one starts and finishes anything anymore. We do little pieces, small precise actions to produce things of no real value. We live in a world of paper towels and paper napkins, of built-in obsolescence. In the process, we have managed to destroy our pride in products and our joy in work.

We pay yet another price. It is not profitable to spend the majority of our time laboring away at something that is unproductive to our pride and unnourishing to our soul, in order to have only a few hours for play or intellectual nurturing. What has happened in the cities of the world is the trivialization of work. To deal constantly in activities that have no beginnings and no ends must lend our work an absurd quality.

With the creation of the factory, which inevitably led to the assembly line, human labor would be reduced to the level of an inadequate machine. Charlie Chaplin's *Modern Times* is a testament to the essential idiocy of spending our days standing in one position, riveting one part to another, starting with a product that is half done by someone else, and passing it on, only incrementally completed, to still another person.

We know that we have now degraded work in many of our industrial plants to the extent that our own product, the robot, is superior to ourselves. The robotization of the assembly line may start a new age of liberating humankind from the pieces of work that are no longer creating whole things out of unwhole things. We have not yet arrived there. What we are doing instead is exporting this kind of labor to less developed countries and to less privileged people. We are closing our steel mills, reducing our assembly lines, and importing more and more of our products from the sweatshops of countries that are one or two generations behind us, either in their development or their aspirations. Still, ironically, most of us work, seek work, and need work.

One danger of having the toil taken out of work was that for many of us the opportunity for any employment would disappear. We are readjusting our economy to more technologic ends, which demands a work force with a greater education and more technical skills. There is nothing new in this; surely something like it happened in the many generations that were necessary to bring us out of the caves and into the sunlight, although probably without the current speed of change, the modern condensation of time. Nevertheless, all through history some craftsmen and artisans existed who performed work that had meaning. There was a time when farmers worked rather than simply labored. Although they produced consumables, these were for others, not themselves, and they were building farms that would outlast themselves. They may have worked desperately hard, as in the nineteenth century, a period that did not honor the sweat of their labor—a period of such vast class distinctions as to repel and disgust our modern imagination. The landed gentry of the English countryside lived off the sweat of freemen whose lot was often not very dissimilar to that of paleolithic man. Modern medicine had not yet been born to cure their diseases, and the Industrial Revolution, which was under way, offered little of the technology that would later emerge to ease their burdens.

The small farmer nonetheless worked in a way that in itself possessed a nobility. It is good to plant seed, nurture it, see it grow, harvest it, separate the chaff from the wheat, produce a product of value and worth. Beginning with one season of planting and ending with another of harvest, it is good to take that wheat and mill it, grind it into flour, mix it with yeast and water, and bake it in bread. It is good to create food, to start with raw materials and end with a product of utility. It was good for the artisan working in his shop to create a chair, a bench, or a table, or, more elegantly, a violin or a cello, which would be used with pleasure and passed on after the death of its user to still another user, thus gaining a kind of immortality across cultures.

Even with the lowest form of work, our culture had so conditioned the population, particularly the male segment, to equate pride and work that the loss of a job was not merely a financial blow but a blow to self-respect. During the recession of the 1970s, television screens were filled with poignant pictures of unemployed mine and mill workers suddenly finding themselves unneeded and useless in industries that were under assault from more cost-efficient cultures.

Our culture does not, for the most part, allow people to starve; unemployment insurance, welfare aids, and various benevolent institutions of government guaranteed that the unemployed laborer and his wife and children would not go hungry. It was not a matter of hunger, but of pride—a matter of what work meant, and therefore what it meant to be without it. The sense of despair and humiliation in the eyes of those blue-collar workers will not easily be forgotten by those of us who publicly viewed their shame.

It was not that their employment was so joyous. Their labor was for the most part miserable. It was mining coal in the hills of Kentucky and stoking fires in the steel mills of Gary, Indiana. This is not work; this is labor. There is no joy or pride, only sweat and toil, backbreaking labor, and risk to health. Yet the man was supposed to be a provider, to "bring home the bacon." It did not matter whether there was bacon in the house independent of his work—it was his job to supply food for his family. His pride, and beyond that his identity, were involved in *his* bringing home the bacon. Unemployment actually relieved these men of heavy burdens, but as they perceived reality, it was depriving them of their manhood.

In recent years, we've seen something approaching a revolution in the attitudes about work and gender. It has been fed by a confluence of forces: the Freudian restructuring of human sensibility; the necessity for a labor force that included women during two world wars; finally, the feminist revolution, which demanded what had already begun to be a financial necessity—fuller access to the workplace for women.

We began to change our definition of "man's work" and "woman's work." And although equality of reward may not yet have arrived, we have begun the process of eliminating the difference. How ironic and unfair it seems that at this moment, when women have gained access to the marketplace, the conditions of labor should have so deteriorated. There is something pathetic in the way we lay waste our powers getting and spending for all of these gadgets whose only purpose is to satisfy status needs, and in the process convert all work, that real source of pride, into common labor. The condition of unrewarding work is egalitarian. It exists for the privileged as well as the disenfranchised or underprivileged masses, for men as well as for women. Now that we are visualizing a labor force of both women and men, it will be a double tragedy if we are not able to reconstitute some of the aspects of work that support pride.

One should not romanticize what labor was in primitive cultures. None of us would have wanted to be a serf under Peter the Great. There were always laborers, and most of humanity during this period only labored. But the emergence of a better, more egalitarian society should have produced a greater conversion of toil into work—not the opposite.

What is needed is more of something good, not just less of something bad. The answer to unrewarding labor is not "non-work." We know that, though leisure time alleviates the strain of toil, it is not a substitute for the empowering aspects of work. It is true that, once we are freed of the constraints of earning money, many forms of "work" should be available. But the evidence emerging from experience with the population of the retired has not been encouraging. In the days when social legislation was first being considered to ease the agony of the human condition, the concept of a government-guaranteed retirement was created. When the principle of Social Security was being born in Germany at the turn of the century, a logical age was sought at which to peg retirement. It was decided to pick the median age at which people would normally be forced to retire because of disability, and set that as an optimal retirement age. When Social Security laws were first passed, at the turn of the century, that median age, at which half the population was disabled or unable to work, was sixty-five. The institution of retirement at sixty-five was then established— not arbitrarily, but with statistical validity.

In the 1930s, when America, under the New Deal, began to structure its Social Security system, the same sixty-five-year cutoff point seemed appropriate. No one at that time could have anticipated the dramatic progress in medicine after World War II, when medicine truly became a lifesaving profession instead of merely a caring and comforting occupation. This has caused a profound dislocation and conflict between the verities of age and the principle of retirement. Our medical progress has made ludicrous and perhaps even destructive the social-welfare programs of the New Deal.

We are not only living longer; we are living healthier and "younger" for longer periods of time. If we were planning today a retirement based on the mean age of disability, we would set the age at eighty-two! This suggests two problems. First, the enormous burden of an aging population will rest on a young population who must labor to support the Social Security system. Second, the so-called free ride of the now vital and not disabled elderly will extract its toll from them, too.

We know from early studies of retirement that some unexpected results occurred. Men relieved of the burdens of modern labor did not flourish. Depression and despair were more likely the lot of the indolent human being, unless he could invent for himself a new occupation. Some found it in games. Those with sufficient income could retire to the "work" of golfing, one of the most exasperating and demanding of tasks. Although games do not fulfill the traditional definition of work, in that they do not create a product, they do involve effort and mastery. I am not at all convinced that a product is an essential of work. What is the product of the teacher, the social worker, or the physician? All three represent honorable and rewarding fields of work. In a world that is increasingly abstract, service and mastery may be as central as a product to a concept of proper work.

Women, on the other hand, tended to do much better in the postretirement period. For most of them, "work," after all, continued essentially unchanged. They were not given the freedom of retirement, since they were never paid for their labors or, for that matter, honored for them. Women simply continued doing what they had always done—cooking, cleaning, tending, if not their children, their grandchildren now, or perhaps an ailing and sinking spouse.

At the same time, it is important to notice that such women's work was never fragmented into meaningless parts. They did actually both labor and work. Given a choice of being an assembly-line worker—beyond the assembly-line worker, a pediatrician who spends his entire day doing nothing but examining well babies with an occasional child in need of a standard remedy of antibiotics—I would much rather be a mother than a pediatrician. *Provided*—and what a proviso this is—that it paid the same, that it commanded the same respect and honor, that it endowed one with the same power. In the early days of the feminist revolution, women assumed that there was something noble about men's work and wanted their share of the marketplace. But the intellectuals who led the feminist revolution were thinking of jobs that *they* could achieve—to be senators, judges, editors of magazines, surgeons. The average man, however, was working in the mill, or the mine, or sorting envelopes in the post office. It is this marketplace that women would be entering. The irony remains that with their final freedom women are free to enter an area that has been depleted of joy for most men.

It is my thesis, albeit admittedly difficult to prove, that there is an inherent biological directive toward work—not just a cultural bias. Obviously such a thesis is harder to prove than the genetic foundation for autonomy, intelligence, imagination, and a romantic sexuality among human beings. But the fact that something needs to be taught does not mean that it is not inherent in the nature of the species; one sees the young leopard being taught to hunt, the young eagle encouraged to fly, even though there is undeniably an inherent biology directing the leopard toward hunting and the eagle toward flying. Human beings are born to work and need work.

Throughout this chapter I have used "work" to mean a special human activity, an exercise of self-imagination and an exploitation of the skills of the body, to produce products or conditions that enhance our life and will outlast us. An absence of work produces a depressing feeling of passivity, indolence, and degradation, so that excuses for these enterprises are manufactured by us and built into the culture.

Why have we not been able to fulfill our expectations that our technology would increase the ratio of work to labor and diminish the need for toil? Why have we not created the robots and the technical aspects for a toil-free existence? To a certain extent we have. It is easier these days to wash dishes, clean clothes, prepare food, traverse distances than it ever has been. However, the freedom thus obtained has not led to a regeneration of real work—or for that matter play—but to an increased involvement in other unrewarding labors and unrewarding leisures. We have increased our need for toil by increasing our desires for more and more trivial items, which serve vanity and insecurity rather than pride. With the conversion of all work into labor, we have destroyed one of the essential joys of our species. We must reverse the process for the sake of pleasure and the quality of life. But, beyond that, our survival itself demands a re-evaluation of modern industrial society.

We have the capacity to change the facts of our existence. A corollary to this is the capacity to change our environment—in negative as well as positive ways. We can create an environment hostile not only to our foes but to ourselves as well. The depletion of the ozone layer, the reduction of the purifying effect of the seas, the creation of acid rain that poisons our forests and our cities are some examples of the many ways in which we are destroying the environment on which we depend. There is a perverse relationship between the degradation of work into toil and the contamination of the environment.

Our consumerist society has reduced most work to meaningless labor necessary to produce meaningless things: overpowered and oversized cars, plastic cups and plastic packaging, throwaway every thing. The manufacture of such objects, as well as their disposal, is managing to contaminate the air and water on which we depend. Would anyone want to make the case that true pleasure has been increased through consumerism? Relief from backbreaking toil, assuredly; convenience, sometimes; but increased pleasure?

We have always intruded in the environment. No current ecology is fixed and optimal. The environment has always been in the process of change, whether through the forces of nature, as in the ice age, or through the activities of *Homo sapiens*. The maintenance of our culture demands massive intrusions on the environment. Such environmental changes are a product of our nature and, indeed, to our credit, according to both Pope John Paul II and Hannah Arendt. Fabrication, the actual work of the human being, by its nature demands "using" and therefore destroying aspects of the natural environment. Arendt states: "Material is already a product of human hands which have removed it from its natural location, either killing the life process, as in the case of the tree which must be destroyed in order to provide wood, or interrupting one of nature's slower processes, as in the case of iron, stone or marble torn out of the womb of the earth. This element of violation and violence is present in all fabrication, and *homo faber,* the creator of the human artifice, has always been a destroyer of nature. The *animal laborans* . . . may be the lord and master of all living creatures, but he still remains the servant of nature and the earth; only *homo faber* conducts himself as lord and master of the whole earth."[12]

We lords and masters may have the privilege of transforming the environment, but we dare not be so irresponsible and self-destructive as to alter the very conditions essential to survival. When we examine what is destroying the environment and measure it against the accretion of joy or pleasure that is offered to justify these contaminations, it quickly becomes apparent that we are playing a fool's game. We seem to have driven ourselves into a peculiar and double dead end. We are not only degrading all work into common labor; we are, in the same process, testing the patience of nature as we exhaust its resources and contaminate the environment.

Somehow, in some way, we must reverse this trend. The answer does not lie in increased leisure time during which we do nothing self-extending and pride-building. We are not a species that thrives on indolence. There have been cultures in which all toil was removed, often through ignoble and unacceptable means. The citizens in Periclean Athens were freed from manual labor by the institution of slavery. They contributed nothing to secure the things that were essential for their survival; all this was done by slaves. Yet the Athenians invented a form of work. They discovered philosophy, theater, science, and the arts. The average Athenian was industrious.

The way out of this dead end is through a re-examination of our quick-fix, passive forms of pleasure, and a rediscovery of work, mastery, and creativity—the privilege of our species—whether paid or unpaid. We need to work to be fulfilled. The good Fairy taught this as a primary lesson to the pathetic puppet who was striving, against his own self-destructive impulses, to become a human being. The good Fairy understood the nature of work.

Pinocchio announced to her that he did not "wish to follow either an art or a trade." When she asks him why, he answers that it tires him to work.

"My boy," said the Fairy, "those who talk in that way end almost always either in prison or in the hospital. Let me tell you that every man, whether he is born rich or poor, is obliged to do something in this world—to occupy himself, to work. Woe to those who lead slothful lives. Sloth is a dreadful illness and must be cured at once, in childhood. If not, when we are old it can never be cured."[13]

We are still young creatures, we human beings. Perhaps we can take comfort in seeing that we are in transition as a species from immaturity to maturity, in process—but a process now in our own hands. We must not unduly prolong our "adolescent" period. Instant, cheap gratification is never gratifying and always dear; the present is not everything; the future *will* arrive. These are truisms that adolescent individuals and adolescent cultures have a hard time accepting. But now there is an imperative for us to give up childish ways. We are running out of time. We are getting so unruly in our adolescent acting up that we may destroy the world which supports our bad habits. In so doing, we will be destroying the future, which is still necessary for our maturation as a species.

We have time—if precious little; time to mature; time to restore our perspectives; time to reorder our values; time to grow up and fulfill the promise of Genesis, the potential of our nature.

CONSCIENCE

~~~~~~~~~~~~~~~~

PINOCCHIO LEARNS TO HONOR WORK AND, more important, develops "a good heart." In so doing, he becomes a real boy. He enters the moral community, if only on the limited scale of responsibility that we ascribe to children. "A good heart" is a most descriptive phrase for that uniquely human function, a conscience. In developing a conscience and in conforming our behavior to its demands, we see the human being in his noblest light. We see ourselves in the image of God. In the absence of conscience, we are reduced below the most primitive and the basest animal forms, who, without choice, are never capable of evil.

This strange creature, the human being, has the capacity to contemplate his own conduct and compare it with his ideals. Conscience is nothing more than the capacity to judge ourselves in moral terms and to adapt our conduct to the standards that we have accepted. Conscience clearly shows the interrelationship of all the factors that make us human. Without freedom of choice, we could never speak of a conscience. But the same is equally true of imagination, prediction, anticipation, and a full range of feelings. The forces that drive us to act according to our ideals reside in the motivating power of such emotions as fear, guilty fear, guilt, shame, and pride, and in such complex human activities as sympathy, empathy, compassion, identification, and love.

Other animals, generally group animals, have been described as exhibiting "altruistic" behavior. What is usually used as evidence

of altruism is the observation of an individual member of a species—whether fish, insect, or bird—sacrificing its own survival to
serve the community.

Few of us would be likely to commend the individual for his
unselfish action or honor him for his nobility when we recognize
that he has no choice: he is commanded by genes to such "altruism."
Mandated behavior is morally neutral. Beyond these and other acts
of self-sacrifice attributed to lower animals—generally related to
protection of the young—lie the heavy hand of genetic determinism
and the tyranny of species survival. Most of us withhold moral
praise for the doe's sacrifice of her life in protection of her fawn,
as we would eschew negative moral judgment of the "bestial"
behavior of the lion who devours her neighbor, or the male tiger
who devours his own cubs if given the opportunity.

Even those who indulge in anthropocentric sentimentalizing
about animals' nobility are unlikely to see the operation of a conscience in such actions. Since the very concept of a conscience
requires the capacities for reason, abstraction, autonomy, and a
broad range of feelings, the concept is of necessity reserved for the
human species. Moral philosophy is—for good or ill—a creation
of the human being concerning the behavior of the human being.
Only human beings make moral judgments, and we should make
them only about our own kind. Inevitably, the inconsistencies of
such freedom will allow for an wide variability in moral behavior.
We can do bad things as well as good. Some people are more
prone to bad than good, and some people are capable of being
grotesquely bad, of committing what has been inappropriately
called "inhuman" conduct.

At this point I must clarify my use of terms. The language of
morality overlaps with the language of other judgments in other
frames of reference. "Good" and "bad" do not necessarily suggest
moral judgments. Indeed, in my dictionary, the definition of "good"
starts with this descriptive and morally neutral statement: "Having
positive or desirable qualities"; it goes on to the next definitions:
"... suitable ... : *a good outdoor paint*"; "Not spoiled ... : *The
milk is still good*"; "... grade of meat"; and on and on. It is only

at the fourteenth definition that we come to "Of moral excellence; virtuous; upright: *a good man.*"[1]

Similarly, "right" and "wrong" need not suggest a moral judgment, or even a statement of propriety. They can simply mean "correct," as in "the right answer to an arithmetic problem." When we are speaking exclusively in moral terms, the two most appropriate words for "good" and "bad" are "virtuous" and "evil." But to many these words have specific religious connotations or refer to special theories of virtue. Generally speaking, therefore, "good" and "bad," "right" and "wrong," as used in this chapter, will refer to "morally good" and "morally bad."

The human capacity for philosophizing has led to a rich literature that attempts to define right and wrong and to understand principles of morality that might be useful in guiding human behavior. I have lived in academia long enough to be aware that "moral sophistication" and "morality" are regrettably not synonymous terms. The Hastings Center is an interdisciplinary research organization devoted to ethical and policy questions emerging from the fields of biology, medicine, and health. We all work together there: biologists, lawyers, philosophers, physicians, historians, theologians, economists, and sociologists. One would expect the moral philosopher to be the most sophisticated, in both analysis and argument, in distinguishing right from wrong. Often, but not always, this is the case. I have seen no evidence, however, that the moral philosophers are in any way morally superior to those less knowledgeable about the nature of ethics. Knowledge and conduct are unfortunately independent functions of human experience. We are less rational than we like to believe. Knowledge of right and wrong is less likely to determine moral behavior than to rationalize our behavior after the fact. The rational reasons we offer for much of our conduct are only rationalizations, as Freud pointed out, for behavior that is emotionally, and often unconsciously, driven.

There is an important but limited condition where knowledge may modify ethical behavior. The term "consciousness-raising"— as popularly used by the feminist movement—though awkward, is generally understood to describe this case. The good person may be doing something unwittingly that is harmful, evil, or painful. If he is a good person and he becomes cognizant that his behavior causes pain, he then can, and will, change his behavior, guided by this new knowledge. But this is, again, a small part of moral behavior.

Unless a knowledge of ethics can be transformed into ethical behavior, it would seem an esoteric and limited resource. One would expect, therefore, to find a literature on shaping human conduct in moral areas at least as rich as that which exists in moral analysis. This is not so. Compared with the libraries full of moral philosophy, the literature on moral conduct is trifling.[2] The psychology of behavior is a young discipline. Its newness is only part of the explanation for the neglect of the moral world within the fields of psychology.

Psychology has been divided into two main streams: the behaviorists, traditionally psychologists and generally influenced by Pavlov, Watson, Skinner, et al.; and the dynamic psychologists, largely psychiatrists (physicians) but increasingly others, who draw on the teachings of Freud and successive psychoanalysts.

Behaviorists had never incorporated the concept of the mind into their field of endeavor; indeed, the concept was alien and anathema to them. Morality would, therefore, not be as logical a point of inquiry as learning, perception, or memory. Further, behavioral psychologists have traditionally gathered data from animal populations. Seeing *Homo sapiens* as in a continuum with lower animals, they made the implicit assumption that the data gathered from the pigeon and the rat, or the chimpanzee and the ape, could then be extrapolated to the behavior of human beings. But since no animals except *Homo sapiens* are moral creatures, no trajectory can be constructed.

The dynamic psychologists, on the other hand, were early incorporated into the field of medicine and the burgeoning medical specialty of psychiatry. Psychiatry applied its insight and energy to the treatment of illness. One of the implicit conditions of illness is the concept of nonculpability. Moral neutrality shapes our attitude

toward the patient, and defines the "sick role." We do not condemn
a patient for his disease, even when it is infectious, such as tuber-
culosis, and can cause serious harm to others. If we do, we violate
a basic moral premise of medicine. The sick role is intended to
secure compassion and care. The patient is viewed as the victim
of his disease rather than the cause of it. Since the world of the
psychiatrist was occupied with the "mentally ill," there was no
place for moralizing here.

Conscience and moral development, therefore, were to become
late entries in the lists of respectable research interests of psychology. In everyday life, however, proper human conduct is a primary
concern for all of us. What makes a person choose good over evil,
and what can be done to encourage such choice, is a crucial issue
in a communitarian species like ours. It is hardly a theoretical
problem. Our very survival depends on it.

Because for most of us morality resides in human actions, not
in human perceptions, we are concerned only that people behave
well; the motives for good behavior have no more relevance than
the motives for bad. I recognize that I may be introducing a
psychoanalytic bias here. In psychoanalysis we do not judge
thoughts, wishes, feelings, or fantasies—only actions. The unconscious and the constrained conscious impulses of every one of us
are presumed to be a rich reservoir of all sorts of unspeakable and
indecent matters. The distinction between the saint and the sinner
is not in what exists in his thought, but in his means of dealing
with impulse and fantasy—his readiness to suppress selectively or
express a different order of things. The saint and the sinner may
share the same unconscious impulse, but he who suppresses the
evil is the saint and he who suppresses the good is the sinner.

I recognize that in certain theologies, the Roman Catholic for
one, thoughts can be evil. This concept has presented me with
some difficulty. If one did not have to struggle with evil impulses,
how could one be judged virtuous? Would one not then be back
with Adam and Eve in the preautonomous age of the Garden of
Eden? It may be answered that the recovery of that state of innocent
virtue is the goal for all of us, and the degree to which we are

capable of recapturing the innocence will be the measure of our virtue. Since it is a concept with which I am neither comfortable nor knowledgeable, I will restrict my definitions of good and evil to doing good and evil.

Assuming that a person knows right from wrong, why does he choose right? More exactly, why should anyone do any action that does not serve selfish survival needs? How can one explain, in this Darwinian age, such behavior as selflessness, generosity, empathy, sharing, caring, and self-sacrifice? Is goodness innate or learned?

Students of human nature have been divided between those who viewed us as halfway to the angels, and those who saw us as the only evil animal. Generally, the latter have held sway. Whereas Genesis saw the human species as being created in goodness and love, after the Fall a new vision of human nature emerged. With the concept of original sin, Christian theology viewed all of us children of Adam and Eve as being born sharing in the sin of our parents. Only through education and service would we be redeemed to a new set of ideals embodied in the spirit and teachings of Jesus.

The concept of original sin had a profound influence on generations of writers and philosophers working from a theological matrix who evolved a notion of an evil nature requiring redemption. In addition, the culture of Christianity extended itself into the realm of the secular. Diverse writers from disciplines other than theology were influenced by their Christian biases. These students of human nature generally saw the child as a dangerous spirit to be tamed or civilized. In this tradition, the adult is always a potential sinner, requiring the constraints of civilization; in this sense, the mischievous and subhuman Pinocchio is a classic Christian creature. Worse than an animal, who can do neither wrong nor right, he does mischief and evil and becomes human only when he is transformed by love.

This negative view of human nature is supported by the fact that we tend to be more aware of transgressions than of virtues, discomfort more than comfort, sickness more than health. When a human being behaves selfishly, when he is aggressive, angry, avaricious, indulgent of himself, he is often described as having given in to his "animal nature." The disapproved of behavior is often seen as a "lack of control." "Control" suggests that the fundamental impulse of the human being is towards selfishness and brutality if uncontrolled by the discipline of culture and education.

Montaigne is a prime and extreme spokesman for this self-demeaning philosophy. He viewed the human being as one of the lesser animals. He found our physical form revolting, and our natures vile. The very traits that are generally proposed as our glories—our freedom and autonomy—are perceived by Montaigne as primarily the freedom to do evil, and as such a lesser, baser phenomenon than the fixed characteristics of lower animals.[3]

So low had we fallen in our own self-esteem by the eighteenth century that the novelist Henry Fielding—in exasperation at the prevailing philosophies of his day—begged for surcease. He sardonically stated that he was prepared to concede that many natures—"perhaps those of the philosophers"—may be entirely free from all traces of compassion and love. Nonetheless, he implored them to "grant that there is in some (I believe in many) human breasts a kind and benevolent disposition, which is gratified by contributing to the happiness of others."[4]

Although human nature has had its defenders, the pessimists and the nihilists have generally held sway. The human being in modern times, particularly after the onslaught of two world wars, the Holocaust, and the atomic bomb, has had few defenders. Lorenz, Fox, Tiger, Morris, and other anthropologists and ethologists have added a pseudo-scientific gloss to the philosophy of man the destroyer. We are viewed as driven by a personal need for survival compounded by an aggressive set of built-in genetic directives for survival, with only the restraining influence of culture to keep the destructive forces in check. This view had been most eloquently presented in modern literature by Sigmund Freud in his influential work *Civilization and Its Discontents*.[5] Yet Freud was a clinician, and the sort of clinician who refused to close his eyes to the empirical and everyday evidence in front of him even when it contradicted his pet theory. His keenly observing eye saved Freud from making the errors of those who spin their theories in libraries and laboratories protected from the messy inconsistencies of actual people. It also explains the internal contradictions that all of his students have found in Freud's work.

From the beginning, it was obvious to Freud that a human nature that was instinctually driven and exclusively survival-oriented could never explain all the complexities of interpersonal relationships. This was particularly evident when one began examining the self-sacrificing behavior of parent to child. The essential biological fact of human dependency was to bring Sigmund Freud constantly back to the confusing and contradictory aspects of human nature, which refused to conform to his central image of an instinctual and self-serving human being.

Freud's original position was a product of the rising tide of individualism that swept through the capitalist democracies of the Western world at the turn of the century. Only when one focuses narrowly on the individual self do generosity and self-sacrifice seem to be self-destructive. We are, as Aristotle insisted, by nature a social or political creature. The group is requisite for our survival. The parent must be generous and unselfish in the service of the weak and helpless infant. This is vital to species survival, given our preposterously dependent young. It would be odd, even impossible, to consider such a fundamental survival mechanism as care and compassion for the infant a lucky accident of developing culture. In addition, sacrificing ourselves for our children is the ultimate self-serving device, for they are the vessels that transport our selves into a future that transcends our corporal survival.

In his earliest works, Freud explained all behavior in terms of an instinctual drive for pleasure and survival, and all neuroses in terms of repression of these drives. From the very beginning of his clinical research,[6] Freud was forced to confront contradictory evidence. In time he began to allude to "an unconscious sense of guilt."[7] By the time Freud published *Totem and Taboo*,[8] he was placing human decency and morality within the very matrix of the species. This book makes Freud the father of sociobiology, in that he drew heavily on Darwin at a time when few of his contemporaries recognized the enormous impact Darwin was to have on modern thought.

Totem and Taboo has been severely neglected, not only by serious general scholars but also within the psychoanalytic community. Its revolutionary message was ignored because it was based on what has since proved to be an erroneous concept of inheritance. Freud assumed, as many of his day did, that acquired characteristics could be transmitted genetically. He was, in other words, a Lamarckian. But when we look at the question metaphorically, we, too, become Lamarckians. Human beings do transmit acquired characteristics to successive generations—but through our culture rather than our genes.

The mythology and specific substance of this book are unimportant; what is startling is the message, particularly coming from Sigmund Freud. He concluded that certain revulsions, certain moral-behavior patterns are so necessary for the survival of the species that they cannot be considered a product of any specific culture, or of culture at all, but must be built into the genetic nature of the species. He was specifically examining the universal abhorrence of incest when he said that this feeling "probably belongs to the historical acquisitions of humanity and like other moral taboos it must be fixed in many individuals through organic heredity."[9]

Any nature-nurture battle eventually becomes polemic and tendentious. When one accepts the essential plasticity of human nature, the indivisibility of these two features becomes apparent. The lesson of Adam and Eve is that we are "created in the image of God," meaning we are different from the other animals but, with the modification of T. H. White, we are only "potential" in His image.

It remains for environment to allow—perhaps to encourage—those features of decency to emerge. It is "natural" for most parents to treat their offspring with love and caring because of a genetic directive to respond protectively in relations with the helpless young. There are, however, abnormal human beings, either by genetic fault or more likely by gross distortions and negligence in their early environment, who have little vestige of this natural inclination toward protection of the young. And so battered children become battering parents, who beget battered children. And neglected children become neglecting parents, who beget other neglected children.

Understanding the complex interrelationship between nature and nurture in the human being, let us put it aside, at least for this time, and examine some of the mechanisms of conscience in formation and in action.

In *Pinocchio* we see a late-nineteenth-century version of the development of proper behavior in a child. Pinocchio is not a misbehaving boy. He has not even earned the privilege of being a child yet. He is a puppet, a mischievous, commedia dell'arte character. But the moral certitude of his Tuscan creator was reassuring. One must learn to be good through hard experience. One learns to be good from doing bad and suffering the consequences. Punishment has an essential and inevitable role in this learning process. But, transcending all, compassion, empathy, and proper models are critical. It is not a bad schema.

What, then, motivates good behavior and limits bad? The most primitive constraint on human behavior is fear. Fear and rage are certainly not specifically human emotions. We see them in a multitude of creatures down the developmental line. In the newborn they are innate. One identifies the rage of a newborn infant in his cry of hunger, and one identifies the facial prototype of fear in his "startle" reflex on being exposed to a loud noise or a falling motion. In the chapter on emotions I have described the common roots of these emergency emotions that are aroused in human beings, as well as other animals, when confronted with a life-threatening situation.

Although loud noises and falling are the basic sources of fear in the child, present even before he can differentiate himself from an environment, the growing child will quickly learn other sources of danger, either directly through experience, or by resonance to the response of the adults that support his existence. He may, for example, learn the danger of heat by touching a radiator or, equally, by witnessing the vehement, protective, half-angry, half-frightened movements and shouts of the parent when he attempts to do so.

He will gradually be educated to those life-threatening aspects of the environment and will incorporate them into the fear mechanism.

Since the primary lesson of dependency is that we are helpless and must have parental approval for our survival, a secondary form of fear will be elaborated in the human child that in its complexity *is* unique to human creatures. This is what I have referred to as "guilty fear," the fear of punishment for having done wrong. Though, as we have seen, animals, particularly domesticated animals, can experience guilty fear, they do not do so in the complex and elaborate forms that shape human experience.

We have abstracted a concept, already a human function, called "punishment" that will determine and shape behaviors in areas quite distinct from the situations in which the original punishments may have arisen. Certain animals fear "authority." They fear what we would call "punishment." But a "concept" of punishment that is transferable outside the specific situation, time, and experience is beyond even the chimpanzee. Human beings take their early experiences with their parent and elaborate a sense of reward and punishment based on "good" and "bad" behavior that they can extrapolate into future, anticipated situations. We use our uncommon abilities for abstraction to relate one idea—making "peepee" in the "potty"—to another situation—getting our homework handed in on time—for which we can anticipate reward rather than punishment. We extend the concept of the approving authority from the parent to the teacher to the boss, and beyond mere mortal flesh to a divine authority. Only human beings can elaborate from the anxieties over parental approval to a concept like "divine retribution," or, beyond that, to the even more abstract principle of the moral good.

The fear of punishment from an internal or an external authority becomes a central mechanism for limiting aggressive and antisocial behavior. Though the amount of anger and hostility generated by any individual will undoubtedly vary with each differing life experience, angry impulses are demonstrably part of every human being's genetic endowment. The constraints of childhood are rooted in the fear of the disapproval of the all-powerful and ever-present parent. These fears will transcend the actual presence of the authority as we gradually learn to internalize the punitive parent in what may be the first step to the development of conscience.

One institution that combines both internalized and external forms of constraint is organized religion. To a fundamentalist, the distinction between God and the punitive parent of his childhood is not all that clear. God will punish for transgression of His laws, and the punishment will be fearful beyond anything we could endure in childhood. Eternal hellfire, damnation, banishment from His loving presence in the Kingdom of Heaven—all of the punishments of childhood, intensified to a nightmarish quality, continue to have validity for the religious fundamentalist, who believes in heaven and hell. Freud, not a religious man himself, visualized the transfer of authority from the father to the Father in heaven as the basic mechanism of religious conviction.[10]

But what of those who do not subscribe to organized religion and who are also decent people? We are all aware of the existence and power of the state. There are laws designed to constrain the aggressor from abusing the vulnerable. We may covet our neighbor's property, but we do not steal it, under penalty of law. But surely it is not simply the constraint of law that governs our behavior. We act appropriately and decently—for the most part—guided by internal directives, with little concern about transgressions of the law. While I am sure that speeding and income-tax evasion would flourish were there no punishments under law, most of us would not murder or rape, regardless of the legal injunctions. Why not? What constrains us?

Also, much of our behavior falls outside state interest, within the jurisdiction of our own autonomy. Certain things are no business of the state. Behaviors that govern interpersonal relationships, except at their most extreme, are not governed by law. How much love I give my children, how much constancy my wife, how much honor I bear with me in my business relationships, how I comport myself with those who have less power than I and those who are dependent on me financially, my attitudes, my dispositions, my generosity or lack thereof—all of these are determined by internal rather than external directives. It was to these aspects of life that Freud addressed himself in his pursuit of conscience, and it is worthwhile to examine his intellectual odyssey through the labyrinths of the moral mind.

One of the more intriguing inconsistencies of Freud's work is that, although he constantly addressed himself to pathology, his real accomplishments were in the understanding of normal human behavior. It was from the sick that he learned about the healthy. Typically, therefore, his understanding of the internalized forces of conscience began with an attempt to understand the disease of clinical depression. The self-castigation of the depressed patient led Freud to the concept of an introjected (swallowed-up) parent who became an internalized observer and punisher of disapproved behavior. The idea of an encapsulated, internalized image of a parent would later be resurrected by Freud as a key element in his first construction of a punitive conscience. Freud's work on depression[11] was to be a prelude to understanding identification. Identification was in turn to become a cornerstone in the building of the "superego," Freud's later term for the conscience mechanism.

Freud's earliest view of conscience had the individual continuing to operate under an instinctual drive for pleasure, controlled only by his fear of punishment. The poor struggling child assumed the parent to be omniscient as well as omnipotent. Worse, the child lived with a ubiquitous parent, always present, because he was carried within the unconscious structure of the child's mind. This image of the parents' role is the foundation of simplistic view of God previously described.

Philip Roth explains this brilliantly when he has Howard Portnoy say of his mother, in *Portnoy's Complaint*:

"She was so deeply imbedded in my consciousness that for the first year of school I seem to have believed that each of my teachers was my mother in disguise. . . . Of course, when she asked me to tell her all about my day at kindergarten, I did so scrupulously. I didn't pretend to understand all the implications of her ubiquity, but that it had to do with finding out the kind of little boy I was when I thought she wasn't around—that was indisputable. One consequence of this fantasy, which survived (in this particular form) into the first grade, was that seeing as I had no choice, I became honest."[12]

According to this view of conscience, we behave well because, whether the punitive parent is present or not, we have the sense of him or her within us. We assume that the parent is like some omniscient Peeping Tom who sees all and is prepared to punish all. Conscience, in this construction, is simply a mechanism to avoid punishment or rejection. Remember that to the child parental rejection is tantamount to death. Conscience at this level is a defensive maneuver—a reluctant sacrifice of pleasure in order to buy safety.

But surely conscience represents more than constraint. This grants too much to the image of the human being as an elegant version of a domesticated animal. We are not driven exclusively by a selfish instinct contained only by fear and guilty fear.

Even this limited view of conscience would still place human beings above the beast, and make of human conscience a special human phenomenon. Anticipation, imagination, conceptual thinking are all essential to the kind of internalization that is represented by Freud's introjected father. Still, the phenomena of conscience cannot be viewed as mere concessions to survival. All generosity is not ingratiation. All selflessness is not a product of political maneuvering. All instances of kindness and charity cannot be simply approval-gaining mechanisms. This concedes too much to the Freudian view of a libido-driven, pleasure-oriented man. Whereas most Freudians were prepared to accept his vision of human nature, Freud was not among them. The master had his doubts. What of his concept of an inherited conscience that facilitated group living, as articulated in *Totem and Taboo*?

Once again, when Freud turned away from the individual patient to examine the peculiarities of group behavior, a broader concept of conscience was to emerge.[13] In his study *Group Psychology and the Analysis of the Ego,* he was to develop a concept that came to be known as the "ego-ideal." In discussing self-respect, he stated that each individual contains within him an internalized image of an ideal self—an ego-ideal—by which the actual self, or ego, would judge its own behavior. We respond with pride when we conform our behavior to our standards of what we can be at our best, and we respond with humiliation, shame, or guilt when we fail our better selves.

This represented Freud's first understanding, or acknowledgment, of the motivating force of true guilt. With guilt, the pain that is experienced is the anguish of personal failure. It occurs when we have dishonored our *own* internal self by falling short of what we ought to be. It has nothing to do with parental displeasure, although the nature and even the presence of an ego-ideal is contingent on the values and models (if any) presented to the child by his parents or their surrogates during the formative years. Guilt is not fear of the other, not fear of punishment, not fear at all. It is disappointment in self. Recall that Paul Ricoeur had described guilt as "a way of putting oneself before a sort of invisible tribunal which measures the offense, announces the condemnation and inflicts the punishment."[14]

With the concept of our own ego-ideal, what we experience when we do wrong is closer to a feeling of failure than to a sense of wrongdoing. The concept of an ego-ideal that operates through pride in fulfillment and guilt in failing the ideal is in every way a richer, more complex, and more specifically human concept, and allows for the explanation of a host of altruistic human behaviors that resist understanding in the cruder, earlier model. One such phenomenon involves what has been called a "social conscience."

This idea of the conscience serving a social purpose, or, beyond that, the idea of a "social conscience," is expressed most eloquently in a scene from *Huckleberry Finn*, the episode in which Huck discovers his own conscience in a way that completely bewilders him, and which was not completely understood by me on my first unsophisticated reading. It seems particularly relevant here, in contrast with *Pinocchio*.

One of the coincidences of literature is that two authors, independently (as far as we know) and at almost the same time, used two such similar sets of rogues as did Twain and Collodi. Pinocchio is flimflammed by the Cat and the Fox. There is no revenge, no retribution, and no moral conclusions drawn by Pinocchio. He is still, after all, only a piece of wood aspiring to be human. In a similar scene, Huck is exploited shamefully by two con men who call themselves the Duke and the Dauphin. These two scoundrels have used and abused Huck, exploited, ridiculed, humiliated, and mocked him, and then comes the scene of retribution and revenge.

When I was a child, vengeance was as sweet to me as it was to Saint Augustine. I loved the literature of revenge—*The Count of Monte Cristo* being a paramount example, because the vengeance was unhurried, deliberate, and deliciously extended through over half the book. So, identifying with Huck, I expected him to respond with sheer joy when the Duke and Dauphin finally got caught and get their comeuppance. Huck watches from a distance as the con men are tarred and feathered. He recognizes them although "they was all over tar and feathers, and didn't look like nothing in the world that was human,"[15] but Huck feels no joy. The forces of evil are conquered, the bad are subdued, the good triumph, virtuous order is restored, yet Huckleberry Finn is peculiarly distressed:

"It made me sick to see it; and I was sorry for them poor pitiful rascals. It seemed like I couldn't feel any hardness against them any more in the world. . . . Human beings *can* be awful cruel to one another."

Huck is haunted by his feelings and does not understand them. He is not nearly so brash as he had been before but feels "kind of ornery, and humble, and to blame somehow—though I hadn't done nothing." Those words are not random choices. Only a student of conscience and a creative genius would have used them. Like most great novelists, Twain intuitively understood human nature in a way that philosophers and psychologists can only approximate through logic and analysis. He expresses through the character of an ignorant boy the nature of social conscience.

Huck feels "ornery," mean-spirited and ugly. He recognizes his kinship not just with the victims, but with the mob, since he must have wished the same and worse many times over for these two scoundrels. He is experiencing the tragic truth that has been acknowledged by most of us: the literal fulfillment of our fantasies rarely offers us pleasure.

He feels humble, reduced, humiliated, because that dark side of human nature characterized by the lynch mob also says something about himself. With the social conscience he possesses unawares, he undoubtedly recognizes that what he saw in others he shares with them as members of the human race. In seeing their meanness, he is seeing the potential within himself for the same.

But how could he feel "to blame somehow," he who had every right to wreak vengeance, to enjoy retaliation? He had done nothing to harm these men. Somehow or other, he shared a common burden of guilt with those who violated decency by treating fellow human beings with such indignity:

"That's always the way; it don't make no difference whether you do right or wrong, a person's conscience ain't got no sense, and just goes for him *anyway*. If I had a yeller dog that didn't know no more than a person's conscience does I would pison him. It takes up more room than all the rest of a person's insides, and yet ain't no good nohow, Tom Sawyer he says the same."

Guilt, shame, pride, love are attributes inherently built into the human organism, but they must be supported to survive and grow. Conscience will evolve only through the proper nurturing of these attributes. Fear, guilty fear, guilt, and shame are all natural human capacities that are incorporated into the conscience mechanisms. But all human behavior is not an avoidance of the negative. There are powerful positive motivations. What about human pride, and human joy in giving to, sacrificing for, and serving other persons or ideals and principles? To understand these most creative and uniquely human facets of conscience, one must understand the multiple meanings of the concept of "identification." It is via this mechanism that much of empathy and altruism will operate.

At this point I will somewhat arbitrarily distinguish two phenomena with quite different dynamics, which lead to similar behavior patterns: I will call the consciously attempted mimicry of parents and conformation to their consciously encouraged behavior "modeling." The unconscious assumptions of models, the auto-matical introjection of the values and the behaviors of the parents, I will call "identification." We are most likely to choose as models those who seem the most powerful figures around us, our parents. We model our behavior to their standards and desires because we see them as the instruments of our survival and stand in awe of them as such.

One way a child in his formative years learns how to behave is by responding to cues from the environment. This learning takes place piece by piece in a mode best described by behaviorist psychologists. Through rewards or punishment, the child is encouraged to express certain behaviors and discouraged from expressing others. The parents will be aware of the direct effects of their rewards or punishments. They will be unaware that their faces, their manners, their general demeanor with the child will mean much more than their specific statements or even actions in shaping his behavior. This helps to explain why children tend to become like their parents rather than like other people's parents, or even like what their parents would like them to become.

Character traits in children emerge through a pragmatic trial-and-error method, particularly in the most early, infantile stages. It is the lesson of *Pinocchio*. Do wrong and see chagrin in the Fairy's face, hear it in the voice of the Cricket's conscience, or note sadness in the expression of the father. What most likely happens is that the typical child, almost like an ameba, tests the environment in all directions, using all methods of survival to see which works. Since the human child does not forage for food, the only important activity for his survival is securing the approval of the parents; they will nurture and sustain him, providing he pleases them. The child will try all means to ingratiate the parents and gain their love.

If through trial and error the child finds that being cute, charming, and cuddly evokes a positive response, or forgiveness for wrongdoing, he will be conditioned to use those behaviors more and more as a means of avoiding punishment and seeking reconciliation.

If, on the other hand, the parent responds to the ingratiation and charm with distaste because he cannot tolerate it, the child may find alternative means of approval. The way to this father or mother's heart may be through "being a good boy" and doing everything that term implies: tidying his room, playing quietly by himself, attending to whatever work is considered appropriate for his age.

This child will be different from the first described. He will see performance and achievement rather than charm and ingratiation as the primary means for gaining approval, and will tend more and more to use the successful devices. Children are masters at reading their parents' moods. They have to be. Their lives—at least as they see the issue—depend on it.

This early social conditioning may explain the "hereditary" nature of personality. It deals equally well with the question of why little Italian children tend to behave like Italians, whereas Swedish children behave like Swedes. More important, it may be a key to understanding gender differences. I am not suggesting that there are not innate gender differences between men and women, but these are not immune to the plasticity of all genetic traits.

In the beginning, the child basically accedes to the demands of his parents. Conscience at that time is experienced as a foreign entity, if at all. With maturation, we undertake the burdens of responsibility for ourselves, but the standards of that early conditioning will be incorporated into the ideal image by which we will judge ourselves. It is through the complex and multiple mechanisms of identifications that we will coordinate our caring and altruistic propensities, and define a moral self.

We need not identify with all aspects of our parents, nor can we necessarily select the parental attitudes that we admire to incorporate into our own characteristic behavior patterns, while rejecting those of which we disapprove. We will frequently discover ourselves later in adult life, often to our chagrin, behaving precisely the way our parents behaved in fashions that embarrassed or humiliated us.

Fortunately, we are not limited to identification only with our parents. We can identify with other persons, more in accord with the wishes and needs of whatever stage of development we may be going through, friends, teachers, heroic figures—all of whom have been encompassed by the generic term "role model." This is a lifesaving mechanism for those whose parents are not suitable models. Some sort of identification, by whatever means, must occur to establish the set of internalized standards and to build the ego-ideal that must exist for the full emergence of conscience.

One's identity is therefore an amalgam. It will involve conscious modeling, whereby certain traits will be carefully selected for emulation, and others that have been, consciously, vigorously rejected. In earliest childhood, when learning is most powerful, the parent is all, and all-perfect. The tendency will be weighted toward emulation of the caring figure, if one is present. We have all seen with a certain amusement a little boy imitate the posture of his father or a little girl imitate the gestures of her mother. But conscious modeling is effective only in the most trivial of personality traits. We can reject the Midwestern or European inflections with which we were raised for the tonier cadences of our college classmates. We can cut our cloth and our hair to whatever is *de rigueur* for our generation, but most of what drives behavior and compels choice will be established by less voluntary and rational choice.

Modeling is as nothing compared with the power of the automatic identification that goes on willy-nilly, even while the child assumes he is rejecting the parental authority. The earliest model, and figure for identification, for both boys and girls, will be the "mother." Here I do not necessarily mean the female parent. In this age of experimentation with gender role, anyone who is the primary caretaker would be the equivalent of the "mother." That first caretaker, who supports the survival of the helpless infant—who cossets, nurtures, feeds, bathes, touches the infant—will become the cornerstone upon which all other identifications must stand. As such, that caretaker exercises the greatest control over the future development of the child's personality.

Identification is a peculiar process. Because it operates on an unconscious level, a mother is more likely to influence the design of a child through behavior over which she, herself, has little conscious control. She may have a detailed design of the kind of child she wants, but what she is may be more crucial than what she desires. This concept of identification is so powerful that it mystifies parents who do not understand the distinction between their injunctions and their actions.

A little boy will often behave as his father wants him to behave out of fear of the father, love of the father, or a need to be approved by the father. But that same little boy will behave like the father—even if this may not be the way the father wishes him to behave—out of a strong and almost automatic process of identification.

Identification is the most powerful of behavior-determining measures. It is a "wholesale" adoption of the forms, habits, and even the values of the parents. Through identification, we adopt behavioral patterns in big, indiscriminate blocks by incorporating the character and identities of others. It is chagrining and humiliating for most adults to find themselves constantly repeating with their children things that their parents did to them, though as children they had vowed, "Never will I do this to my children."

It is through identification that we assume the role of a mature individual guided by our own standards, rather than the wants of others. Understanding the mechanisms makes it clear that we never free ourselves of the "wants of others." But when they are internalized, are they not fairly construed as constituents of the self we have built? We assume the full mantle of autonomy, even though we are not as autonomous as we would have ourselves believe. Our moral behavior and conscience, however constructed, will be the function of an internalized image of authority, which we will come to regard as an abstract system of standards and values. It will no longer be some other thing that we fear or feel subordinated to. Conscience will be woven into the fabric of the self. When we follow the dictates of our conscience, we will seem to do what we want to do, not what someone else wants. Not even someone within us. We will be acting out of aspiration, not out of intimidation.

The central thesis I have attempted to outline briefly here is that, given our genetic potential for conscience and caring, there are two routes to develop patterns of unselfish and good behavior.

We learn to behave in a socially approved manner even when it contradicts our selfish interests at the moment, initially out of fear of punishment and need of approval of the authorities on whom we are dependent. This presumes the presence of parental figures who are, first of all, present, and who themselves have the values that underlie decency and responsibility. Later we will internalize a model of goodness, an ego-ideal, the person we would like to be, the person we feel we ought to be. This internalized model will be the standard by which we measure ourselves. When we fail this ideal self, we will have betrayed a sense of our own potential. We will have done an injustice to which we aspire to be, and to what we might have been. What we will then feel is not fear, which is the emotion of the beast, but guilt, the uniquely human emotion. When we find ourselves behaving according to the standards of this ego-ideal, we will feel suffused with the warmth of self-pride. Our achievement of this goal demands the presence of models. The child must be attended to in the earliest stage by loving primary caretakers who set standards of behavior, if he is to grow into an adult with a conscience.

Still another form of identification must be discussed, for it contributes to the focus and strength of empathy. For want of a better term, I have referred to this as "downward identification." The traditional identification, which I have called "upward iden-tification," or simply, "identification," is typically represented by the child's identification with the parent and is what I have been describing. Downward identification is another thing entirely.

What is one to make of the almost instant identification that the parent makes with the child at its moment of birth? This sense that I experienced at the birth of my own children, and at the birth of my grandchildren, was like an epiphany. As a phenomenon, it seems much more closely related to the instant bonding of a duck for the first object it sees moving than to traditional human modes of response. Unlike friendship, which takes time to mature; unlike love, which requires experience, sharing, vulnerability, trust, and commitment—this had the quality of chemical reaction.

Why even call it "identification"? It doesn't have the trappings of traditional identification. We don't model ourselves after our children. We don't say that we look like our children: they look like us. We don't adopt their mannerisms, their tastes, their judgments, or their values. If we are lucky, we are delighted to find them adopting some of ours. However, the basic ingredient that defines identification is not modeling but, rather, the fusion of the self with another, the blurring of the boundaries of the self.

With upward identification, we incorporate the parental figure and then fuse with that "introject" to the point where we no longer know where we end and they begin. With downward identification with a child, the process of fusion tends to be total and instantaneous. If anything, the confusion about where I end and they begin is more profound in this direction than the other. To do damage to my child is to injure me, is to cause me perhaps the greatest pain. The grief over the loss of a child is the equivalent of the open, festering, and agonizing sore of Philoctetes, which is destined never to heal.

What has happened here in my identification with my child? I have not swallowed her up, introjected her. I have somehow or other catapulted myself into her shell. My children are containers, and fragile ones at that, which cradle not just my hopes and my ambitions, my aspirations and my vanities, but my essential self. They are me.

In some mysterious way, with this kind of identification we locate our core within another's corpus. We have our faith and our destiny packaged in a body under someone else's control. If my child does something irresponsible or willfully self-destructive, the pain will be experienced by hapless and innocent me. In great part this explains why no one is capable of enraging us as much as our own children. They carry the helpless parent within them during all their foolish and sometimes treacherous escapades. How dare they risk the purpose of my existence, my only immortality, my existential "meaning," by endangering themselves?

Downward identification has the power and fixity that are associated with biologically driven and species-preserving devices. It is a human variation on the traditional animal theme of maternal instinct. It brings to the fore all of the protective devices necessary in a parent during the dangerous period of existence before society itself adopted some of the protective functions. Like the protective behavior of a doe, it will ensure the survival of the species. By sacrificing herself for her offspring, the mother, animal or human, carries genes forward beyond that which would be capable in the limits of her lifetime. Her child will transport essential components of her self to her children, and to future generations. With civilization, these primitive mechanisms are less essential for the species, and carries too great a force given the current realities. Social institutions will support the survival of the species; the marauder is rarely at the gate.

We must not allow this powerful identification, this fusion, to become so powerful that we forget our primary responsibility as a parent. It is not to make a clone of ourselves, but to nurture a child to a point of autonomy and independence. The child is not created to extend our narcissistic selves, to become compensatory mechanisms for our frustrations and failures. We must not encourage the child's dependence on us. Nor must we do worse by denying the child the right to become an independent and unique creature. Too often the child is viewed as a new self, offering us an opportunity to rectify the inadequacies of current existence. It is not just that the child will be forced to attempt to become the writer, ball player, musician that we were unable to become. Some parents view the child as the reincarnation of the failed self—the "I" that never was. These parents will see the child not just as an ally or extension of themselves but as a corrected self.

When we treat the child as an instrument for the fulfillment of our own frustrated dreams, we violate the Kantian moral imperative to always treat a person as an end rather than a means, and we do it to the person who is most precious to us. If the parent obsessively serves his own frustrations through too powerful a downward identification, it can be a nightmare for the child, who will eventually find ways to wreak vengeance on the overly manipulative parent.

These processes of identification are helpful in understanding some of the contradictions in the workings of conscience. Why, for example, are we more capable of being committed to those people who are separated from us in time—that is, future generations—than to those who are separated from us in space, like the tragically dispossessed inhabitants of the underdeveloped world? In an age when the inheritance-tax laws were more flexible, fortunes were left to unknown people of unknown character who just happened to be biological descendants. Since few of us have any capacity to envision our forebears of a few generations back, about whom we have some information, how can we feel a responsibility to, or affection for, our descendants a few generations forward, about whom we know nothing? Somehow we can envision grandchildren who do not exist as replications and continuities of ourselves.

The answer lies in a phenomenon I have labeled "proximal identification," which is best understood by comparing our responses to tragic events. Proximal identification is not a moral principle but a psychological reality, an indisputable, universal phenomenon.

There is no question that an injury to my child, even of a trivial sort, hurts me more than a major injury to the child of a friend. In my sensibilities, my child's pain has a transcendent importance over your child's pain. I am not pleased by this observation—it represents a limit on my capacity for empathy—but I am convinced it is true. If I extend the argument further, it becomes more horrifying but no less true. A severe trauma to my child, a scarring that would affect her life over a lifetime, would grieve me more than the death of hundreds of thousands of children from starvation in the sub-Sahara.

Let me clarify what I am saying. Of course I am distressed by the agony and injustice exemplified by famine in Africa. When I witness this tragedy on the faces of real people through the pictures on television, or only in my imagination while I am reading the newspapers, a sense of true grief overcomes me; it is not simply an intellectual response. But this grief has a pathetically ephemeral experience. Although I may maintain my intellectual involvement and moral commitment through relief activities, my true emotions will not be the same as those caused by the everyday awareness of an injured child who shares my life. The most refined of consciences, the most overdeveloped capacity for guilt, will nonetheless defy our logical sense of justice and override our sense of proportionality when dealing with our own vis-á-vis others.

Having dealt with human suffering on the most intimate level in my work with patients, I know that true suffering is a proximal quality. Only those rare academics who are sheltered from the grief of others by the insulating wall of their theoretical constructions propose that the great burden oppressing our children is the threat of atomic warfare or other such universal existential constructs projected out of our political concerns. The old joke about the division of labor in a marriage holds true. The mind may take care of the "important" issues like worldwide hunger, the depletion of the ozone layer, and the threat of atomic war; the heart is grieved and pained by the "unimportant" factors—how will my child ever get into college if he doesn't get his priorities in order; how will I take care of my mother, in a nursing home or in my own home; how will we manage to pay for either on the money I am now earning? The *importance* of conscience is in its capacity to drive us to transcend selfish interests; the *limits* of conscience are set by proximal identification.

We are grieved by the everyday, by what we see. The priority of the daily papers and television programs in projecting local news over international news is testament to the interests of the audience. More true grief and tears were generated in the weeks before Christmas in 1988, in the New York area at least, by the crash of a London-to New York Pan American airliner than by the loss of as many as 150,000 lives caused by the earthquake in Soviet Armenia. More exact comparisons could be made with the downing of an Iranian airline in the Persian Gulf by an American warship, the *Vincennes*. Here was another aircraft packed with civilians, totally destroyed. What grief may have been felt was minimal and only too quickly replaced by a defensive anger, necessitated by the political significance of the act. What official contrition may have been felt we never knew, since the response of our government was outrage that the plane, on a scheduled flight, should have intruded on the space of our missile.

The nearby disaster has more meaning, even though lesser than the distant one. It is not a new idea. As Hume observed over two hundred years ago: "Pity depends, in a great measure, on the contiguity and even sight of the object."[16] Maybe proximal identification does not require the physical closeness to or sight that Hume suggests but it requires something comparable.

The concept of proximal identification will allow us to form kinships that extend into a future too far for us to envision and back to a past we never experienced. The chaos in Ireland, taking the lives of hundreds of innocents, will touch the Irish American who has never been to Ireland more than the loss of a hundred thousand lives in Iran. A terrorist bomb placed on a bus full of Israeli children will break the heart of an American Jew who has never been to Israel.

These linkages—ethnic, religious—with the limitations of empathy they imply, for good or bad, can be seen as deriving from important survival patterns built into our genetic matrix before the anticipation of modern culture. Proximal identification may seem irrational and unjust in our current period, when we are approaching a global culture, but it must have been a biologically adaptive mechanism at a more primitive time. The units of survival in prehistoric times were much smaller than those of today. There were no nations, and there was no consideration of the universality of man. There were only family clusters. Survival of the species, particularly of the independent human young, demanded an overvaluation of, and extreme sensitivity to, the needs of the young who are our own specific charges.

In herding animals, the herd is best protected when the antelope protects her offspring, and hers alone, from the marauding lion. If every mother were concerned about all the young, none would survive. The propensity of human beings to overvalue their own offspring is a part of the biological inheritance we share with these lower, communal or herding animals. It is given a new meaning and new enhancement by the processes of identification that are so specifically human. In herding animals, the female protects her own young, and the male protects the general herd. In the human being, with the intense capacity for identification with our own that will last a lifetime, both male and female will continue to idealize and overvalue their own "young," long past the children's age of dependency has passed.

Let me return to the thesis that began this chapter. Morality is exclusively a human enterprise, and conscience is the ultimate expression of that morality. Clearly the authors of Genesis regarded morality as exclusively a human attribute. This is a conviction held by almost every serious student of ethics to the present. For an action to have a moral significance, it must involve some executive choice on the part of the actor. Things that are mandated, by whatever means, cannot be judged evil. All significant actions of animals are dictated by their genetic constitution. For this reason, only the behavior of human beings can be judged "good" or "evil." The ravaging of a baby gazelle by a pack of wild dogs who tear the flesh from the bones of the living creature may be disgusting and offensive in the eyes of an observing human being, but we do not judge the dogs evil. Their behavior is in the nature of the hunt and the necessity of survival. It is, we will say, the "nature of the beast."

When we talk of animals doing wrong, it is most likely in relation to domestic animals, which have been imbued by us with human characteristics and on whom we project a humanoid type of morality. "Bad dog" is said in a stern and moralistic tone to suggest our lack of approval an approval we have conditioned the dog to need. It is, however, a simple command, like "Heel," "Stay," or "Fetch," to indicate behavior that is socially acceptable or unacceptable to the human being. It is a training device, not a moral judgment. Moral values are reserved for actions of the only truly autonomous creature, the human being.

I started with the assumption that only human beings can be judged as moral, and that such judgment is based on an evaluation of their behavior, not their fantasies or thoughts. One aspect of the perceptual mind that is valid when ascribing moral judgment is intention. With human beings as well as animals, when we sense that some action is beyond their control, we reduce our sense of their responsibility. This is most clearly seen when we translate morality into law. The very definition of what is criminal is conditioned by the voluntariness of the action and the mental state of the actor, his perceptions and his intentions. The psychic state of the accused is encompassed by the legal term *mens rea,* and it dominates our attitudes about the most heinous of crimes, even to the point of determining what we will label a crime.

A man who falls off a ladder onto another man kills him by the force of the fall. No civilized person or state would call this "murder," or act as though the man falling from the ladder were criminal. It was clearly an accident; there was no intention involved. All of this is taken into account by the legal definition of *mens rea.* The mental set of the individual, his intentions and purposes, is inherent in the definition of the legal judgment of culpability, and also in that of our moral judgment.

There are conditions in which the intentions of the action are not taken into account. If a drunkard was climbing the side of a building in a public space and fell, killing a passerby, we would find him guilty—not of murder, but of a lesser charge, such as "reckless endangerment." If a man accidentally killed a man while committing a felony, some jurisdictions would treat the accidental death as murder.

"Homicide" literally means "person (man) killing." But there is "justifiable homicide" and there is "first-degree murder" (always reserved for the most heinous and calculated of crimes), and between these two offenses is a series of intervening charges that express the state's sense of mitigating conditions. Each downward modification, or lightening of charge, implies that the state's moral judgment finds the crime somewhat less of an evil.

To murder someone in cold blood in order to rob him of his possessions is different from killing that same person in a passion after a sense of personal betrayal. Both constitute evil wrongdoing in the most crucial moral sense, but one is considered more evil than the other by our society. Different cultures will make different judgments. In all, however, there will be a lessening of responsibility because of either the intention of the individual or the conditions surrounding the act. Ultimately, if the homicide is done in defense of self or family, it is considered neither morally wrong nor criminal. Similarly, if done by an insane person who is deemed not to have the capacity to distinguish right from wrong, the person will be found "not guilty by reason of insanity." Obviously both of the above are not only innocent of crime, but morally innocent of wrongdoing. At the heart of all moral judgments resides the idea of freedom, and its consequent though conveniently forgotten correlate, responsibility. Only human beings are freed from the strictures of gene and instinct. Only human beings are moral agents.

Since only human beings are capable of doing evil or being virtuous, it seems appropriate that concern about morality is also a specifically human function. We can safely assume that there is no animal besides *Homo sapiens* who agonizes over the propriety of a piece of behavior. If there is hesitation before action in an animal, it is to judge the safety or the propitiousness of the action, not its moral implications. We analyze our own behavior, and feel guilty when we recognize, for example, the unfairness of some aspects of proximal identification. Why are we ashamed to admit that we still grieve over our child's lameness, or merely our child's disappointment, long after we have ceased to feel any emotion about the children who died in the last drought in Ethiopia? The antelope does not feel guilty for overvaluing her child. It is the very nature of human conscience, so precise and distinct from anything that exists in any other creature, that allows us even to question a basic integrative and organizing biological directive that served our species well for the millions of years before culture, and may once again be called upon to serve our species if we destroy the vestiges of culture in some atomic madness.

The operations of conscience exhibit the nobility of what we can be, and the violations of its imperatives distress us, for we are failing to fulfill our potential. This feeling of having violated our own ideals of self is a specifically human grief. It is the grief of Pinocchio, a grief near love. The same Pinocchio who greedily ate the pears that Geppetto had brought for himself—all of the pears— will give his last forty pence to buy "a mouthful of bread" for the poor sick Fairy lying in bed at the house.

In the beginning of *Pinocchio*, Geppetto sells his coat—a coat that is needed for warmth, not vanity—to buy Pinocchio a spelling book. Pinocchio, narcissistically and cynically, uses the money to see a puppet show. Even though I am aware that *Pinocchio* was written serially in a newspaper, one chapter seeming to follow the other with no particular concern for smoothness of story line, Collodi was, after all, a writer, and it must be that in his last chapter he sees the need to make an organic whole of his tale. It cannot be by chance that he returns to the symbol of the coat. The forty pence that Pinocchio had given to the Fairy was what he had saved to buy himself a new coat:

"'Oh, poor Fairy, poor Fairy, poor Fairy! . . . If I had a million I would run and carry it to her . . . but I have only forty pence. . . . Here they are; I was going to buy a new coat. Take them, Snail, and carry them at once to my good Fairy.'

"'And your new coat?'

"'What matters my new coat? I would sell even these rags that I have got on to be able to help her.'"[17]

This expression of the possession of a "good heart" endows Pinocchio with his humanity. He has become a real boy. Real boys do not always behave well, as the Blue Fairy acknowledges, yet their humanity is not predicated on perfect behavior, but on the possession of a human sensibility, a good heart:

"'Well done, Pinocchio! To reward you for your good heart I will forgive you for all that is past. Boys who minister tenderly to their parents, and assist them in their misery and infirmities, are deserving of great praise and affection, even if they cannot be cited as examples of obedience and good behavior. Try and do better in the future and you will be happy.'"[18]

Pinocchio will continue to do good *and* bad, because he is a human being, not a saint, but he will hear the voice of conscience and suffer when he violates the standards that have now become his own.

This capacity for empathy, compassion, and self-sacrifice goes beyond conscience and approaches the ultimate attainment of the human being, the ultimate expression of our humanity—mature love.

LOVE [1]

~~~~~~~~~~~~~~~~

CONSCIENCE DISTINGUISHES AND ELEVATES OUR SPECIES. It encompasses all the inbuilt devices that guide us, at least occasionally, to making morally right decisions. But the term itself has a distant and mechanistic ring, suggesting sobriety, duty, and self-denial. It is of the vocabulary of duty, rather than that of nobility and celebration. "A good heart," by contrast, has an ebullient, almost merry quality, and suggests more than just good behavior. It describes the whole character of a person and predicts the nature of his life and relationships. To say that John is goodhearted is to bring us closer to describing a loving nature than simply to say that John has a conscience. "A good heart" evokes connotations of affection and joy. It suggests that we not only behave well but get pleasure from such behavior. It brings the relationship of one to another to the forefront: it bridges goodness and love.

The Fairy with the Blue Hair plays multiple roles in *Pinocchio*, but mostly she is the teacher of love in all of its forms. Pinocchio first meets the Fairy when he is pursued by assassins. He is frantic for help, almost despairing, and ready to succumb to the assassins. He sees a house in the distance and knocks agitatedly at the door, kicking and pummeling with all his might. In response to his clamor, a window opens and "a beautiful Child appeared at it." She has blue hair and a face as white as a waxen image. She announces that there is no one in this house. There is no help for Pinocchio there; they are all dead. Pinocchio pleads with her. "At least open the door for me yourself," shouted Pinocchio, crying and imploring. "I am dead also" is her answer, as the window closes.[2]

With each reappearance throughout the story, the image of the Blue Fairy changes. Poor Pinocchio is apprehended by the assassins. They attempt to kill him by stabbing him, but of course he is not a boy, he is a puppet, and the hard wood breaks their knives. So they hang him and wait for him to die, "but at the end of three hours the puppet's eyes were still open, his mouth closed, and he was kicking more than ever."[3]

The Blue Child reappears shortly, and it is now apparent that she is a fairy. From this point on, she will take a maternal role toward Pinocchio, guiding him toward proper and good behavior. It is she who teaches him he must not lie, that lying is "the most disgraceful fault that a boy can have."[4]

In saying this, the good Fairy joins all the social-contract theoreticians in that great philosophical tradition that elevates truth-telling—in that it underlies all trust and confidence that binds people together—to the transcendental virtue. Pinocchio's punishment for lying is that his nose becomes long and ridiculous, exactly like that of the snout of an animal or the nose of a wooden puppet. It takes him further from his goal to become a real boy, reducing his stature and diminishing his "humanity."

Pinocchio, not seeing his own nose, is bewildered at how the Fairy knows he lied, in exactly the same way a child is overwhelmed by the seeming omniscience of the mother who accuses him of eating the forbidden jam when she sees it all across his face. To the discerning parent, the innocent and ridiculous lie of a child is always as plain as the nose (or jam) on his face.

The Fairy seems to forgive all. She is always compassionate, a word that is repeated constantly in describing her. She is the understanding mother who adores the child with all of his imperfections. She represents the true love that all of us will seek to replicate through our lifetime—a love that is unearned and undeserved, that is unconditional.

Pinocchio delights in the loving nature of the Fairy and declares his love for her, but of course he does not love her, even though he thinks he does. He is as yet incapable of love, for he does not understand its ingredients. He makes the mistake that too many adults in our narcissistic culture are likely to make—the assumption that the delight in being loved is an equivalent to loving or having a loving nature. In a mature relationship, being loved is assuredly one of the components in a complicated and unpredictable system of giving and taking. It cannot, however, be used as a substitute for reciprocity. In a mature love relationship, we can indulge our need to be loved. Mature love is rich and generous enough to adapt to the specific needs of each partner. There is a pleasure in knowing that you can feel free to be childish and vulnerable, allow yourself to be cared for—comforted by the knowledge that when your partner also has this need you will then be capable of being the nurturer, the caretaker, the responsible parent.

Mature love requires—and enjoys—this flexibility. What is pathetic in so many of our modern relationships is the preoccupation with the passive role. In a peculiar way, we seem to elevate the role of the infant above that of the parent. It seems preferred, more desirable. Romantic love requires two adults mature enough to tolerate their partners' being childish at times and prepared to give up their own childish needs during these periods. Something strange is happening in our modern culture. The crib seems preferable to the nuptial bed, and both partners are fighting to crawl into it. This situation will not allow romantic love to flourish.

The narcissist in our midst not only craves to be loved always; he craves to be loved in a specific way. He wants to be loved "for himself," not for what he does. He values love that is "freely bestowed," not earned, as though somehow any effort to earn that love would diminish it.

What can it possibly mean, to be loved for oneself alone—not for one's virtues, one's actions, one's body, one's beauty, one's mind? What else is one except the sum of all these behaviors, actions, and perceptions? There is no "inner self" that is independent of our character and our form. It can only mean one thing. There is only one time when one is loved for oneself independent of one's behavior, and that of course is in the first stages of early infancy.

There is little about the *behavior* of a newborn to delight anyone. His eyes are usually out of focus; he is likely to disturb our sleep and exhaust our energy with demands that cannot be fulfilled; his cries of rage are coercive demands for—what? We cannot always know. And when he sheds tears of pain, we often fail to discover a source that can be corrected. He violates all the rules. He behaves in a way that will be greeted with dismay and disapproval even in the young child: he will interrupt our dinners, refuse to maintain any reasonable schedule, pass gas, urinate, or defecate in public. He demands everything and gives nothing. And we adore him. This is what is meant by "true love." This represents being loved not for what one "does" but for what one "is."

Even if Pinocchio has learned the pleasure of being loved but not yet the capacity for love, at least he is taking one step toward that goal. Pinocchio, like the newborn child, originally accepted the tender ministrations and noble sacrifices of his adoring father, Geppetto, as his just due. But throughout the book, Pinocchio is learning. By the middle of the story, chapter 25, he has determined to become a human being. Here he once again encounters the little Fairy with the Blue Hair, but this time she is in the form of a woman. The Fairy has undergone her own transformations: first a child, now a sister, and eventually a maternal figure.

Pinocchio is amazed at how rapidly the Fairy has grown and matured. It is reminiscent of Mark Twain's oft-quoted statement: "When I was a boy of fourteen my father was so ignorant I could hardly stand to have the old man around. But when I got to be twenty-one I was astonished at how much he had learned in seven years."[5] It is Pinocchio who is changing as he is exposed to both the kindnesses and the harshness of human nature and the real world.

Pinocchio recognizes the Fairy despite her transformation, and when asked by the Fairy how he recognized her, he answers: "It was my great affection for you that told me."[6] This affection, again, sees beyond the form and the shape of the individual. It is a sign of the maturing Pinocchio. He wonders why the good Fairy can change so rapidly but he never changes. She informs him that puppets never grow: they are born puppets, live puppets, and die puppets.

The human being changes dramatically in the course of his development. He is born helpless and incomplete, with all his adaptive capacities existing only in potentil form. The nature of environmental differences will determine the degree to which the potential is realized, if at all, and the form that the potential will take. This explains both the remarkable divergence in behavior of the immature and the mature human, and the extraordinary variations (as compared with all other animal) among adult human beings. The capacity for mature love represents the most complete expression of humanness. Its achievement requires an environment of loving, and the capacity to grow over an extended life experience.

The good Fairy instructs Pinocchio in what he is to do to become a real boy—he must be obedient, learn to work, speak the truth, and diligently go to school. She does this because he has already demonstrated that he has the stuff of humanity within him, through the following exchange. Pinocchio tells the Blue Fairy that he had believed her to be dead, having viewed her gravestone:

" 'If you only knew the sorrow I felt and the tightening of my throat when I read 'Here lies . . .' "

" 'I know it, and it is on that account that I have forgiven you. I saw this from the sincerity of your grief that you had a good heart; and when boys have good hearts, even if they are scamps and have bad habits, there is always something to hope for.' "[7]

It is through the *loss* of love that Pinocchio first understands the *meaning* of love, and it is through the same loss of love in any of its various forms that most of us become exposed most nakedly to both our need for love and the meaning of love. In a certain sense, death of a loved one is sometimes more tolerable than abandonment or rejection. Much crueler is the knowledge that the absence was by choice. Even more unbearable is the awareness that it was the choice of one we had idealized and cherished. With such rejection we experience humiliation and self-diminution, in addition to loss.

Rejection or abandonment by a loved one is in many ways the opposite of the exhilarating experience of falling in love. Rather than the delight of anticipating imminent passionate fusion, there occurs an unexpected mutilation—the unexpected cleavage of the self. We are left in a transient period of confusion. Who are we? We do not seem to be the same. We do not recognize our own "self." We seem incomplete.

The entire scenario of bereavement can be played out with any abandonment. Mature love is so much a part of the fabric of life that we do not recognize the threads out of which it is constructed until some of those threads are ripped out of the whole. Mature love does, indeed, press into consciousness most cruelly at the moment of its loss.

If loving is not the same as being loved, and if love goes unnoticed in our ordinary existence while still nourishing us, what, then, is love? What are the essential elements that in our view constitute the human capacity for love, and what is the nature of the experience of love?

Love is the cohesive and civilizing force in human life. This was perhaps most eloquently expressed in the classic writings of the Greek philosopher, from the fifth century B.C., Empedocles.[8] Here love was seen not as in conflict with reason but in contrast to strife. Aphrodite was the bonding, compassionate, and unifying force in nature, here considered the antagonist of Ares, the god of war and destruction. This concept of two life forces, which Empedocles called "love" and "strife," was to be replicated at its strongest in the late nineteenth century with the concept of a life force, "élan vital," to use the term of the influential French philosopher Henri Bergson Vitalism, the concept of an internal force that drove human behavior, was to influence almost all of the major thinkers at the turn of the century, including Schopenhauer, Nietzsche, and Freud.

The image of the heavenly Aphrodite, the consolidating force of love, is seen at its purest in the relationship of parent to child. Here is something close to the bonding that occurs with animals, although no animal so tries the patience and endurance of the parent as the human child with its exaggerated period of dependency and growth.

Love is not to be equated with the genetic bonding of animals—it is less and more. It is surely less immutable, as is evident from the number of neglecting parents and even more so from the existence of barbaric parents who beat and batter their children. But the bonding of animals is usually directed upward from a newborn animal to the first object in its visual field. It is unrelated to ideation or even emotion. Its intense fixity has been demonstrated in those ludicrous examples where a young duckling will inadvertently see a cow, a horse, or even a garbage pail before its mother and bond to that visual object. The duckling will remain bonded to the cow, for example, following it with a "devotion" that is in every way equal to the behavior of its fellow ducklings who managed to focus on the proper imprint.

The human infant is born too incomplete to imprint at the moment of birth. The neurology is not yet set. The tissue will demand the stimulations of an environment to develop slowly, so that neurons may be myelinated, multiply, and grow. Cortical tissue must yet evolve to permit this complex and autonomous, self-determining and self-designing, agent that is a human being to be capable of the elaborate human emotion of love.

Nonetheless, the response I had personally experienced of almost instantaneous bonding on viewing my first grandchild shocked me with its rapidity and its irrationality, and impressed me with its chemical and automatic nature, so similar to animal bonding. It was such a profound and mysterious experience. I knew my entire sensibility had changed—that a new "me" existed—and it happened immediately. I experienced it as an almost painful sense of fullness, a sense of "too much" that made me seem stretched to the limits of sensitivity and vulnerability. A secret message had entered my nervous system, readjusting all the patterns of my consciousness. To the lifetime of experiences that had shaped my characteristic perceptions and behavior, a new one had been added of such a magnitude that I would never be quite the same. If I were experiencing this, separated in space by a nursery window and from the actual time of birth by an hour, what must a mother experience at the moment of birth, seeing this creature emerge from the self?

Literature is full of mothers' responses to seeing their new children and their sense of immediate and instant dedication. It is rare to find literature indicating that a father can also feel this way. It is why I cherish C. P. Snow's description of a father receiving his newborn son into his arms. He is shocked at his own response. He feels utterly alien from this being presented to him, but at the same time he was "possessed by the insistence, in which there was nothing like tenderness, which was more savage and angry than tender, that he must live and that nothing bad should happen to him."

"Partly I felt I could not get used to it, it was too much for me, it had been too quick, this was only a scene of which I was a spectator. Partly I felt a tug at the fibers as though I were being called on in a way I did not understand; as though what had entered into me could not yet translate itself into an emotion, into terms of anything I could recognize and feel."[9]

I am aware of historic studies indicating that in some societies, and at various times, children were not highly valued. The conclusions that are drawn from this seem patently erroneous. Authors go on to assume the value of the child is a recent discovery, rather than recognizing that societies that placed so little value on the life of a child were societies in which the majority of children would die. The casual acceptance of death, the embracing of a religion ennobling the afterlife, and the apparent stoicism were simply defenses against the inevitable. The death of a child represents the ultimate pain and sacrifice in the religions and mythologies of diverse peoples across too many cultures and too many time periods to be considered other than a universal feeling of the species.

It is a mistake to see the child's love of a parent as a parallel phenomenon to parental love. I know children love parents, but I do not think their emotion has the same order or even the same quality as the parental love for a child. Parental love of a child is the most instinctually fixed of all love patterns—of necessity, because it is the ultimate guarantee of the survival of the helpless newborn. The child, on the other hand, must learn to love the parent. In the process, the child learns to love the services before the person. His is consequently a selfish love, not an altruistic one.

The energies, the love, the devotion, and the life of the parents are the resources to be consumed by the child in building his own capacities to be such a parent.

Like Pinocchio, a child probably does not love or need to love until he comes of age. At each step he will enhance his capacity for loving but may never experience the full measure of filial love until the parent is either "rediscovered" when the child is an adult or rediscovered by identification when he himself becomes a parent.

But filial and parental love are still not romantic love. They are considered by most to be nonsexual kinds of love. Romantic love is the most difficult form to experience and the most difficult to sustain. It is a volatile mixture of two potent forces which must coexist in one relationship: the caring and tender aspects on the one hand, and erotic desire on the other. Romantic love, in fusing these two passions, creates something quite different from the elements that compose it.

There are three processes essential to the development of mature love: fusion, idealization, and commitment. The first two occur in an automatic way beyond the control of the individual; his imagination weaves the experience and produces the effect. Commitment is another story. It demands an act of faith, courage, and trust.

Fusion may have existed as the very earliest experience of the infant, the very first stage of awareness. In the imaginary scenarios that all psychoanalysts spin in trying to fathom the thinking of a newborn, there exists a popularly held one that assumes we were born in a state of fusion. Margaret Mahler proposes that the first sensibility of the individual was not as a self but as a thing joined with the mother, a dyad.[10]

In this way Mahler, whether wittingly or unwittingly, was repeating the myth of Aristophanes that occurs in Plato's *Symposium*. Aristophanes also assumes that the human being was originally constructed as a fusion of male and female and through the jealousy of the Gods was sundered. In this delightful, romantic image, we are incomplete, searching for our other half until in love we once again rejoin ourselves. In the words of Aristophanes:

"Human nature was originally one and we were whole, and the desire and pursuit of that whole is called love."[11]

This capacity of an adult human being to form a state of oneness with another human being is what I call "fusion." It is one of the essential components that helps to define not just romantic love but all forms of loving. The presence of fusion relates the love of parent to love of child, to love of spouse, and for that matter to love of God, country, or ideal. I am uncompromising in the way I use "fusion." I use it literally to mean the loss of one's identity in that of another, a confusion of ego boundaries, a sense of unsureness as to where I end and you, the person I love, begin—the identification of your pain with my pain and your success with my success, the inconceivability of a self that does not include you, and the inevitability that your loss will create a painful fracture of my self-image, which will necessitate long and painful rebuilding of my ego during a period of grief and despair. The common ingredient of all love is this merging of the self with another person or ideal, creating a new identity.

But isn't it axiomatic in almost any psychology that a normal person ought to know who he is? Someone who is not sure of his own identity, who confuses himself with another being, must be a madman. Isn't this the cliché of the psychotic with delusions of being God, Jesus, or Napoleon?

It is true that in psychosis there is a loss of self-boundary; the inability to know where the self begins and ends is a sign of a delusion. Loss of ego boundaries is a very serious psychopathology *except* in one condition: the condition we call love. This very blurring of boundaries is the essential hallmark of fusion and of loving.

Freud was aware of this and was not at all sure whether, in addition to occurring in "madness," fusion could not also exist in "love." "At the height of being in love the boundary between the ego and the object threatens to melt away. . . . A man who is in love declares that 'I' and 'you' are one and is prepared to behave as if it were a fact."[12]

Many philosophers had difficulty with the idea of "merger." Christian theologians clung to a sense of the psychological world that was consonant with the world of actuality, and that therefore must conform to the laws of logic inherent in that world. Psychoanalysis was shaped to the models of German idealism that dominated thinking during the period in which Freud created this new field. The "real" world that we live in, according to psychoanalysis, is not some "actual" world out there. The internal world of our own perception is the reality to which we respond, that shapes our personal heaven and hell.

The Christian philosophers of the Middle Ages describe this phenomenon I have described with words like "being joined" or "glued together": "Thou art in me and I am Thee glued together as one and the self same thing." Or "like rain falling from the Heavens; into a river or spring there is nothing but water there and it is impossible to divide or separate the water belonging to the river from that which fell from the Heavens."[13] In Christian philosophy, "merger" was a heretic concept except when used for the human relationship to the divine.

I will reserve "merger," then, for the theologians, and will use the term "fusion" for what occurs in love. The dripping, sinking, immersing liquid roots from which the word "merge" derives (from the Latin mergere, "to dive, plunge") are more suggestive of the spiritual world, anyhow. "Fusion," with its literal meaning of "melting by heat," allows for a physical passion more appropriate to love.

Words gain fresh meaning within differing cultural contexts. In our modern economic terminology, "merger" is now linked with "acquisition" and possesses a connotation of the possessive, expansive self-interest of the corporate world. It is pedantic, dull, statistical; whereas "fusion" has the frightening but awesome connotation of nuclear power. "Fusion" in our modern world is indeed the more appropriate metaphor.

The closest Freud ever came to love, and the closest to "merger" or "fusion" in the main body of his theoretical work, was in the title I have previously cited on identification. The concept of identification was so close to that of fusion that one wonders why it was not quickly and readily extended. Perhaps this failure to extend the concept of identification was due to the fact that in early Freudian theory all character formation was assumed to be limited to the first few years of life. Only with post-Freudian psychology did we begin to appreciate that we could find our "introjects" throughout life. Fusion, while common to all forms of love, differs with each form of love, but in all of its forms it is exclusively and nobly a functions of the human mind and heart.

Idealization, the second component of love, undoubtedly exists in all of the forms of love. "My dad can lick your dad" and "My mother is the most beautiful in the whole world" are common statements of childhood that testify to the child's idealization of the parent. But idealization is apparent at its most intense, and in that sense at its most distorted, in early parental love and in romantic love. The early parental idealization of the child, which allows each mother to see her child as the most beautiful and most precious, is obviously rooted in the same automatic devices previously described as essential for survival of the species. It is a fixed and rapidly induced phenomenon that suggests the chemical or instinctual bonding of lower species. The mechanism of its induction is quite different from the idealization that will occur in mature romantic love.

Freud had the imagination and intuition to have discovered all the elements of love without having had the inclination or motivation to put them together into an integrated theory of love. It probably was a reflection of the richness of his imagination—so many insights piling one on another, the storerooms full of raw materials; one lifetime simply could not encompass building everything that could be created out of these wonderful deductions

Freud saw human desire as arising from almost the opposite direction as animal desire. The pheromones (olfactory stimulants) released by the female animal in heat automatically trigger the sexual behavior of the male animal and drive him to her. In Freudian theory, exactly the opposite occurs in human beings. The desire does not arise from the loved one; instead, the sexual appetite originates within ourselves, male or female, and we invest that sexual energy in some love object, at which point, to use the awkward vocabulary of psychoanalysis, we are said to have "cathected the object."

The human male or female may release some pheremones, but if so they have little to do with sexual desire, and less to do with sexual activity. The diminished sense of smell in the human being as compared with other animals is further evidence of the dissociation between smell and reproduction. Rather, we cathect the object of our love with our own sexual energy. In so doing, we have enlarged the person we love and created an idealized image. What we are passionately drawn to, then, is not the unadorned and uninvested sexual object that exists in some real world of which we are unaware, but a sexual object we have created by investing her with attributes that *we* have supplied. In this discussion, Freud constantly confuses desire with love. He is talking of the mechanisms of sexual appetite when he uses words like "cathecting an object" but is describing a phenomenon that is central to love and absent from lust.

Pygmalion is the ideal mythic character to illustrate the classical Freudian theory of idealization. Pygmalion, according to Freudian theory, would not have fallen in love with Galatea except that he had created her to his ideal image of womanhood. It is not the creation of another sculptor with whom he falls in love. That would have been a different story, a lesser one, and inconsistent with the Freudian view of passion. Galatea must be the product of Pygmalion's artistic imagination in exactly the same way that every romantic love is a creation of the artistic imagination of the lover.

Stendhal anticipated Freud's concept of the idealization of a loved object with his imagery of crystallization. In the salt mines of Salzburg, it was traditional to strip a bough of its leaves in winter and throw it into the depths of the mine. In spring it would be retrieved, covered with brilliant crystals. Stendhal saw this phenomenon as a symbol of what happens between lovers, using the term "crystallization" to describe "that process of the mind which discovers fresh perfections in its beloved at every turn of events."[14]

Those of us who love are all Pygmalions. Romeo and Juliet, Dante and Beatrice, Héloïse and Abelard are all joint creations of nature and the imaginations of their beloveds. We all create for ourselves the loved persons we require. None of us acknowledge that this happens, that these traits are only in our imagination. We insist on seeing them as the actual stuff of the person.

This does not mean that the loved object is selected by chance. There are indeed limits. We are not likely to fall in love with anybody. The idealization is not randomly determined. It will be shaped by our own culture and also by the specific facts of our personal histories. Beauty or sexual appeal will have different definitions to different people. These esthetic biases will determine the values we set on the "raw materials," whether they be clay, wood, or marble, whether the person be fat, thin, black, white, passive, or aggressive. Basic attraction will be conditioned by our cultural, as well as our personal psychodynamic past.

Once these essential criteria are fulfilled, we can start the idealization process and are free to supplement the actual attributes of the individual with those we want him to possess. We endow him with the attributes we admire, independent of their roots in reality. Then we will begin a second stage of idealization. We will begin at the same time to romanticize whatever traits are actually part of the package.

Here I am going beyond Freud's conception of idealization and introducing a somewhat different, two-step event. It is not just anyone we choose to romanticize. We start with an ideal image conditioned by our past, perhaps our memories of our mother or our reactions to her—and even here it will not be our mother as she was but as we perceived her. Then, given the minimal illusion necessary to start the process, we will begin to see in the loved one what we need to see, what we choose to see. We will begin the process of idealization.

There may be yet another step, beyond idealization. The latter implies simply that beauty (or virtue or value) lies in the eye of the beholder. With less assurance than I hold for idealization, let me suggest that there may be a transforming aspect of love. The loved object may not only seem to be what we wish him to be; he may become that.

Consider the familiar story of "The Frog King," popularized by the version of the Brothers Grimm but already in existence for some three hundred years before that. Briefly, the story involves the obligation of a beautiful woman to live with (in some versions, to kiss) a frog. Repulsed by the slimy creature, the beautiful woman is nonetheless commanded by duty and honor, and in time she fulfills the commitment. With the fulfillment of the contract, the frog is inevitably and magically converted into a handsome prince. "The Frog King" is part of the genre that Bruno Bettelheim has labeled the "animal-groom cycle of fairy tales."[15] These tales include "Cupid and Psyche" and "Beauty and the Beast." Though Bettelheim analyzes the components in traditional psychoanalytic terms, with an emphasis on the ambivalent fascination that the genitalia have for the young girl in her emerging sexuality, these tales also clearly indicate the transforming nature of love. The Frog King, as a frog, not only ceases to be repellent to the young beauty; eventually he is transformed into a handsome prince. There are two distinct phases, both in this story and in "Beauty and the Beast." In the first phase, the heroine becomes conditioned to what the frog (or beast) is and begins to love what he is. In the second phase, the nature and fact of her developing love influence the reality of what he is perceived to be. The frog may not ever change except in the perception of the beauty and in his own perception, but, then, he may never have been a frog except in those perceptions. And, as in most aspects of human sensibilities, perception is all.

As with Mark Twain, the imagination and sensibility of all great creative artists often transcend the analytic intelligence of the philosopher or psychologist. I am on less firm ground here, but I am convinced that the vision of us held by our loved ones enters into and modifies our self-awareness. What we feel ourselves to be in turn contributes to what we will become. Love does transform us.

Fusion and idealization are the hallmarks of love, distinguishing the genuine thing from the tinselly infatuations and dramatic *folies à deux* that often pass for love. Fusion and idealization happen to us. They are unconscious phenomena that emerge despite ourselves and usually without our acknowledgment. But romantic love is more than the fiery and acute phenomenon depicted by the penetrating fire of Cupid's dart. It is a chronic condition, grown over time. Mature love does not just happen; it must be patiently constructed.

The third and least glamorous component of love, commitment, is of a different order. It requires patience, compromise, courage, and maturity. In order to understand the importance of commitment, it is essential to differentiate between "falling in love" and "loving" and to understand the nature and meaning of "passion."

"Passion" itself is a confusing term. It is too often used to define the intense experience, delightful as it is, that occurs in the initiation of a relationship, when we are falling in love. Here I will draw on the insight in Francesco Alberoni's recent book, *Falling in Love*.[16] In this book, Alberoni draws a distinction between "falling in love," which he describes as an act or event, and "loving," which is a phenomenon that occurs in time, a process, something that goes on.

Falling in love, happening at a moment in time, is a unique experience with its own particular joys. It happens *to* us; it does not issue from us. He calls falling in love a "nascent" state and the word seems particularly apt, for it means "coming into being, being born."

In chemistry, the word has a very specific meaning and, when applied here, a particularly informative one. A "nascent element" is an element that has just been released from a compound; *because it is new, it has unusual properties*. The nascent chemical acts differently from the chemical it is about to become because the atoms of the element have not yet combined to form the molecules that will give the element its fixed characteristics. Nascent chlorine, at the moment of its release from the compound, will not behave like the product it is in the process of becoming. It is different: in the nature of its behavior, in the predictability of its reactions (indeed, there is a certain unpredictability about all nascent states), and in its essential character.

So, too, falling in love is different from love. The elements that will finally be integrated into the mature state of love exist during the period of falling in love in an unstable association only. All of the elements of love are there, but the character of the two states is quite different.

Alberoni does not really deal with love itself until the end of his book, and then he decides that love must be the process of "repeatedly falling in love" with the same person. It is a romantic concept, but I am not sure it is necessarily so.

There is a process of rediscovery that occurs in love, and in other aspects of life as well. Lost in everydayness, in the actuality of living, we tend to be numb to the magic and mystery that are part of existence. Then, in some moment, we will re-examine the stars. We will notice, really notice, through the frame of a library window, the arch of oaks that have stood there unattended for weeks or months or years. We will see our loved one approaching from a distance and actually perceive her. We will have a heightened awareness of that person in some casual moment whose origin may be bound in mystery but which nonetheless catches us at the heart. We will rediscover love.

In the early stages of love, one sees passion at its most intense and most intimately bound to sexual drive. Sexual passion may be most intense during adolescence. With maturation, passion must be fed from a variety of different streams. The fervor of the "first touch" will inevitably diminish in time, but the familiar touch that replaces it has its own special excitement. There is a "knowing" quality about the familiar touch—with its shared secrets and common history—that can serve and sustain the passion of a mature love. Mature adults may nostalgically miss certain aspects of the adolescent period; we may wish for youth again and bemoan the burdens of aging; but very few of us would want to relive our teens. One cannot always live at a fevered pitch. Maturation means learning to appreciate the passion and joy inherent in the quieter nature of mature love. When love has ripened, passion survives well beyond the point where endocrines cease to circulate. This postfertile passion that exists only in human beings is empirically supported by evidence, not just a hypothesis of mine.

I do not want to deprecate the exhilirating titillation of falling in love. There is excitement in the new, a special passion in the anticipated and dangerous. One need not deny the specific pleasures of the state of falling in love in order to make claims about the pleasures of being in love. If you can have both at the same time, so much the better. The concept of passion can be broad enough to include both infatuation and commitment, and love can carry within itself the memory of falling in love.

We must not forget the true joys of loving. They are easy to forget, because they are so much quieter. It is so much more difficult to appreciate the process than the event. As C. S. Lewis put it, there is "no sudden striking an emotional transition [with love]. Like the warming of a room or the coming of daylight, when you first notice them they have already been going on for some time."[17]

Nothing about human love—no component, from the sexual aspect to the ripening of mature love, including idealization, fusion, passion, falling in love, or what I have described as mature love—can be equated with animal instinct or animal bonding. One cannot imagine the goose—which is always being presented by sociobiologists as being more faithful in its monogamy than the human being—ever falling in love or ever truly loving. Imagination is at the heart of human love, as it is at the basis of all our art and our culture.

But what of the flight from mature love, the almost frantic abandonment of commitment in pursuit of adolescent forms of passion, that now seems epidemic in our culture? I suspect it says more about the condition of our culture than it does about the nature of love. Though women are certainly having their problems with trust and commitment, I see the difficulty at its most extreme in middle-aged men who are compelled to abandon their mates for younger women. I view it here as more a manifestation of the fear of death, the worship of youth, the distorted emphasis on power and machismo—demanding of the aging man that he reassert his position among other males in the sexual world by pursuing a younger mate—than as a statement about the nature of passion. Beautiful young women constitute the modern middle-aged man's jewelry. He wears them to announce his power, position, and status. His choice says very little about love.

Stendhal referred to this reassuring aspect of love as "vanity-love." Today we are likely to dump these needs into the increasingly inflated category "narcissism." "The great majority of men, especially in France, desire and possess a fashionable woman as they would possess a fine horse, as a necessary luxury for a young man. Their vanity, more or less flattered and more or less stimulated, gives rise to rapture. Sometimes sensual love is present also, but not always; often there is not even sensual pleasure. The Duchess de Chaulnes used to say that a duchess is never more than thirty years old to a snob."[18]

What is necessary for true loving goes beyond power and status needs. It requires security and self-confidence, risk, and, more important, commitment. As Stendhal phrased it: "Love is an exquisite flower, but one must have the courage to go and gather it on the brink of a dreadful precipice."[19]

If love is the greatest form of pleasure, it is also something beyond pleasure. It describes a state of existence of two people, a set of contracts between them, a moral arrangement and changed sensibility, an altered identity. Trust and commitment are essential to both of these; though they are quite similar, we must look at how they differ.

"Apart from ridicule, love is always haunted by the despair of being abandoned by the beloved and by being left nothing but a dead blank for the remainder of life," Stendhal says.[20] This demands the strength and courage of a competent self, and also a trust of the highest order in the other. Trust is an act of faith. It demands a firm belief of confidence in the honesty, integrity, reliability, and justice of another person. Trust is love's testament.

If trust is an act of faith, then commitment is an act of will and a statement of intent. It is a promissory note to love. When we commit something to another, we are of course entrusting it to them, and when it is love about which we are talking, what we are giving in trust to the other person is nothing less than ourselves. Commitment comes very hard these days.

Commitment means more than merely the deliverance of our destiny to another for safekeeping. It also means a pledge to do something. Commitment can occur in loving relationships beyond marriage, but it was the institution of marriage that epitomized the contractual bonding of one to another. It was not so long ago that the act of marriage was for a large part of our population an irrevocable and inviolate commitment to a shared fate and a shared experience. Most of us in our marriage ceremonies did "solemnly swear" to love, honor, cherish, obey, trust, or any combination of the above. We swore it even while knowing it might be anachronistic. We swore to do so "till death do us part."

In these days of overripened individualism, with our emphasis on the here-and-now rather than the long-range, with our elevation of pleasure over purpose, of fulfillment over duty, of right over responsibility, *nothing* is likely to exist "till death do us part."

The dissolution of the bonds of marriage has always been a possibility for the elite—at least since Henry VIII. Now it has become so for the mass of population.

Marriage just isn't what it used to be—to which many would hasten to add, "Thank God." Entrapment of women, particularly in a loveless and unfulfilling marriage, was no joy, and I do not want to romanticize the indissoluble state of marriage that once existed. Nonetheless, a fixed commitment over time—some contract—ought to be in operation beyond the caprices of daily inclinations, in order to allow the time necessary for the ripening of love. Marriage is a noble state, and if in its realization it fails to satisfy its anticipations, it is still an ideal worth aspiring to.

Marriage has been referred to by psychologist Ned Gaylin as "the institution for civilizing" sexuality.[21] Civilization is certainly a human enterprise: the process of creating social organization of a high order. To civilize anything, whether passion or sexuality, is to "elevate" it, to "improve" it, and to "refine it." Civilization of sexuality means bringing sexuality and the passions in general out of the wilderness of adolescent frenzy and into fusion with concepts of trust and service, justice and commitment, altruism and responsibility.

Marriage involves not just the joining of two people but the joining of their aspirations, and it demands a collective accommodation of their dreams and desires. Love is the underlying fusion of identities that, when it works, will make this common fate a possibility. Despite the lowered state of marriage in our current culture, it is still generally approached with respect, even awe. Most of us do not enter into marriage lightly, and though most marriages may not endure, the termination is usually enacted in pain and disappointment.

With all the failures, it is still touching that most people about to marry make the assumption—perhaps a self-deluded one—that theirs is to be a permanent arrangement. Divorce may have a diminishing stigma in our society, but on an individual level it is almost always viewed as a failure, a betrayal, or both. For the bulk of people in our culture, marriage is the central life goal, and a marital state is part of their articulated future.

Recently marriage has come under attack not just from burned and bruised ex-spouses but from philosophers. The basic argument offered by Derek Parfit, for example, is that marriage represents a promise extended over such a length of time as to make it unbelievable and implausible. Since only short-term promises can be kept, he asserts, only short-term promises should be made. I suppose he is advocating either a trial marriage or a marriage contract that has a renewal clause or termination clause in it.

Another British philosopher, Susan Mendess, exposed the absurdity of this concept by saying, "It is bizarre to respond to: 'Wilt thou love her comfort her and keep her?' with: 'Well, I'll try.' "[22]

Mendess makes some telling points about the nature of commitment, the primary one being that commitment is not an announcement of fact, not an unconditional guarantee, but a statement of intention. And she wisely recognizes that statements of intention are important factors in determining what is about to happen. We are actors in our own drama, but we are also writers of the script. The very fact of the commitment determines what we are prepared to accept as the possible solution.

This theoretical argument is best supported by a practical example. When a parent is presented with a quandary about how to handle a recalcitrant, irritating, and exhausting four-year-old, she never considers abandoning the child as an alternative. She is committed to its care and does not conceive of "divorce" as a possible solution. She must look to more imaginative and less extreme actions.

Obviously the contractual moral responsibility we tacitly make to our children is beyond what most of us are prepared to grant to a marriage: marriage is not essential to survival of the species, and care of the child is. Still, the trivialization of marriage is not an attractive alternative.

D. H. Lawrence, of all people, firmly supported marriage. He argued for it on the basis of tension between family and state. He saw marriage as a freedom for the twosome, if not the individual, from the overwhelming intrusion of the state into family matters. "Man and wife, a king and queen with one or two subjects, and a few square yards of territory of their own, this, really, is marriage. It is a true freedom. Because it is a true fulfilment."[23]

Despite D. H. Lawrence's seemingly florid 1920s romanticism, his apprehensions were realistic. We see the rising power of the state in areas to which it previously had no access in our modern life. Traditionally the rights of the helpless have been vested within the family; it was the mother or father who spoke for the helpless child or senile parent. Certain "rights" movements (fetal rights, rights of the retarded) have been progressively demanding a real-location of power, either because of the absence or dissolution of the family, or simply because of the distrust of the family.

Distrust of the potentially destructive family has led us to take the decisions for caring for their helpless and placing it in the warmer and softer hearts of the courts and the state legislatures. Thus we are fulfilling the prophecy of D. H. Lawrence in seeing the decline of the family as creating a vacuum that would be filled by the expanding state.

It may be that marriage has had its day. Surely enough crimes have been committed in its name; as an institution it has housed its share of misery as well as security and bliss. Still, some kind of commitment one to another is necessary. At least sexual, emotional, romantic, and loving pleasure must be cast in terms of the twosome. We cannot degenerate into a narcissistic pursuit of individual plea-sure without any commitment to one another.

Lawrence understood this, too, when he said:

"Sex goes to the rhythm of the year, in man and woman, cease-lessly changing. . . . Oh, what a catastrophe for man when he cuts himself off from the rhythm of the year, from his unison with the sun and the earth. Oh, what a catastrophe, what a maiming of love, when it was made a *personal* [my emphasis] feeling taken away from the rising and setting of the sun. . . . This is the matter with us. We are bleeding at the roots, because we are cut off from the earth and sun and stars, and love is a grinning mockery, because, poor blossom, we picked it from its stem on the tree of life, and expected it to keep on blooming in our civilized vase on the table."[24]

Lawrence defends commitment and marriage by tracing the varying relationships of passionate love from its dawn to its sunset. Men and women differ at thirty, forty, fifty, sixty, and seventy, he acknowledges, but he finds some "strange conjunction in their differences" and he sees through it all "some unseen, some un-known interplay of balance, harmony, competition like some soundless symphony which moves with a rhythm from phase to phase, so different, so very different . . . and yet one symphony . . . made out . . . of two strange and incompatible lives, a man and a woman's."[25]

We have seen in America particularly, and in most of the West-ern democracies, an extraordinary and progressive overemphasis on the individual. But individual fulfillment at its highest is never achieved except through relationships. From the beginning, our fates are bound one to another. We left the Garden together by choice.

The deterioration of the concept of pleasure into the superficial gratification of a pampered self is like the corruption of loving, a product of a larger tendency in our society to glorify the artifact of modern misunderstanding—the isolated self. By now it should be apparent to all that there is no such creature. It is a chimera. The isolated self cannot survive to maturity without others; even if a child manages to survive isolated from contact with its own kind, it will become a humanoid creature rather than a human being. Surely this is the message of *Pinocchio*.

No animal—with the possible exception of the human pet—is

capable of love. Some may wish to consider the dog, for example, as loving, but manifestations of love in the dog have the same ironic occurrence as animal speech; dogs tend to reserve these special qualities for their relationships with us, not with their own kind. No animal is capable of fusion, and none has the mental resources for idealization. They can be committed, but that act of commitment is not one of freedom or will, but the mandated response of behavior to a genetic trigger. The goose can no more be said to love or be committed to his monogamous mate than the salmon can be said to love his breeding ground. The mating bird can be committed to its winter home, but one would hesitate to equate this with patriotism or love of country, even though the bird might be more "devoted" than a person in the literal sense.

Love as we know it is only a human experience, and the ultimate expression of our humanity. If we accept this, it is then necessary to consider whether the potential for loving is a universal part of the human condition. Certainly we can say that the human being carries within him a potential, and beyond that a genetic directive, for loving. Yet, looking around us in this not always beautiful world we occupy, we see that all people are not equally capable of loving, and some people seem incapable of loving at all.

The capacity for loving should be viewed as a spectrum, and where on that spectrum we fall as individuals will be determined by the nature of our particular experiences. One such "experience" might be as basic as our gender: is there a gender difference in either the capacity for loving or in the experience of love?

There is an unfortunate tendency on the part of some to see asking such a question in itself as a sign of sexism. This is a silly, superficial, and ultimately self-defeating attitude. If there are different genetic influences operating on men and women, they would be of a limited magnitude and easily modifiable, given the general looseness of genetic control over human behavior. Whatever differences may exist, they are minimal when compared with the shared traits between genders: intelligence, imagination, caring, and a mutable nature.

Let us take one step back in human history and presume that

there is a genetic directive for aggression and hunting in men, and for domesticity and child-rearing in women, and that, in some prehistoric yesterday, people behaved according to those directives. We know that people today do not behave the way people behaved yesterday. This statement would be true in almost any "today" in relationship to any "yesterday." In all behavior not directly linked to survival, cultural directives almost always dominate. When we examine the phenotypes (the developed person) as distinguished from the genotype (the genetically mapped person), we see dramatic variations in the nature of male and female behavior: culture has overriden genetic suggestions. Cultural directives, once set, can have the fixity of a biological trait.

During a revolutionary period, when a struggle for justice is in process, it may be necessary to assume, even to insist, that there are no distinctions or cultural variations between black and white, homosexual and heterosexual, man and woman, Christian and Jew. It may seem mischievous and impolitic to point out the considerable differences between them, for these differences could be used po- litically, and—worse—punitively.

That black culture is different from white culture, that homo- sexual object choice and homosexual love can serve different dy- namics from those of heterosexual object choice and heterosexual love, that even within the homosexual community the patterning of lesbian culture is often antithetical to the patterning of male homosexual culture, and that women and men may operate with a different set of biological influences—all this can only be discussed in a climate that does not automatically equate "different" with "inferior," and that understands we can then decide, *independently of biological directives,* which features serve pleasure, adaptation, and our social values, and which do not. At that point a society is free to modify cultural directives. But all such modifications must take into account the biological nature of the species, so that we do not tread too closely to the limiting conditions of humanhood.

The data we have today suggest that the two genders have different biological directives vis-à-vis attachment and caring and ultimately different attitudes toward romantic love. We know that

boys and girls develop at different rates and develop various skills
at different ages—cognitive and verbal skills, on the average, mature much earlier for girls than for boys, just as muscle capabilities
are generally more developed in boys at any given preschool age.

Margaret Harlow, from her studies with higher primates, concludes that there is also among human beings a difference in male
and female protective attitudes toward the young, with the female
having a more fully developed maternal instinct. She has compared
these gender differences in humans with those of chimpanzees and
has found the variations to be much less in human beings. In
almost all subhuman primates, the paternal role is to protect and
comfort the entire group—all the young, not just his own. He
takes care of the herd. The mother is the only official custodian
to her own children. One can see an adaptive purpose in this. As
I have previously described, if no one places special emphasis on
a given child, he might be lost in the group. The mothers will
look after their own, and the fathers will see all as their own while
being less attentive to any specific child. This collaborative effort
would seem to be admirably suited to protect the horde from attack.

Human variation is somewhat less marked. Harlow insists that
the human protective system is stronger in males, and she sees this
as undoubtedly an influence of culture. She makes a telling case
that we can ignore gender differences, both genetic and hormonal,
and institute the proper early conditioning, which is after all essential to the maturation of any biological trait. Both are dependent
on the same thing—the capacity to establish affectional ties to others
of the species—and this was clearly tied to early conditioning by
the pioneering work of her husband, Harry Harlow.[26]

The feminist movement raised the consciousness of all of us to
the hidden prices, beyond even the obvious explicit costs, that had
been paid by women because of gender stereotyping. The price
that men pay for gender stereotyping may not be as evident; but
it has been considerable. To be denied the pleasure of caring and
loving, to be made to feel ashamed of one's own sensitivity and
sensuality, to feel guilty for dependency desires—this is to court
the sterile world of power that is currently considered the proper

goal of masculine endeavor. It is tragic to deny either gender access to the pleasure of either of the great activities of the human species—loving and mastery.

What Western culture had done was to distort a biological difference that may once have existed and made adaptive sense into an absolute and artificial division that makes absolutely no sense under the current conditions of our culture. It might have been defensible in that primitive time when the mass power of the male body was necessary to move giant stones and to race after the antelope, but none of this pertains today. Yet, until very recently, Western culture tore apart the two foundations of human pleasure—*Liebe und Arbeit*—and assigned work to men and love to women, and in the process corrupted the pleasure in both.

This cleavage of work and love influenced the way both sexes conceived of love, as well as altering the innate capacities for love. I am convinced that in our culture most men only vaguely appreciate the full experience of love. This is apparent in the fantasies and anxieties of the patients on the couch as well as their actions in distress. For one thing, men rarely commit suicide over the loss of a loved one, whereas this is the preponderant reason for a woman's suicide. Men commit suicide over the loss of their business or other representation of position or power. This should not be interpreted to mean that men *value* their businesses more than their wives or children. If he were given the choice in advance, I have no doubt that the typical man would save his child over his business. But in suicide we are dealing with an internal reality in which the symbol transcends the actual. With the loss of a loved one, a woman will often see the loss of her capacity for survival. Women had been trained to vest their pride, confidence, and identity in their attachments; men were more likely to vest these same things in their achievements and their positions.

The feminist revolution has enabled women to begin to find their way into the world of power and mastery. One fervently hopes that, in grasping for the privileges of power inherent in the masculine role, they will not find themselves trapped in the loneliness and lovelessness that have characterized that role for men.

At least women know where the power is—it is found in the world of work and money. But men seem unsure how to locate or enter the world of love. Where in this world are the proper marketplaces? There are no law- or medical-school equivalents in this world of relationship to facilitate the transfer from one role to another.

The survivability of our species may depend on the character traits we encourage or suppress in our progeny. In great part, the human being can become what we choose it to become; we can design our descendants. If we desire our children to be lean or strong or more generous, less competitive, more courageous, less narcissistic, less gender-stereotyped, more empathic, more giving, loving, caring, committed, less hedonistic, more imaginative, more honest, less self-deceptive, more sensitive, more decent, wittier, and more spontaneous (to indicate a few of my biases), there are ways to encourage these traits.

I am not saying that these are the only traits that ought to be encouraged. You may have an alternative or opposing list. We need not argue about the nature of the lists. We only have to acknowledge that such character traits as the ability to love are shaped by the directives that emerge from the value systems of the general culture and are further modified by the specific conditions of the individual's history, the biases of the family, or the absence of a family.

There are two special categories of people who seem incapable of loving that are instructive to examine, the autistic child and the psychopath.

Autistic children are biochemically and genetically flawed: they seem incapable of love and, beyond that, to relatedness at all. I recall with pain and horror a training clinic in which a young psychiatric resident interviewed the mother of an autistic five-year-old boy. He had never seen such a case before, and he asked the typical clichéd questions—had the mother ever held, embraced, or offered her child love in the first year of life? The mother, hurt, angry, and defensive, answered, "Have you ever tried to embrace an icicle?"

The mother was correct. These children are different, and respond differently; one has the sense that no amount of early conditioning could modify what must be a genetic flaw.

Another group outside the broad range of normal variation who seem incapable of guilt, conscience, empathy, or love is the so-called congenital psychopath. With the psychopathic personality there may be a genetic factor at play, although the category is much more poorly defined and may include two quite different groups, those with a genetic flaw—the "constitutional psychopaths"—and those whose early deprivation was so severe that the environmental influences are confused with genetic flaw. Here, one senses, psychiatry may have originally erred in the opposite direction from autism, attributing to genes much that was a product of very early environment. Children raised without family, care, or love are likely to become uncaring and unloving adults.

Traditionally, psychiatrists had avoided the psychopath by refusing to label him as "sick": he was simply abnormal. The reason was that psychopaths do not suffer because of their developmental abnormalities; they make those about them suffer. Therefore, they do not fall within the traditional definitions of sickness.

The psychopath also has a severely impaired capacity for foreseeing the consequences of his acts, or for anticipating a future in which he will be forced to pay for his transgressions. His behavior is viewed as criminal, not sick. Most cultures cannot afford to allow amoral, exploitive, cruel, and conscienceless behavior to be exculpated by labeling it as sickness. Psychopaths are recognized as untreatable by most psychiatrists, and they represent a large percentage of the criminal population. They *may* respond to the threat of swift and certain punishment. After all, though they are deficient in the emotions of shame and guilt, they do retain the primitive emotions of fear and rage that we share with animals.

There is a third, less obvious population deficient in their capacity for loving: extreme narcissists. Here one begins to appreciate the critical importance of the human beings' extended period of dependency. It is in this crucible that the elements will be mixed that will form the mature adult. Nature has given us the time necessary to develop so complex a figure, a figure that must take a role in a society as different from that occupied by other higher primates as chimpanzees are from the fishes of the sea. The connection between the narcissism of an adult and the early narcissism normal in an infant was recognized by Freud when he suggested two stages of narcissism: primary, the normal state of the infant, and secondary narcissism, the regressive or arrested state of some adults.

The narcissist does not need love; he needs reassurance—he needs to be loved. He is concerned with his safety and survival, and he vests these in the approval of others. He seems to be seeking love, but what he is seeking is approval. For the narcissist, popularity and adoration are not luxuries, not true pleasures. They are insurance policies and safety measures. Unfortunately, narcissistic reassurances are only quick fixes. Like a cocaine high or an alcoholic binge, they create an illusion of well-being and safety that is only too quickly diminished and more often than not will lead to a rebound reaction of despair and dread, driving the poor approval-addict for yet another and another quick fix.

A Don Juan is a kind of love junkie who never gets the reassurance of real love. He has no idea what fusion means. He is always separating himself from the very thing he so desperately needs, a loving partner. Women are objects to be used as instruments for reassurance. He treats them as mirrors on the wall from whom he is insistently demanding to be told that he is the loveliest of them all. He is a cracked vessel, and no amount of affection poured into him will ever fill it to the brim.

None of us is immune to the early lessons of childhood. All of us want to be loved. All of us have narcissistic elements. Fortunately, most of us have gone through an early development that is not quite so crippling as those that have been discussed. Most of us have some capacity to love, but the nature of our loving may be conditional by certain degrees of insecurity. We may require of our loved one a bonus beyond loving and commitment, some security measure, some socially enhancing aspect—beauty, wealth, power—that will support our own insufficient self-esteem.

I am asked whether ours is a more narcissistic time than others.

This is a difficult question to answer. There are cyclic periods of history that tend to repeat themselves. Ours may only be the age that has discovered the term "narcissism" and uses this new definition to reclassify old problems. What we do know is that culture makes a profound difference in our psychology and morality, and it has certainly made a difference in our attitudes toward sex and love.

In the midst of a revolution, it is not easy to isolate the positive and negative aspects, but certain things seem apparent. For love to flourish, the following conditions seem essential: the courage to risk being hurt, the capacity for identification, an ability to trust, a willingness and courage for commitment, and the necessity for all of us to relinquish our hunger for instant, superficial gratification in order to allow us to experience the more profound pleasures of delayed gratification. True loving is worth that risk.

Loving has suffered because of a pervasive aberration of our time. Ours is an age that has not honored any concept of community, even the community of two. There are few hosannas heard for commitment, duty, responsibility, and dedication to purpose. It would be surprising if love were not a victim of these trends, since commitment is such an essential part of mature love. Sociological data are not easy to come by, but there seems at least some indication that there has been a failure of commitment in our time; a serious decrease in our confidence in relationship; a sense of increasing isolation and existential angst; and a doubt about the nature and purpose of life which is compounded by an erosion of our trust in the traditional institutions—marriage, religion, government—that no longer seem to serve our purpose. If commitment is difficult, then the same can be said of trust and fusion.

The case for loving is so urgent and powerful that it must be made now. The painful lesson learned by our hero, Pinocchio, was that selfishness is ultimately not self-serving—not when we consider the larger self. Through giving of ourselves we become enlarged, not diminished. At the turn of the century the great Russian philosopher Vladimir Solovyov said: "The meaning of human love is the *justification* and deliverance of individuality through the sacrifice of egoism."[27]

Love, Pinocchio learned, transforms our definition of pleasure. It is a dedication of the self, through trust and commitment, to an expanded existence. Because love uses all of our noblest human capacities—generosity, altruism, empathy, service, self-sacrifice, and devotion transcending a narrow concern for self—it defines what sets us as a species apart from all others.

If our culture is eroding the conditions required for love to flourish, we must change our culture. We must spend at least as much time concerned about personal relationships as on environmental deterioration. The contamination of our rivers and streams is of course an urgent problem that must be solved, but it is no more severe than the adulteration of our trusting relationships. The binding force of love is the only thing strong enough to support the weighty burdens of our complex modern community, and each and every individual is linked in survival to the stability of the community in which he resides. The human community is the moral and esthetic world. It is the world that God in Genesis saw as very good. It is in our hands.

After being rebuked by God and being told they could no longer occupy the world they had inhabited, the perfect world of the Garden, man and woman went out to create a new world, a world that is the antecedent of the one we occupy. And they did it together.

EPILOGUE

DR. FRANKENSTEIN AND

THE IRISH ELK

~~~~~~~~~~~~~~~~

In 1816, Mary Godwin (Shelley to be) was holidaying in the Swiss mountains near Geneva, staying at the Villa Diodati with her lover, Percy Shelley. "It proved a wet, ungenial summer, and incessant rain often confined us for days to the house." Mary, though still unmarried, had already experienced the death of her first child in 1815, and had just given birth to a son, William, in the winter of 1816. She was all of nineteen at the time.

In this dismal season, Mary and Shelley spent much of their time in the house reading "some volumes of ghost stories translated from the German into French . . . [which] . . . fell into our hands." One evening, along with their neighbor, Lord Byron, and their physician friend, Polidori, they decided to try their hands at writing ghost stories. Byron, as one might have expected, was off and running, quickly drafting his tale. He never finished it. Shelley also soon lost interest in his story, the narrative form never having held much appeal for him. The third male member of the group fared no better:

"Poor Polidori had some terrible idea about a skull-headed lady who was so punished for peeping through a key-hole—what to see I forget . . . [that] he did not know what to do with her and was obliged to dispatch her to the tomb of the Capulets."[1]

Mary, at first, proved even less capable than her male friends. She seemed blocked, unable to conceive of an idea. Shelley urged her to continue trying. Being of a more persistent nature than any of the men, she did precisely that, but a central idea on which to frame her story eluded her. As she says in her introduction, "Everything must have a beginning . . . and that beginning must be linked to something that went before." She wanted a story "which would speak to the mysterious fears of our nature and awaken thrilling horror—one to make the reader dread to look round, to curdle the blood, and quicken the beatings of the heart." Mary felt "that blank incapability of invention which is the greatest misery of authorship."

" 'Have you thought of a story?' I was asked each morning, and each morning I was forced to reply with a mortifying negative."[2] Then, one night, Mary had a vision or a dream in which the root idea of her story appeared to her in a frightening and complete image:

"I saw the pale student of unhallowed arts kneeling beside the thing he had put together. I saw the hideous phantasm of a man stretched out, and then, on the working of some powerful engine, show signs of life and stir with an uneasy, half-vital motion. . . . His success would terrify the artist; he would rush away from his odious handiwork, horror-stricken. He would hope that, left to itself, the slight spark of life which he had communicated would fade, that this thing which had received such imperfect animation would subside into dead matter, and he might sleep in the belief that the silence of the grave would quench forever the transient existence of the hideous corpse which he had looked upon as the cradle of life. He sleeps; but he is awakened; he opens his eyes; behold, the horrid thing stands at his bedside, opening his curtains and looking on him with yellow, watery, but speculative eyes."[3]

Even in these pre-Freudian days, Mary was sufficiently sophisticated to know that dreams are rooted in the experiences of reality. Probing for reasons why this bizarre image had occurred to her, she recalled that, during the intemperate weather when they were confined to the villa, they would fall into philosophical discussion on the nature of man and the nature of the principle of life. They talked particularly of "the experiments of Dr. Darwin." More specifically, they questioned whether there was any probability that the essential nature of life might be discovered and its nature communicated. "Perhaps a corpse would be reanimated; galvanism had given token of such things: perhaps the component parts of a creature might be manufactured, brought together, and endued with vital warmth." These discussions were consistent with fashionable speculation at the beginning of the nineteenth century.

The story was intended to be a diversion for the author and an amusement for the poets. Yet this lightly conceived work, which was published in 1818 as *Frankenstein, or The Modern Prometheus*, was to ensure Mary Shelley's immortality and would probably have a greater impact on the sensibilities of our time than the monumental works of those two giants of nineteenth-century romantic poetry, Percy Shelley and Lord Byron. I do not mean to imply that the collected works of either poet do not stand as a towering achievement in literature that dwarfs this small novel. Nonetheless, in the imagination and perceptions of our culture, the Frankenstein myth has taken a central role beyond any individual work of either noble poet.

In 1818, we were at the beginning of the modern scientific revolution. The idea of one human being fabricating another was pure metaphor; the feat was presumed impossible, beyond human imagination, a grotesque exaggeration. It was a gothic tale, a device whereby the author could express her philosophical concern about the questing nature of the human being and the potential dangers inherent in this ambitious poking, prodding, nervous, unsatisfied attempt to know everything, to control everything, to confront the forces of nature, and to conquer them. We were intended to identify with Dr. Frankenstein, the nineteenth-century man committing the classical crime of a Greek poet of the fifth century B.C., the crime of hubris —overweening pride.

In classical Greek mythology, the basic flaw of the hero was always in his aspirations, not in his failures: in his refusal to accept the limitations of the human role and in his reaching too dangerously toward the powers reserved for the gods. Dr. Frankenstein was a "modern" version of Agamemnon, Oedipus, and Ulysses.

There is an eccentric correlation between the early nineteenth century and our modern times. Europe had then been wracked by the experience of two major revolutions, the American and the French. In addition, the Napoleonic Wars, which had started with such excitement and promise, had ended in the corruption of the dream. Napoleon was the source of inspiration for Beethoven's Third Symphony. By the time of its completion, however, Napoleon had revealed himself as more of a despot than a liberator, and Beethoven stripped his name from the title, labeling it simply the *Eroica*, a tribute to heroes and heroism in general.

Diane Johnson, in her introduction to a new edition of *Frankenstein*, says of that period:

"Authority crumbled. God had been questioned for a century, tyrants more recently, and the romantics were beginning to look at parents too. The industrialization of Europe, and especially of England, resulted in a rapidly increasing middle class and a dramatic population shift from rural to urban living, with consequent dramatic changes in social stability. Questions of property and democracy were raised . . . and Mary Wollstonecraft [Mary Shelley's mother] raised, in the *Vindication of the Rights of Women*, fundamental questions of freedom and education for half the human race.

"Everybody was interested in discovering the nature of man and of the social contract, matters in which . . . the previous century had barely been questioned."[4]

The Prometheus legend dominated the thinking of many of the intellectuals of the time. That very summer, Lord Byron was working on his major poem *Prometheus*, and Shelley would eventually write his *Prometheus Unbound*. And Mary's work was subtitled *The Modern Prometheus*.

The legend of Prometheus was an inevitable symbol for that time, as it is becoming a central myth of ours. Certainly the preceding quotations indicate an astounding parallel with our times, with one terrifying distinction. We live in a supertechnological society where almost nothing need remain in the world of fantasy anymore, where almost anything is within the grasp of our technology.

The over two thousand years that separated Mary Shelley from Aeschylus had certainly witnessed a rapid expansion in our understanding of basic scientific principles. But in terms of the technological capacities to use that knowledge—particularly in the biological sciences, which were to develop much later than the physical sciences—the two thousand years were as nothing compared with the 170 years that separate Dr. Frankenstein from the molecular biologist and the genetic engineer of today.

At the time of the creation of *Frankenstein*, the biological sciences were still only potential and promise. The technological age consisted primarily in the excitement of anticipation. Science was ascending, and the only terror was that in our hubris we would offend God by assuming too much and reaching too high—by coming too close. The scientist was the new Prometheus.

Prometheus had violated the rules of the gods by creating man out of clay and water, and in the very image of the gods. In addition, he had given man the divine fire, the basis of the technology that would eventually enable a Dr. Frankenstein to rival the very gods by creating life.

Prometheus created modern man: if he did not actually create man, as some myths would have it, he created civilized man through his gift of fire and technology. For this elevation of man to a proximation of godliness, he would pay dearly. Chained to a rock, he would have his limbs and liver continuously devoured by the avenging eagle of Zeus. But that modern titan, the twentieth-century human being, need fear no retribution from the gods.

By the end of the nineteenth century, the scientist was more than a rival to God: he *was* God. Technology had surpassed even its own expectations. There was nothing it would not eventually solve. We were too arrogant even to recognize arrogance. We did not have to fear God, for we had replaced Him. Up to that point, the whole of history seemed to have contrived to serve the purposes and glorify the name of *Homo sapiens*.

Now, as we approach the end of the twentieth century, we find that the myth of Frankenstein has become an everyday reality. With the miracle that is modern surgery, we use patches and parts, manufactured parts, and real parts borrowed from ourselves, other human beings, or cadavers, and we stitch them together with sutures of nylon or pins and staples of stainless steel. The development of such an elegant technology, which gives ambulation to the lame and life to the dying, is a glory to our species.

That we are prepared to trivialize our powers through vain and narcissistic uses painfully symbolizes the dissonance between our abilities and our values that so characterizes the time we live in. We modify our noses to some patrician view of elegant beauty, while being careful to rationalize it as a medical procedure; the "deviated septum" becomes both our protection against the crime of hubris and our economic defense, allowing us to maintain an image of humility while preserving our purse.

We have come a long way from those modest early days of cosmetic surgery. But while we were progressively enlarging our capacities, we were trivializing our mission. In an age of scarcity, where medical resources must be husbanded, vanity and youth-worship prevail. Now, in addition to reductive procedures, we have added supplemental ones. The unwanted fat can be sucked out of one section and plastics can be inserted into another. We play with the human body as if it were modeling clay, creating protuberances and hollows that start by serving some image of beauty but end in futile attempts to mitigate our terror of aging.

Modern surgery, guided by the new technologies of advanced anesthesiology and the miracle drugs that guarantee protection from bacteria, rejection, inflammation, and immune mechanisms, can do truly wonderful things. Skin can be taken from unexposed areas along with, bone, tissue, and fiber to reconstruct a face destroyed by genetic or traumatic disaster. The selfsame procedures that seem common and trivial when used to support human vanity are ennobled when they work to satisfy the basic need for socialization, community, self-respect, and pride, and diminish the pain of isolation and rejection.

Thus the fabrication of a human being is no longer mere metaphor or literary device, but an everyday fact in the operating rooms across the country. The inconceivable has become conceivable. Twentieth-century human beings are indeed patched together out of pieces and parts. We will reattach a recently severed arm, and we will fix shattered hips in place with metal spikes. Beyond that, we will create a plastic hip to completely replace an eroded or damaged one, or patch arterial tubing with plastic, or salvage corneas from the dead and kidneys from the living or dead. Pacemakers are inserted to control the rate of speed of the heart, and certain automatic pacemakers may be placed in the brain to control aberrant behavior. We have artificial limbs, artificial teeth, artificial joints, and artificial kidneys; artificial hearts are in the state of preparation. Organs that resist manufacture may be borrowed from the living or newly dead: corneas, lungs, hearts, livers, and who knows what is next. Dr. Frankenstein is at work in every major city of the modern world. We honor, we revere, we respect and need him. We wish him well and urge him on. An artificial heart, a brain transplant? Go further. An artificial placenta? Go further.

This is an achievement from which we should take pride. Why, then, does it still have the power to terrorize us? The tragedy lies in the dreadful fact that, with the realization of the promise, we have somehow or other switched identities. We have stopped identifying with Dr. Frankenstein, and now identify with his monster. Perhaps that is an overstatement: perhaps the real dilemma is that we now identify with both.

The fears have been relatively unorganized and inchoate within the field of surgery. Surgery has a long and incremental history, a gradual development, a story line that can be followed step by step by any intelligent layman. It is not so far, after all, from Captain Ahab's ivory leg to a modern prosthesis responding to an electronic impulse; and if we can adjust to the concept of an artificial limb, why not an artificial organ?

Each step in modern surgery has prepared us for the step to follow, and all have been judged good. All are in the service of health, survival, vitality, youth, or productivity.

But even in surgery we are approaching the boundaries of doubt and insecurity. Where will the patching end? How far can the remodeling go? Is a transsexual operation a medical procedure or a mutilation? Is a person tied to an artificial heart, which bears more of a kinship to a gasoline pump than to a human heart, capable of living a normal life? How many parts can we take, manufacture, make? How far can the experiment be pushed? And on whom? And will there be some unavoidable price in some future time in some unanticipated and horrifying way?

But forget surgery. What of the miracle of modern genetics! Those of us who may have struggled with traditional human genetics had no preparation for this strange and glorious world of molecular biology. We barely mastered an understanding of the teachings of Darwin and Mendel. Which of us still remembers the simple-minded rules of inheritance? Do you really have clearly in mind the distinctions between dominant and recessive? Do you remember why a child has brown or blue or perhaps hazel eyes but no intermixtures? How is left-handedness controlled? If a disease is dominant or recessive in both parents, what percentage of the offspring will have the disease? What percentage will be healthy and what percentage will be carriers? Are you at home and at peace when your child asks you to define "autosomal recessive," "sex-linked dominant," "penetrance," or "expressivity"? Do you remember anything of your elementary genetics from high-school days?

Then how can we make the leap into molecular biology—into DNA and recombinance; into gene splicing and the manufacturing of new species, chimeras; into the potential of introducing genetic materials and the traits they command from one individual to another, and from one life form to another? What about this new capacity to design our descendants? No longer need we depend on the crude and distasteful methods of the old genetics—diagnosis followed by selective abortion. Now something formerly thought unimaginable is within our grasp: the defective or missing gene can be replaced.

At the time I am writing this manuscript, the genome map, the pathway through all of our significant genes, while eagerly pursued, has yet to be performed. I suspect that at the time of the publication of this book, it will already have been done.

In *The Wall Street Journal* of July 13, 1988 (p. 28), there was an announcement that a team of scientists at the National Institutes of Health had pressed an application to extend recombinant-DNA technology from microbes, mice, and monkeys to humans. That very day, a biosafety committee reviewed proposed experiments for the first legal gene transplants in human beings. The first gene transplant is a modest one—simply to monitor a cancer trial—but Dr. Michael Blaze is quoted in the article as saying that he will examine his work in the test tube and see if it is still behaving; if so, he will extend it to future therapeutic experiments. "We can see if we can soup them up [the cancer fighting cells] to make them more effective."

The researchers are aware of some of the dangers involved in altering the basic genetic makeup of a living human being, and they have many safeguards, but not the ultimate one. "The only thing that would make me feel better . . . would be to put a second marker gene as a failsafe to allow you to kill all the cells of that lineage at will if something went wrong," an anonymous researcher stated, but he acknowledged regretfully that such technology was not available. "If a gene has not been inserted, it inevitably will and when it does there is a whole host of conditions waiting for gene therapy."

As of this writing, we have identified the genes and located their source of action for some forty-seven inherited diseases, from acatalesemia to von Willebrand's disease.[5] In addition, we have already marked the site for twenty-four other diseases. There is no question that, by the time of the publication of this book, the list will have grown considerably. Some genetic diseases are exotic and relatively rare phenomena, like Tay-Sachs, but the list includes widespread diseases such as sickle-cell anemia, and extends from cystic fibrosis, that destroyer of children, to Alzheimer's disease, that humiliating tragedy of older people.

We are on the threshold of a new world, as inconceivable to us as the modern world of biology and technology was at the turn of the last century. At the close of the nineteenth century, who could have anticipated the lives we lead, the advances in physics and chemistry, television, supersonic transport, computers, space travel?

Were they even susceptible to the imagination in the specific forms in which they occurred? A rocket to the moon was a lyricist's or a playwright's metaphor, not an actual event. The great legal scholar Paul Freund insisted that the biological revolution would surely transform our lives in ways we cannot anticipate, changes as profound and unpredictable as those the Industrial Revolution has made in our lives in this century.

Yet, to this date, the new genetics seem to have generated more anxiety than jubilation. We are more terrified by high-technology ways of influencing human behavior than by equally potent low-technology ones. It is clear to me that an unanalyzed, irrational element has entered the debate on research with recombinant DNA.

Within my limits as a person relatively unsophisticated in molecular biology, I have attempted to read everything I could understand about gene-splicing. It represents an extraordinary potential and a major new direction of research. This is unquestionable. There are, as always, risks when one is entering unchartered areas. My own judgment—and I offer my conclusions with no great assurance of authority—is that the anticipated benefits are well worth the risks.

I recognize that people of good will disagree and that the experts are divided, thus further confusing the public. But something else is happening. The extra, irrational variable that I believe to be distorting the public debate, I have called the "Frankenstein Factor."[6] I define this as having two major components, both of which are likely to enhance anxiety about research.

The first is that high-technology research, being basically incomprehensible to the average layman, will generate an air of mystery that will be more frightening than low-technology techniques that effect the same ends. For example, treating depression with electric-shock therapy is more feared than modifying behavior with drugs, which in turn is resisted more than modifying behavior by conditioning—even though all three bypass autonomy and rationality, and even though the level of safety for the patient may well be in reverse order.

Similarly, experiments to modify behavior with electrodes or

psychosurgery (such as prefrontal lobotomy) caused massive political upheavals, much more so than drugs have done. Drugs, in
turn, cause more concern than operant conditioning. Yet all three
of these procedures bypass rationality equally—they do not use the
traditional procedures of education—and thus could be defined as
manipulative.

Years ago, after a two-year research project on the potential
values and dangers of electrode implantation and psychosurgery
(the bêtes noires of those days), it became apparent that as modifiers
of human behavior they had a limited effect, but were relatively
harmless.[7] You would not have known it from the spate of novels,
plays, and hysterical political movements that thrived on the technological fears. When all is said and done, the only difference that
could be discerned between the implantation of an electrode and
the implantation of an idea was that the electrode was easier to
withdraw.

The second factor operating in the Frankenstein Factor concerns
a bias about the field of study. Research that is seen as changing
or controlling "the nature of the species" or controlling behavior
will always be received with a special fear that equally risky research in other areas does not engender. Even success—particularly
success—is frightening. Research and devices that save and extend
life aggrandize both the discoverer and the patient. Such research
seems empowering: the ability to control death, although still not
the immortality of God, is a cut above the helplessness of the general
animal host. Behavior manipulation through technological means
such as electrode implantation, psychosurgery, and mind-altering
drugs initiated organized, and often hysterical political movements.
Why? This is an instance in which we identify not just with the
researcher but with the research animal. Such research reasserts
man's kinship with the pigeon, the rat, and the guinea pig. The
more technological the control devices—the more mechanical the
method—the scarier it all seems.

Genetic engineering is even more terrifying, with its inherent
implications of tampering with the stuff of life itself and in the
process reducing people to the level of manufactured items. The

new capacities for genetic engineering enable researchers to seem frighteningly close to playing God. Here again, we identify not only with the creator but with the creature.

What should we do about this bias? Recognize it for what it is, an irrational anxiety. Obviously we cannot—should not—glorify the pretechnologic society. Technology has elevated our species, and there is no going back. At any rate, given our undeveloped state at birth and our easy modifiability, "natural" man is always the collaborative creation of nature and man himself. We must not be afraid of changing our nature, because it is our nature to change our nature. We are created with a plasticity that invites such change. Our freedom from instinctual fixation invites—demands—that we meet new contingencies in a world that is constantly changing, that often we ourselves are changing. We meet these environmental changes by adapting our nature to flourish in the new conditions of survival. Antitechnology is a self-hatred that we cannot afford and must not indulge.

Remember that no other animal significantly and *purposively* changes its larger environment. If the environment is modified by nature—if nature strips the forest of its leaves, if a drought occurs—the herd will die or be forced to migrate to a new and alien environment. In that migration, they will either find conditions similar to those they have just left—rediscover their old world and thrive—or most assuredly die. Most animal species cannot adapt to even modest environmental alterations. One thinks of the dependence of so highly developed a species as the panda on the leaves of the eucalyptus, a dependence that may presage the extinction of the species.

A certain form of survival does occur via the process of subspeciation. Throughout the world, there are closely related deer, sheep, rabbits, frogs, snakes, fish, birds, butterflies, wasps, flies, mollusks, sponges—and on through the animal kingdom. Similar in appearance, they are actually different species, incapable of interbreeding. The death of the species may take generations, and during that time a mutant form may emerge that finds the new environment amiable. Subspeciation then occurs: a new relative of the species will emerge. But it will only be a close relation. The original species will have died. The tropical hare and the arctic hare may look alike, but they are species apart. One can even predict the variations. An arctic form will be stubbier, rounder, with shorter appendages. This is a device to conserve heat. A sphere has the smallest surface area in relation to mass of any form. It explains why we curl up into a ball-like shape when we are sleeping in the cold, and why we spread out in the heat, exposing as much surface as possible to dissipate the body heat we generate, and to encourage the surface evaporation of sweat, which are our primary cooling devices.

We human beings do not manufacture new forms via mutation. We might, but the odds are against it. The length of time for such a favorable mutation to occur—since the vast majority of mutations are negative and could not survive at all—would be extremely long, well beyond the relatively brief time of human history. Instead, we are masters of adaptation.

This adaptability explains why we are the most far-ranging of creatures, and the most variable. Unlike certain insects, which are totally dependent on one specific nutrient, we can make do with a remarkable diversity of comestibles. We tolerate major modifications in our environment. We can survive in extremely variable climates, but we also have the imagination and powers to change the environment; we are not passive victims of it. We protect ourselves from inclement and inhospitable weather by insulating clothes, generating artificial heat, and devising forms of protective shelter. We invent central heating. And after generations of success in living in cold environments, we recognize that we can reverse the process and survive—nay, flourish—in the arid heat of desert lands, through air conditioning and transported water. We move massive populations into the Southwest of our country. We invent, God forgive us, Palm Springs. Eventually, merely by extending the principles of some of that same technology, we may send pioneers to cultivate the moon.

Yet, technological devotee that I am, I am nonetheless concerned. Although we can change our nature in glorious and unpredictable ways, there are limits to such change. We must be sure that we modify ourselves in such a way as to enhance our survival and, beyond that, our humanness. For what do we gain if we succumb to a tyranny of survival that is indifferent to the nature of the creature that survives? If what survives is devoid of feeling, imagination, and love, it is not worthy of the name *Homo sapiens*. It can be argued that each generation will be newly born with those same potentials, and that therefore survival at any cost is justifiable. But such a position requires a very long view indeed. Besides, the conditions favoring survival generally tend to favor the presence of human qualities as well.

To protect our humanism, we must fully value and understand what makes us human. The problem is a nightmare of contradictions. Think again of B. F. Skinner's concern that by overvaluing autonomy, perhaps the most widely appreciated aspect of being human, we are in a position to destroy our planet and our species. His fears were real. His solution was an easy one—for him. Since freedom is only an illusion to Skinner, he says we should abandon it: give up those silly myths of human freedom and dignity, and get to work with intelligent and rigorous early programming of children in order to create a more predictable creature that can secure our survival.

But what about those of us who believe in autonomy and see our diversity as our last hope for survival? We perceive the same dangers as Skinner does: our freedom is bringing us close to disaster. We even acknowledge, with him, that all early conditioning constitutes a form of mitigation of autonomy. We want a child to feel guilt when he does "wrong." We work to create such a child by various forms of explicit and implicit indoctrination. Yet we honor freedom and wish to create an adult with maximum capacity for free choice. We who believe in freedom must walk a perilous path. We encourage the emergence of an adult—by the way we indoctrinate the child—who will, guided through conscience and identification, "choose" to do good and eschew evil, yet an individual not so constricted and obsessive that he cannot recognize conditions in which he may feel obliged to change or defy his own rules. That is no mean feat.

Further, we can only maximize autonomy in an environment that also encourages pride, guilt, empathy, identification, love, duty, obligation, unselfishness, and hope. We do not currently live in such a society, and we are critically close to a point of no return. Our present culture, with its overripened individualism and its contempt for community, is dangerously close to a tilt point that will either lead to its destruction or to draconian reversals in the extremis of a struggle for survival.

Let me turn to another story that illustrates what I believe has happened to our modern Prometheus. Stephen Jay Gould, in one of his delightful essays, discussed the famous case of the Irish elk.[8] This magnificent beast, during the course of his adaptation, developed progressively grander and more elaborate horns. Those animals who had the largest horns won the battle of survival by attracting more females and by threatening their potential rivals. Eventually the Irish elk (ironically, neither Irish nor an elk, but actually a deer) evolved such a massive and ornamental headdress that it got caught in the trees and could not flee from predators. Its former glory became a source of its own downfall. What had originated as adaptive had become destructive.

At this stage, modern civilization is in many ways becoming like the horns of the elk. There are indications that technological society has estranged us from certain necessary conditions of survival as human beings. Unawares, we may have passed the apex and slipped onto the downward slope of the curve of adaptation. What was formerly our glory and power—our technology and the culture it has spawned—has begun to reduce us. We feel increasingly impotent in the face of the pleasureless social institutions that we ourselves created, but which now seem to control us.

But how are we to know, poor creatures that we are, when we go astray, when we venture too far? How can we tell when we have reached the edge of the abyss? What are the guidelines? We cannot, as an earlier, primitive time would have us do, avoid the "unnatural." There are no strict natural laws to obey. To say that something is "natural" is difficult with the human species, because we change our nature. We are invited by our nature to tamper with our nature. We can never, therefore, define the good exclusively in terms of the natural. But even beyond that, it is clear that to say something is natural is not to say that it is good. We will always need to analyze and define the kind of life we value.

I recall very clearly a debate between a distinguished Jesuit philosopher and a physician in the days just prior to the first achievement of in-vitro fertilization. The theologian, though liberal, was esthetically and intuitively offended by in-vitro fertilization, but had difficulty articulating a logical defense of his position. Finally, pressed hard in public by a relentless opponent, he was driven to a corner and, without his usual elegance, simply stated that it was offensive because it was such an unnatural way for human beings to beget children. It was "inhuman."

Whereupon the biologist gleefully pointed out that, quite to the contrary, in-vitro fertilization was the only specifically and uniquely human way of creating children. Copulation and sexual intercourse were shared with a number of lesser and many loathsome creatures; "test-tube babies" were the unique production of the human mind and human sensibility. The theologian was caught in his own rhetoric. What he had hoped to do was to make his case for reproduction through the traditional and natural fusion with passion and tenderness that exists in the human act of lovemaking. Technology was not the villain. What concerned the theologian was some of the consequences he anticipated resulting from the use of in-vitro fertilization. There is little in the workings of a modern obstetrical ward—from the surgical gowns, antisepsis, delivery table, and stethoscope to the fetal monitor, sonogram, and caudal anesthesia—that is "natural" in some God-given sense, and little that is not "natural" to Franklin's tool-making man.

In a sense, by asking the question "What's so special about being human?" I suggest my bias: being human is indeed special. In enunciating the attributes that distinguish us from the beasts, that define our humanness, I have implicitly listed attributes of our life that must be encouraged and enhanced to maintain our status "in the image of God." Acknowledging that one of the primary aspects of our humanness is the capacity to modify ourselves, I would hold that the criterion for testing the value of change would be the

degree to which the change encourages or discourages the emergence of the other noble human qualities I have analyzed in this
book: a life of imagination, esthetics, and hope; autonomy; a range
of feelings that includes joy, pride, guilt, and shame; romantic
sexuality; work (as distinguished from labor); conscience; identification, friendship, and love.

In guarding these central human attributes, we must not ex-
aggerate the danger of the technological, because in so doing we
will take our eye from the sociological and psychological factors
that to this date, and probably into the near future, have had the
most profound impact in changing human nature. We will be
victimized by the Frankenstein Factor—intimidated by the
method, rather than focusing on the effect. No technology to date
has been able to dehumanize and demoralize with the power of
poverty, neglect, or despair. Usually, when we fear the technological, further assessment reveals that the untechnological contains
the greater threat.

In the powerful sense I have previously indicated, we are always
designing our descendants. The unprecedented incompleteness of
the human being at birth and its prolonged dependency have been
recognized by scholars for years. Any comparison with other higher
animals has led to an awareness of the unusual degree and duration
of the dependency of the human infant. The human is born an
alert fetus, ready and able to learn. We are, in our roles of parent
and child, Dr. Frankenstein and his monster. We are constantly
creating ourselves across generations.

We continue to see the influence of the Frankenstein Factor at
work in our distorted concerns about modern society. We are right
to be worried about maladaptive cultural and scientific changes
that might reduce our humanness, but our priorities are skewed.
More attention has been given by television, magazines, and newspapers—and, worse, the academics, the courts, and the legislators—
to the problem of the surrogate mother than to the infinitely more
dangerous problem of the unmarried teenage mother. The surrogate mother, while representing complex and intriguing moral
dilemmas, is no great threat to our society and warrants much less

concern than she has attracted. The unattached, unsupported, and immature teenage mother is a knife at the throat of modern culture, and a mortgage on the future vitality and hopes of, especially, the black population in major cities where teenage illegitimacy is now the condition of a majority of births.

Why am I placing such importance on the illegitimacy rate? Beyond concerns of compassion for the children born without hope of proper care extend the sociological implications of such illegitimacy. In the complex human being, each aspect of his humanhood is dependent on and conditioned by the others. For a child to develop a conscience, a positive identity, a sense of duty and responsibility, a capacity for empathy, identification, and love, ambition, and hope, he must receive loving care during the period of his dependency.

The problem with the alienated ghetto adolescent, whether male or female, is a complicated story with multiple derivatives. It is a story, however, that is singularly suited to illustrate the interrelated problems that modern urban society has generated for the human species. Some fifty years after the end of the Great Depression and the humanitarian social reforms that it spawned, a black underclass seems as firmly and persistently entrenched as ever. A recent explosion of violence and a boycott of Vietnamese businesses in a black ghetto led to an anguished outcry from a black resident of the neighborhood. He observed that Jewish store-owners had given way to Italian store-owners, who had given way to Greek store-owners, who had given way to Hispanic store-owners, who had given way to Korean store-owners, who were now in the process of giving way to a second wave of Central American and Oriental entrepeneurs. "When," he asked, "will we see the day of the black store-owner?" When indeed? But as important as when is how and why we have not seen them in the past.

How have these successive waves of impoverished immigrants, some burdened by confounding language barriers as well as the visible and palpable bigotry to which they have been exposed, managed to leapfrog over the black community in their race into the middle class? This question, based on empiric observation,

makes it only too apparent that the purely economic explanations
offered by most sociologists are grossly insufficient to explain the
black conditions that now exist in the ghetto. Poverty may be a
necessary but not sufficient explanation for what has been happening in our black ghettos. What distinguished most of the im-
migrant groups that arrived after the end of slavery in this country
was that they brought with them their bourgeois values, their
bourgeois aspirations, their bourgeois pride, and their solid, though
humbled, bourgeois identities. They knew who they really were,
and therefore knew where they were going. And if they didn't
quite make it, their children would. A sense of a future is a middle-
class luxury.

Civilized social behavior demands some identification with the
group, with society and its values, with its institutions. Most of us
will not do harm—not calculated, gratuitous harm—"to our own."
We will not soil our own nests. Unfortunately, for some there is
no "own" with which to identify. If people are alienated from the
mainstream of society, they will cling and clutch to any offering
of a group identity, even if it is with a gang of marauding, antisocial
teenagers like themselves. A gang, after all, is still a community
or a group, and better than the total isolation that is a living form
of the grave.

The streets of suburbia are usually well tended. The streets in
slum neighborhoods are usually not. This has been explained by
the paucity of public services in ghetto neighborhoods, but the
latter is only a partial explanation. Suburbanites are concerned
about "their" streets. The ghetto residents are aliens, forced to live
in an alien world. The street is not "theirs," and they have no
identification with it. The garbage is in the street not just because
there is poorer collection service, although God knows that is true,
but also because slums create slum attitudes and slum despair, and
these in turn are capable of creating more slums and more people
with slum mentalities.

Again, I do not mean to trivialize the debilitating and humiliating effects of poverty and deprivation. But what the alienated
minority in our society is deprived of is more than its equal share

of material goods. That might be tolerable; there are poor societies in which the median standard of living is well below our minimum. They are deprived of an equal share of self-pride and self-respect, and the independence and power that issue from such positive identification. We must seek the sources of alienation within the processes of identification that I have previously described in this book.

The roots of antisocial behavior are set in childhood. The antisocial behavior is our due payment for our neglect of the *biologically determined* needs of the dependent child. Care is his natural right. We dare not deprive him of his most basic due, his very birthright. If the neglect and deprivation are severe enough, the developing adult may become an antisocial individual, immune to any corrections except those of fear, punishment, confinement, and aging. Street crime is the avocation and occupation of the young. If we have no effective treatment for crime that is a product of psychopathic character and behavior—and for the most part we don't—at least we can concentrate on prevention in succeeding generations.

But we minimize the problem of the neglected child, who will breed a neglected child without our support and guidance. Our institutions of help are inadequate, and our social and economic inequities compound the risk. A frighteningly high percentage of inner-city children have been isolated from a sense of past as well as future, deprived of ties of community or family, raised without models or aspirations. The phenomenon of casual violence that exists there, often as gratuitous as it is heinous, is testament to that deprivation.

Early neglect of any child will produce, at the least, a vulnerable child. We compound this by exposing the child to an environment that would test the endurance and integrity of even the strongest: an environment of poverty, filth, and neglect in which he will be tormented by the chasm between promise and reality, by his awareness of deprivation in the midst of plenty, of alienation from the world of privilege, his degraded sense of self and depleted store of hope. These are the essential ingredients to build a permanently

deprived and hostile underclass—the psychological and sociological
chains that bind the black Prometheus to his rock of perpetual
torment.

To respect others, one must respect oneself. To respect oneself,
one must feel respected by others. If our only goal were obedience
to law, that could conceivably be established through fear and
terror, but, given the current state of our society, it would have to
be at such an extreme that the society would be a nightmare not
worthy of preservation. The social order is best protected by citizens
who care, who see their environment as part of themselves, and
who can see a future of hope. We must find ways of creating a
community with which all can identify.

I deal with the problem of the alienated teenager in the ghetto
briefly and inadequately. This is not a treatise on the massive
problem of deprived minorities. I realize only too well the limitations of the preceding discussion. It is offered here as an example
of one of the massive problems of our civilization that have resulted
from a failure to recognize clearly the things that make us human,
and the conditions necessary for the nurturing of our humanity.
Ghetto life is not only an affront to the dignity of the residents; it
is creating the conditions that will confine *their* children to a life
sentence among the dispossessed.

Another problem is that we are destroying the family through
the freedom of divorce. This, compounded by the necessities and
interests that remove both parents from the home, has created an
environment in which the majority of children need some new
and imaginative institutions of caring. We have seen that, beyond
survival, the infant requires caring to develop capacities for love
and empathy, for conscience and attachment. The child requires
caring to become, in other words, a caring adult. New methods of
child care that go beyond the custodial are essential for the survival
of a humane species. These will not be labor-efficient institutions
and the costs will be staggering. As we lower the age of infants
turned over to custodial care and increase the time they will spend
in such institutions, we will change the definitions of a preschool
program. With four-year-olds, a safe environment may be all that

is necessary. With one-year-olds and less, it must be a caring and stimulating environment. This cannot be accomplished if there is one caretaker for forty or even twenty infants. One to four or eight is a more appropriate ratio. The costs will be of an order that could be supplied only by the federal government, but they will have to be met. The future safety of the community depends on adequate child care, just as it does on national defense. This *is* a form of national defense.

We have too often concerned ourselves disproportionately with the civil liberties of the individual, ignoring in the process the biological needs of the individual. Central to those needs is a recognition of the Aristotelian verity that we are social animals through and through. If you protect the individual and degrade the community, you will destroy the individual, whose very existence as a human being demands community. A bloated concept of individualism is our greatest danger these days.

The glory of Western democracy rested in respect for the individual. Who would not prefer the excesses of individualism to the corruption of the overvalued community or state as represented by the almost indistinguishable totalitarian Leviathans of modern fascism and communism? But rampant individualism is becoming the horns of the elk. We have created an artifact, the isolated self, *that does not exist in biological truth*. In the service of this isolated self, we have seen a deterioration of the concept of pleasure and a reduction of joy to the most primitive hedonistic level, a passive model of immediate and effortless gratification free of pain, immersion, or commitment. We have enshrined the quick fix. Crack is not only the actual poison that is contaminating our urban environments, but the ultimate metaphor for a society that overvalues the individual moment and the individual self.

In the service of this isolated self, we have seen a vulgarization of the concept of rights and an abandonment of a commitment to duty, respect, and responsibility to the larger group. In the name of autonomy, we have made paternalism a sin, and all beneficence suspect. Not only are the mentally ill permitted to freeze to death in the streets, but this is argued before the courts to be a privilege of their autonomy. One would expect as sophisticated an organization as the American Civil Liberties Union to understand the relationship between true autonomy and cognitive capacities. A paternalistic protection of those who temporarily, or permanently (the organically senile), are incapable of determining their own self-interest is an act of decency, not arrogance. It is our moral duty. Such care should be seen as our ethical responsibility, but responsibility and duty are undervalued currencies in the current social marketplace.

We are also destroying the public spaces with the personal indulgences, ugly manners, and antisocial behavior that make portions of our cities mine fields that even the police dare not enter. Finally, our self-indulgences are destroying the *larger* public spaces—the very air we must breathe, the waters which cleanse, and the land which nurtures us. A greedy, shortsighted industrial bureaucracy, in collaboration with passive and cowardly public servants, in the presence of an apathetic and narcissistic population, seems determined to destroy this earth on which our future depends. With the immaturity and recklessness we associate with a four-year-old who knows only that he wants his candy and he wants it now, we are creating a culture of anomie and an environment that soon may no longer be able to sustain the needs of this so promising creature, *Homo sapiens*. We are no longer just reordering the elements of the environment—we are destroying the substratum on which we are dependent. Though we have invented the potter's wheel, we are still dependent on the clay and water. We cannot destroy them without destroying the potter. From now on, it will not be God who will shape us, or our world, but ourselves. We will shape ourselves and our institutions through our conscious designs and our unconscious biases. We need the integration of all the resources of the human species to shape our destiny and avoid our possible destruction.

Our incompleteness has allowed us to design ourselves, perhaps into obsolescence. But we cannot say that we usurped this role or acted arrogantly. It is the nature of our design, whether by the hands of God or of evolution, that demands that we be coauthors of our own existence. No longer should we ask, "What hath God wrought?" but, rather, "What have *we* wrought?" In defense of our individualism, we have mitigated our commitment to marriage in the interests of sexual freedom and pleasure. We have invented the loveless and rootless life of the unattached and uncommitted, for the sake of freedom and "fun." But we have trivialized sexuality to a degree that no lower animal could possibly imagine or effect. Animals, after all, are controlled by their biology; we, only by our sensibilities. The promiscuity and vulgarization of sex have led to some of the most profound social problems of our day: teenage pregnancy is on the increase; venereal disease, once thought to be near eradication in the Western democracies, is now once again on the rise; added to the traditional scourges of syphilis and gonorrhea, we have rampant epidemics of genital herpes, chlamydia, and now AIDS. We have made a tragic nightmare of modern sexuality. And it isn't all that much fun.

We take comfort in the strangest things these days. "Sexually the current uncertainties about AIDS have at least one 'silver lining,' that is, the opportunity to increase one's sexual behavioral repertoire, to go beyond the standard intercourse and discover the many means of giving sexual pleasure without depending solely upon intercourse." This astonishing comment was part of the statement of a distinguished medical group.[9] One would think that one emergent and agonizing conclusion to be drawn from the AIDS tragedy is the danger of thinking in such terms as "a sexual behavioral repertoire." The problem may already have been our overexpanded repertoire. But never mind—more important is that we find ourselves, in these narcissistic days, reduced to settling for such tarnished silver linings.

In depression, *Homo sapiens*, that most resourceful of all creatures, abandons hope in his own resources—his capacity to cope and survive. He passively awaits his pleasureless and inevitable decline. Without struggle or desire, he is helpless. Despair is the condition that ensures its own anticipated end.

The reasons for despair seem obvious, the reasons for hope less so. Look around, and the world seems a mess. But it is neither the best of times nor the worst of times. Violence, brutality, hunger, injustice, bigotry, war, personal abuse, inequity exist in our generation as they have in all preceding generations. One suspects they exist less now, but takes little comfort from the fact. When one plays the game, prompted by John Rawls's *A Theory of Justice*, of selecting a time in which we would choose to live, with the understanding that we cannot choose who we would be in that time or culture, there are few who would risk the fate of being the lowest in other places and other times.[10] We tend to return, in embarrassment, to the comfort of the contemporary.

Our despair lies not in the state of the world at large, but in the failure of our aspirations and the abandonment of our dreams. We have looked at the best of us, at our most civilized, at our most progressive, and have found that it, too, seems not to work. The dream of the nineteenth century is defunct, yet we see no alternative, for that dream was based on personal glory, on a sense that our own intelligence, through the instruments of technology, would solve the nature problems of existence, bring us surcease from pain, and herald a life of justice, pleasure, and pride. The inequitable distribution of resources was depressing enough when it involved just material goods; it is particularly offensive when it extends to the very source of survival. How can we have sympathy for a world in which the anguish of the hungry is paralleled by the anguish of the obese, who suffer from their self-indulgence?

It is the observation of the most successful in the most successful of societies that is particularly discouraging. It is the joylessness of middle class American and Western European life written about by middle-class American and Western European writers that destroys the hope which defends against despair. Technology, even when it fulfills our aspirations, seems to betray our needs. We have been to the moon, and it is a cold place.

If the world does seem in more desperate straits than ever before, this stems from the fact that the only solutions that are obvious to us now (because they were solutions that were so effective in the past) seem not to be effective anymore. Further, those very past successes that technology achieved seem to be contributing to today's failures. For example, we are, because of technology, moving toward a homogeneous small world. With all of the differences that may or may not exist between communist China and the United States, the similarities are just as apparent. When Periclean Greece and Imperial Rome talked about the destruction of civilization, they narcissistically referred to their small corner of the world. We are now one small world, and we will rapidly become even smaller. When we talk about the destruction of civilization, we mean the destruction of the world—a conceivable possibility in a way it never was before. Contagious disease may be limited by physical contact and community boundaries, or by the broad expanse of oceans; the contagion of violence, thanks to nuclear weapons and advanced rocketry, knows no boundaries.

And so we despair, not because we are abandoned by God—it was we who abandoned Him—but because we think that we have used our best and it was not enough. We despair as a group in the same way we despair as individuals when we feel impotent and unable to cope. To think, however, that we have exhausted the potentials of our true technology—in other words, our imagination—is preposterous. It is as though we have recognized the limitations of the balloon and not yet discovered the airplane. Our first models served us so well that we needed to explore no others. Now we need something new; we must begin to find different designs, different models, and different motivaters. The problems are not what we once thought they were, and that is a good thing to have discovered, for we can now seek different solutions.

I do not despair at the state of the world; I despair at the current state of passive disenchantment and self-denigration. Given knowledge of the nature of the human being, such worry is warranted. And psychological definitions of the human state tend to be self-fulfilling prophecies. We may not be what we think we are—but what we think we are will help determine what we are to become. We must not design our future in terms of our disillusionment with self, for such designs, even if erroneously conceived, will influence the future development of our species.

Coming face to face with our increasing capacity to destroy

ourselves, our kind, and indeed our world has led many, particularly among the young, to reject not just the specific models but
the generic ones. They have given up not just on one person or a
specific group of people, but on humanity itself. I see evidence of
this in the so-called right-of-nature movement, and to a frightening
degree in the antiperson bias of much of the man-versus-nature
talk.

If there is nobility in our world, it is the presence and consciousness of *people* that conceptualizes that nobility, and thereby
creates it. There is no innate grandeur in a sunset; grandeur is a
transcendent feeling of the human species shared by no other animal. In fact, the sun does not really set, except in human perception.
Of course, the garbage in the rivers, the litter in the streets, the
destruction of the forests, and the pollution of the air offend me.
They offend me because they diminish the environment in which
human beings live, and will thereby diminish them as human
beings. To talk, however, of what a good place the world would
be if it weren't for the vile and destructive nature of man is foolish,
particularly when such a position is articulated by a member of
that species. It is silly to praise a nature in which "every prospect
pleases, and only man is vile." Pleases *whom?* We are returning
once again to a cycle of self-contempt.

Our diminishing expectations now are directly traceable to the
abandonment of certain dreams. Cynicism and pessimism are nour-
ished by the death of hope. We cannot afford to abandon our grand
dreams. To unshackle the bound Prometheus that is modern man,
we must—to quote that most romantic of nineteenth-century poets,
Percy Shelley, "Hope till hope creates from its own wreck the thing
it contemplates."

It was hope that sustained Pinocchio through his travails, even
though it was only the naïve hope of a child—wish fulfillment, if
you will. Surely it is hope—as well as faith—that informs the story
of Genesis. The miracle of Genesis is epitomized in that magic
moment to which I have been drawn again and yet again in this
book: the moment of banishment. To me, the glory of human
existence is inherent in what is absent from that critical scene.

There is no abandonment by God and no abandonment of God. There is no expression of regret by Adam. Gone are the hiding and the whining; there are no imprecations, no requests for a second chance, no self-recriminations, no shirking of responsibility. Adam accepts mature accountability for his own actions, and he sees, perhaps only dimly, the liberating force even in defying God, if that is the price for attaining freedom, because in freedom lies the true creation of the species. And a new species will emerge. He renames his wife. In calling her "Eve," or "Life," he is anticipating the generations to come.

The new Adam and Eve are the personification of human hope. Never mind what they lost; the future will be theirs. The departing Adam and Eve respond not as though they have been banished from the Kingdom of Heaven but, rather, as though they had been released from the monotony and senselessness of an all-good world in which choice was not exercised and labor not necessary and therefore work not rewarding; where growth was not possible and change was limited to variations on an immutable theme. They were leaving the secure and loving world of childhood to enter the unpredictable but expanding world of the adult. By their faith in themselves and each other, by their exploitation of that most human of attributes, hope, they converted their exile into a pilgrimage. Facing an unknown destiny; forewarned of its difficulty, of the pain and travail; knowing there was no return—these two pioneers set forth, not with fear but with hope. They were the first aspiring human beings, and our best models for today.

The freedom they chose is a powerful and potentially corrupting gift. We have seen the abuse of that freedom only too often in the unspeakable and inhuman actions that permeate our history. The capacity to do evil is a risk of freedom, but it is also a component in defining the good, and in defining the only species in which good and evil abide. I center my hopes on those special attributes of our species: loving, caring, imagination, anticipation, empathy, compassion, and—yes—that most dangerous of attributes, our freedom.

From the moment we left the Garden and stepped into that

unpredictable world east of Eden we were embarked on a unique
journey, fraught with danger and immersed in pain, but a journey
that only our species was capable of undertaking. We were privileged to abide in the Garden, but we are equally privileged in our
journey from it. We are, in the words of T. H. White, both the
once and the future king. We are born underdeveloped, and will
remain that way all of our lives, but only this "eternal embryo,"
the human being, always remains "potential" in the image of God.
In our quest for that which we may become, we inevitably assume
the mantle of Dr. Frankenstein, but we dare not ignore the lesson
of the Irish elk. Both the knowledge of the past and the potential
for the future are the special burdens of *Homo sapiens*. We are,
indeed, something special.

NOTES

All quotations from *Pinocchio* are from the following edition: *The Adventures of Pinocchio* by C. Collodi, trans. by M. A. Murray. New York: Grosset & Dunlap, 1946.

All biblical quotations are from *Pentateuch and Haftorahs*, ed. Dr. J. H. Hertz. London and New York: Soncino Press, 1987.

All quotations from Freud are from *The Collected Works of Sigmund Freud*, Standard Edition. London: Hogarth Press, 1955. Figures refer to volume numbers and page numbers in the above edition.

PROLOGUE
WHAT'S SO SPECIAL ABOUT BEING HUMAN

1. Genesis 1:27–28.
2. Sophocles, "Antigone," in *Oedipus the King*, ed. and trans. P. D. Arnott, Crofts Classics Series, lines 327–33.
3. A. Stern, "On Value and Human Dignity," *Listening*, Spring 1975, p. 78.
4. I. Kant, *The Doctrine of Virtue*, trans. M. J. Gregor (New York: Torchbooks), p. 99.
5. T. Dobzhansky, *Mankind Evolving* (New Haven: Yale University Press, 1962), pp. 346–47.
6. Quoted in M. Midgely, *Beast and Man: The Roots of Human Nature* (Ithaca, N.Y.: Cornell University Press, 1978), p. 218.
7. I. Kant, *On History*, ed. L. W. Beck (Indianapolis: Bobbs-Merrill, 1963), p. 58.
8. Genesis 3:16.

ADAM AND EVE: ON BEING HUMAN
LIVING IN TWO WORLDS

1. Genesis 1:26.
2. Genesis 1:24.
3. Genesis 2:18, 19.
4. Genesis 2:20–22.
5. Cicero, *De inventione*, trans. H. M. Hubbell, The Loeb Classic Library, 1.1: 2.2, p. 5.

6. J. Rousseau, *Second Discourse*, in *The First and Second Discourses*, ed. R. D. Masters (New York: St. Martins Press, 1964).

7. N. Chomsky, *Language and Mind* (New York: Harcourt Brace Jovanovich, 1968), ch. 3, pp. 65–100.

8. J. Bennett, "Thoughtful Brutes," A. Philosophical A. Proceedings, suppl. to vol. 62, no. 1 (Sept. 1988), p. 202.

9. E. Wilson, *On Human Nature* (Cambridge, Mass.: Harvard University Press, 1978), p. 63.

10. H. Terrace, *Nim: A Chimpanzee Who Learned Sign Language* (New York: Washington Square Press, 1981).

11. Genesis 17:5, 7.

12. Genesis 17:16.

13. Genesis 32:28.

14. Genesis 35:10.

15. Genesis 2:19.

16. Ovid, *Metamorphoses,* trans. F. J. Miller, The Loeb Classic Library, 1:7.

17. S. Tax, *Evolution After Darwin* (Chicago: University of Chicago Press, 1960), vol. 3.

18. E. Cassirer, *Essay on Man: An Introduction to a Philosophy of Human Culture* (New Haven: Yale University Press, 1962), p. 24.

19. Ibid., p. 25.

20. J. Rousseau, *Emile*, pp. 82–83.

21. E. Becker, *The Denial of Death* (New York: Free Press, 1973).

22. S. Freud, *The Future of an Illusion*, 1927, 21:3.

23. J. Rousseau, *Emile, 2*, pp. 80–81.

24. I. Kant, *Critique of Judgement*, sect. 76–77.

25. Genesis 3:19, 20.

FREEDOM AND CHOICE

1. Genesis 3:7–13.

2. *Pentateuch and Haftorahs*, ed. Dr. J. H. Hertz (London: Soncino Press, 1981), n. 17, p. 8. P.

3. I. Kant, *On History*, ed. L. W. Beck (New York: Bobbs-Merrill, 1963), p. 55.

4. Genesis 2:16–17.

5. In this discussion, I draw heavily on the guidance and work of my colleague Bruce Jennings, and his unpublished manuscript "Rousseau: A Geneva of the Mind."

6. J. Rousseau, *The First and Second Discourses*, ed. R. D. Masters (New York: St. Martins Press, 1964), pp. 113–15.

7. Ibid., pp. 114–15.

8. R. Dubos, *So Human an Animal* (New York: Scribners, 1968), p. viii.

9. *American Heritage Dictionary*.

10. B. F. Skinner, *Beyond Freedom and Dignity* (New York: Knopf, 1971).

11. T. H. White, *The Once and Future King* (New York: Putnam's, 1958), p. 195.

FEELINGS

1. For a more detailed analysis of human feelings, see W. Gaylin, *Feelings: Our Vital Signs* (New York: Perennial Library, Harper & Row, 1979).

2. W. Cannon, *Bodily Changes in Panic, Hunger, Fear and Rage* (New York: Appleton-Century, 1915).

3. Genesis 2:18, 20.

4. Genesis 2:25.

5. Genesis 3:7, 10.

6. M. Kingston, *The Woman Warrior: Memoirs of a Girlhood Among Ghosts* (New York: Knopf, 1977).

7. M. Buber, in *The Knowledge of Man*, ed. M. Friedman (London: George Allen & Unwin, 1965), p. 133.

8. S. Freud, *Totem and Taboo* (1913), 13:1.

9. J. Timmerman, *Prisoner Without a Name, Cell Without a Number* (New York: Knopf, 1981).

10. N. Mandelstam, *Hope Against Hope* (New York: Atheneum, 1976).

11. P. Ricoeur, "Guilt, Ethics and Religion," in *Conscience: Theological and Psychological Perspectives*, ed. C. Nelson (New York: Newman Press, 1973), pp. 15, 16

12. Aristotle, *Rhetoric*, in *Basic Works of Aristotle*, ed. R. McKeon (New York: Random House, 1941), bk. II, ch. 6, p. 392.

13. Ibid.

14. *The History of Herodotus*, trans. G. Rawlinson, ed. M. Komroff (New York: Tudor Publishing, 1956), bk. I, p. 3.

15. A. Kardiner, *The Psychological Frontiers of Society* (New York: Columbia University Press, 1945).

16. G. Steiner, "Night Words," *Encounter*, Sept. 1965, p. 18.

17. P. Roth, *Portnoy's Complaint* (New York: Random House, 1967).

18. Genesis 1:3–4.

19. Genesis 1:10.
20. Genesis 1:16–18.
21. Genesis 1:25, 31.

S E X

1. Genesis 1:28.
2. Genesis 2:25, 3:7.
3. Song of Solomon 4:9–11.
4. S. Freud, *Three Essays on the Theory of Sexuality*, 1905, 7:125.
5. E. Wilson, *On Human Nature* (Cambridge, Mass.: Harvard University Press, 1978), p. 140.
6. Ibid., p. 141.
7. Sophocles, "Antigone," in *The Complete Plays of Sophocles* (New York: Bantam Classics), p. 135.
8. Virgil, *The Aeneid*, trans. R. Fitzgerald (New York: Random House, 1983), pp 97–98.
9. E. Pagels, *Adam, Eve, and the Serpent* (New York: Random House, 1988).
10. Ibid., p. 132.
11. Ibid.
12. Ibid., pp. 140, 141.
13. A. Ryan, "The Nature of Human Nature," in *The Limits of Human Nature*, ed. J. Benthall (New York: Dutton Paperbacks, 1974), p. 9.
14. P. Rieff, *Triumph of the Therapeutic: Uses of Faith After Freud* (Chicago: University of Chicago Press, 1987).
15. C. S. Lewis, *The Four Loves* (New York: Harvest/Harcourt Brace Jovanovich, 1960), pp. 134–35.
16. R. Unger, *Passion: An Essay on Personality* (New York: Free Press, 1984), p. 176.
17. W. Aaron, *Straight* (New York: Holt, Rinehart and Winston, 1973).

Pinocchio: On Becoming Human
DEPENDENCY

1. I am grateful to Nancy D. Sachse, author of *Pinocchio in the U.S.A.*, for her invaluable help in sharing her knowledge of the history of Pinocchio with me.

2. D. Redmont, "After a Century, Pinocchio Still Enchants the World," *Wall Street Journal*, December 2, 1980.

3. M. Blount, *Animal Land* (New York: Avon Books, 1977), p. 56.

4. A. Portmann, *Animals as Social Beings* (New York: Harper & Row), pp. 75–76.

5. S. Freud, *Inhibitions, Symptoms and Anxiety* (1926), 21:223, pp. 139–40.

6. Ibid., 20:7.

7. The work of Harry Harlow with various collaborators, including his wife, M. K. Harlow, is now legend. Perhaps the best introduction for the uninitiated would be H. Harlow, *Learning to Love* (New York: Aronson, 1974).

8. These remarkable experiments are summarized in H. F. Harlow and M. K. Harlow, *The Affectional Systems*, vol. II, in A. M. Schrier, H. F. Harlow, and F. Stollnitz, eds., *Behavior of Nonhuman Primates* (New York: Academic Press, 1965).

9. R. Spitz, *The First Year of Life* (New York: International University Press, 1965).

10. J. Bowlby, *Attachment and Loss*, vols. I, II (New York: Basic Books, 1962, 1973).

11. M. Klaus and J. Kennell, *Parent-Infant Bonding* (St. Louis: V. V. Mosby, 1982).

12. Ted Bundy was an extremely attractive, boyish-looking mass murderer who specialized in killing young college girls. When finally apprehended he was implicated in the murder of dozens of women.

13. I have documented this specific phenomenon in W. Gaylin, M.D., *The Killing of Bonnie Garland* (New York: Penguin, 1983).

14. D. Hume, *A Treatise of Human Nature* (London: Oxford University Press, 1949), p. 363.

15. J. Gewirtz, ed., *Attachment and Dependency* (Washington, D.C.: V. H. Winston, 1972). Also J. Gewirtz, "The Course of Infant Smiling in Four Child-Rearing Environments in Israel," in B. Foss, ed., *Determinants of Infant Behavior*, vol. III (New York: John Wiley, 1961–1969), pp. 205–48.

16. *Pinocchio*, p. 254.

WORK

1. *Pinocchio*, p. 19.
2. *Pinocchio,* pp. 19–20.
3. Pope John Paul II, "Laborem Exercens," *Origins*, vol. 11, no. 15 (Sept. 24, 1981), pp. 225–27.
4. Genesis 2:17–19.
5. Genesis 2:5, 8.
6. Genesis 2:2.
7. Pope John Paul II, "Laborcm Exercens," p. 229.
8. H. Arendt, *The Human Condition* (Chicago: University of Chicago Press, 1958), p. 7.
9. Abath di Rabbi Nathan, quoted in *Pentateuch and Haftorahs,* ed. Dr. J. H. Hertz (London: Soncino Press, 1981), p. 8.
10. W. J. Bate, *Samuel Johnson* (New York: Harcourt Brace Jovanovich, 1977), p. 299.
11. H. Arendt, *The Human Condition*, p. 124.
12. Ibid., p. 139.
13. *Pinocchio*, p. 151.

CONSCIENCE

1. *The American Heritage Dictionary of the English Language*, ed. William Morris (New York: American Heritage Publishing Co., 1969).
2. In 1958, a young psychologist presented a Ph.D. thesis on moral development at the University of Chicago. Lawrence Kohlberg was to devote his life to research and writings on moral development. His stages of moral development were established early in his writings, and further elaborations did not dramatically enlarge upon his original insights. Though frequently cited, his work did not father a school of scholarship in this area. See L. Kohlberg, *Essays on Moral Development* (San Francisco: Harper & Row, 1981).
3. See "Apology for Raymond Cibonne," *Essays of Montaigne* (New York: Modern Library, 1946).
4. H. Fielding, *Tom Jones* (New York: Signet, 1963), pp. 226–28.
5. S. Freud, *Civilization and Its Discontents* (1930), Standard Edition, vol. XXI.
6. S. Freud and J. Breuer, *Studies on Hysteria* (1893–95), S.E., 2:253–307.

7. S. Freud, *Character and Anal Erotism* (1908), 9:167.
8. S. Freud, *Totem and Taboo* (1913), 13:1.
9. Ibid.
10. S. Freud, *The Future of an Illusion* (1927), 21:134.
11. S. Freud, *Mourning and Melancholia* (1917), 14:237.
12. P. Roth, *Portnoy's Complaint* (New York: Random House, 1967), pp. 3, 4.
13. S. Freud, *Group Psychology and the Analysis of the Ego* (1921), 18:69.
14. P. Ricoeur, "Guilt, Ethics and Religion," in *Conscience: Theological and Psychological Perspectives*, ed. C. E. Nelson (New York: Newman Press, 1973), pp. 15, 16.
15. This and subsequent quotations from the episode are from M. Twain (S. Clemens), *Adventures of Huckleberry Finn* (New York: Harper & Row, 1896), pp. 331–32.
16. D. Hume, *A Treatise of Human Nature* (London: Oxford University Press, 1848), p. 370.
17. *Pinocchio*, p. 254.
18. Ibid.

LOVE

1. For a fuller discussion of love, see W. Gaylin, *Rediscovering Love* (New York: Viking Penguin, 1986).
2. *Pinocchio*, p. 80.
3. Ibid., p. 51.
4. Ibid., p. 98.
5. It was, I believe, my father who first brought this quotation to my attention, perhaps when I was fourteen. I have been unable to locate its source despite inquiries to various Mark Twain associations. It was quoted in the *Reader's Digest* of September 1937, and is also included in R. Flesch, *The Book of Unusual Quotations* (New York: Harper & Brothers), p. 88. Neither source offers a citation.
6. *Pinocchio*, p. 147.
7. Ibid., p. 150.
8. Empedocles in W. K. Guthrie, *A History of Greek Philosophers*, vol. II (Cambridge University Press, 1975).
9. C. P. Snow, *Homecoming* (New York: Charles Scribners Sons, 1956), pp. 75–76.
10. M. S. Mahler, *The Psychological Birth of the Human Infant* (New York: Basic Books), 1975.

11. Plato, *Symposium*, ed. B. Jowett (New York: Tudor Publishing, 1956), p. 318.
12. S. Freud, *Civilization and Its Discontents* (1930), 21:64–65.
13. I. Singer, *The Nature of Love* (Chicago: University of Chicago Press, 1984), vol. I, pp. 221, 222.
14. Stendhal, *On Love* (New York: Liveright, 1947), p. 6.
15. B. Bettelheim, *The Uses of Enchantment* (New York: Alfred A. Knopf, 1976), pp. 277–310.
16. F. Alberoni, *Falling in Love*, trans. Lawrence Verruti (New York: Random House, 1983).
17. C. S. Lewis, *A Grief Observed* (New York: Bantam Books, 1976), p. 71.
18. Stendhal, *On Love*, p. 2.
19. Ibid., pp. 156–57.
20. Ibid., pp. 156–57.
21. N. Gaylin, in M. Farber, ed., *Human Sexuality: Psychosexual Effects of Disease* (New York: Macmillan, 1985), pp. 40–54.
22. S. Mendess, in *Philosophy*, vol. 59, no. 228 (April 1984), pp. 243–52.
23. D. H. Lawrence, *A Propos of Lady Chatterley's Lover* (New York: Bantam Books, 1983), pp. 354–56.
24. Ibid., p. 347.
25. Ibid., p. 345.
26. M. Harlow, in *International Encyclopedia of the Social Sciences* (New York: Macmillan Free Press, 1968), vol. I, p. 124.
27. V. Solovyov, *The Meaning of Love*, trans. G. Bles (London: Centenary Press, 1945), pp. 22–23.

Epilogue

DR. FRANKENSTEIN AND THE IRISH ELK

1. M. Shelley, *Frankenstein* (New York: Bantam Books, 1981), p. xxiii.
2. Ibid., p. xxiv.
3. Ibid., p. xxv.
4. Ibid., p. xi.
5. H. Ostrer and J. Hejtmancik, "Prenatal Diagnosis and Carrier Detection of Genetic Diseases by Analysis of Desoxyribonucleic Acid," *Journal of Pediatrics*, vol. 112, no. 5 (May 1988), pp. 679–87.
6. W. Gaylin, "The Frankenstein Factor," *New England Journal of Medicine*, vol. 297, no. 12 (Sept. 22, 1977), pp. 665–67.

7. W. Gaylin et al., *Operating on the Mind: The Psychosurgery Conflict* (New York: Basic Books, 1975).

8. S. J. Gould, *Ever Since Darwin: Reflections in Natural History* (New York: W. W. Norton, 1977), pp. 79–90.

9. *Intimacy and Sexual Behavior* (New York: National Hemophilia Foundation, 1985), quoted in *Hastings Center Report*, August 1985, special suppl., p. 10.

10. J. Rawls, *A Theory of Justice* (Cambridge: Harvard University Press, 1971).

INDEX

Aaron, William, 120
abortion, 9
    definition of human and, 32
Abraham:
    Isaac sacrificed by, 145
    name changed from Abram, 30–31
acid rain, 173
Adam:
    animals named by, 31
    Eve named by, 123, 270
    work done by, 156–57, 162
    see also Adam and Eve
Adam, Eve, and the Serpent (Pagels), 110
Adam and Eve, 16–17, 23–123, 184,
        239
    autonomy of, 25, 71, 151, 154, 180
    as clothed by God, 36
    creation of, 17, 25–26
    Fall of, 26, 46, 47–48, 71, 79, 101,
        122–23, 157, 161, 181, 269
    hope and, 269–71
    sexuality of, 100–101, 122–23
    shame and, 79–80, 87, 90
    see also Adam; Eve
adolescence:
    prolonging of, 175
    sexual passion in, 224
Aeschylus, 247
Agamemnon, 145, 245
agriculture, discovery of, 164, 165
AIDS (acquired immunodeficiency syn-
        drome), 266
Akiba, Rabbi, 33
Alberoni, Francesco, 223, 224
altruism, 78, 190, 239

of animals, 176–77
    identification and, 192, 196–97
ameba, survival of, 73
American Civil Liberties Union, 265
American Heritage Dictionary, 94
American Revolution, 246
anger, humiliation and, 88
Animal Land (Blount), 129
animal-rights movement, 11–14
animals:
    Adam's naming of, 31
    altruism of, 78, 190, 239
    amorality of, 203
    bonding of, 213–14, 225
    conscience lacked in, 177
    domestication of, 164–65
    feelings of, limited range of, 72, 73,
        74, 230–31
    feelings of, as shared by humans, 76,
        81–82, 186, 236
    God figure for, 24
    instinctual behavior of, 33, 36–37,
        44–45, 49–50, 56–58
    language use of, 28–29, 30
    play of, 160
    proximal identification by, 202–3
    sexuality of, human sexuality vs., 98–
        101, 104–6, 108–9, 116–18, 119,
        120, 122, 219–20, 225
    subordination of, to humans, 4, 5,
        11–14, 25–26, 31
    thinking of, 26–27
    work not done by, 159
    see also specific animals
anthropology, 10, 14